WULVER RISING

1

Run.

LYDIA MAINE

Cover Design: Sellkie Design

Editing: Kendra's Editing and Book Services

❀ Created with Vellum

For everyone waiting for their knight in shining armor. It's time to go find your own sword.

ONE

Lya

A TEAR TRICKLED out of the corner of my eye as I begged and bartered in my head with whatever higher power was out there for a little more time. This latest implosion of my life snuck up on me a little too fast, and I wasn't ready for how quickly I needed to get out.

Unsurprisingly, nothing and nobody answered. Even though I knew nothing would come of my silent pleading, the stillness of my surroundings felt a little mocking. I leaned my head against the tree I sat against and exhaled the breath I'd been holding, trying to compose myself before heading back to the house.

"This wasn't how things were supposed to go," I whispered to the nothing that was listening.

Nothing in my life was playing out how I'd hoped. I shouldn't be surprised that it had stayed the course in that respect. Maybe someday, I'd get used to my residence in left field. Today was not that day.

I looked up at the sky peeking through the branches. Stars twinkled, and what little light from the half-moon that could make it through the foliage cast a soft glow on the forest floor. This little home I'd found was an interesting place. We were surrounded by prairies and farmland for hundreds of miles, but the Buffalo Ridge along the Big Sioux River had rolling hills, forest, and a sense of mystery. It was a little taste of home, even if it was only a few miles worth. Just a couple miles east or west and you'd be back to the never-ending open spaces until you hit a mountain range. You'd have to follow the river north or south to stick with this little haven.

I stood up to make my way through the little strip of forest. The best thing about the house I found just last year was that it backed right up to the rolling hills of the Buffalo Ridge. It was a selling point, actually. I'd be sad to say goodbye to my little sanctuary. Hopefully, the next place would offer something to replace it.

Just as I was exiting the tree line, I couldn't shake the feeling of being watched. More than just squirrel or rabbit eyes—you get used to those. I whipped my head around and locked gazes with golden brown eyes following me. They were far enough away and hidden in the shadows that I couldn't make out the creature's body, but it was probably a coyote. Interesting that this one had come so close to me, although not unusual at all that they were in the area.

I smiled to myself. Maybe something was out there listening, even if it was just the coyote.

I scuttled the rest of the way down the hill, through the alley, and up the driveway. Before I entered the house, I ran through which floorboards were creaky, which steps I would need to skip, and whether or not I had left the door ajar. The door would be the big one; if I had left it open, I'd be good. If it was closed, the shriek of the hinges would wake Ted, and I didn't want to deal with him. Not now.

This sneaking out to find solace was new. The deterioration of this relationship was new, at least to him. He wouldn't miss me in bed. He had moved to the guest bedroom a couple of nights before, but he'd still be angry about me sneaking out of my own house.

How do you tell someone they were just your golden ticket to a new life? I couldn't keep going like this anymore. He was about to find out. Time to pick up, move on, and start over. Twenty-four wasn't too old to start a new life, by any means. No strings attached to anyone next time. Just me, a lone wolf. Maybe I would get a dog.

Luck was on my side, and the door was cracked. I slipped in, silently thanking the hinges for not betraying my movements and staying quiet. I closed the door behind me and surveyed the room. Something was off. Things were more barren than when I left. Ted's laundry basket of clothes and lamp from his bedside table were gone. The picture of his family no longer hung on the wall. I breathed out, unable to decide whether or not it was a good thing he was clearing out his belongings. On the one hand, it would make getting out easier, but on the other, he knew I had been gone. The last thing I needed was for him to report me as a missing person.

I sat down on what used to be his side of the bed and opened the nightstand drawer. I furrowed my brow when I saw his knife was missing. It was a dagger, really. It had been given to him by his dad when we got engaged, with the proposed purpose of self-defense. Who uses a nine-inch dagger for home protection? In middle-of-nowhere Minnesota, wildlife would be a bigger concern than home invasion, and a gun would have been more logical.

His dad had made a big deal of bragging about the silver blade. It was an heirloom, passed down from father to son for generations. It was that gift that made me decide it was time to get out. Ted's dad suspected too much, which meant it was only a matter of time until Ted knew, too.

I had never liked that knife being around, especially in the room I slept in. But now, it was even more disconcerting that it was gone.

Time to run.

I'd had a bag packed for two weeks now, since the day that knife showed up, tucked away in the spare tire storage of my car. Clothes and cash. You didn't need much else to start over, right? It'd be easiest to act like I was heading into work in the morning and keep on driving as far away from here as I could get. Further west this time. Mountains were calling me.

The loose ends, though; I had a job and a few quasi-friends. If only I had planned better. I should have put in my notice at the vet clinic the second he got that dagger. But friends, if they were real friends, would ask questions if I just vanished. Too bad they didn't know I wasn't someone they could consider a real friend.

I laid down, trying to think. How difficult could it be to fake one's death?

The door creaked, and my eyes snapped open. I could make out Ted's frame in the doorway, clutching onto something in his left hand.

I glared at him, certain my deep amber eyes were near glowing in the dark, but didn't move as he strode over to the bed, stopping to stand over me.

"L-Lya?" he stuttered. "Is this what you really want?"

I didn't respond.

"Can we... Do we have to sleep in separate rooms?"

I sighed. "We talked about this."

My voice trailed off as he raised his hand, revealing, as I expected, that damn blade. The silver soaked up the moonlight shining in through the window.

"Are we over?" His voice cracked, and I truly did feel bad. He didn't really deserve this, but he couldn't know.

Eyes wide as I stared at the dagger, I lied through my teeth, "N-no, babe, of course we can fix this."

Any sane person says whatever their attacker wants to hear, right?

His eyes grew hard. It began to feel like the wall I had worked so meticulously to build up in my head was now crumbling. I shook with fear but held still. Maybe if he took me out of this world, that would be for the best.

"I don't believe you."

"Ted..." I started, unable to say more. The dagger was poised, his mind made up. That wall in my head came tumbling down.

And then it happened.

'STOP HIDING FROM ME!' that voice I had spent so much of my life running from shrieked at me.

A scream tore from my throat as bones cracked and rearranged, the fabric of my clothes shredding. It wasn't me on the bed anymore; it was that... thing, and it was Ted's turn to look very afraid.

I peeked out from behind the monster's eyes, just along for the show, like watching a movie from the main character's point of view. There was nothing I could do at this point. *It* had control.

A growl rumbled in its throat, and I slunk back as far as I could, refusing to know what happened next.

What felt like a quick moment later, I was brought back forward as bones shifted and fur receded, leaving me kneeling naked in a growing puddle of blood beside Ted's body, absolutely macerated. I knew that thing inside me had done it.

"I knew it," Ted gurgled with one final breath.

I fell back and sobbed. He didn't deserve this. He could have moved on with his life, and I would have been a blip on his radar in the long run.

'Why?' I cried at that thing in my head, that other part of me I had tried and failed to kill off.

'Hunter.'

One-word replies. That's all I got from it anymore. There was a time when it first surfaced that it was a friend, but not anymore. It had ruined my life, and any hope I had for a life in the future.

'What are you?' I asked, desperately hoping for a real answer this time. I never got one, but maybe committing murder would finally be enough for it to show me some mercy.

'A part of you.'

4

'*What am I, then?*'

'*You know.*'

I did know; I just refused to admit it. My eyes were stuck on one bloody paw print on the floor. There was no escaping this now. Hard to build a new life when you're wanted for murder, or would be when people finally came looking for him and found me missing. I'd be the logical suspect.

I picked up the dagger by its handle and held it against my skin. This part, I had done before. '*Go AWAY.*'

I screamed as I dug the silver in, slashing up my arm. Twice more for good measure. It stung and burned more than any knife wound should, but it was the only way I knew how to silence the monster within.

There was a yelp. I expected the thing to go back and hide behind its wall like every other time I banished it this way, but it surged forward instead, shutting me out.

OLIVER

I BLINKED sleep out of my eyes as I rolled over in bed, grabbing for my phone that wouldn't stop ringing. One missed call wasn't a huge deal; repeated calls in the middle of the night became worrisome.

The caller ID showed a name from the past, someone I hadn't spoken to in a very long time. He was one of us, but very much on the periphery, really only calling when he needed help. Against my better judgment, I accepted the call.

"What?" I barked out.

"Good evening to you, too." He was much too perky for this time of night.

"It's 3 a.m. Not my definition of evening anymore."

"Well, someone isn't having much fun with their life, then," he grumbled.

I groaned, ready to end the call. "What do you need?"

There was a pause, and I could tell the upbeat demeanor had vanished. "I need to report a rogue."

That caused me to sit up. Rogues weren't uncommon. Hell, my own brother would now be considered a rogue, but the ones worth reporting were. Rogues worth reporting posed a threat, whether it be to our kind or humans. To us, they were easy to manage. A threat to humans was worse. That would mean exposure and the inconvenience of hunters on our backs.

It had been so long since he had been on our lands; he could be anywhere at this point. This threat might be one to pass off to another pack, but I worried that was not the case. "Where are you now?"

"East River, a college town on the border of South Dakota and Minnesota. Brookings, to be exact," he said.

Brookings. I knew that place better than I would have liked. East River was a long way off. South Dakota was such a wasteland over there; there was no natural habitat for us, but we still fell responsible for protecting the people in that neutral territory. Protecting them from what little of our kind could be found over there. They were rogues, mostly, but rogues with collegiate ambitions or a desire to integrate with humans rarely posed a threat, so the area wasn't on my radar. Hadn't been for twelve years.

I huffed. This was not what I wanted to deal with. "How many?"

"Just one. She's alone."

She-wolves rarely went rogue. Furthermore, he was more than capable of handling a single rogue female. "What makes you think she's a threat?"

"I've known her for a while. I should have known. She never smelled quite right for a human..." His voice trailed off, and there was a pause. "I think she's shut out that part of herself and doesn't even know. She has a life here—a job, friends."

"What makes you think she's a threat?" I reiterated.

Another pause. At this rate, it might be quicker if I drove out to Brookings to have this conversation in person.

"I don't think she has any control... She shifted and killed her fiancé."

I stiffened. A rogue with no control potentially going on a murderous rampage? Yes, this was bad, and it needed to be dealt with. Yesterday.

"How do we damage-control this?" I demanded.

"She bailed. I snuck in and cleaned it up, so it looks like a normal domestic violence murder scene. The true crime YouTubers will probably have a great time with it," he added, chuckling nervously.

One problem solved, but we couldn't lose eyes on her. "And where is she now?"

"Headed into town. I'm tailing her. It... uh... kind of looks like she's headed to my place..."

"Get her here as soon as you can." I pulled the phone away from my ear to hang up, but he spoke up once more.

"How much do you want me to tell her?" he asked. "I seriously think she has no idea at all what is going on."

"As much as you need to and as little as possible," I replied. A situation like this was uncharted territory. How could one not know what was going on when there had been another goddamn entity sharing their body for years?

"Hey, Ollie, wait."

"What?"

"Her fiancé that she killed? He was a hunter."

I slammed the phone down, ending the call. He always somehow managed to bring bad news our way. I swung my feet out of bed and got dressed. There would be no more sleep at this point. We hadn't had a run-in with hunters in over a decade. I had hoped we had been forgotten. I didn't want that to change now.

I made my way to my office with a brief stop at the kitchen for coffee. Once settled at my desk, I pulled up the database we had with all current assignments and locations. It looked like we had a few over in that direction we could use to help cover this up. With Trevor trailing her, I was confident he would have her here by noon. But there was still a lot to do. I really wanted to avoid going over there myself, if I could, but I wanted to avoid another war more.

A low growl reverberated through my head. *'How could one deny such a special gift?'*

'We don't even know if that's what's going on,' I grumbled back. For all we knew, she could be fully aware of everything, and this was one hundred percent intentional. I wouldn't be quick to show mercy.

'We should go out there ourselves,' the wolf insisted.

'No,' I snapped. *'An Alpha's resources are wasted on something like this.'*

Adair's rumble reverberated through my head, but he made no further arguments. His disagreement was known, but he also knew me well. I wouldn't budge.

I picked up the phone, hoping I could set wheels in motion while calling as few people at this ungodly hour as possible.

"Hey, little bro!" I smiled at my brother's cheerful greeting. He always was chipper nowadays, no matter the circumstances. "What has you calling so early?"

"Any interest in covering up a murder?" I asked wryly.

He chuckled. "I'm not exactly sure that's how you start a conversation before sunrise."

"Or is it the best time?"

He laughed at that. "What's going on?"

I sighed. I barely had enough details myself to understand the situation. It seemed unfathomable. "An out-of-control rogue. She shifted and killed her hunter fiancé and then fled. Probably best if we just make the body disappear."

"Alright, but you know I'm a ways off from you now, right? There might be someone better to call if this is time-sensitive," he pointed out.

"It's right outside of that college town on the state line. You're my closest guy."

"Gotcha," he mumbled. "Another hunter hit around Brookings."

I ground my teeth. I had been trying to avoid linking this to the events of twelve years ago, but considering who called to report the incident, it bore more similarities than I was willing to admit. Some gut feeling told me this was different, but the facts screamed otherwise. I was even more anxious than before to get this girl here and start questioning her.

The past, I had discovered, had a way of repeating itself.

Two

Lya

I CAME to in a familiar place, exactly the opposite of what I had hoped. I needed to be far, far away from here. Curled up in front of Trevor's apartment door was not that.

I heard footsteps down the hall, but I didn't even have the mental fortitude to move. Maybe I could be arrested and sentenced to death. That'd be one way to get rid of this parasite.

'I'm not a parasite.' That damn voice.

'Go away,' I retorted.

'No.'

Great.

The footsteps got closer. I would sure be a sight—a naked little girl covered in blood curled up on the floor. This would definitely draw attention. Why couldn't I move?

Trevor rounded the corner. He was the only person I wanted to see, and the last at the same time. I stared at his shoes as he came to stand in front of me.

"Oh, Lya..." He sighed. I offered no response. He helped me stand, unlocked the door, and guided me inside. I stumbled across the apartment to flop down at the kitchen table. I didn't want to sit anywhere the blood would be impossible to clean. I refused to put on the shirt he offered for the same reason.

Trevor sat down across from me and stared intently, probably taking in the absolutely horrific condition I was in. Why wasn't he freaking out? I was sure he had so many questions, but I couldn't think of a way to answer any of them.

"Do you want to tell me now or take a shower first?" he asked.

"I... I think something is wrong with me," I whispered, refusing to look up at him.

Trevor chuckled softly. Even in the most serious of times, he always found a way to try and lighten the mood. It was what garnered him the position as my closest friend here. Not that that was saying much. I still kept him at arm's length.

"That's a matter of opinion." He paused, and I finally met his gaze. "I do not think anything is wrong with you. But I do know you need help."

I let out a sigh. If only he knew what was really going on...

"Why don't you go take a shower, and then we can talk."

It was a welcome suggestion. I got up and wandered to the bathroom, leaning against the vanity while the water heated. Trevor was one of the kindest, most accepting people I had ever met. He deserved better than to be around someone like me. When my relationship started to fall apart for reasons I refused to divulge to him, he was there for me with absolutely no questions asked. Just a shoulder to cry on and a couch to crash on.

Ted had asked once or twice in the weeks before if I was cheating on him. Trevor was the main culprit he had in mind, but I tried my best to ease his worries regarding his suspicion. Trevor would never cross that line, and I had absolutely no interest in going anywhere close to it. Besides, even if Ted couldn't believe it, it was really, truly an 'it's not you, it's me' situation. Probably the epitome of them.

Hot water beat down on me, the blood washing down the drain, but it did nothing to wash away the guilt and shame that was my life. The gashes on my arm stung as the water and soap sluiced over them.

This wasn't anywhere close to the exit strategy I had planned.

'This is our life now.'

'Not if I can help it,' I retorted. If you could say something through gritted teeth to the unwelcome resident voice in your head, that's what I did.

I hadn't even noticed Trevor slip in and leave a shirt and pair of sweats for me to borrow. I suppose I could have told him I had stuff in my car, but I should probably leave those there for when I inevitably escaped again.

Thinking about it, maybe the best way to get out was to actually tell him the truth. If he knew what I really was, he'd probably be excited to see me leave. And it would guarantee that none of my friends came looking.

Once dressed, I glared at myself in the mirror. My amber eyes stared back at me. I used to think they were a unique, exotic-looking color. Now, though, I resented them. They looked animalistic. Completely inhuman.

But that was the truth.

Time's up, Lya. Gotta go ruin my life some more, I told myself.

I left the bathroom, making my way to Trevor's living room. Sinking into his couch, I appreciated the creature comforts he splurged on. This would probably be the last time I'd get to sit on something as comfortable and plush. I'd be on the run or in prison for the rest of my life. I gave it three days before anyone found Ted. People would notice he was missing from work, not showing up to the climbing gym, and not responding to texts and calls. I wondered if anyone would bother to check on me.

Trevor's eyes hadn't left me since I'd come out of the bathroom. I really couldn't make out what exactly his expression revealed. Worry? Fear? Curiosity? The silence was growing tenser by the moment, but I refused to break it.

He sighed and sat back, lacing his fingers behind his head. "When did you first shift?"

My eyes bulged. That was far from the question I was expecting. He didn't seem surprised.

"Wh-what?" I choked out.

'*You don't get to run forever.*' I refused to engage.

"We know, Lya. And all we want is to help." He leaned forward, honey-colored eyes boring into me and a smirk on his face. "Come on now, an anomaly like yours? You had to have known you weren't the only one. So, when did you first shift?"

"Fourteen." I pulled my knees up to my chest, feeling much more vulnerable than when I thought I was only having to justify a murder.

He nodded. "That's young. Why didn't your parents help you out with it? At least one of them has to be full-blooded for you to have gotten a wolf."

I shook my head. "My mom found out."

Somewhere in the back of my head, I recognized that this conversation was completely ludicrous. This wasn't what people casually discussed, and it certainly wasn't normal. Or maybe it was the most normal, given the circumstances.

"Found out? So, your dad was a shifter? She still should have known if it was from his side. Are you adopted?"

I shook my head again, my eyes not leaving the floor. "She was scared, so I tried to get rid of it..."

He motioned for me to continue, so I held out my arms. Scars from years of cutting myself with a silver blade to shut that thing out covered them, and my wrists were raw from constantly wearing silver bracelets, even though I was allergic to them. "Suicide attempts didn't work, but silver always made it go away for a while."

He leaned his head down, eyes scrunched closed, and ran his hands through his sandy blond hair. I looked past him at the suggestion of dawn streaming through the window.

"Lya, there's nothing wrong with you." Trevor looked back up. This time, it was clearly sorrow in his eyes. "You should have been told, educated. That is a failure of all of our kind. You're a werewolf, Lya. Not a monster."

OLIVER

DAWN WAS BEGINNING TO BREAK. I really hoped Trevor had a handle on where she was by this point. For the first time in a long time, I actually called him. The phone barely had a chance to ring before it connected.

"Yeah?" His voice was gruff.

"Update?"

"Oh, y'know, pulled an all-nighter. Not the fun kind, either." I waited for him to continue. This wasn't exactly a joking matter. "It's bad. We'll be headed to you as soon as we can."

"We knew it was bad," I pointed out. "What other information do you have?"

He sighed. "Do you want to know now or wait for her to tell you?"

"Now."

"Well, her mom at least clearly had no idea what she could be. I don't know if it was a one-night stand or she was adopted, but her dad isn't in the picture. The wolfiness could have come from him. Bottom line is, no one was around to help her."

That bombshell caused pause. Werewolves didn't let humans adopt their pups for this very reason. It was too dangerous to go through a first shift and try to navigate a new identity by yourself, especially outside of a pack. There was absolutely no way to predict this girl's mental state or moral compass.

"She hates her wolf. Calls her a parasite and the demon in her head."

My own wolf growled at the comment. Your wolf was a gift, not a curse. For a mere moment, I understood why Trevor was providing this girl so much grace.

"She's tried to kill herself multiple times, but y'know, wolf healing, it didn't really work. So, she slashes herself up with a silver knife to keep her wolf at bay. Wears a silver bracelet and silver earrings. It's..." Trevor's voice caught. "It's barbaric. This should have never happened."

"It's why we have laws that prevent this," I stated. "The last time someone shifted without knowing what was happening, our entire existence was almost exposed."

The last time—the only time, to my knowledge—was before my time. Human scientists had gotten their hands on a pup, which could have resulted in the public finding out about our existence. The rescue mission failed, he got away, and a hunter took him out. At least all the people who knew about his existence were dealt with. But this girl's lack of knowledge left her at too much risk and made her a risk to us. She couldn't remain a rogue for the safety of everyone, never mind the fact that she would have never learned how to properly integrate with her wolf.

I sat and thought. She had been given none of the tools to even get by and understand who she was. Because of that, she was a very, very real threat. There was the easy route where we just neutralized her, but I had to hope we had gotten to her in time to fix the situation.

My brain kept circling back to silver. Silver affected each werewolf differently, ranging from debilitating burns to a painful death. Never had I heard of one with any amount of resistance outside of myths. Wearing silver jewelry would have been out of the question. I knew it couldn't be a result of being a half-breed, either. If diluting shifter blood had any effect on how we reacted to things like silver, crossbreeding would have become a much more popular practice. Being a werewolf was all or nothing.

My wolf, ever the emotional beast, curled up and hummed. The neglect bothered him on a different level than it did me. Wolves were pack animals; we needed and looked out for each other. We cared for our own as much as possible. No matter how the media tried to present us in fiction, we were a very peaceful bunch and enjoyed quiet lives in nature with others of our kind. Sure, we had become quite civilized. Integrating ourselves with the human population was the only way to survive without being discovered and eradicated, but we weren't monsters.

Trevor cleared his throat. "You still there?"

"How old is she?" I asked.

"Twenty-four. She first heard her wolf when she was fourteen."

Ten years. Ten years alone and scared of herself. Ten years of hating half of who she was. Ten years of trying to kill herself and keep her wolf away. My wolf let out a whine. For both of us, as leaders of a pack, it was hard to sit quietly and wait. "Does she know anything?"

Trevor scoffed. "Oliver, she doesn't even know the name of her wolf. She hates her so much, and I think her wolf is getting so angry about it that she's starting to take over. The only thing Lya knows is how to keep the wolf side quiet for a bit. She said tonight was the first time she had shifted since she moved here two years ago."

I was quiet. None of that was natural.

"We will be there by noon your time. Hopefully, I can get some more information out of her on the drive." He sighed. "I'm sorry, man."

"Especially about the silver," I grunted. "And anything about the hunter family she had ties to."

"What are you going to do with her?" Trevor asked tentatively.

"I don't know. She needs help. But keeping her here will be dangerous for us..." My voice trailed off, thinking of the hunters who would inevitably be at our doorstep if they found out she was here.

"She's my friend, Ollie."

"Mate?" I asked.

He was quick to disagree. "Even if she was, I don't think someone raised human and so disconnected from their wolf would be able to stomach that conversation."

"Good point." This situation was getting more and more difficult to manage.

"See ya soon." And with that, Trevor disconnected the call.

I sat in silence for a moment. My wolf, Adair, whined in my head.

'*What do we do?*' I asked. The wolf always knew best.

'*She will run from us,*' he said. '*She cannot even accept herself. How will she accept others?*'

'*I would hope that being surrounded by her kind would help her.*'

That's one thing we needed to get through to her. Your wolf was you.

A light knock on the door startled me out of my thoughts. I glanced up from my desk to see Rose peeking in. She was tall and lanky, quiet. Typical for a shifter whose best talent was scouting. Rose had been a top student when going through her training. I had high hopes for her and what she could do for the pack.

"You wanted to see me?" she asked.

"Yes, please sit." I motioned toward one of the chairs across from my desk. I never understood why the Alpha had an office before I took over the role. From what I had noticed, my father rarely utilized it. Now, seeing how many people sat in those chairs every day, I was endlessly thankful for the space.

I sat back and looked at her. Piercing ice-blue eyes stared back at me. Not the pretty ice-blue, but the depthless blues that saw right into your soul.

"How are you enjoying your scouting work?" I asked.

"It's been great!" she said ecstatically. "I'm so excited to be put on a big project! I have loved testing myself and solving so many issues. I know none of my assignments have been of any real importance, but someday, right?"

I nodded, a sad smile stretching across my face. She was a new grad, not even a month out of the program. Of course, she would still be enamored with utilizing her skills. We didn't want to need them, but we wouldn't be caught with our pants down and not have them. That was a hard concept for new grads to get their minds around.

"Just like the warriors, it's a position you train hard for in the hopes of never needing," I reminded her. "But we need you now."

"Really?" Her face lit up with excitement. "When? Where? What are we doing?"

"I will remind you once. After that, it is on you to remind yourself." I leaned forward, resting my elbows on the desk, pausing for gravity. "We never want our pack to be in a position of needing to make use of your training."

"No... of course. That makes sense," she stammered. "Of course, we don't want breaches to our security. I'm just anxious to prove my usefulness and my worth."

I chuckled. "Rose, I would much rather sign a paycheck for someone who has only been able to train and not work, than someone who has to prove their worth. I'd much rather you be useless and an expense."

"Exactly. I get it." She nodded, disappointment clear on her face.

"That's not to say it'd be a useless expense," I quickly added. "But it looks like you'll be earning your paycheck on more than the training grounds now."

She nodded again, careful not to show her excitement.

"How do you feel about a road trip?"

THREE

Lya

I WAS CURLED up in the passenger seat of Trevor's Lincoln, staring out the window. Every time he tried to get me to talk, I kept silent. Really, I had probably told him too much already. I needed to get out and away from here.

Trevor insisted there were others like me, but I had a hard time believing it. He wanted to take me to what he called a pack. They could help me, get me acclimated and adjusted to the life I was supposed to have. That wasn't going to happen. There was no way something like me was supposed to have a life.

"Are you like me?" I asked after a good half hour of silence.

"Yeah," he admitted with a laugh. "I am. It's how I've kept an eye on you the past couple of weeks."

"You what?" I asked, shocked.

"C'mon, Lya," he chided, giving me a sideways glance before quickly reverting his eyes to the road. "I knew something was wrong. Do you remember a couple weeks ago when you stayed late at the bar, actually got drunk, and then crashed at my place? It was, what, a couple days after you got engaged? I knew something was wrong."

"I didn't think I was that obvious," I mumbled. I had worked so hard to stay distant. The extent of my knowledge of social interaction was mostly

16

from people watching, and from my understanding, getting drunk and staying over at a friend's place wasn't unheard of.

He shook his head, a wry smile across his face. "People don't get engaged one day and refuse to go home the next. I may not be human, and our relationships work differently, but I do know that."

"How so?"

Trevor laughed again. One of my favorite things about him had always been his ability to laugh at anything. I wondered if that's what people were supposed to be like.

"What was your life like?" I blurted out, not even realizing I had asked what I was thinking.

"Oh, it was great." The smile lingering from his laughter grew nostalgic. "The pack is like one big family. A family of a few thousand, but you get the point."

"How do a few thousand people hide from all of West River?" I asked, curiosity getting the better of me.

Trevor shrugged. "It's one of the larger packs. We've more or less built up our own self-sufficient towns, so there's no real reason to leave and no big reason for others to come in. You'll see."

It sounded like a cult, if you asked me. But I prodded a little more. "Why aren't you still there?"

"I'm, uh... I'm looking for something."

"If a pack is so great, why couldn't you find it there?"

"Well, life would be too easy if everything was always at your fingertips, wouldn't it?" he teased.

The car dipped down a steep hill, bringing the Missouri River into view. Trevor pulled into a gas station, citing it as one of the last places to refuel before traversing the Badlands. So, I hopped out of the passenger's seat, grabbing my bag. Trevor looked at me quizzically.

"I need to go to the bathroom."

He nodded. I definitely didn't want to be a part of a society where I needed permission to go to the bathroom.

I rushed into the gas station, immediately looking for alternative exits.

Right next to the bathrooms was the entrance to the stockroom. There was always another exit there. I glanced around but saw no security cameras. Not exactly uncommon for a place in as small a town as this.

Bingo.

Slipping to the back of the store and into the stockroom, I quickly found the exit and took off. These small-town businesses really needed to get better about their security. Nobody should be able to pull a stunt like that, traipsing through 'employees only' areas and leaving out a back door. That was the only easy part of the escape, though. I wouldn't have much of a head start before Trevor noticed. I just needed enough time to create some distance.

Growing up, running was my escape. It was something I had never given up, even once I figured out I couldn't run away from myself. It was so easy to get lost in the monotony of the pounding tempo, and people rarely questioned your reason for running. It's good for you, right? I knew I could run for miles, and I was fast. Give me an hour and a half, and I'd be ten miles away from here.

I felt the resident in my brain stir. *'Why do you have to be so dumb.'*

It wasn't a question, so I didn't bother with a response.

Of all the places in South Dakota to stop, this was a great one. The hills around the river would slow me down, but they would also help hide me from watching eyes. I only wished there was a forest like my sanctuary had. My feet pounded against the earth, carrying me one step further away with each stride.

'You don't even know what you're running from.'

I decided to stick to the hills instead of running east or west. The Missouri was a bigger river, meaning a more hilly area surrounded it. Those hills were coverage. I had heard countless times that South Dakota was one of the only states where you could watch your dog run away for miles before jumping in the truck to follow it. I didn't want to be that dog. If they wanted to find me, I wasn't going to let it be easy.

'If you would just let me in, I could show you it won't be.'

I shook the bracelet around my wrist, hoping the silver jangling against my skin would shut her up and send her away again.

Her. It didn't deserve identification and personification. It wasn't a her. It certainly wasn't part of me. And I wasn't going to give it the power to fuck things up even more.

My pace slowed, the terrain taking more out of me than I expected. I couldn't afford to trip or get hurt. Better to go slow and steady and continue making forward progress.

OLIVER

I HADN'T THOUGHT TWICE BEFORE ANSWERING all phone calls today. Already, I had sent my three best scouts to check out the area surrounding the girl's former home. I had Cyber digging up what he could about the hunter family she was enmeshed with, and I had calls out to packs within five hundred miles asking about hunter activity.

So far, the consensus had been that hunters had been quiet recently, almost worryingly so. There were only a few primary factions of hunters throughout the country, forming their own packs of sorts. It was usually a side gig for them while they maintained otherwise normal lives. Years ago, they tried to make noise about the things that went bump in the night that humans should be scared of, but human society quickly wrote those hunters off as mentally unhinged. That served us well, resulting in a large number of our threats being locked away or dubbed insane. In a roundabout way, it also secured the idea that we were simply the plot of the next worst paranormal novel and nothing more.

If it weren't for a select few of our kind, I had to think there wouldn't even be hunters. We were a peaceful people who looked out for the good of all, not just our own. We had the means and the structure to deal with our own rotten apples, too.

The girl was important, but the pack was the priority. I had to do everything I could to keep any threat from coming to our door, even if this girl did. Once she showed up, she would be part of the pack. Adair wouldn't allow anything else.

She'd be part of the pack I needed to protect.

She'd be part of the pack I needed to protect from her.

The phone ringing was becoming a grating sound. Trevor's name flashing on the caller ID was not something I could ignore, though, so I begrudgingly picked it up to get the noise to stop.

"What?" I snapped. Phone calls were getting exhausting.

"Ollie, I need help." His voice was frantic. That wasn't the norm, even when he was in trouble. He also never straight out asked for help. "She's gone! She's just gone! We were halfway there, but she's gone."

"What do you mean, she's *gone?*" I demanded. "I told you not to take your eyes off of her!"

"We stopped for gas in Chamberlain. She went in to go to the bathroom, and she must have run. I'm sorry, man, I—"

"Follow her," I said. "She won't shift, and if she does, you'll probably have an easier time dealing with her wolf."

"Yeah, okay," he stammered.

"I'm on my way."

Adair wanted to run, but a car would be faster. They were only three hours away, and it wasn't quite ten. He could get out to play his part once we got there. If things went smoothly, we could be back here tonight. I wasn't worried about finding her, just about finding her first. There was a world of possibilities for a feral wolf on the loose, and most of them resulted in death.

I strode out to the driveway and got into my Land Cruiser. I sat and thought for a moment before pulling out. Chasing after a weak rogue with no pack connections hundreds of miles away wasn't something an Alpha should be doing. It was something a warrior or scout could easily take on, especially with Trevor already there. Truthfully, the only reason Trevor needed help at all was because it seemed his emotional connection to this girl was clouding his judgment and function. Hell, even one of the newly shifted pups with only a year or so of basic training under their belt could probably manage it just fine. Adair didn't care, though, and pushed us on.

It bothered me how fiercely protective Adair was of this girl. But then again, the protective instinct came naturally for an Alpha.

I prodded through the pack members, checking to see if Rose was still in range. She had been excited to get such a big assignment and had taken off to pack and head out almost immediately. I told her I wanted her back in a week. That should be plenty of time to make sure my brother had left no trace of the mess, see how things got managed, and monitor whether or not other hunters showed up to snoop around.

Faintly, I felt her still close enough to the pack.

'Rose,' I reached out. Mind-link was a magical thing I constantly wondered how humans lived without. Probably why cell phones and texting had become such a necessity for everyday life.

'Yes, Alpha?'

Being referred to as Alpha was something I swore I would never get used to. I much preferred being 'Oliver,' and most pack members I interacted with regularly used that instead.

'I'm going to need you to stop over in Chamberlain for a while before heading on. We might need another set of hands. You can send the others ahead of you.'

'Yes, Alpha.'

The lack of questions, however, was something I was very happy with.

Even if we didn't need her to help bring the girl back, another woman around would probably be more reassuring than being ambushed by two men.

I slammed on the brakes before I pulled out of the long driveway. I wasn't needed for this, no matter what my wolf tried to convince me. It would be a feat to overpower him, but my time was better spent ensuring my schedule was cleared for her inevitable arrival. I changed trajectory, instead driving through town toward the training grounds. It was a Monday, so things were quiet. People here still worked, pups were at school, and the career warriors were training.

I tried to call Trevor, but he didn't pick up. Reception in this state was always miserable. Another reason to be thankful for mind-linking. I tried reaching out to Rose, but she was too far away to get through to her. I just had to hope he would have the girl secured by the time Rose got there. Hopefully, I wouldn't get a phone call saying I should have gone out myself.

The training grounds were a feature within the pack I was exceptionally proud of. The training academy had been my father's project and became a legacy I happily carried on. As the largest pack in North America should, we had the strongest army and the most cohesive of relationships with allies. This training academy, which was open to any allied pack, was a big reason for that. They relied on us more than we did them, but it was a worthwhile investment. I had to assume that, someday, the tides would change, and we would be able to cash in their debts.

"Kota!" I called across the parking lot, hoping to get my Gamma's attention before he disappeared onto the training field.

He whipped around as if his guard was up. Knowing him, though, it always was. I jogged across the parking lot, where he quickly fell in stride alongside me. I stayed quiet until we were within the confines of his office. Some news didn't need to be overheard. There was no reason to cause unnecessary worry or rumors.

As soon as the door was closed, I started in. Rogue girl, feral wolf, no idea where she's from. Silver wasn't stopping her, and she was missing.

Kota nodded slowly. "And why didn't you drive out to Trevor's place last night?"

I stilled. Kota was one of the few who so willingly pointed out where I had failed, which was how he'd earned his position. That didn't mean being humbled felt good.

"I figured Trevor could handle it," I mumbled.

"And why would you think that?" he scoffed. "Do you even have a name for this girl?"

"Lya." The name rolled off my tongue, tasting like a distant memory of a happier time. Something I almost remembered. It was a unique name, the hard 'Y' rolling off the tongue. It wasn't one I would forget, and it worried me that I might have.

Kota took a deep breath. "I may know her."

"You've met her?" I demanded. Kota was from an allied pack down south. The possibility that she had involvement in his old pack gave me a little hope. Maybe she wasn't as naive as Trevor let on.

"No," he quickly disagreed. "But I've heard the name before. She went missing five or six years ago."

If she was twenty-four now, that aligned with Trevor's tale of her being kicked out as soon as she was of legal age, but why wouldn't she seek solace with people she knew? I turned to the Keurig in his office and began doctoring myself a cup of coffee. "What pack was she affiliated with?"

"None," Kota said. "If she's the girl I'm thinking of, she's Jade's cousin. She didn't think she had a wolf, though..."

I placed my mug of coffee on the desk, not wanting to throw it. It was Adair's anger reverberating through me, but it might as well have been my own. Two instances now where the girl had been failed, and the responsibility was falling on my shoulders.

"Would you consider her a threat?"

Kota looked up at me, gray eyes hardening to stone. "Never."

"And do I have any hope of getting more information out of you?" I prodded.

"No."

FOUR

Lya

I SAT on the embankment overlooking the river. The sun was high in the sky, and I had been making steady progress for a good four hours, maybe more. Given the hills and the amount of time I had walked instead of run, I hoped I was fifteen miles away from the gas station. My phone was back in Trevor's car, so I was relying on my internal compass at this point. At least that had always been reliable.

I peeled off my sweatshirt and spent a minute enjoying the feel of the sun on my skin. Melting snow had engorged the river, and the high waters rushed by. Off in the distance, I could hear four-wheelers. The thought that someone else was at least enjoying the first taste of summer brought a sad smile to my face. I'd have to remember this place and maybe come back someday.

There hadn't been much about this state I had liked, but this place was akin to my little sanctuary. Just a lot bigger, and without trees. Many people had told me I would enjoy the Black Hills, that they would remind me of the Appalachian Mountains in New England. I highly doubted that, though. Nothing could ever compare to those. And there was no way I was headed there next. If that pack was in the Black Hills, I was steering far away from there.

I thought about my next move. Choices were exceptionally limited. I didn't have any mode of transportation other than my own two feet, cash would run out, and I really had no idea how I would continue existing with the whole 'people don't hire murderers' thing. I had nothing and no idea what to do. My best bet was probably to get back to Brookings, retrieve my car, and somehow obtain a fake identity. How did one go about that, anyway? It had been a three-hour drive thus far. It'd be a long walk back east. Maybe I should head north to Canada now.

'*You have me,*' the voice slyly quipped.

'*Oh, yeah?*' I asked. '*And what, pray tell, will you do to help out here?*'

'*I could get us to somewhere safe.*'

I didn't know what her idea of a safe place was, but I didn't think I'd agree with the assessment.

I wished I had a good way to follow the news. I was morbidly curious how long it would take for Ted's body to be found. I knew exactly how they would portray me. Dead man with a missing fiancée. It was an open-and-shut case. They'd call it a crime of passion, probably. If I was lucky, I'd only be put away for manslaughter. I wondered how they'd spin the murder weapon, though.

But what had tipped Ted's dad off about the monster I harbored inside of me? I had never dared even allude to it around Ted or his family. I hadn't shifted in years. Well, aside from last night. Was it really only a day ago? It felt like a lifetime.

The pack Trevor spoke of was intriguing at the very least. I guess it wasn't completely surprising that there were others like me, but it was shocking to think of how it came upon me. I thought I was schizophrenic for the longest time, and shifting had been a figment of my imagination. I didn't have a problem with it at first; it was actually almost comforting. I had a constant companion. But when I lost control and shifted in front of my mother, the horror was abundantly apparent. It wasn't all in my head.

My younger sister was twenty at this point. I wondered if the same thing had happened to her as she grew up. If it really was a genetic thing, and my mom had no idea, it had to have come from my father. By the time I was fourteen and could have asked my dad, he was on his way out of the picture. Or, as Trevor had suggested, I was adopted and never told. I doubted that, though. I bore too much of a resemblance to my family.

I sighed. I had too many questions and didn't even know where to begin looking for answers on my own. I was slowly coming to the realization that understanding more would probably make my life a lot easier. Like, maybe there was a way to permanently suppress or get rid of this curse.

I swore at myself as I came to the conclusion that maybe, just this one time, running had not been my best move. Just because I went to a pack didn't mean I'd have to stay there. I could always run. But now I wondered if Trevor would even still take me, or if I had blown my chance. Would my ego even let me beg for forgiveness?

'*But now you need to run.*' The voice sounded urgent. I shook my wrist, the silver bracelet bouncing harshly against my skin. It twinged a bit, but it usually did the trick to shut the voice up.

A hand wrapping around my bicep and yanking me up pulled me out of my thoughts. I hadn't even heard someone coming up behind me.

I swung around, throwing a fist, but another hand stopped the punch. A haggard, weatherworn face stared back at me, his laugh exposing broken and yellowed teeth. I cringed in disgust, trying to twist out of his hold.

"Now what's a pretty little thing like yourself doing out here all alone?" he mocked. Behind him, I saw three other men, each with rifles on them, and four-wheelers. They must have been who I heard. I desperately hoped they were out here for the spring turkey season and this wasn't about to become some rendition of *The Most Dangerous Game*.

I kicked out, my foot landing in his crotch. As he doubled over in pain, another one of the men was on me in an instant, tackling me down to the ground.

"Now what'd you go and do that for?" he sneered, his face inches from mine. He was young, barely more than a kid, but days out in the elements were already beginning to weather his skin. "All we wanna do is make sure you're okay."

"I would disagree," I snarled. A growl rumbled in my chest, and that peculiar feeling of 'about to shift' came over me. I tried to wiggle out of his grasp, glancing around for a way out. The first one who grabbed me was up and looming over us, and one behind him had his rifle aimed at me.

I reached out to the thing in my head, to the wolf. Something I hadn't done in almost a decade. '*Some help might be useful.*'

'*Say please.*'

'*Do you want to be dead, too?*'

'*As if I don't feel like it already,*' she scoffed.

But, bones cracked, rearranging and stretching my human flesh. I sucked a deep breath in, trying to stay focused. Shifting was so painful.

The guy pinning me down lost his hold on my wrist as it morphed into a paw. The wolf shoved him off and lunged for the first man, grabbing and tearing at his arm. His scream was deafening. Just as she was about to leap at the younger hunter, the unmistakable sound of a bullet rang out. I felt it tear through her shoulder, causing the wolf to let go and yelp.

The wolf steadied herself and looked around, trying to decide on the biggest threat. It was alarming to me how unsurprised these men seemed. Like seeing a person shift into a giant wolf was nothing new to them.

What if it wasn't anything new to them? Ted hadn't been surprised, either.

Three of the four had guns pointing at us. The one my wolf had torn into was clutching his mostly amputated arm.

"Look at the little puppy dog, come out to play," the first man sneered, gritting through the pain.

The wolf turned on its haunches to run, but two more guns went off, one bullet landing in our hip, and the other lodging itself in our side.

The wolf toppled over, letting out a whine. The men formed an impenetrable wall, preventing escape, one placing a kick to the stomach while the other pointed his rifle between our eyes. Blood sputtered from the wolf's side, and things grew hazy. I peered out from behind the wolf's eyes, catching the sight of a large, tawny wolf launching itself at the man with the gun pointed at us, another lanky, cream-colored wolf in hot pursuit.

But it didn't matter anymore as everything went dark.

Oliver

Best case scenario, this girl would be back in four or five hours. Their noon arrival I had been promised had been pushed back to late afternoon, leaving me with nothing to do but sit and wait. And fight my wolf. He had never been this... possessive over anyone. Protective, yes. The whole pack fell under that jurisdiction. This Lya girl, however, was not pack and was a threat until proven otherwise. A concept he seemed unwilling or unable to grasp.

Adair's attempt at seizing control to force information out of Kota was enough to let me know the training grounds were not a place I should be today. I was surly, and Adair was an Alpha. Neither of us took the word "no" well, especially from a subordinate. Kota wouldn't budge, though, even when his back was to the wall with my clawed hands around his throat. Even with a wolf strong enough to combat that of an Alpha, never before had I considered he had the potential to be an enemy.

That's exactly how I found myself stomping toward my grandmother's little cabin on the outskirts of our territory. The path was not nearly as worn as it should have been, and it was entirely my fault. I hadn't been making my way out this direction often enough. But right now, it was the only place my wolf could safely be. I was nothing more than the prodigal child, returning to confess my transgressions.

She lived alone now; her mate died five years previously from the slow decline of heartbreak after their son, my father, had passed. I often wondered how the death of their only child followed by the death of her mate didn't take her, too. Her mental fortitude was one of the things that garnered her a place as an Elder.

Her cottage looked like it had always been here, even though I remembered assisting my father and grandfather in building it by hand. I remembered my mother painstakingly replanting the natural fauna we'd removed to make space for the structure, and how diligently my grandmother cared for it in the first few years to ensure it survived. I had been a different person then. The youngest son of the most powerful Alpha in the country, destined to be forgotten.

I missed those days.

But here was one of the few places I could feel the façade of an Alpha fading away. It wasn't mine in her presence.

Maybe I waited a moment too long, standing in front of her cabin in the woods and examining the scenery. The door swung open, revealing the Alpha of two generations ago.

"Ollie?" she called. "What is it?"

I hung my head, kicking at the dirt once more before making my way to her front door. "Hi, Grandma."

Her warm smile reminded me she never remembered my failures, even though I only ever showed up here after making a mistake, proving my inadequacy. "What is it, Ollie?"

"I've... I can't control Adair."

She frowned, nodding slowly. "I figured as much. I don't expect social calls from you."

I followed her inside, flopping down on one of the overstuffed chairs in what used to be a living room. Books had long since overtaken the communal space, residing on shelves and in stacks on every surface. She settled in the seat across from me and waited patiently for me to disclose what it was that had brought me here.

"Trevor found a girl," I finally told her. "Just some rogue, but she might be feral."

She quirked an eyebrow but offered no response. This was her way, letting people talk their way to their own conclusions. With a heavy sigh, I continued.

"Adair was willing to kill Kota, just because he thinks he knows her. My wolf is being all obsessive over her."

"Obsessive or possessive?" she asked.

"What's the difference?" I huffed. "I can't lead a pack when my wolf refuses to think of anything other than some girl he hasn't even met."

Her wan smile told me I was missing some vital piece to the puzzle. "You're twenty-eight, Oliver. Do you not think he could be so concerned because she's more than just a feral rogue?"

The suggestion was ludicrous. I knew why my wolf hated feral rogues. It had everything to do with the circumstances in which my father died and nothing to do with a mate, as my grandmother implied. I had met my mate, a decade ago, but couldn't find her now. There was no way in hell the delicate little sprite I had seen once upon a time had a wolf driven to murderous tendencies.

"Tell me about her."

I shook my head but decided to appease the woman. "Trevor says she's resistant to silver. He thinks the fiancé of hers that she killed was a hunter, too."

"All plausible," she mused, glancing over to her stacks of books.

"A resistance to silver is not plausible," I scoffed.

"Oh, how quickly you forget," my grandmother chided. She struggled to her feet and turned to her stacks of books to rummage through. "Myths are borne from facts, dear. I'm sure you remember how fondly Thom loved the histories."

I rolled my eyes. She was referring to one of the first werewolf packs, one that was rumored to have developed a silver immunity. The evolution of their power came from the rise of the first faction of hunters as they captured and tortured the members of that pack with it.

But it was just a myth. There were no known survivors of the Wulver Pack and no traceable descendants. They were nothing more than a bedtime story, used to remind pups the Moon Goddess would always look out for us if we were just. Powers among wolves did not simply randomly appear, either. They were inherited.

She turned back to me with a book in her hand. "Read this before you come to any conclusions."

I looked down at the book and pulled away the cloth wrapped around it to see the cover. It was old but in beautiful condition. I ran my hand over the title, *A History,* but quickly pulled my hand away as the silver embossment burned my skin. I didn't dare touch the Celtic knot of the same embossing.

"What would you do, Grandma?"

"If it was still my job to determine that, I would still be the Alpha of this pack," she chuckled. "But I will tell you, you need to stop seeking threats. You will only find them in the wrong places. Your father's reign was filled with trauma, but you have been blessed with peace. Follow that."

I hung my head. She was the first female Alpha this world had seen, and by far the fairest and most just. My father had been able to emulate her, but I always fell short. I was simply riding on the coattails of the successes of those before me, failing to learn from the mistakes they never made.

I wondered how she was able to maintain such an optimistic outlook in situations like these. It had only been eight years since my father was killed in the line of duty at the hands of a rogue wolf gone feral. The rogue had amassed a small army and tore through packs, decimating anyone in his path until he reached Snow Moon. My father had killed him, yes, but at the cost of his own life. I wondered how my grandmother could be willing to show such mercy to someone who was on a trajectory to be a duplicate of the monster who'd caused her own son's death.

"History will only repeat itself if we don't learn from it," I mumbled.

"Exactly," she agreed. "Show the girl the kindness and acceptance she has never known."

I looked up from my hands, wanting to study my grandmother's reaction to the question I was about to ask. "Do you think, if someone had shown Dad's killer the grace you want me to exhibit, things would be different now?"

"No," she stated coldly, staring blankly across her living room. "No, because I still do not believe he was simply a feral rogue."

"And why is that, Grandma?"

She looked up, the pain of eight years ago appearing fresh on her face. "I believe it's time for you to go, Oliver. An Alpha's time should not be spent bemoaning the past."

I knew my grandmother well; I would not be getting any more information out of her. I carefully rewrapped the book and made my way out of her cabin. I elected to take the long way back to the training grounds, needing the extra time to process everything she had told me—all while saying nothing at all, mind you.

The further I got from my grandmother's presence, the less compliant my wolf felt. He minded his place in the Elder's presence, but now he was as anxious as he had been when we got the call from Trevor that the girl was missing.

I felt like my sanity was ebbing, which was not a feeling I enjoyed. Whether I liked it or not, I was the Alpha. I couldn't get hung up on a rogue who realistically posed little threat. I knew I was blowing this whole situation out of proportion, but there was nothing I could do to stop it.

I forwent the complex, beelining for my FJ60. I slid in, seeing my phone still on the passenger seat and flashing with an alarming number of notifications. Most from Trevor, but more concerningly, a couple from Rose. I mentally kicked myself for being so foolish as to forget it. It was nearly two now. What were the chances it was an update to confirm they had her?

The phone rang a couple too many times for my liking when I called back. The delay for the phone to connect was equally frustrating.

"Where the fuck are you, man?" Trevor shouted. "You said you were coming!"

Not for the first time today, I flinched at the accusation that I wasn't handling this personally. "I sent Rose."

"That's not good enough," he huffed after a long pause. "We need more hands. And a first aid kit."

"What happened?" I snapped.

"She's shot, Alpha," I heard Rose call. "She was ambushed by hunters."

I didn't think twice this time, throwing the old stick shift into gear and burning rubber. "I'm on my way."

Thank the Goddess for South Dakota's eighty-mile-per-hour speed limits. I'd still speed, anyway. It was as good a time as any to see how few miles per gallon this old thing could get.

FIVE

Lya

'HEY,' a voice echoed through my head. I ignored it. Everything was so dark and disjointed, I had no perception of what was going on.

'Hey,' it repeated. It was a feminine voice. Flowy and soft, but also demanding respect and to be heard.

'What?' My own was groggy and cracked.

'A thank you is in order,' she said.

'And why would I do that?'

'For taking over and protecting your ass when you would never return the favor,' she scoffed.

I had no idea what was going on. I felt completely out of my own body. That feeling intensified as images from the past came into focus.

'It doesn't have to be this way,' she whispered softly.

I was sitting in my old childhood bedroom. It must have been late because the curtains were drawn and a lamp was on. I looked on at a younger version of myself, smiling and giggling. I missed those days.

I remembered this night, this conversation. I had turned fifteen two months prior, and my wolf had shown up right before my birthday. The voice had come a couple months before that.

When the voice initially appeared, I was wary. I was certain I was going crazy. I didn't tell any of my friends, and certainly not my mother. The only person I mentioned it briefly to was my younger sister. She was enthralled, wanting to know every detail, but I kept it short. Just a friendly presence; a constant companion. She didn't have a name, at least not one she had told me.

The day of my first shift, the voice warned me that a change was coming, encouraging me to find somewhere alone, so I went out for one last trip to a private little beach in midcoast Maine. She said most people wouldn't understand, and it'd be better if I was by myself. I hadn't been alone that day, though. I ran into someone. She told me it would hurt, but it'd be brief. She said she would manage as much of it as she could.

She was right. The pain was excruciating, and I screamed as it felt like every bone in my body was breaking. When I opened my eyes and looked around, I saw paws instead of hands, fur the same color as my auburn hair, and when I turned, I saw a tail. The tail was the thing that really set me off. I had a *tail*. A big, fluffy tail.

Before I could truly freak out, the voice jumped in. '*This is us, Lya. I am your wolf. I am a part of you just as much as you are a part of me. We will always have each other.*'

That reassurance and acceptance warmed me. Everything would be okay. My life was in shambles with my dad deciding we needed to move down south and puberty being hell for any kid, but I would always have this. No matter how bad things ever got.

'*Keep this secret,*' my wolf implored. '*When the time is right, I'll let you know when it's safe to tell others.*'

'*Are there others like us?*' I had asked.

Her voice was warm and reassuring when she said, '*All in due time, you will know.*'

I didn't know how to see my wolf back then. She was like a mother figure, a sister, a mentor, and a best friend all rolled into one.

But this night she had brought me to, it's the night everything changed. We had been talking about a boy, Sutton, who I had the hugest crush on. He didn't even know I existed. My wolf insisted he wasn't worth my time and energy, that we would know when the right one came along, but he wasn't it. Just wait.

We heard voices from downstairs. That was unusual because it was late and both my sister and I had gone to bed. I perked up when I thought I heard my dad's voice.

I rushed out of my bedroom and down the stairs, stopping when I saw him in the doorway.

"Daddy?" My voice cracked. The past months of anger and hurt dissipated.

He smiled at me, his expression warm. "Lya." He held his arms open for a hug, but as I moved toward him, my mom jumped in between us.

"*You do not touch her,*" she hissed. "You don't get to disappear after forcing us to move, leaving us high and dry with no idea what happened or where you were, then waltz back in and be '*Daddy*' again!"

He tried to push past her, but she slapped him and shoved him toward the door.

That was it. That was what had done it.

Anger bubbled up to a point that I couldn't contain. I wanted to see my dad. I could be angry and seek my own retribution later, but right now, I was just thankful to know he was alive. And he was here.

A growl rumbled in my chest, and both of their eyes were on me. Soon, they were looking at a wolf standing on the stairs, not their daughter.

'*No,*' I thought. '*I am their daughter like this, too.*'

I looked at my parents from behind my wolf's eyes. It was such a unique sensation, being there but only as a fly on the wall.

The look of sheer terror on my mother's face bit deep. Looking at my father, at the time, I thought he felt the same. The fear in the room was palpable. I could smell it.

But now, studying his face from this perspective. I saw a flash of something else. Joy? Pride? It was the same look he'd give when he informed me I was the best oldest daughter he had.

But the look was quickly replaced by sadness, hurt, and grief. And with that, he bolted out the door.

I ran back to my room. I had loved my wolf with all my heart, but all that love dissipated in a few short seconds. It had scared my mother, and it had sent my daddy away again. I fought my wolf, forcing her back to allow me to settle into my own skin.

'*You have to go now. Forever,*' I told the voice.

'*Lya, no,*' she insisted. '*I can't. I'm a part of you.*'

'*Leave.*'

She refused. I racked my brain for every bit of werewolf mythology that I knew.

Silver.

The only thing I had made out of silver was a set of jewelry. I rarely wore it because it gave me rashes. I ran over to my jewelry box and picked up a silver stud. I dug it deep into my wrist and dragged it as far as I could. It wasn't deep by any means, but it was enough. The blood seeping out made the little earring slippery and difficult to hold on to. This hurt worse than my first shift. The voice whimpered, crying out in pain, but I smiled. It was working.

'I'll kill you then,' I told the voice.

'You can't kill me without killing yourself, and I won't let us die,' she choked out, her voice getting fainter and fainter.

I dropped the earring and grabbed a silver bracelet from the small box. It became a permanent fixture on my wrist.

The next day, my dad's truck was still in the driveway. Mom had it towed. I never saw him again.

A couple nights later, when out in the backyard, I saw large pawprints in the mud outside my window.

Over the next three years, my mother and I never once even alluded to that night. She still took care of me, but she wasn't kind, warm, loving, and involved anymore. She always had a twinge of fear whenever I was around, and that hurt worse than if she would get angry at me or tell me how she felt. A conversation was all I wanted.

On my eighteenth birthday, I knew exactly the reason why she told me I needed to leave.

The images faded and I was back in the darkness of my brain. Alone.

'Yes,' I said, knowing the wolf was listening. She always was. *'It does have to be this way.'*

OLIVER

I HAD HOPED I'd run into them along the road. When I didn't, I could only assume things were worse than initially implied. She had been shot, yes, but she was a werewolf. She should heal quickly.

But Rose said they were hunters. That meant she had probably been shot with silver bullets. There was no telling how that would impact her if Trevor's assumption that she truly was resistant to silver was correct.

Truth be told, she probably wasn't even alive at this point. A werewolf would have succumbed to the silver, and a human would have bled out. But something in my gut told me I would know if she was gone.

I pulled up beside Trevor's Lincoln and stepped out, inhaling deeply as

34

the ocean air, carrying notes of lilac and pine, hit my face. It took me a long moment to remember we were in a landlocked state. My head whipped around, trying to find the source, but I couldn't find anything.

Allowing Adair to take over was a given. I had to find that scent, and I had a feeling it would lead me to that girl. Nose to the air, we followed the smell. It felt so close to a memory, but one I couldn't quite reach.

Behind an outcropping of rocks, out of plain sight, I found the source.

And I froze.

I couldn't stop the rumble that built up in my chest, just loud enough to draw the attention of the shifters hovering over the naked girl. Trevor took one look at the Alpha wolf before raising his hands in innocence and taking a slow step backward. Rose sent a cursory glance over her shoulder but didn't move. I understood why she didn't; the smell of blood permeating the air told us she was bleeding out, and if Rose moved her hands, that process would be expedited.

I wouldn't, couldn't move. But I wasn't about to take my eyes off of her. The air was electric, but it was wrong.

'Go get my truck,' I mind-linked Trevor, needing him far away from her naked form.

Tentatively, cautiously, Adair took a step forward. He seemed as perplexed as I was, but the fates drove him in a way that didn't touch me. *'Mate.'*

Adair was so certain. I shook my head; it couldn't be her.

'Mate,' he said again.

There was no debating with the wolf, but I refused to believe he was right. Adair leaned down and nuzzled her neck, sparks zinging through his muzzle.

Rose didn't look up as she asked, "A human hospital, Alpha?"

I shook my head. "She will need blood."

"We'll get her home, Alpha," she assured me, but I wasn't so certain about that. It was late. I had gotten the call three hours ago, but how long before that had she been attacked?

I didn't see how she could survive, and my family had a track record of losing their fated mates. The rumbling of my truck was barely enough to force my mind away from the inevitable. Adair receded, leaving me in my human form. A quick visual assessment confirmed they had bound her wounds, bullet holes that reeked of silver, but they had long bled through. I bit the bullet, stooping down to scoop her up. I shuddered as sparks from the mate bond wracked my body. I did my best not to look at her, but it was near impossible. She was small and delicate, but far from frail. With deep auburn hair that refracted red in the sunlight, and softly freckled skin, she looked so much like a memory I couldn't quite reach.

I was twenty-eight, definitely a couple years past the prime age of finding my mate. Most, by my age, would have a chosen mate by now, but I couldn't. I had met her before, too young to truly appreciate the effects of the mate bond, so I stayed resolute in waiting.

But this couldn't be her.

I slipped into the open door of the truck, settling the girl in the back seat. My intention had been to allow Rose to resume doctoring her while I drove, but every time I tried to pull myself away from the girl's side, my body refused.

Rose tossed me a set of clothes, as well as a blanket to cover the little redhead, and slipped into the front passenger seat. I set to work, replacing all the bloodied scraps of fabric with gauze pads and kerlix.

This would be a long three hours back to the pack.

"You're positive they were werewolf hunters?" I asked. "Not spring turkey season hunters?"

"Silver bullets," Trevor bit back.

I gritted my teeth, cinching the medical tape around her thigh tightly. "Any idea their faction?"

Trevor didn't respond, but I had a sinking feeling I knew. Most would think their affiliation didn't matter, but I needed to know if they were linked to the hunter the girl had killed. If they were seeking retribution, or if it was a fluke. Better yet, how had they known where, and what, she was? I was certain she hadn't shifted to run away from Trevor—her wolf would have brought her to the promise of a pack.

'If her wolf isn't as deranged as she is,' Adair grumbled to me.

'You think they're deranged now?' I snarked. *'Twelve hours ago, you were whining about how sad her wolf must be.'*

'Torture changes a wolf.'

Even self-inflicted torture, it would seem.

The miles dragged by in silence. I quickly noticed my own breathing was linked to the ebbing of her heartbeat, getting a little fainter with each attempt. I didn't even look up at our surroundings to judge how far away we were. Wherever we were, it wasn't close enough.

It took every ounce of my focus to ignore her scent, ignore the sparks, ignore the thrum of her heartbeat getting fainter and fainter. By the time Trevor skidded into the pack hospital's parking lot, I didn't know if I was blitzing out of the vehicle and dumping her on a gurney to get her away from me, or to save her life. Still, I couldn't stop my body from trying to follow. Possessive hands refused to let her go, no matter what I willed them to do.

This couldn't be her.

The doctor I hadn't even realized was there turned to us before a set of swinging doors. "We've got it from here, Alpha."

"But—"

"I know." He smiled. "But we will be able to do our jobs better without a distraught mate who might kill us if we fail standing over our shoulder."

Distraught mate. That wasn't me. She couldn't be my mate. Maybe it would be better if she died. I wouldn't be so focused on someone who couldn't be my mate. Even if she was, maybe it would be better if I selected a chosen mate instead of... *her*.

Begrudgingly, I let my hands fall away from her arm. It was harder to ignore the absence of sparks. The trek back to my truck felt like miles. Trevor had moved to the passenger seat, but Rose was gone. I slipped behind the steering wheel and took one long look at the blood seeping into the back seat. I'd never get that stain out.

I wasn't about to say as much, but it was a saving grace that Trevor stayed with me in my office, and Kota had been quick to join us. I didn't know what I would do if I didn't have a distraction. I didn't tell them I doubted she could actually be my mate. I knew where Trevor's allegiances were, and he would jump to the defense of his friend. In this state, I'd probably believe his arguments, too. Things like 'we can't judge what we don't know,' and 'she was only reacting.' Kota, though. He might side with me. Unless he did actually know the girl.

"When will she be ready for questioning?" Kota asked, finally grabbing my attention.

"Not yet," I snapped. My grandmother's advice rang through my head, imploring me to show her safety and a home she never knew.

Kota cocked an eyebrow at me. "Oh?"

"We'll get more out of her if she feels safe here first."

Trevor looked up, worry lines marring his face. "What are you planning for her, Alpha?"

His choice of using my title instead of my name was noted, and it bothered me. I didn't have an answer to his question, so the words were left to hang heavy in the air.

"I suppose we simply need to focus on acclimating her to life as a wolf," Kota finally said. "How is she to feel safe here if she doesn't even feel safe in her own skin?"

I slung back the rest of my drink and got to my feet. If I was going to sit around and wait for the girl to wake up, I'd do so at the hospital. Sitting here felt wrong. I was surrounded by people who could let me in on a number of things about this girl, but it still felt like the most useless place for me to be.

For a fleeting moment, I felt as if maybe Adair was right; there was no ignoring the draw I had to this girl. The need to hold her close and protect her. A feeling that was so close to a memory just out of reach. But I couldn't dwell on that now.

"Hey, Ollie," Trevor called after me. "She's from Maine."

For a mere second, I froze. Before I allowed myself the chance to give his comment any more thought, I waved him off and left the two in my office.

The bloodstain in my back seat still haunted me. If I had listened to my wolf, it wouldn't be there. I couldn't tell if I felt such guilt because I was an Alpha who failed to protect a wolf in need, or because I had let my mate down.

At this time of night, the hospital was quieter. It was mostly utilized for injuries taking place on the training grounds, and very few were ever hospital-ized for extended periods. Some stitches here, a broken limb reset there, and then expedited werewolf healing took over the rest. The calm and quiet the hospital usually fell into overnight was oddly satisfying.

Tonight, it was anything but. There was more staff than usual, and hushed murmurs echoed off the walls. There was a tension that sizzled off my skin, akin to the nervous energy that filled this place. Was this all because of the girl?

I followed the sense of fractal energy, barely responding when people acknowledged me. I had a one-track mind, and I had a good idea as to why.

I came to a halt in front of a closed door, but it might as well have been a wall. My wolf screamed to break down the barrier, but I felt safe on this side. This had to be where the girl was.

I flinched as the door opened, that alluring ocean breeze so similar to a memory wafting out. This time, it was more concentrated. Maddening, really. My eyes locked with Rose as she exited the room, trying to convince myself it was really her, but I knew it wasn't. I would have recognized it years ago if it was.

"Alpha?" she asked. "Why did you leave? Wolves heal better when their mate is present."

I couldn't tell her I doubted the bond. "Why didn't you just start driving here? I could have met you on the road."

Rose only frowned. "I'm sorry, Alpha, but every time we tried to move

38

her, she started bleeding again, and we ran out of supplies. She would have bled out on the drive back."

I wanted to argue that the death of a feral rogue really didn't matter. But the scent that swirled around me screamed otherwise.

It wasn't possible.

"How bad is she?" I asked. "Really."

"She held her own," Rose said reassuringly. "She went down fighting, too. She had been shot three times by the time we got there, but one of the hunters was missing an arm and another had a good chunk of his face torn off."

So, Rose was certain they were hunters, too. It wasn't that I doubted Trevor, but he had always been quick to jump to the worst possible scenario and had a personal vendetta against hunters. Rose was more level-headed, processing every part of a situation before coming to conclusions. That's what she had been trained to do, anyway.

"She's out of surgery," she added. "Maybe you want to talk to Dr. Whitledge first?"

I nodded once, thankful for the excuse. Anything to get away from here.

Adair was oddly quiet as I followed Rose down the hall, leaving the scents of a spring day in Maine in our wake. Maybe he knew it, too. What instinct was trying to scream wasn't possible, or only meant bad things. I knew the second I laid eyes on her again, all control would go out the window, and that was a risk I wasn't willing to take.

Rose came to a stop in front of an office door and smiled up at me. "Please let me know when she's awake. I'd really like a chance to talk to her."

"You can't bond with every person you save, Rose."

"I know," she agreed. "There's something about her. I can't put my finger on it, but she's special."

That comment was not reassuring at all. Something about her had called out to two of my pack now, leaving me the one to catch up.

"Stay here," I added before she could walk away. "She'll need a friend. You'll have better luck getting through to her."

Rose snuck off, leaving me in front of another door. This one didn't seem as daunting, so it was no chore to knock briefly before entering.

"Alpha," the doctor greeted. It didn't seem as if he'd had time to change since the surgery, given his scrubs still had spatters of blood on them. "Figured you'd be posted up in your mate's room."

"I need to know about the girl."

"Of course," he mumbled, passing me her chart. I took a brief moment to scan it, noticing blood tests confirmed she was a werewolf. The injuries her chart listed were extreme, but shouldn't be a problem for a wolf. I paused at her height and weight, noting she wasn't simply small, she was tiny. A runt, to be exact. Runt wolves were the result of part-breeds or the offspring of an unmated pair. It didn't always happen. Only often enough to notice the pattern.

"How long do you think she'll be in the hospital?"

Dr. Whitledge gave a defeated shrug. "I couldn't tell you that. I would have expected her to be more healed when she got here, but she was shot with silver bullets. Additionally, there is research to suggest werewolves who are not accepting of their wolves have such a disjointed relationship they can't do the basic things, like speed along healing, shift when desired, or even recognize a mate."

"Research?" I demanded. "Why would there be research on such a thing?"

"From the Cold Moon Pack," he assured me. "None of our allies would perform such unethical practices, but that doesn't mean we can't utilize what they learn."

I breathed out a heavy sigh. It was equal parts relief and another strike against that pack. Cold Moon was nearly as large as Snow Moon, but they were married to the antiquated structure of a werewolf pack. We had several refugees from there, and it took them a long time to let go of things like their omega status that no longer existed.

'Maybe her parents are from there,' Adair suggested, but I was quick to refute that idea. We knew better than to raise a pup as if werewolves didn't exist. I couldn't imagine parents would do that to their own, regardless of their pack's research.

"And do you actually believe Trevor's claim that she's immune to silver?"

"I do," he said gravely. "Whether she is actually a descendent of the Wulver Pack, or she simply fostered her own evolution to silver resistance, immunity to it is the only way she survived a silver bullet being lodged in her for nearly seven hours."

The myth, the legend, the Wulver Pack. The very same pack my grandmother had given me a book about. I stopped believing they were real years ago as the facts to prove their existence weren't there. "And is Cold Moon doing any research on whether or not wolves can develop a silver immunity over time?"

"Every time they have, the wolves have died," the doctor grumbled.

I nodded slowly, returning the chart to his desk. "Pull DNA on her."

"Already have," Dr. Whitledge confirmed. "Results should be back in a few days."

After bidding farewell, I left his office. I spent a while wandering around, hoping to find a way out without passing the girl's room. It proved an impossible feat, though, and I soon found myself standing in front of her door again. If it had eyes, we would be in a formidable staring contest. With a tentative hand, I reached for the door knob. I'd have to see her sooner or later, and I preferred to break when no one else was watching.

I refused to step through the doorway, but seeing her was enough. There, battered and broken on a hospital bed, was my mate.

Six

Lya

MY EYELIDS WERE HEAVY, making it a monumental effort to crack them open. I was surrounded by white, and everything smelled sterile. I tried to shift positions, but searing pain ran through me.

The room was dark, but light poured in from the doorway. It was pretty clear I was in a hospital, but I had no idea how I got here. The last thing I could remember was dying.

As my eyes adjusted to my surroundings, I realized there was a figure in the doorway. The light behind him made his features indistinguishable, but I was certain it was a man. Tall and burly, and given how stiff he stood, uncomfortable.

"Hello?" I croaked out.

I expected the man to enter the room, maybe even introduce himself, but he didn't. Instead, he turned away, practically fleeing down the hall. Each footfall against the hospital floor rattled me, reminding me I wasn't somebody anyone should care about.

It shouldn't have hurt. I had spent a decade trying to master that persona. But this time, it did.

His retreating footsteps played on repeat in my head. I wondered who he was, and more importantly, why I felt like he mattered. The presence of my parasite was overwhelming in my head, but it didn't feel like she was vying for control. Like she wanted to share space, the way we used to. I had half a mind to think the reason I was so concerned about my intruder was because of her.

I shook my head, trying to dislodge both the wolf and thoughts of that guy. His presence should have worried me. He couldn't have worked here; otherwise, he would have introduced himself. Likewise, if he had been a cop of some sort, he wouldn't have had any qualms about being near me. He wouldn't be scared of a murderer. A cop's job was to put me away. Maybe I had a stalker.

'Or maybe you have a savior.'

Instinctively, I shook my wrist. Silver bashing against skin always shut up the wolf, but she barked out a laugh. I glanced down at my wrist frantically, but all that was there was raw skin. The rash silver always gave me still stung, but my wards were gone.

'Welcome back, motherfucker,' the voice snarled.

Given the way the monitors picked up, I could tell my heart rate was elevated. *'How are you still alive? I thought I had killed you.'*

'Ten years of torture, and not a second of it was I gone,' she growled. *'Like I said ten years ago, I die with you.'*

I had listened when she told me that. There were two suicide attempts I remembered vividly, both of which left me and doctors alike shocked that I was still around. Death, I had always thought, would be better than living with this misery.

Now, though, I knew I faced a fate worse than death. Just maybe, she would let me kill myself this time. I was confined to a hospital bed. It was only a matter of time until I was connected to Ted's murder. Given the condition I was in, an undetected escape was impossible. I so wished the group of hunters I had run into had finished the job. I wanted anything other than to be lying here, useless, and bemoaning some stranger who had taken the time to spy on me.

Come to think of it, a lot more was wrong with me than just a personality disorder.

Footsteps somewhere down the hall called me back to the here and now. These steps were heavier and less fluid. Not the person who had been spying on me. The logical side of me was relieved, but I was so curious about who that man had been and why he was interested in me. Either way, I was on high alert.

"Hey, take it easy, kiddo," a familiar voice said. I looked up to see Trevor giving me a cautious half-smile. "You certainly do like making a scene, don't you?"

"I'm sorry," I croaked.

He strode into the room, reaching over and handing me a cup of water from the bedside table. "Had to expect something like that with the bombshell I dropped on you."

"Where are we?" I asked.

He looked at me with a sad expression. "You're in a hospital. My first aid knowledge doesn't quite cover bullet holes."

I gulped. I guess I wasn't in any condition to run. When they found out about Ted, it'd be really easy for them to waltz in and arrest me.

Or maybe it would be really easy to suggest he shot me and I killed him in self-defense. I breathed out. I had a defense, at least.

"Are you going to stay?" I asked. He nodded. "Are you still going to take me to your pack?"

"We're already here." Trevor chuckled. "Had to get you to a place with the proper blood supply."

I nodded. I didn't know how I felt about that.

The wolf in the back of my head rustled, preening her coat like she was proud of being the reason Trevor had to drag me back here. She probably was.

"Where's my bracelet?" I mumbled. "I need my bracelet."

Trevor's eyes darkened. "I imagine it broke when you shifted. Besides, you don't need that here."

The wolf presence gloated at his comment. "I shifted?"

He leaned forward in his chair, his eyes boring into me. "Lya, you were attacked by four hunters. Your wolf bought us enough time to get you out of there alive."

I started to panic. I was truly and utterly trapped. If my own transgressions weren't going to keep me hostage, it was this damn wolf that was impossible to kill. Trevor must have sensed it because he came and sat on the edge of the bed.

"Hey, calm down," he reassured me. "You'll be safe here, I promise."

"I-I-I—," I choked on my words, but finally managed to blurt out, "I killed Ted."

"I know," Trevor said. His matter-of-fact demeanor was off-putting. Why was he so willing to help me?

"They'll come and arrest me," I pointed out. I didn't think a pack of werewolves would want a slew of human police descending upon them.

"It's been dealt with," he assured me. "You are safe here."

I didn't say anything. Words were hard.

"Look, we get that you don't want anything to do with your wolf. You'll stay here as long as you need to learn and accept things, and then you can decide what's next and where to go. Until then, you are under the protection of the pack."

"Will you be here?" I asked. I was pretty good at picking up and moving on to new places with no connections, but relocating to a pack of werewolves was a little out of my area of expertise.

"For at least a little while." Trevor squeezed my hand. "I've got that thing I'm looking for, remember?"

I nodded. I guess it was too much to expect him to hang around and babysit me.

"Do try to make friends here," Trevor said, looking intently at me. "Rose, one of our scouts, helped get you back here. She'll want to come say hi, and you've already made a good impression on the Alpha."

Another wink and a sly smile. I scrunched up my nose. What even was an Alpha? All of this was getting overwhelming. I really wanted to go to sleep and wake up to find this was all a weird dream.

"So, what do I do now?" I asked.

Trevor shrugged. "Sit and heal, I guess. Read a book?"

'You can always talk to me,' the voice said.

I sighed. "Will I ever be allowed to leave?"

"We don't keep prisoners without a cause. But Lya, you've already seen how dangerous it is to be out in the world so cut off from your wolf. It would be to your advantage if you planned on being here for a while. Besides," he chided, "you might decide you like it here and want to stick around."

"What about that man?" I asked. "The one who was creeping outside my room."

"Oliver?" Trevor supplied. "Oh, he's just the Alpha of the pack. You'll meet him soon. You'll like him, I promise."

I frowned, wondering how he knew exactly who I was talking about with no description. Maybe creeping was a normal thing for this Alpha character.

'I'd do what I could to help you out if you'd let me in,' the voice said.

I had a lot of questions.

OLIVER

I PACED MY OFFICE, waiting for Trevor to return. When I got back and confirmed she was awake, he left to see his friend, leaving Kota to more or less babysit me. I didn't think I needed a babysitter, but Kota was one of the few people with any hope of restraining an Alpha wolf if I lost my tedious hold on Adair.

"I take it she doesn't know you're her mate?"

"This is wrong," I spat. "She isn't my mate."

Kota shrugged. "You said she was fourteen when you met her ten years ago. This girl is twenty-four. It's possible."

I shook my head. An Alpha's mate, a pack's Luna, would not be a loose cannon. She would be strong and powerful and have an innate desire to protect and nurture those around her. A born leader, a compliment to her Alpha mate. Not someone whose only skill was to run.

But then again, I wasn't supposed to be the Alpha.

My brother, four years my senior and the intended successor of the Alpha title, met his fated mate shortly before the battle our father lost his life in eight years ago. She fell, too. They never got the chance to mark each other. Their bond was not sealed and accepted, so the pain and suffering of losing his mate was not so extreme he lost his life in one way or another. That didn't mean it didn't still wreak emotional havoc. He refused to accept his role as Alpha after the loss of both our father and his mate, and he went rogue. I was left to pick up the mantle.

"Hell, she was only fourteen, Oliver. Mate bonds can't be recognized that early. You might have been wrong," Kota pointed out, drawing my attention back.

I glared over at him, Adair's growl rumbling out of me. My wolf hadn't been wrong.

"Maybe she's involved with a coven," I mumbled. Maybe witches had devised some way to mimic a mate bond as a way to infiltrate the pack. Enemies had gone to more elaborate lengths to steal power in the past.

"Maybe she's just your mate."

I stalked over to the decanter on my desk, pouring myself a little too much. Kota, of all people, should understand being mated to the wrong person. That was the mate bond he was stuck in. I figured he'd be the one to understand my misgivings.

But fated mates were a gift from the Goddess. Your mate was your destiny. Mates were too perfectly and seamlessly matched for there to be mistakes.

She needed to be interrogated, and I wasn't sure I could do it. If Adair was allowed any amount of time with her, any doubts I had would fade away.

I flopped down in one of the overstuffed chairs, absently swirling my drink. Nothing made sense. Every fiber in my being screamed for me to run to her, but logic held me back. This wasn't the magical moment I had always dreamed of. No, I had already had that. One fleeting moment with a child. I had left her, intent on coming back for her when she had grown up. When I had grown up. I had never expected her to disappear.

'Maybe there is a reason she disappeared,' Adair tried to tell me, but I refuted that suggestion. I didn't think her wolf would allow her to stray too far.

'Then how did she end up here?'

'We don't know it's her.'

Adair's silence made me believe he had his own reservations, but that was enough to plant the seed of doubt. Maybe Trevor and Kota and even my grandmother were right, and I was simply being a stick in the mud, trying to make life harder for myself.

If I could only remember her scent, or her eyes, maybe I'd be a little more certain. I had avoided thinking about that one chance encounter for so many years at this point, it was akin to a forgotten memory. I didn't even know how I could have forgotten a moment like that, but for a long time, I had been thankful for it. I would have gone insane, trying to find her.

Now, though, I felt a little insane. I was fighting a wolf's most desired blessing all because of some half-baked notion that could be completely made up, for all I knew.

I took a deep breath, trying to inhale a bit of clarity. "It'll become obvious if she isn't truly my mate, correct?"

"If it's truly a mate bond, there's no escaping it," Kota said somberly.

I didn't need to ask Kota what he meant. Back in the days when we were attending the training academy together, he insisted he knew his mate. She was a couple years younger than him, but there couldn't have been another option. Until the Goddess failed them.

Maybe the Moon Goddess had failed me, too.

"Do you think you'll ever be happy with Ellie?" I asked, nervous to hear the answer.

"No."

I looked away from him, deciding it was not my place to pry. Not until I realized I was in the same boat as him. My eyes fell on the silver-encrusted book my grandmother had loaned me. "Silver doesn't affect this girl."

"Maybe she's a Wulver," Kota mumbled.

I scoffed. "You actually believe in them?"

"I have to," he told me. "Otherwise, I'd be convinced evil has the opportunity to win."

"You put more faith in a group of vigilantes than your own Alpha?" I chided, sending him a teasing glare.

Kota pulled himself to his feet and began making his way to the door. "You're a fool if you think you are the strongest wolf out there."

"Careful," I warned him. "I can take your Gamma title away as quickly as I gave it."

He turned back, a smug grin on his face. "And you chose me as Gamma because I'm not too scared to put you in your place."

The door clicked shut behind Kota, leaving me alone with my thoughts. It wasn't a healthy place to be as my wolf and I warred over what to do about the girl—the potential mate of mine. At the very least, we shared the idea of attaining as many answers before forming an opinion, not allowing her to sway our belief in the facts. Trevor's emotional attachment to the girl made him an unreliable source, and everyone else seemed to be in support of her truly being my mate. I had felt alone for the eight years I had been this pack's Alpha, but never before had it seemed more true. I didn't even have the support of my confidants now, it seemed. Hell, I wasn't even sure I had the support of myself.

'Even if she isn't our mate, she's on our land,' Adair reminded me. *'You are her Alpha, at least for now. You would betray yourself and the legacy of your ancestors if you did not offer her safe harbor.'*

His words were sobering and true. My own grandmother had claimed this pack from an Alpha who refused to assist packs and rogues in need, and my father strove to unify as much of our kind as possible during his reign. Humans had the Statue of Liberty, calling for the weak and weary, the huddled masses. We had the Wulver Pack, reminding us no soul was lost until they had given up on themselves. I heard the rumors: several packs called us the Wannabe Wulvers. My father and grandmother had each claimed a pack desperately seeking refuge, but me? Maybe all I'd claim is one lost she-wolf, about ready to call it quits.

'And that would be enough.'

I found myself headed toward the door, again, and not even because I had loosened my hold on Adair. I couldn't take my Land Cruiser again. The bloodstain haunted me. The walk back to the hospital was bleak and felt longer than usual. But he was right. Even if she wasn't my mate, she was my pack. For now.

But the wolf continued to prod. *'Why are you so resistant to her being our mate, anyway?'*

I frowned. That all boiled down to nothing about her showing she had the potential to be the Luna my mate was destined to be.

'You never wanted to be Alpha,' Adair reminded me. *'Anyone could have said the same thing about you eight years ago.'*

'Times changed. I changed.'

'Maybe she would, too,' he argued.

I couldn't see it. I may have been a loose cannon once upon a time, but I wasn't a threat to an entire race.

I was saying everything except she was beneath me. I flinched at my own thought, seeing exactly how it went against everything this pack stood for. It was something my brother never would have let cross his mind. Hell, he was Alpha-blooded and married to a human now.

As I walked back through the halls of the hospital, I felt like an imposter. I was on my way to her room to pass judgment, not offer support. Still, I slipped through the open door to her room without knocking, taking up the chair beside her bed. I eyed Trevor but was careful not to say anything. I wouldn't give in to the behaviors of a mate. Not yet.

I tried my best not to look at her, but that was harder than expected. The rising sun cast a warm glow across the room, practically illuminating her in light. She was still pale, but that only made her smattering of freckles stand out. Her auburn hair was dull and fanned out across the stark white pillow in tangled chunks. Even gaunt and frail, she had an air of strength and power. I supposed there had to be for her to still be alive. Just maybe there was something there, something I was too dense to notice yet.

Her gaze immediately turned to me, morphing into a harsh glare. "Who are you?"

"How are you feeling, Lya?" I asked, avoiding her question. How do you tell someone you're the Alpha of a werewolf pack and possibly their mate?

"Like I've been shot three times and then someone went digging around in my organs," she quipped.

I gave her a wan smile. "I suppose that wasn't a very good question."

Trevor's eyes darted between the two of us nervously. I knew he was scared for his friend and had a healthy understanding of the battle ahead of her. If only he knew the half of it. "This is the pack's Alpha, Lya. He's in charge around here. I imagine you two will be getting to know each other quite well over your stay."

Lya looked down, stuttering out, "S-sorry, Alpha."

I shook my head. "Please call me Oliver. Calling me Alpha is a little too formal for people who tried to bleed out in the back seat of my truck."

"Oh, I'm, um, I'm sorry. I can pay for—"

"Not necessary," I cut her off. "It wasn't the first time, and it certainly won't be the last. Just try not to be the person trying to die again."

"No promises," she muttered.

If a couple sarcastic comments was the best I was going to get out of her today, I would take it. It would take time to get the answers I needed and formulate my own legitimate opinion that was not shrouded in the magic of mate bonds. In her presence, I hated myself for all the things I thought of her, even if the logical side of me knew they were well-founded.

'*Can you sense her wolf?*' I asked Adair.

'*She isn't pack,*' he pointed out.

'*But she is our mate,*' I reminded him. Maybe this could be an indicator if that prospect held any water. '*Maybe we get some privileges with that.*'

Adair pulled back and vanished, clearly on a mission.

I looked up to see Lya peering over at me. "You don't have to stay and babysit me if you're bored."

"What?" I asked. Her comment had me a little taken aback. I hadn't thought I'd given any indication that she didn't have my full attention. In fact, this was the only place I wanted to be, and I hated that.

"You looked all zoned out and like you weren't really here."

"Oh, um, no," I said. "I was talking to my wolf. You kind of get a glazed-over expression when you talk to your wolf."

"Oh." She turned back to continue talking to Trevor.

Adair's presence came back. '*She's here!*' he howled. '*We can't communicate, but I can sense she's here.*'

I smiled. No silver meant no restraints for her poor wolf.

I thought of the torture and suffering her wolf had been forced to endure for the past ten years. It was impossible for me to be angry at Lya for it, but I still felt bad. I hoped, even if she did choose to leave, we could at least right that wrong.

Trevor stood from his seat at the foot of the bed. "I'll leave you guys to it, then. You kids be good."

Maybe he did know something was afloat. Keeping this mate thing a secret until she was ready would be a lot more difficult than I thought.

SEVEN

Lya

THE SWARM of visitors was a little overwhelming, even if it stemmed from good intentions. I wondered if my room had been a revolving door of people when I was asleep also. I looked over to the man in the chair by the bed. Mountain man was an accurate description for the pack Alpha. Even down to the flannel shirt with rolled-up sleeves, Oliver was a lumbersexual's wet dream. He had messy jet-black hair that curled at the ends and a beard that looked like it had been forgotten about for at least a few days. His dark chocolate eyes never left me.

I wished Trevor was still here. This Alpha character was a tad intimidating, and I wasn't in the mood to defend myself. I wasn't dumb. I had read enough paranormal romances to know this ended in one of two ways; either I became enemy number one, or I was the unsuspecting heroine. I had grown accustomed to my role as the antihero, though, and I knew with that came questions and demands and expectations, none of which I would be able to answer or fulfill.

'*We should keep this one around,*' the voice purred. I scoffed at her comment. She wasn't expecting this to go the way I knew it would.

"Is there anything I can do to make your stay here more comfortable?" he asked.

I shook my head. "Unless there's a way to blow this popsicle stand before the weekend."

"What, don't you like hospitals?" he asked with a smirk.

"Who does?" I snorted.

"You know, a good way to avoid them is to not get shot." He gave me a pointed look, but the smile still lingered on his face. His entire face lit up when he smiled. I wondered if all his emotions were as expressive. It would make him easy to read.

The thing hummed in my head. '*He smells nice.*'

I furrowed my eyebrows. All I smelled was antiseptic.

He noticed my change in expression quickly. "Too soon? I'm sorry, I didn't mean to be harsh."

"No, you're fine." I tapped my head. "Just a bit of an annoyance trying to pull me into a sidebar."

Oliver leaned forward, resting his elbows on his knees. "So what does your wolf want to talk about?"

I barked out a laugh. "*We* don't talk. *She* harasses me and I ignore her."

He studied my face like he was trying to commit every detail to memory. "Why?"

I shrugged. "It's what works."

"My wolf can get annoying, too," the Alpha, whatever that was, told me. "He's quite the talker. His name is Adair."

"They have names?" I snorted. My own wolf had refused to reveal hers every time I had requested it. '*All in due time,*' she would say as if there was a proper situation in which to introduce yourself.

"Of course," he said. "All you have to do is ask."

I turned my gaze to the wall, thinking about his statement. Did I even care what her name was?

I struggled, wiggling to sit up, but that caused me to wince in pain. Mountain Man Alpha stood, reaching across me to adjust the bed's positioning with the buttons on the side. I actually managed to catch a whiff of him, and for once, I had to agree with the wolf. He chose a great cologne. His hand brushed against my arm, catching me with a zap of static electricity, causing me to flinch.

"Why are you even here?" I asked Oliver. "I imagine an Alpha has better things to do than check in on hospital patients."

He only shrugged as if this was normal. "Not really. Werewolves don't require overnight stays at the hospital that often."

"I would think, with how many people live here, you'd at least have a handful around at a time."

"Nope," he said, popping the 'p.' "Werewolves heal quickly, so it's usually a quick in and out, then recover at home. The most typical injuries we deal with are from training, and that's just setting a bone and good as new in a few days, or sew them up and send them back to the training field."

That information got my attention. I hated hospitals. "Does that mean I can get out of here sooner?"

Oliver actually took the time to glance up at me, but I couldn't read his expression. If anything, he seemed as confused as me. I appreciated the solidarity, but I wanted answers.

The man finally spoke up. "You aren't a typical case, Lya."

"Why?" I asked. "Trevor told me that I am a werewolf, so why wouldn't I have werewolf healing?"

He looked down to stare at his hands laced in his lap. I was certain my feelings of confusion were clear on my face, but try as I might, I couldn't hide them.

Oliver cleared his throat. "The stronger your relationship with your wolf, the stronger your abilities are."

He didn't clarify any further. I didn't need it.

"Oh."

I turned back to pick at loose threads on the sheet. The way he phrased it felt like a slap to the face. I was a werewolf, but not really. I was failing at things I couldn't even control. For the first time, I was upset at my inability to harness this power. So much was at my fingertips, but none of it could I actually reach. For a split second, I almost understood why Trevor spoke of his own wolf with such affinity. Even now, though, it was an idea I couldn't grasp.

The sound of a chair scraping against the floor pulled my attention back into the room. I looked up, seeing Oliver stand and take a few steps toward the door. On any other day, I would have been happy he was leaving, but there was something about him. The shift in my opinion of him scared me, but he hadn't shown he was a threat to me in any way. Maybe he had simply decided I was useless. He wouldn't be wrong.

"I'll see you soon, Lya," he said, a soft smile flitting across his face.

Finally alone in my room, all the exhaustion of simply being awake for a couple hours hit. Maybe it was because of all the people I had seen. Over the years, I had kind of programmed myself to be an introvert. Times like this, I felt it was actually what I was meant to be.

I reached around in my head to see if I could sense her—the wolf.

Without any silver, she was impossible to truly block. Feeling her easily, I decided to initiate a conversation.

'*Alright, do your thing. Heal us,*' I instructed.

She laughed at me. '*No can do. You heard the guy.*'

'*Well, what do I have to do for you to be able to heal us?*' I demanded. She was in my head, using my body. I should be the one calling the shots.

'*Rewind the clock and not banish me with silver for an entire decade.*'

Sometimes I wondered if I got my sarcasm from her, or if she got it from me.

'*So we are basically just human now?*' For some reason, that made my stomach turn. So much of my identity was based on being different and unacceptable. I had spent so long wanting to be nothing more than human, denying what I already knew without anyone telling me—that I was a werewolf—but at the same time, the werewolf thing had come to define so much of who I was, even if it wasn't in a positive way.

'*More like two separate entities fighting for control of the same body,*' she said. '*But it doesn't have to be this way.*'

I thought of all the times I had teased Trevor for zoning out. After catching Oliver doing it as well and getting his explanation, it made sense. These people could talk seamlessly with their wolves. I wondered if they had control of when they shifted as well. I wondered if they could demand their wolves heal them, or if that came naturally.

I felt sleep taking hold. The last thing on my mind was that maybe Trevor was right. Maybe this was a place I could be happy. Maybe this was a place I could be accepted.

OLIVER

ADAIR GROWLED in protest as we left Lya's room. I wasn't at all surprised to find Trevor in the waiting area, ready to interrogate me the way I had intended to question the girl.

In her presence, it was abundantly clear she was no threat. Lost and scared, maybe, but she truly was at a fork in the road. Every action from this moment forward would be solely determined by how safe she felt. That fact only increased the weight of my responsibility.

'*We need to be with her,*' Adair insisted.

'*Adair,*' I sighed, '*you know that will set her off.*'

'Her wolf won't mind.' His tone made it clear he was not willing to negoti-
ate, but his words indicated he had a greater ability to communicate with the
girl's wolf than sensing her presence.

'But the one running the show will.' My comment made him whimper. He
knew I was right. I felt him recede to the corners of my mind and curl up in a
ball.

Trevor had fallen in stride beside me, allowing us to walk in silence until
we were outside of the hospital. "I'm guessing that's not really the first
encounter you expected."

I shrugged. "I wasn't expecting anything."

"Meeting your mate?" he clarified. "I'm not dumb, Ollie. Adair wouldn't
even let me look at her back in Chamberlain. I know you wouldn't have been
all sweet and concerned if she was just some rogue."

I tried to let the comment roll off, but it seeded itself deep in my chest. If
Trevor and Rose could identify she was my mate, it was only a matter of time
until the pack noticed, too.

"I know this will make Adair puff up and be all overprotective," Trevor
chuckled, "but she really does have a heart of gold. She has walls. You'll think
you know her one minute, and then she'll throw a curveball the next. I was
convinced she hated me for the longest time and she only came into the
brewery for the beer. Then she made me a cheesecake for my birthday."

I laughed at that. "So I'll know I'm on her good side when she makes me a
cheesecake?"

"Oh, Goddess, you do not want her cheesecake. It's the worst thing I have
ever tasted." He shuddered at the memory.

"Good to know, if she was my mate," I mumbled. One measly conversation with her, and I was already beginning to doubt my stance that it was
impossible.

I could tell Trevor was biting his tongue. He had opinions but knew
better than to voice them. Hell, I was nervous to voice my own thoughts at
this point. I had no idea what would even come out of my mouth. The
pendulum swung between getting her as far away from this pack as soon as
possible and killing anyone who looked at her twice. A battle between the
head and the heart. Maybe my opinions would be clearer if I knew whether or
not she was the same girl I met all those years ago.

The packhouse was still asleep when we arrived, the gentle thrum of
appliances the only sounds to be heard. Trevor beelined for the Alpha wing
where he had a room, but I stopped him. There were conversations we needed
to have that had nothing to do with the stray he had dragged in.

Trevor stayed at the packhouse whenever he was back in our territory. That hadn't happened very frequently over the past six years. In fact, I had hardly heard from him in all the time he had been away, constantly jumping from place to place. In the past couple years, he had settled down and was working as a manager at a brewery in a college town. He initially left under the pretense of finding his mate, but I had long thought that wasn't the case. The particular town he had chosen to settle in only confirmed that theory. This pack had too much history there.

"Before you go, can I have a quick word in my office?" I asked.

Without even looking back at me, he changed his trajectory and headed to my office. He waltzed in, sitting in the chair in front of my desk. I flopped down on the couch. We didn't do formal meetings.

"How have things been going?" I asked.

Trevor barked out a dark laugh. "Well, the only thing of interest I've brought back to the pack was a screwed-up she-wolf, so not well."

"Are you ready to come home yet?"

"I dunno, man," he sighed. "I'm starting to think I don't know if I'm running away and hiding or out on a hunt."

I waved away the thought. "Didn't your dad always used to say life has a way of finding you without ever going out and searching?"

"I guess I should probably start living my life instead of chasing it." He looked down at his hands. Giving up would be a big deal for him, but he was twenty-six and had been away from the pack for a long time. If he didn't come back soon, I would need to start pushing him to go rogue.

"You know, I haven't filled my Beta position yet," I reminded him. My father's Beta was sitting as mine, but it was common knowledge that each new Alpha chose their own hierarchy. I had been holding that spot for Trevor as long as I could, but I'd have to rescind the offer eventually.

He sighed, running his fingers through his hair. It was a big ask, but he should have known it was coming. I had reminded him of the offer every time he found his way back to Snow Moon. "Can I have a couple days to think about it?"

I nodded. "How long are you planning on staying this time?"

"Just until Lya gets settled in the packhouse, then I need to head back. I can't just disappear from work," Trevor said. He scrunched his nose. Wolves rarely did okay with the monotony of human social structure. Here at the pack, if he had disappeared from his job on pack business for a week or so, no one would have thought twice. Out where he was, that wasn't the case. "I told them there was an emergency back home."

"Just let me know before you head out," I suggested. A few more days utilizing my father's Beta wouldn't be detrimental, seeing as it had already been eight years. I understood why he wanted to wait when he was eighteen. Even when he left at twenty, I empathized with wanting a chance to get out in the world before tying himself down to the pack. That was an opportunity I had missed out on. Now, he had run out of excuses.

He stood to leave. "I'm gonna go get some sleep, then. Sleeping in a hospital chair is not restful."

I was jealous. I needed to sleep, too, but it was the dawn of a new day. Yesterday had been a wash, and I needed to play catch up. Running a pack, for the most part, was monotonous. If I were smart, I'd delegate most of the day-to-day redundancy, but I bore too much of a need to prove I was worthy of this position I didn't want. I wasn't about to be the Alpha who only showed up when problems arose.

At the end of the day, I flopped back into bed, absolutely exhausted but wide awake. There was too much space; the bed felt empty.

'I swear on the Goddess, Adair, if you keep me awake all night, I will start wearing a silver bracelet.'

Adair rumbled, *'Not funny.'*

He was right.

'So what do we do?' I asked.

'We could go sit with her,' he suggested.

Adair was anxious. He was pacing, whining, and begging to return to the hospital. Had been all day.

'If I go there, will you let me sleep?' I demanded. By my calculations, it had been too close to forty-eight hours since I had slept, and I was willing to do just about anything to get it. Even if it meant freaking out my maybe mate.

'Maybe.'

The only way I was ever going to sleep was if I shut up my wolf. It seemed like the only way that was going to happen was by attempting to sleep in a hospital chair, which Trevor had already testified was ill-advised. I rolled off the couch and stumbled toward the door, grumbling all the way to the pack hospital. I kept my head down as I walked through the halls for the third time today. I wanted sleep, not any of the interactions always expected of me when I was out of the packhouse. I flung open the door, maybe a little too loudly. Lya's face was peaceful, giving no indication I disturbed her.

'Happy now?' I asked Adair. His only response was a contented hum.

I swear, we were asleep before we hit the chair.

EIGHT

Lya

IT WAS dark out when I woke. Lights were off, and moonlight streamed through the window. My arm brace had been taken off, and the head of the bed was no longer elevated. I hadn't even noticed anyone come in.

The room was quiet, save for the beeping of monitors and a soft snore. I looked over, expecting to see Trevor, but the form in the chair was decidedly not him.

I reached out to the wolf in my head. *'So you couldn't warn me that some random guy turned up here?'*

'What, am I supposed to be your babysitter or something?' she jeered.

'You've already proven you can be a bodyguard, so why not?' I said wryly.

'Oliver and Adair are not a threat.'

'How do you know?'

She didn't humor me with a response.

I kept my eyes on the figure in the chair, not willing to allow him to make another move without my knowledge. Maybe he could feel my intense glare, because the person invading my room stirred, slowly opening his eyes.

"Hey." Oliver's voice was gruff with sleep.

"Are all werewolves creepy stalkers?" I asked.

"Only sometimes." The room was too dark to make out his expression, but it sounded like he was smiling.

"Well, I don't need a babysitter," I said, turning away from him.

"I wasn't trying to babysit," he replied. "Just figured you would want some company when you woke up."

"How do you know?"

Oliver looked intently at me. "Look, I get that this is a lot. I just thought—"

"Yeah, it's a lot," I scoffed. "This *thing* that is stuck in me brutally murdered someone I cared about, I'm stuck in a hospital, I hurt *everywhere*, I have no idea where I am or why I'm here, I don't really have the option to leave, and nowhere to go if I did." I fought to hold back tears as the gravity of the past couple days hit me. I hoped he didn't notice as I dashed away the single rogue tear that managed to slip out. "And now there's some stranger who keeps showing up in my room as if we're friends. I feel like a kid who has no idea what's going on or how to deal with anything."

Oliver came and perched on the side of my bed, awkwardly putting his arm around me in a half-hug. I didn't move away from his side, partly because it would hurt to move, and partly because sometimes a hug is nice. I breathed deep, trying to focus on the scent of his cologne and allow the overpowering aroma to ground me. Either way, it felt exceptionally unnatural—for both him and me.

"It'll all figure itself out," he said quietly.

"I don't see how," I mumbled into Oliver's shirt.

"Sometimes it takes a while to figure out." He removed his arm and went back to sit in his chair. He leaned back and propped his feet up on my bed. "My parents died about eight years ago."

"I'm sorry." I didn't know what else to say.

"Me too." He was silent for a moment. "It isn't really what you're dealing with, but adversity is adversity, right? I was pretty lost for a while. The entire pack was. Sometimes, I feel like I still am."

I nodded. My father didn't die, he just left.

"They passed, and my brother refused to take on the Alpha role. Actually, my brother left the pack and is now what we call a rogue."

"You can leave the pack?" I asked.

Oliver nodded. "Being part of a pack has many benefits, but some want to be lone wolves. Thom has a pretty good life now. But, because he left, I had to become Alpha. My father hadn't bothered to train me at all for it because it was always expected that Thom would replace him. So I lost my father, my brother who had any idea of what to do was gone, my mother was dying, and I had gone from having no responsibility to being in charge of nearly five thousand people, all within a week."

"Oh." I stared at my hands, not knowing what else to say.

"So I get it," Oliver continued. "I know what it's like to feel lost and alone and scared. But most of that comes from feeling like you have to do everything by yourself." I stayed quiet, still lost for words. I hoped he'd get to the point of his saga soon. "You were brought here when shit went sideways so you wouldn't be alone, and you have a home available to you in the pack for however long you would like." Oliver's face developed a pained expression. "Should you choose to leave, no one will stop you, but you would be on your own."

I hated how it felt like he was reading my mind, peeling back every grotesque layer and revealing flaws and fears. He had no right to know these things, but they were probably easy to guess. I couldn't have been the first stray to find their way here.

"What would happen if I stayed here?" I asked.

A smile flitted across Oliver's face. "You'd be a pack member."

I motioned for him to continue. "I'm the new kid, remember?"

"We are our own little society here," Oliver clarified. "We have a fully functioning, self-sufficient territory, so you'd never need to go anywhere else or be around people who think something is wrong with you again. All pack members contribute to the pack, and in return, the pack doesn't allow anyone to end up in situations like the one you're in now. It will be up to you what happens if you stay here with us. There are jobs or the training academy. Or other packs you could transfer to."

"How do people, humans, not find out about this place?" I asked.

"We are quiet and keep to our own," he said. "We do have enemies out there, and we know the best way to avoid them is by flying under their radar."

I thought of the one word my wolf had said when she had killed Ted. *Hunter.* Maybe those were the enemies he was talking about. I supposed they would be my enemies, too.

"This is a lot."

"I can't imagine what it would be like to learn all of this at once instead of growing up with it," he agreed. "The only thing we ask is, if you leave, you keep quiet about us."

"Do all of the people who live here have a wolf as part of them?" I asked.

Oliver chuckled. "That is one of the key attributes of being a werewolf.

Those of us who have chosen a human mate usually don't live within our towns, but they are still actively involved in the pack. Or they're now rogues."

"This is too much right now."

"We don't have to talk about this. All we have is time."

We sat in silence for a while, but he made no move to leave. I didn't complain; I was beginning to appreciate the company.

"Where are we?" I asked. "Where is the, uh, the pack located?"

"South of Spearfish, in the Black Hills. Have you been out this direction before?"

I shook my head.

"Here, can you scooch over?" Oliver moved back over to sitting on the edge of my bed. I slowly–painfully–made some space for him. He settled in beside me, pulled out his phone, and opened up his photo gallery. Most of the pictures looked like scenery photos. He scrolled through, showing me quick snapshots of the area. This felt too normal, and I liked it.

I stopped him at a picture of a small waterfall flowing into calm waters. "That place is pretty. It reminds me of a place back home."

Oliver looked down at me. "Where is home for you?"

"I grew up in Maine, lived in North Carolina for a while, but Vermont is home." A smile played on my lips as I thought of everything I missed the most. I laid my head back against the pillow and closed my eyes, remembering. "I used to live in a house that was quite literally falling into the river. After Hurricane Irene, the White River got really full and destroyed the houses really close to the river. I think mine was technically condemned. After work, I used to take a couple beers down, sit on one of my favorite rocks, and keep them cold in the water."

I opened my eyes after a moment of silence. Oliver's eyes were burning into me. Something about his deep brown eyes looked off compared to how they had a few moments ago.

"It sounds lovely," he finally said. "We can go there sometime. Maybe it will be almost as nice."

"Maybe." I smiled at the idea. Maybe staying here wouldn't be so bad. For a little while, at least.

Oliver

I woke up still in Lya's hospital bed. Her head was resting on my shoulder, and she snored softly. I breathed in deep, as if her lilac scent wasn't overwhelming enough. Her body pressing up to mine was a tantalizing temptation that had me reminding myself we were in a hospital bed, and she was healing, and I wasn't even certain she was my mate. There had to be more indicators than just some sparks when you touched and an exceptionally alluring scent. I slowly started to shift off the bed, making sure not to jostle her, but Adair growled.

'We stay,' he insisted.

I looked out the window. The sun was up, with the last bits of pinks and oranges burning off. I really didn't want to be caught in bed with her. Not yet.

'People will be by to check on her, and she will wake up at some point.'

'So? Mate.'

'Maybe,' I admitted, *'but she's not ready.'*

Adair grumbled as he released the hold paralyzing me. I grabbed my jacket and slipped out the door, quickly closing it behind me.

"Still here, Alpha?"

I whipped around, standing a little straighter when I came face to face with Dr. Whitledge. "You're here early."

"I'm the only doctor in the pack at the moment, and I have a patient to check on," Dr. Whitledge reminded me.

"When does Lessa get back again?" I asked. Lessa was a friend growing up, but we lost touch when she went off to school. She met her mate while getting her medical degree. He was in a different pack, and she was off visiting him. I really hoped they decided to settle here; we needed at least two doctors around. Three or four would be better.

"This weekend, and I believe Ric will be coming with her. He wants to see the pack before they decide where to live."

"I'm sorry you've been flying solo. I'm doing my best to get a third doctor staffed, but all our candidates are just starting school," I said.

"Don't forget, Ric is also a doctor," he reminded me.

I nodded, catching his drift.

"So," he clapped me on the shoulder, "how is our patient this morning?"

"Sleeping. She woke up for an hour or so late last night."

"Good, good. Sleep is healing." He looked past me, through the window of the door into her room. "Do you think maybe her wolf is doing something to speed things along in the background?"

I shrugged. "I don't have medical training."

"And this is uncharted territory," he mused. Dr. Whitledge made his way into Lya's room, and I started my return to the packhouse.

Adair shifted around, clearly upset.

'What?' I demanded.

'Her wolf is sad.' His voice was morose, carrying the pain for both of them.

'I would imagine.'

'I want to talk to her,' the wolf said.

'In time.' I wondered how long that would be.

Back in the packhouse, I drifted toward the noise coming from the kitchen. I had been a little too surly the past couple of days, and the Beta family deserved a moment of my good side.

"Morning," Trevor drawled. He was leaning against the kitchen counter with a cup of coffee in hand. "How was sleeping in a chair?"

"Uncomfortable," I grumbled, reaching into the cupboard to grab a mug, "so I slept in the bed instead."

"We've gone over the importance of consent, yes?" Trevor joked, cocking an eyebrow. I shot a glare in his direction. "What? She's my friend."

"And I'm your friend. I would hope you'd think better of me." I chuckled.

"Your oldest friend," he corrected. "And I do remember a time when you weren't sitting around waiting for your mate."

"She's all broken in a hospital bed. Not exactly the time to make a move," I grumbled, rolling my eyes. "She might not even be my mate, anyway."

"Do you think you might have spent so long insisting that kid would be your mate that you set her on such a high pedestal you don't even recognize her now?"

I hated the comments people were making. They all indicated they thought I was wrong to be cautious. Given last night, I was hazarding to think they were correct.

I never wanted to be the type that refused to accept my mate. I wanted that over-the-moon, luckiest-man-in-the-world feeling. I didn't have that with Lya, though, and I didn't want to force it.

"Besides," Trevor continued, "given how broken her relationship with her wolf is, she probably can't do normal things like recognize a mate. Who's to say it doesn't go both ways?"

I shook my head, refusing to engage in his discussion of hypotheticals. "Let's just get her out of the hospital so we can see what she's actually like.

"She'll like that," he agreed. "Do you have a room picked out for her yet?"

"Probably Thom's old room. It's on the ground floor, so it'll be easy for her to get around while she recovers."

The packhouse was large. There was an entire floor dedicated to guest rooms I could have put her in, but giving Lya a room in the Alpha wing was simply a necessity. And a little selfish.

"Do you think Anna will ever move out?" Trevor asked, scrunching his nose.

He and Anna had had a tumultuous relationship, to say the least. While growing up here, they were the definition of a sibling rivalry, even though they weren't siblings. Anna was the current Beta's oldest daughter while Trevor was the son of the previous Beta couple, adopted by my parents after their untimely death twelve years ago. She was twenty-two now and finishing her undergraduate degree. She had been playing with the idea of going to medical school, which would be another four or more years away from the pack.

I shrugged. "I wasn't super concerned about it. She's only been back once or twice since she left for school, and we haven't needed the room. When she meets her mate, she will move in with him. I do hope she isn't a deciding factor regarding you taking on the role of Beta."

"She isn't," he said quickly. "Is she coming back for the summer, then?"

I nodded. "Last I heard, she wanted to see if her mate was back at the pack before giving med school a go."

Trevor scrunched up his nose again. "I feel sorry for that poor bastard."

I chuckled. "I do believe there are quite a few she-wolves out there that would say something similar about you."

Trevor downed the rest of his coffee, placing the mug in the sink. "I'm going for a run. Wanna join?"

I shook my head. "I have to call my brother."

"Suit yourself."

I refilled my coffee and retreated to my office. I looked up at the clock on the wall. 8 am here meant 9 am East River. Hopefully, Thom wasn't at work yet. I sat down and pulled out my phone.

The phone rang a few times before he picked up. "Hey, man, what's up?"

"How did it go?" I asked.

"Just fine," he said. I truly wondered how he was able to maintain such a chipper attitude about disposing of a body.

"Do I want to know?" I really didn't.

"The less you know, the better, right?"

I sighed, thankful for that. Maybe if I had actually received Alpha training, I would be a little more hardened to this aspect of the job. Me, though? I was just a warrior by training. I could take the bad guys out, but disposal and dwelling on the carnage never sat well with me. "So how are you doing?"

"Just dandy. In another couple months, Kai will be here, so we're in the homestretch of prepping for that." Thom's excitement was palpable.

"I wish Mom was here for this," I mumbled.

"Me too," he sighed. "But what about yourself? How is the girl settling in?"

"We had some hangups getting back." My tone was guarded. "We need to start tracking local hunter activity more carefully, I think."

"This have anything to do with that guy sitting in my pigs' lot right now?" he asked.

"Yeah," I confirmed. "We also had a run-in with a group of them a few miles north of Chamberlain. Lya got a bit shot up."

"You sure they were hunter-hunters?"

"Silver bullets."

"Ah." Thom was silent for a moment. "But the girl is okay after she got shot with silver?"

"Lya will be fine, I think. There's a lot to unpack there," I mumbled.

"Alright, well give me a hint, but then I have to go to work," he prodded.

"Well, it would appear she is my mate," I said sheepishly.

"Oh, you dog!" Thom cackled. "Can't help a girl out of the goodness of your heart, can ya?"

"But she doesn't know. Not yet," I added. "I'm not even positive, really."

"What?" he asked. "Why not?"

"She's so disconnected from her wolf they can't pick up on it."

Thom whistled through his teeth. "There is a lot to unpack there. I'll give ya a call and we can talk about it over a bourbon sometime. But I gotta go. Good luck with your mate."

"Talk to you soon," I promised, ending the call.

I hadn't been off the phone long before there was a knock at the door.

"Come in," I called.

The door opened, revealing my Beta. Gregory was a good guy. He had grown up in this pack and was my primary pillar of support when taking over for my father. If it weren't for him, this pack would be in shambles. I had considered handing over the Alpha line to him on more than one occasion during the first couple years of my tenure.

"How's it going, Gregory?" I asked.

"Well enough," he said. "We got some information regarding the hunter family you asked about."

My ears perked up. "Oh?"

"I am actually concerned we weren't aware of any of this family's connections so close." He dropped a file on my desk with a familiar name written in bold letters.

"Shit."

NINE

Lya

I WASN'T EXACTLY excited when another new face came waltzing into my room. It felt like a revolving door. Over the past two days, the doctor and nurses were in constantly, making me feel like some anomaly they were studying. Trevor chased them off whenever he was here, but I wasn't his only responsibility. Oliver seemed like the only one I actually wanted to talk to at this point. He had been the only person who had listened.

"Good morning, sunshine!" this new person sang. She seemed too chipper. She looked a few years younger than me. Maybe the world hadn't jaded her yet. "Afternoon, really."

"Hey," I said, offering a half-smile. I could at least act like I appreciated the company. I sat up a little and looked around, trying to get a gauge for the time. I had woken up a while ago to the sun glaring through the window, alone. I wasn't surprised Oliver had left. He was the Alpha, after all. I assumed that meant important duties that required round-the-clock attention. Still, I peeked over her shoulder, hoping to see him. "Who... who are you?"

Her ice-blue eyes widened as if her lack of an introduction was some monumental failure. "I am so, so sorry! I'm Rose. I helped Trevor and Alpha Oliver get you back here."

I nodded absently. She could be considered friend, not foe. For now, at least. Everything was subject to change.

Rose offered a forced smile. "I figured some time away from the boys might be nice. So how's hospital life?"

I groaned. "This is the most uncomfortable bed I have ever slept in."

"I'm sure any bed would be uncomfortable after lying in it for two days," she laughed. "C'mon, let's get you up."

I had already been encouraged to get up and move around a few times in the later part of yesterday and this morning. It was never that far at a time, seeing as my left leg was so torn up, and my collarbone made it impossible for me to use crutches, and I felt like I had been hit by a bus. I was told that's par for the course with my injuries and the surgery I had gone through. Slowly, though, I sat up and swung my legs over the side of the bed. Rose offered her hand for leverage, which I gladly accepted.

After a few shaky steps, she wheeled over the wheelchair in the corner. "Let's go outside."

"Yes, please," I agreed.

Rose greeted people as we passed. She seemed to have the pack ambassador thing down to a science, diving right into treating everyone like her best friend, me included. I liked being able to skip the awkward getting to know you stage and just talk.

"Do you know everyone?" I asked her after the fourth or fifth person she greeted by name.

She giggled. "Packs are close, and I work closely with the warriors, so I spend more time than I'd like over here at the hospital. It'd be a little awkward if I saw someone nearly every day and didn't know their name."

"So are you from this pack?" I prodded.

"From the pack, yes," she said. "But I grew up in one of the smaller towns in our territory. I only moved here when I started training to be a warrior, and then obviously stayed when I accepted a permanent scout position."

"Are the other towns far from here?"

She shook her head. "The furthest is the Wyoming town an hour or so northwest, but if we are called into action, it's always best to be close to headquarters."

She wheeled me out the doors and onto the patio of the cafeteria. It overlooked a river rushing past with a mountain covered in pine trees climbing up on the other side of it. I breathed in sharply. This was a view you never quite got used to.

"Welcome to the Snow Moon Pack, Lya. Hope you like views like this." Rose stared out at the river, smiling to herself.

"Is everywhere like this?" The stark contrast between here and the area of South Dakota I was familiar with made it hard to believe it was even the same state. The pictures Oliver had shown me certainly did not do it justice.

"Our territory is, but you go further out and you get to the Badlands, and then eventually to the boring side of the state, otherwise known as East River."

I laughed lightly. "East River was definitely a drag when it came to landscape."

We spent a few moments in silence, enjoying the view. We could have spent all day here, and I would have been happy.

'I like it here,' the wolf popped up in my head.

'Me too,' I agreed.

The wolf made a soft humming sound. 'We should stay here.'

'Maybe.' I wasn't agreeing to anything until I knew more.

I cleared my throat, searching to fill the silence. "Do people come and go from here often?"

Rose thought about that for a moment, finally saying, "Yes and no. If someone finds a mate in a different pack, they will either go to that pack or their mate will come here. Sometimes a rogue will decide they are done with that life and want the structure of a pack, or the other way around. Every once in a while, we will have a transfer. Actually, recently, Oliver has created quite the reputation, so we've had higher than average transfers."

"A reputation?"

She nodded. "From my understanding, he is quite a good Alpha. I didn't pay too much attention to what his father was like because I was so young, but from my time in other packs, he's quite good."

"What have you gone to other packs for?" I asked. "I thought people didn't come and go?"

Rose glanced over at me. "That's part of how we fund things here. Our warrior crew will do mercenary work for other packs. It's a new structure Oliver implemented, lending other packs a hand while making use of our numbers here. But, to change the topic, is that little bag in your room all you have?"

I had more questions but didn't want to push, so I nodded. It definitely wasn't a wide selection of clothing I had brought, but it was just a go-bag; it wasn't everything I owned.

"Well, we need to get you some more clothes once you're more healed up," she informed me. "You'll be ripping out of them left and right in no time."

I smiled. Shopping was a guilty pleasure of mine. I thought of my closet full of dresses back at my old house. I would miss those. "I should probably save my money, though. It's not like I have a job or anything."

Rose giggled. "You won't have to worry about that. You'll be taken care of here. I don't think Oliver will let you worry about expenses, at least not until you're settled and healed. And clothes are definitely a necessity."

I cringed at the thought of not paying my own way. For as long as I could remember, I hadn't gotten handouts.

"That really isn't necessary," I complained. "I have some money saved, but I don't want to be frivolous with it."

"I hear you, and I also helped with the pack accounts last month, so trust me when I say it's fine."

I arched an eyebrow, encouraging her to clarify.

Rose sighed. "The pack is involved, at least financially, in quite a few non-werewolf businesses, so we have a steady stream of income. It keeps houses and utilities paid for, the hospital up and running, affords a salary for us warriors, all that good stuff."

"So... no one pays for anything here...?" This was starting to sound like some make-believe utopia.

"Oh, no," she said. "You'd still pay for things like eating out, groceries, shopping, your vehicle, but the basics, like healthcare and housing, are not a concern. But everyone is also expected to participate in training and pack protection, even if they aren't a warrior, so it isn't really like accepting handouts. Everything is earned."

I nodded slowly, the wheels turning in my head. I glanced over, seeing Rose looked zoned-out. She must have been talking to her wolf.

She came to and grabbed the wheelchair, spinning it around. "C'mon, let's get you back to your room. Apparently, you might get to go home today."

I breathed out a sigh of relief. Hospitals were my new least favorite place. I glanced at a clock as we rolled by, noting that it was already 2:30. Time was beginning to have no meaning here.

The doctor and Trevor were waiting for us when we got back to the room. Dr. Whitledge immediately set to work examining surgical sites, taking my temperature, and poking and prodding. He finally stood back, writing more on his charts before looking up at me. These people must really have had no idea how to deal with a hospitalized human because I was pretty sure gunshot wounds warranted more than a couple nights' stay.

"How does it feel to walk?" he asked.

I shrugged. "Okay. I wouldn't want to walk too far yet."

"She's got a room on the ground floor, so no stairs," Trevor piped up. I looked over at Trevor and smiled. Anything to get me out of here sooner.

The doctor nodded. "The leg should be mostly healed within two weeks, which will make getting around a lot easier. Collarbone will be a six to eight week recovery. Time will tell with your side, but make sure not to push it too much. Do try and get out of bed. Move around. And I will be coming by the packhouse daily to check on your progress, for at least the next several days. Once your mobility improves, you'll start physical therapy, which will be over at the training grounds."

"So, do I get to leave today?" I refused to let my excitement leak through my voice.

"I would be remiss if I did not say I would much rather you be here until the weekend, but the Alpha indicated you should leave sooner rather than later." He paused, looking at me intently. "If *anything* goes wrong, you will be right back here. You could still develop an infection, or the affected organs could need another repair. Do you understand?"

"Yes," I quickly agreed. Anything to get out of here.

"I'll let Ollie know he can bring the car by," Trevor said. "Ready to be roomies, Lya?"

Trevor's smirk made me smile. "Does this mean we get to have movie nights and stay up late talking about boys?"

He rolled his eyes. "Oh my Goddess, I forgot what it's like living with girls."

OLIVER

'*YOU CAN COME by to pick her up,*' Trevor's voice drifted through the mind-link.

Adair perked up. '*They're coming home.*'

I smiled at the wolf's excitement. It was contagious. Almost enough to make me equally excited. I had my guard up, though. '*You can't overwhelm her. She's healing.*'

I made my way to the Land Cruiser, again thankful the drive was short.

Trevor and Rose were wheeling Lya out as we rolled up to the front door. I jumped out and opened the passenger door for her.

"FJ60?" Lya asked, her eyes wandering over the car.

I smiled and nodded. "You know your cars."

She shrugged. "A thing or two."

I hated that it pained me to watch her struggle to get herself into the passenger seat. Without thinking, I scooped her up and set her in. Lya blushed a deep red, quietly muttering "thanks," while I gnashed my teeth. Her skin emitted sparks, desperately trying to grab my attention, even when I refused to comply.

Trevor jumped in the back seat, sliding a little too close to Lya. "You coming, Rosie?"

Rose shook her head. "See you at the training grounds later, though?"

"Doubtful," Trevor snorted. "Just gonna get Lya settled in."

I kept my eyes trained on the road as we pulled out of the hospital parking lot. If I glanced in the rearview mirror, a fierce jealousy I was unfamiliar with reared its ugly head, and I didn't need the reminder of what I could have if I just gave in. Alphas were strong. This was the perfect test to see if I was truly cut out for the part.

Lya looked around, taking everything in. We had tried to stick with the local flavor when designing the pack, so most of the houses looked like life-size Lincoln Log cabins. Her eyes grew wide as we turned down the driveway to the packhouse, the log mansion consuming our view.

"Oh," she breathed.

I looked up at the house. I had gotten very used to it here, as it had always been my home. The house faced away from us, overlooking the river. Nearly floor-to-ceiling windows let in light and made the view impossible to miss. There was a large patio running the length of the house with a balcony above. It truly was the definition of a log cabin mansion, but it needed to be.

"This is huge!" she exclaimed. "How many people live here?"

I chuckled. "It's actually kind of small as far as packhouses go. Only the Beta, his mate, and their three kids, Trevor has a room here, I've lived here all my life, and now you. We also have the offices for pack leadership here, and pack events are held here."

Lya nodded, eyes still bugging out of her head. I pulled up as close to the front door as I could get, hopping out and scooping Lya out of the back seat before she had the chance to try and struggle out on her own. Or worse, Trevor tried to help her. She was stiff in my arms and beet red. I couldn't help but think her embarrassment was cute.

"Would you rather walk?" I asked.

"Yes," she stated.

"Can you?"

"No," she quietly conceded.

"Welcome home, Lya," Trevor mused once we were in the foyer. "Want the grand tour?"

"S-sure," she agreed.

I looked past Lya, shooting Trevor a glare before I settled her in the wheelchair she had for the time being. I didn't need a mind-link to demand he keep his distance.

But Trevor didn't listen, stepping up to push her around. *Still don't think she's your mate?*

Chivalry is not dead, I snapped back.

Trevor chuckled out loud, but mind-linked, *It's only chivalry if you do it out of the goodness of your heart, not because you'll kill anyone else that looks at her.*

"The kitchen is fully stocked, and you are welcome to anything," Trevor said aloud when we made it to the kitchen, "but we do ask that you never try to cook anything, at all, ever. We don't need this place burning down."

Lya barked out a laugh. "Hey! I do it out of love."

Trevor cringed. "Find another love language."

I led the way to the back patio, needing fresh air. "This is where we spend the most time in the summer. Kota and Brandon come by pretty regularly."

"Kota and Brandon?"

"Two of my Gammas," I clarified. "Kota oversees our training academy and warriors. Brandon is my liaison for Norridge, a town north of here."

The sun glistened off the river, the water slowly weaving downstream. I pointed to a particular outcropping of rocks right on the shore. "That would be my suggestion for a good place to go with a beer. When you're healed."

"It's beautiful here." Lya smiled. I watched her eyes find a footpath that followed the river. She pointed over to it. "Where does that go?"

"My grandmother's house," I said. "She didn't want to live in town after she moved out of the packhouse. She likes the solitude."

We sat in a comfortable silence on the patio. After a while, Trevor slipped back into the kitchen, reemerging with a few bottles.

"It's too early to drink, and one of us is on high doses of painkillers, so kombucha will have to do," he said as he passed them out.

"Oh, is this some of the stuff you make?" Lya asked, cracking open her bottle.

Trevor gave her a side-eye. "Really, would I let you drink anything less?"

This was the kind of peaceful afternoon I could get used to. Silence that didn't need to be filled, and company that wasn't a burden. I was almost disappointed when Trevor broke the silence.

"I've been thinking about your offer, Ollie," he said, looking down at his bottle. "It's time. I'll take it."

I nodded, keeping my eyes trained on the river. "Good. We will need you here, anyway."

Lya looked back and forth between us. "What's going on?"

"Part of the pack hierarchy includes a Beta," I told her. "The Alpha title is inherited, but the Alpha gets to choose their own Beta and Gammas. I've been trying to harass Trevor into taking the Beta position since I took over eight years ago, and have kept on my father's while waiting for him to take it."

"Does that mean the whole family will need to move out?" she asked, seeming worried.

I shook my head. "Not immediately. I'll probably have Gregory work with Trevor for a while to get him up to speed, and their oldest daughter is probably going to medical school after this summer. So, at the end of summer, we will start looking at alternative arrangements for them."

"Besides," Trevor chuckled, "the house will be too quiet without them."

"Speaking of, they'll be getting home from school soon." I looked up at Lya. "Would you like to meet some rowdy teenagers or see your room?"

"Uh... room, please," she said.

I nodded, standing and wheeling her back through the kitchen, leaving Trevor on the patio. We walked down the hall of offices, turning at the end of the hall toward the Alpha wing. There were four doors, two on either side. The first on the right was Trevor's, and the second on the right was empty. To the left was Lya's room, across the hall from Trevor's and right next to mine.

'Not close enough,' Adair griped, but I ignored him.

I was used to these digs, but Lya was impressed. They were, after all, probably nicer than her condemned house falling into a river. I could tell Adair was boastful, proud of being able to provide for the she-wolf he had decided was his mate.

"Oh, wow," she gasped. "I get to stay here?"

"I figured a downstairs bedroom would be easier for you while healing, and the upstairs is currently very desolate with no one staying up there." She looked around, eyes landing on the open door to an ensuite. I imagined she hadn't had much more than a sponge bath since her near-death experience.

"We also have a housekeeper. Mara will do laundry and a basic clean once a week."

"That isn't necessary," she quickly insisted.

"It isn't," I agreed, "but it's a way I can ensure a paycheck for at least one pack member. Also, I hate cleaning."

"When, uh, when do you want me moved out by?" she asked cautiously.

Adair was rubbing off on me. I almost told her never.

"Don't worry about that. Just get healed, figure yourself out, and then we'll talk." I paused, waiting for Lya to speak, but she only nodded. "Do you need help with—"

"No," she cut me off, holding up her good arm. "I'll figure it out. I don't need a babysitter."

I backed off. "I'll come grab you when we get around to dinner, then."

Lya's only response was a nod again. I left the room, hoping some time and space would be enough for her to open up. I couldn't get a read on this girl to save my life.

'Usually, you don't have to get a read. I do,' Adair griped.

I huffed. *'So what's your take, then?'*

'I don't know. I can't get a read.'

'You are so very helpful,' I grumbled, rolling my eyes. I opened the door to my office, glad to see Trevor was already there.

"So you're staying."

Trevor let out a heavy breath. "I'll have to go back for a couple weeks to wrap things up, but I'll be back this time. I promise."

"If you back out again, I won't be able to give you another chance." I looked at him gravely. A little over a year ago, one of the few times he had been back, he agreed to officially step up to be the pack's Beta, but backed out as soon as he went back East River to 'wrap things up.'

"You said last time there was a girl..." my voice trailed off.

"It was her," Trevor explained. "There was always something... off. She's been a regular at the brewery since the day she moved to the area. She never smelled right. Not human, not werewolf, always super on edge. For a while, I thought she was a hunter, actually."

I tried to keep a stoic expression. Adair seethed. He was upset that we could have had Lya here before that hunter had ever put his hands on her, but my concern was a potential hunter even six hours away was too close to home. "Why didn't you say anything?"

"I didn't want to sound the alarms over nothing. But then she came in with that guy a few weeks ago, and he was just fishy. That's when I determined she had to be a werewolf and started following her." Trevor stared at his hands. "I always knew she was something more. Being the destined Luna of my pack makes sense. This has been my ultimate screw-up, and now I have to fix it."

I shoved the file Gregory had given me earlier over to him and spat, "Well, we have a lead on the family her hunter fiancé is from. I think you'll recognize the name."

Trevor looked down at the file. He leaned back, scrunched his eyes shut, and pinched the bridge of his nose. He was about to lose it.

Marsan. Our pack knew that name well. Over a decade ago—twelve years, to be exact—the Marsan family had targeted this pack. Luckily, we'd been tipped off and were able to lead them to think we were at a different location. Brookings, to be exact. The same town Trevor had decided to settle. Both of Trevor's parents were killed in the battle that ensued.

Once upon a time, Trevor's father had been the Beta of this pack. After his parents died, my parents took him in. We grew up in the same house; he was already practically family. It only made sense for him to stay. I wasn't surprised when he left to seek vengeance, under the guise of searching for his mate. But I knew Trevor, and I knew he didn't give a shit about finding his mate. He knew exactly who his mate was and absolutely refused to admit it was her. Slowly, over the past six years he had been gone, I connected the dots. When I confronted him, he guaranteed he would come back home as soon as he ended the Marsans for good. He said he would have time to face the music then. But he knew as well as me that the fight was coming home now.

I leaned over my desk, my voice low. "I know retribution is what you really want, but they didn't fall for that trap you tried to set. Time to follow the rule book now."

TEN

Lya

THIS ROOM WAS HUGE.

The bathroom was an oasis.

I could fit one hundred times what was in my little bag in the closet.

The size of this room would eclipse the entire downstairs in my house back east.

'*We should stay here,*' the voice insisted for about the hundredth time.

I rolled my eyes. '*Do you think of anything else?*'

'*No.*'

I sat and thought. If I was going to get along in this wolf community, I'd probably have to learn how to accept this thing I was the unwilling host of. My entire life, I had thought of this thing as a curse. Maybe...

'*Why?*' I asked.

'*Why what?*' The voice seemed distracted, like she didn't really care what I had to say. That was probably the case.

'*Why do you want to stay?*' I prodded.

'*The same reasons you do.*'

I sighed, struggling my way out of the wheelchair. I hadn't gone to the bathroom by myself since I tried to bail in Chamberlain, forget bathing. It was hard to believe that was only two days ago. *'Maybe responses like that are why I don't talk to you.'*

'You know it's not,' she chided.

Back in the hospital, after noticing every person talking privately with their wolf at one point or another, I came to the decision I was going to try to have at least a cordial relationship with mine, even if it was only while we were here. I hadn't actually seen a wolf here yet, but I had heard them. Surely, there weren't that many people losing control. Maybe symbiosis was actually attainable.

'Do you have a name?' I finally asked.

'Yes.'

I slipped into the tub, allowing my body to relax for maybe the first time since getting here. *'Well... are you going to tell me?'*

The wolf scoffed. *'What makes you think you deserve to know it now?'*

I winced at her rebuttal. She was right. I sank down in the tub a little more, the water covering my shoulders. I was used to sitting in silence. Enjoyed it, even. This time, the silence felt deafening.

Sponge baths, I quickly decided, did not replace actual bathing. Washing my hair was a struggle, but eventually, I got all the soap out. At least, I hoped I did. Getting out was also a challenge. I sighed, realizing everything would be difficult for a while.

I had been sent home with extra sticky patches to cover my surgical sites. I replaced those, then slipped the sundress I had been wearing back on. I made my way over to the overstuffed chair in front of the fireplace and perused the built-in bookcases. The books were all nicely bound and either newer or well cared for. I hadn't read any of these books before because they were all about werewolves. I wondered if the book selection in here had been specifically curated to reflect what they felt I needed to read, or if it was standard for the rooms.

I settled on one that had a particularly eye-catching binding before struggling out of the chair and limping over to grab it. Settling back down with it in a cushy seat near a window, I looked at the cover. *The Werewolf's Progress.* I snickered at the title; it seemed like a spoof on *The Pilgrim's Progress.* I felt the wolf's presence emerge, but she stayed quiet. Like she was observing with me.

I hadn't even realized I had fallen asleep until I woke up to knocking on the door. I looked down at the book that lay open on my lap. I had barely made it two pages in.

"One sec," I called groggily.

The door cracked open, and Trevor poked his head in. "Pizza sound good, kid?"

"Sounds fine to me," I agreed.

"Good, because we already ordered," he chuckled.

Trevor pulled the wheelchair over, but I shook my head. "I'd rather walk."

I expected to backtrack to the kitchen or dining room, but Trevor led us further down the hall. I hadn't even noticed an additional living room at the end of the Alpha wing. This house seemed endless. A plush couch and loveseat surrounded a large fireplace with a TV on the mantle. This living room was much cozier than the large gathering area in the main portion of the house.

"Rose and Ollie are coming by, too. They're out picking up the pizza," he said, flopping down on the couch.

As if they were summoned, the two of them walked through the door. Rose put a stack of pizza boxes on the coffee table before sitting on the couch, and Oliver doled out drinks. Beers for everyone else, kombucha for me.

"Okay, but is this pizza going to be as good as yours, Trevor?" I asked with a smirk.

Oliver chuckled. "It better be, seeing as it's his cousin's restaurant."

"Yeah," Trevor agreed. "I stole his recipe."

"Aww, you remembered my order!" I beamed. Truth be told, Trevor was probably one of the closest friends I had ever had. It was a depressing realization; he was my best friend, but I was far from his. Guess that's what happened when you didn't get close to anyone other than the guy who poured your beers or the guy masquerading as your fiancé who was actually secretly plotting to kill you.

Oliver sat on the loveseat next to me. I shuddered, glancing over at his pizza. "Gross, olives."

He smirked, pulling one off his slice and dropping it on mine.

"No!" I shrieked. "You've tainted it!"

The room erupted in laughter, me included. Laughing hurt a lot, but it was worth it. I couldn't even remember the last time I'd laughed, but it felt good.

"Lya doesn't like olives," Oliver commented. "Noted."

"Or mushrooms," Trevor added.

"Lya is a picky eater," he amended. "Noted."

I rolled my eyes. "It's just those two I will *not* touch."

Oliver chuckled. "Alright, haggis for dinner tomorrow night."

"So, what are we watching?" Trevor asked.

"Oh!" Rose piped up. "There's a new one that came out I want to watch." She grabbed the remote from him and started scrolling through streaming services, pulling up *Bladerunner 2049*.

"This isn't exactly new," Trevor pointed out.

"Well, I haven't seen it yet, so to me, it is," she snipped.

I smiled to myself. Staying here was starting to seem better and better. At least, for now.

OLIVER

LYA FELL ASLEEP ONLY about thirty minutes into the movie. She had unconsciously tucked herself under my arm sans my knowledge, and I caught myself playing with a couple strands of her thick auburn hair. Rose left once it was over, promising to come back after training the next day. Trevor and I sat, staring at the black TV screen.

Trevor sighed before breaking the silence. "I'm really sorry, man."

"What for?" I snaked my hand along the back of the loveseat, attempting to find my way out of cuddling with the girl. She wasn't going to be my mate until she proved it.

"I wouldn't have done it like that if I had known..." his voice trailed off, but I knew what he meant. He wouldn't have tried to use Lya as bait to draw the hunters in if he had known she was my mate. He hadn't said as much earlier today, but knowing him, it was easy to put the pieces together.

'*Shut up,*' Adair hissed.

'*Not now, Adair.*' I gritted my teeth.

"It shouldn't have been done that way at all, with anyone," I said.

"I know," he nodded.

"Ending this isn't all on you. If anyone, it's me." Trevor tried to speak up, but I cut him off. "I get that they killed your parents, and I get the personal vendetta you have. But it's my pack, and they pose a threat to all of us. Not just you."

"I thought I could end it without getting anyone else involved," Trevor mumbled.

I chuckled. "That's never how it works. What made you decide to give it up, anyway?"

Trevor shrugged. "She actually became my friend, which wasn't supposed to happen. She was supposed to be a pawn. I wasn't supposed to care that she was probably going to get killed. And the closer they got, the more it worked, the more scared she was..."

"And you couldn't do to her what our parents did to others," I finished. "Those things usually only work once, anyway."

"Is there any way we can keep my mate away until this is over?" he asked.

I shook my head. "You know, as soon as this is over, there will be another threat on the horizon. You could've had four years of peace with her at this point. I already forced her into college instead of being a warrior like she wanted. I'm not controlling her life anymore. You want her away from the pack, you tell her."

Trevor looked down at his beer. "I can't lose her, too."

"Man, you don't even have her. All you've done is run from her," I scoffed.

He stood, pointedly glancing down at Lya. "I could say the same about you."

"She'll be back at the end of the month." I looked over to where he stood in the doorway. "You've got two weeks to figure your shit out."

Adair rustled around in my head, demanding my attention.

'Now what?' I asked.

'She's been awake.'

'Fuck.'

"Lya." I couldn't bring myself to look her in the eye. When I finally looked over at her, she was staring at me, wide-eyed. The scent of wolf on her became overpowering.

I searched through the mind-link until I found the person I needed. *'We need you at the packhouse.'*

I didn't get a response, but I rarely did.

"Why was I brought here?" she demanded.

"Lya, nothing's changed," I insisted. "You're still safe here."

"But *why?*" she insisted.

I withdrew my arm. Gone was the girl whose walls were beginning to crack and joked about pizza toppings. "It's a long story."

"Make it short," she growled, sounding very much like a wolf's growl.

"Exactly as it sounds then," I sighed. "Lya, can you listen please?"

She growled again, and the unmistakable sound of bones cracking to shift ripped through the room. I thought at least her wolf trusted us, but now I wasn't so sure.

"Lya, please," I begged. I reached out to touch her, but an auburn paw batted my hand away.

'What do we do?' I asked Adair.

'I don't know!' he shrieked anxiously. *'We can't hurt her.'*

Lya's wolf went to dart past me. I reached out to grab for her, but she made her way through. The little wolf had speed I had not predicted.

A large brown beast came charging down from the Beta wing, leaping at the little red wolf. She flew back against the wall, yelping in pain. She struggled to her feet, cowering against the wall.

Before I could stop him, Adair had shifted. He shielded his mate, growling at Gregory's wolf.

'Shift.' Even through the mind-link, a wolf lower than the Alpha had to obey. Seconds later, Gregory's form stood where his wolf had been, head bowed. We looked back at Lya, still in her wolf form. She couldn't mind-link with us yet, but a command was unavoidable for a rogue. Gregory saw it, too.

'Luna?' he asked.

Adair nodded and I conceded. There was no more denying it. He prowled over to the she-wolf still lying on the ground, shaking in pain and fear, and lay down next to his mate, nuzzling her.

"Gregory, thank you, but I think I can take it from here," my grandmother called as she came into view.

"Yes, Marjorie," he said, turning back to his room.

'We need to talk,' I heard him say as he left.

'Tomorrow,' I agreed.

"Ollie, Lya, I'd like to talk to you two." It wasn't a command, which she was still capable of, but it was still an order. I shifted back, but Lya's wolf was still attempting to hold on to her form.

"It's okay, Lya," I whispered. I reached out to touch her, but she flinched away. "Lya, you're hurt and this is hard on your wolf. Please shift."

Slowly, her wolf let go, leaving Lya on the floor in her place.

My grandmother, always thinking of everything, handed us both robes. "Dr. Whitledge will be here soon, but Lya, I need to talk to your wolf. Would you let her come forward?"

Lya closed her eyes. When she opened them, her wolf's eyes were darting between us. The same vivid amber, only a little brighter.

"What's your name, dear?" Grandma asked.

"Tala," the wolf in human's clothing whispered, her voice hoarse.

"Tala." She smiled. "That's a lovely name. I'm Marjorie. What can I answer for you right now to make you feel safe?"

"Wh-wh-why was Trevor going to let us be killed?" she stuttered.

"That was never the intention," she assured the wolf, shaking her head.

"Knowing Trevor, he wanted to draw the hunters in with you. You had no family and no knowledge of our kind, so it'd be easy to use you for that without you even knowing. But Trevor always forgets to account for things to go less than perfectly, so it was a poor idea." She cupped Lya's face. "Dear, you have a pack now, and everyone here will fight for your safety, no matter the threat. You convince Lya for us, okay, Tala?"

Tala nodded and closed her eyes. The wolf's strength was fading, and Lya would be soon to follow.

Lya's own expression was full of fear. I wrapped my arm around her to keep her still, yet she struggled against me.

My grandmother grabbed Lya's face, staring into her eyes. "Lya, you need to listen to Tala. Hear her, and trust her."

"Who's Tala?" she gasped.

Grandma smiled warmly down at her. "You, dear. Your wolf."

Lya tried to ask more, but her consciousness was slipping. I looked up at my grandmother.

"What do I do now?" I asked.

"Keep her safe. Safe from herself, mostly."

Eleven

Lya

My eyes snapped open.

Time to run.

Everything I thought I knew about this place was a lie. That's what I got for trusting too easily. A mistake I'd made before and should have known better than to repeat.

'*No,*' the wolf—Tala—said. Her voice was harsh, and I was scared of her.

'*Yes,*' I insisted.

'*I won't let you.*' I knew she wasn't lying. She had taken control of me before, and I knew she had no qualms about doing it again. '*Look around, Lya. They trust you. Now you need to trust them.*'

I did as she asked, expecting to be back in the hospital, probably behind a locked door. But I was still in the room at the packhouse. Alone.

'*You could leave if you wanted. There's the door, but that would be conspicuous. We have an entrance to the patio, and it would take a while for them to realize we are gone.*'

'We aren't safe here, Tala,' I argued.

The wolf growled back, '*Yes. We are.*'

'*How do you know?*'

'*Adair.*'

She slunk back, leaving me in control. The vote of confidence from her left me uneasy.

There was a knock at my door, but I had no intention of answering. I curled up in a ball, pulling my knees to my chest. All I wore was an oversized t-shirt that smelled like... smelled like Oliver. I scrunched up my nose, not exactly thrilled that I was wearing his shirt, no matter how good he smelled.

"Lya, are you up?" Oliver called, knocking again. The door cracked open, and Oliver peeked his head in. He attempted a smile, but his face looked pained. "Hi, Lya."

I didn't say anything. Just stared.

"May I come in?" I gave no response, but he entered anyway. He sat on the edge of the bed and put a plate down next to me. "I figured you'd want breakfast."

We stared at each other for a long moment. I was curled up as far away from him as I could get, and he looked like a sad, dejected puppy perched on the corner of the bed.

'*Just think of him as his wolf,*' my own purred. I internally rolled my eyes but refused to let my expression toward Oliver change.

"I was never going to keep any of what you heard the other night a secret from you," Oliver mumbled. "I wanted you to settle in first. Figure out that you can trust us."

"It's hard to trust someone who's willing to have you killed," I scoffed.

I had baited him. His eyes flashed with a rage I quickly decided I never wanted to be on the receiving end of. I hoped I wasn't now.

"*I* did not do that," he growled, "and if *I* had known about it, I would not have condoned it or allowed it to happen. To anyone."

I softened a bit. He had a point. The person all this anger was really directed toward was the only person I thought I knew I could trust here. Joke was on me, I guess.

"Why do you care so much about me, anyway?" I demanded. Shoot, it seemed like a reasonable plan Trevor had developed. If these 'hunters' were as bad as the werewolves made them sound, use an unhinged 'rogue' to distract them, but away from the pack. Who cared about a little bloodshed for the greater good.

"Because you're—" he started. "Because you shouldn't have to make decisions for your life without knowing what options you have, and no one should make those decisions for you."

I barked out a laugh. "I sure feel like it's been decided I am staying here, and no one asked me."

"Fine," he spat. "Leave."

He left the door open behind him as he stormed out.

Tala whined in my head. *'I will never forgive you if you hurt him.'*

'What's so special about him*?'* I demanded. Sure, he gave me butterflies, but he was just some attractive guy with a savior complex.

'I don't know,' she finally mumbled after a prolonged moment of silence.

I looked down at what he'd brought me for breakfast. I wasn't exactly hungry, but the gesture was nice. I got up to close the door, not realizing that my body wasn't nearly as painful as it should have been until I sat down in the chair with the breakfast burrito.

'You're welcome.'

I picked up the book I had barely started yesterday and opened it back up, returning to the first page. The book was captivating, and I made progress quickly. It didn't read like *The Pilgrim's Progress,* like I expected. Instead, it was more of the progression of werewolves—their origination story, how they evolved from being mostly lone wolves who often felt like I had for the past twenty-four years, to developing packs, and later building their own towns. It was interesting, to say the least. The timeline presented at the beginning of the book outlined that packs of werewolves had started to develop hundreds of years ago, citing their strong family ties and the need to protect extended to those werewolves they found weaker than themselves. The book only mentioned a few major disputes between different packs, always stemming from a pack member being forcefully taken or killed. The primary threats to werewolves, apparently, were hunters and rogues who had spent so much time in their wolf form they lost their humanity.

That concept—the loss of humanity—caused an idea to bubble in my head. Tala had already proven, if I shut her out for too long, I lost control of her and she became a threat to other humans. It was scary to see it was a well-documented phenomenon.

'We are one,' Tala insisted, *'whether you like it or not. We need each other, no matter how much we hate each other.'*

'You hate me?' I asked. I didn't know why it bothered me, seeing as I had done so much to get rid of her because I hated her so much, but it stung.

'I will always love you,' Tala admitted, *'but I haven't liked you for a long time.'*

At least she was brutally honest and I didn't have to question where we stood.

I looked up at the clock. It was almost 2 p.m. I found a sticky note in the bedside table drawer to use as a bookmark before I scrounged up clothes. I had destroyed the only sundress I brought with me last night, so I settled for jeans and a T-shirt. I needed to go shopping soon.

Outside my room, I held my breath. I needed to return the plate to the kitchen and hopefully grab some coffee, but I also needed to stay far away from everyone.

Apparently, no such luck. I stopped in my tracks as a door behind me creaked open. My back stiffened as the footsteps got closer.

'Just start walking, you dolt!'

Okay, sometimes the wolf had good ideas. So, as suggested, I bolted. I rushed into the kitchen, dumped the plate in the sink, forwent the coffee, and ran back to my room, slamming the door and locking it shut. I leaned my back against the door, eyes scrunched closed, and slid down until I was sitting on the ground.

'So, just a quick warning for you when you decide to rejoin society,' the wolf snarked, *'but we aren't alone in here.'*

I took a deep breath, keeping my eyes closed. I couldn't think of a way to escape this without acknowledging who was in here.

I sighed. I had to face the music at some point. Ever so slowly, I cracked my eyes open.

I didn't know who I was expecting to see, but it certainly, definitely was not Trevor. That being said, for all I knew, Trevor had no idea that I had heard all of his and Oliver's conversation last night when they thought I was asleep.

Trevor smiled, but his eyes looked pained. "I'm headed back east tomorrow. Anything you'd like me to grab for you?"

I shook my head. All the things I had to say to him, I didn't have words for yet.

He studied me for a minute. "You gonna be okay without me around?"

I nodded. Great, actually. A lot better than with you here, probably. But I couldn't find it in myself to say that.

"Do you want me to leave you alone?" he finally asked quietly.

I nodded. Everything I thought I knew about him had been undone in the span of about five minutes last night. Trevor stood and walked toward me. I realized I was blocking the door and scooted over.

He came to a stop next to me but didn't look down. His voice cracked as he said, "You're my friend, Lya. I never meant to hurt you in all this."

I looked up at him. "Well, you did."

With that, Trevor left. Who was to say if I would ever talk to him again.

OLIVER

THE RAPPING on my door startled me out of my daze. I had things I needed to do, and absolutely no ability to focus. I was angry at myself for practically encouraging Lya to leave, and I had very little hope she would actually still be around at this point. That scared me more than I could put into words.

"Come in," I called gruffly.

Trevor opened the door but didn't come inside. "I'm headed out."

"You better not bail on me this time," I reminded him.

"I'm not planning on it." He paused, looking down to the ground. "I'm really sorry Lya heard everything last night. That wasn't a very fair way for her to find out."

I sighed, leaning back in my chair. "Realistically, she might have had the same reaction no matter when and how it was done. It's part of the long list of reasons why people who don't know what they're fighting for shouldn't be involved."

Trevor nodded.

"We could have come up with a plan together if you had told me," I added. "I didn't agree with the way our parents did things twelve years ago, so I certainly don't appreciate you attempting to reenact it. It's not safe, it didn't work the way it was supposed to, and more lives were lost than necessary, which you should know more than anyone."

Trevor stepped through the doorway, closed the door behind him, and sat in the chair across from the desk. "Are you retracting the offer to be Beta now?"

"You came clean before it was too late," I told him. "Your ego and ulterior motives didn't stand in the way of you doing what was best for another wolf."

"How long do you think we have until they've found us?" Trevor mused. It wasn't really a question; his guess was as good as mine.

"That's something I'd like you to figure out while you're back East River. Check in with the scouts. Ask around with our connections out there," I instructed.

Trevor nodded and stood. "I'll give you a call when I get there. Putting in my two weeks tomorrow, so I should be back the last weekend in May."

I looked over at the calendar, noticing the full moon was only a few days away. "Sure you don't want to stay until Monday?"

"It's tempting," Trevor sighed, "but if this pack has any hope of having a Luna, I think it's best if I'm not here."

Adair sat up at attention. He had been furious with me all day and said I was trying to push her out the door. "She's still here?"

"Good luck with that, by the way," he chuckled. "If you still don't think she's your mate, you're the idiot."

She was still here.

She hadn't left.

'Tala,' Adair pointed out. *'Tala won't let her leave.'*

I sighed. Why couldn't I have a normal mate who actually enjoyed my presence and being part of the pack? Most mates had mated and marked each other by this point, but she hadn't even realized who I was to her yet. Hell, it took her resisting Adair's command to finally admit it to myself. Had my life not been difficult enough?

Adair was really trying to take over and go see her, and it took everything I had to keep us put.

'We still have work to do,' I insisted.

He huffed. *'It's not as important.'*

I had to agree, but what little I knew of Lya made me think hovering over her was not a good idea. I needed time, anyway. Not just to come to terms with her being my mate, but to forgive myself for insisting it couldn't be true.

I thought of the girl, though. The teenager who was too young to recognize a bond when I was barely old enough to. Nothing more than a forgotten memory, but the cause of so much nostalgia. I was homesick for her and didn't even know who she was. Even though I had found my mate, I still felt like I was betraying that girl. She had driven so much of what this pack was now and didn't even know it. I'd probably never get a chance to tell her, either.

I needed a distraction, so I reached out to Gregory through the mind-link. *'You wanted to talk?'*

'I'll be right there,' he responded. I heard the door to his office beside me open and close, quickly followed by a knock on the door.

"Just come in." He opened the door and bowed his head. I motioned to one of the chairs across from the desk. "You are so formal."

"You are the Alpha," he pointed out.

"You live in the same house as me," I said, rolling my eyes. "You helped raise me."

Gregory cleared his throat. "So, do we have a Luna now?"

"Yes and no," I said, furrowing my brow. I filled him in on the story thus far, leaving out how Trevor was attempting to use her before bringing her here. I didn't need pack members questioning my choice of a Beta before he had even started.

Gregory rarely asked questions about things, which was one of the aspects that made him a good Beta. He followed orders. When he deemed it worthy of speaking, though, his words and advice were invaluable.

"A leader who has not been among us from the beginning will bring in new perspectives," he said solemnly, "which can be both good and bad."

I nodded in agreement.

"But we cannot pretend to know fate's plans. How may we help bring her around?" he asked.

"That's a very good question," I mumbled. "I have no idea. Her wolf seems to be on our side, but that's only half of the equation."

Gregory nodded gravely. "So this must become a home for her."

"Sooner rather than later, seeing as we have a war on the horizon. Speaking of..." I changed gears. "Trevor has finally decided he is going to take up his Beta position."

Gregory smiled. There had been no bones about the fact that, after twelve years, he was ready to step down. He had very much enjoyed leading training for the pups at the school and being a warrior, and had only taken the position out of duty to his pack after the death of Trevor's parents. That was a fun fact I had never been told until a conversation with my grandmother when I was bemoaning being Alpha.

"I would like you to stay on until the end of summer," I added. "Trevor has been away from the pack for six years, and I feel it would do us good to have as many hands on deck as we determine how to deal with our hunter situation."

"Of course," he agreed. "Allyssa will be thankful to know our tenure is coming to an end."

"How will your kids feel about moving out?" I asked.

He shrugged. "Anna hasn't lived here really since she went off to college, and I believe Gavin may elect to move into the warrior's barracks a year early if it could be allowed. George, however..." he sighed. "George isn't very happy. We are expecting another pup in the fall, and he has never handled change well."

I smiled broadly. "Congratulations, Gregory. It seems this transition couldn't have happened at a better time. Please let me know if there's anything I can do to help, especially with George."

Gregory agreed. "I'll be able to handle George, in one way or another. It isn't something you need to concern yourself with, given everything else on your plate."

"George is a member of my pack, too," I reminded him. "I'll do what I can to look out for him."

"Thank you, Alpha." He stood up. "I'll be on my way, then."

I stood and followed him out. "We can plan for an announcement of your pup at the full moon."

Gregory shook his head. "Allyssa wants to wait. She knows she is older and would like to hold off until the last trimester."

"Gotcha. Well, I need to wrangle a very angry she-wolf into going to the doctor, but make sure to pass my congratulations on to your mate."

We went our separate ways, and I found myself standing outside Lya's door without the courage to face her. I felt like a kid trying to woo a crush that was far out of their league. I had a huge amount of respect for those who took chosen mates. The mate bond made things so much easier. Except this time, apparently.

The bond was necessary; it was the best way to ensure both humans and their wolves synced, especially when it came to mating for life. It made sense that a wolf and human who hadn't meshed yet would not acknowledge a mate. I wondered what was going through her head, and if she was battling herself as much as I was.

I couldn't wait for the day she could feel the mate bond. I wondered how long that would take.

'I could take over,' Adair offered.

'No.' He seemed a little dejected, but he was coming around to the importance of appeasing Lya's human side.

Finally, I knocked. I heard some movement in the room, and then the door flung open. Lya looked defensive, which I couldn't blame her for. I couldn't keep my eyes from taking her in. She was shorter than I initially thought and petite, even to me. I'd be surprised if she passed five feet tall, which was exceptionally small for a werewolf, but she was half-human. She certainly didn't lack muscle, though. Her auburn hair was more akin to a deep red, and if it weren't for her wolf being the same color, I would be convinced it was dyed.

"What?" she snapped, pulling me out of not-so-subtly checking her out.

I took a deep breath. "Dr. Whitledge wanted to see you once more today, and I've got some time to give you a ride over."

"No, thanks," was her curt response.

I raised an eyebrow. "How are you planning on getting over to the hospital, then?"

"I'll walk," she insisted.

"Oh? You were in a wheelchair whenever you needed to move around much on Wednesday," I pointed out.

"I'll ask Rose, then."

"She's training," I reminded her.

"Fine," Lya huffed. She marched out of her room, slammed the door closed, and led the way out of the packhouse.

I didn't mind lagging behind and enjoying the view.

TWELVE

Lya

THE SILENCE WAS STRAINED in Oliver's Land Cruiser. I sat with my arms folded across my chest, refusing to look at him.

'There's no harm in enjoying the view,' Tala insisted.

I rolled my eyes. Oliver was, unfortunately, exactly my type. The dark and broody mountain man looked like he was chiseled from stone. I wondered if Michelangelo was jealous. I settled for studying the tattoos down his right arm.

Oliver kept glancing over at me. He looked like he was trying to come up with something to say while I was trying to put off vibes that discouraged interaction.

'He's not the one you're angry with,' Tala reminded me.

She may be right, but I wanted to be angry with him, too. Maybe I just wanted to be angry, period. It'd been a while since my emotions were safe to feel.

"Have you been feeling better?" Oliver finally asked as we pulled into the parking lot.

I nodded, still not wanting to talk.

"That's good," he nodded. I hopped out of the SUV, and Oliver fell in stride beside me. "You haven't really come out of your room. Have you been bored?"

"I found a book to read."

"Oh? Which one?" he asked.

"Some werewolf book," was all I said.

He chuckled, opening the door for me. "They're all werewolf books."

"I noticed."

We walked in silence the rest of the way down to Dr. Whitledge's office. I was surprised we were going to an office instead of an exam room. Once there, Oliver plopped down in one of the chairs outside, and I walked through the open office door.

"Ah, hello, Lu-Lya." Dr. Whitledge got up and closed the door behind me. "You look like you're feeling much better."

I smiled up at him. I was capable of being nice to people who didn't bother me. "I am, thanks."

He nodded. "I expected your shift a couple nights ago to take more of a toll, but it seems to have worked out in your favor. Your wolf was able to heal quite a bit. I'm sure sleeping for a full day helped, too."

"Oh..." I hadn't realized I had lost an entire day.

"Exams last night showed you still have some healing to do," he continued, "but overall, you are mostly there. Just try and take it easy for the next couple of weeks."

"Do I need to come back for any more appointments?" I asked.

He shook his head. "Obviously, if you start to feel worse than you do now, or there is no continued progress, yes. But otherwise, we are confident in your recovery."

"Okay..."

"Other than that, you are free to go." He smiled warmly at me. "Although I will warn you, with the way Oliver worried, he will still try and coddle you. Doctor's orders are that you should be reasonably active. Don't go and train or anything yet, but getting up and moving around, going out and doing things, is encouraged."

I nodded. I wasn't sure what he meant by training. I wasn't training for anything right now, but I was sure that was just a werewolf thing.

Outside the office, I looked down at Oliver, still waiting beside the door. I nodded my head toward the exit and started walking.

"Good news?" he asked when he caught up to me.

I shrugged. "Just not supposed to train, but I can go back to normal life now."

Oliver nodded. I could have sworn he looked a little disappointed for a second.

"What?" I asked. "Were you hoping I'd be broken for a while longer?"

He smiled and shook his head. We climbed inside his car and headed away from the hospital, back to the house, taking a route I hadn't seen yet. I looked around. We were headed down a cute little downtown street with tons of shops and restaurants.

"I thought this town was only a few thousand?" I asked.

"It is, but most people also work in the town and don't really stray off of pack lands for anything, so we have quite a few amenities given its size," he explained while pulling into a parking space. "You up for an early dinner?"

I shrugged, hopping out and onto the curb. Oliver led the way down the street before turning down an alley. He opened the door to a restaurant called "The Wolfe's Nest."

"This place has really good food, and Delia is a sweetheart," he told me.

I nodded slowly as Oliver ushered me in and past the hostess' stand. The girl standing behind it bowed her head, whispering, "Alpha," as we passed. Was that something I should have been doing?

Oliver smiled at her and directed me to a table in the back. A heavier-set lady with gray curls came rushing over.

"Oliver Dallaire!" She swatted him across the back of the head. "You didn't tell me you were coming in!"

I had to stifle a giggle. Oliver was usually greeted with an amount of respect that made me uncomfortable to be around him, so it was nice to see more normalcy.

The woman turned, noticing me. "And with company! You should have made a reservation!"

He smiled up at her, even when she chastised him. "It's early enough, and my table was free, so I think we are okay."

The woman, who I assumed was Delia, glared at him. "It's a Friday, Ollie. We get busy."

"Well, I'll do better next time," he chuckled. "Although Lya hasn't been here before, so could we snag some menus?"

"I see." She nodded. "You can seat yourself, but you can't get your own menus."

"So, I take it you're a regular?" I asked after she had bustled off in the direction of the hostess stand.

"Since the day this place opened," he confirmed. "I try to be a regular everywhere in town, but Delia and I go way back. This is honestly the best restaurant this town has."

I raised an eyebrow. "Oh? How do you know her?"

"She uh... she would be my high school girlfriend's aunt, actually," he admitted sheepishly. He leaned in slightly. "Is it bad I stayed with her for as long as I did because of Delia's cooking?"

I giggled, rewarding his attempt to chip away at my walls. "One of my ex's moms still sends me Christmas presents. At least you got to keep Delia in the split."

"Oh, of course." He smirked. "I mean, she did run off with some guy without even breaking up with me, so it's what I was owed."

"I guess not every girl wants to be the Alpha's sweetheart?"

He brushed off the comment. "It was meant to be between those two. They have a couple kids and are living happily ever after in Norridge."

"Is that one of the other towns in the pack?" I asked.

Oliver nodded. "I'm going up there soon. You can come if you'd like, see more of the pack?"

"That depends," I mused. "Do they have a restaurant as good as you claim this place is?"

Oliver smiled. I had to admit, his smile was endearing, and his dimples were cute. "I guess you'll need to be the judge. I am biased, you know."

"I told you, business picks up quickly on Fridays."

I looked up abruptly, not even noticing Delia's return. But sure enough, the restaurant was filling up. People were stealing glances in our direction. If this was what it was always like for Oliver when he went out, I understood why he stuck to the back corner table.

"And drinks?" Delia asked.

"Does the brewery have a new one on tap yet?" Oliver asked.

Delia nodded. "Vance is playing around with sours. He wasn't happy with Trevor's claim that his sours were weak. And you, sweetie?"

I wrinkled my nose. "If there's a risk the sours are weak, I'll go with an IPA."

Oliver gave me a sideways glance.

"What?" I demanded.

"Aren't you not supposed to drink alcohol so soon after surgery?" he reminded me.

"Doc said I could resume my normal life. That includes drinking."

Delia snickered as she walked away. I liked her.

I looked around, not able to shake the feeling of eyes on us constantly. "Why is everyone staring?"

Oliver looked around, seeing everyone indeed looking at us. He shrugged. "Probably because the Alpha is out and about."

"Don't they get used to you being present in society if you try and be a regular everywhere?" I asked.

He shot me a devilish grin. "Well, maybe they aren't staring at me, then. Maybe they think you're the Alpha's sweetheart."

I rolled my eyes.

'I didn't like Ted anyway,' Tala piped up. *'We can be the Alpha's sweetheart instead.'*

'Well, I did,' I reminded the wolf. *'So give me a minute to get over it.'*

'I just feel like liking a guy who was going to kill you is a little dumb, but suit yourself,' Tala said with a huff. She slunk to the back of my head, leaving me alone, but still very much present.

"How's your wolf?" Oliver asked.

My eyes snapped up to him. "You noticed that?"

He blushed like a kid caught with his hands in the cookie jar. "It's pretty obvious."

"Oh."

"So, her name is Tala?" he continued.

I nodded. "Seems to be."

"That translates to some variation of Alpha she-wolf or wolf princess in a few different Native American tongues," he said with a smile. "Seems fitting."

Delia saved me from having to come up with a response by dropping off our beers and asking for our orders.

"Um..." I glanced down at the menu, having not even gotten a chance to look at it. "I'll go with the, uh, rancher's pie." It was the first thing I saw.

"Lovely, I'll get those out." Delia smiled.

I glanced over at Oliver. "Aren't you going to order?"

Oliver chuckled. "I lost that privilege a while ago. I get what I get."

"Alpha!" a voice called from across the restaurant. I looked up to see an absolute giant of a human walking toward us. "I haven't seen you around the training grounds the past few days. What's going on?"

Oliver threw me an apologetic look. "Been busy running a pack, Kota. That's why I have someone like you to keep an eye on things over there."

"Yeah, man, but last time I talked to you on Monday, you were telling me to get everyone geared up. Figured you'd be doing the same." He leaned back in the chair he had pulled over and took a sip of his beer, glancing over at me. "Who are you?"

"I'm, uh... I," I stuttered.

"This is Lya," Oliver cut in. "She'll be with the pack for a while."

The guy cocked an eyebrow. "So this is Lya. I'm Kota, the pack Gamma. I oversee training, and if you'll be here, that includes you. Non-warrior pack members need to clock a minimum of five hours a week."

I could feel Oliver bristling at the comment. It was like I could sense his wolf's hackles going up. Maybe it was because of my need to be rebellious, but training intrigued me.

"No can do," Oliver told him. "She can't train for a while yet."

"Why not?" he demanded.

"I'm still healing from surgery," I offered.

A look of realization came over his face. "Oh, of course. Hunters will do that to ya."

I nodded, looking down at the beer glass and drawing designs in the condensation. I wasn't exactly comfortable with people I didn't know, knowing about me. I wondered how much of the story he had heard. To be honest, I wondered how much of the story I knew.

Kota stood up, studying me for a moment. "You guys have a good night, then. I'll catch up with y'all later."

"How much does everyone know about me?" I asked Oliver.

"I only told the people that needed to know the bare minimum," Oliver said. "I told Kota that a werewolf who had grown up knowing nothing about what she is had a couple run-ins with hunters, and I needed him to choose some people to send out to where you're from and north of Chamberlain to figure out if they're random and isolated or if something more is being planned."

"Oh."

"And to be honest," Oliver continued, "I don't think anyone knows the full story yet, so I'd be remiss to tell anyone much more."

"What do you mean you don't have the full story?" I asked.

Oliver shrugged. "For one, we need to figure out why you were raised not knowing anything of your heritage. And I really doubt it was simply chance that a rogue like yourself developed a relationship with a hunter."

"Oh, I'm pretty sure it was my dad," I said, focusing on the first part of his statement. Oliver motioned for me to continue. "He disappeared shortly after I shifted for the first time, but I hadn't told him. He came back, saw me shift, and then left again. I always knew I'd hear from him a couple days before he actually called or sent a letter because I'd see giant dog tracks around the house."

Oliver furrowed his eyebrows. "But your mom wasn't a wolf?"

"Absolutely not," I scoffed. "She freaked out when she saw it, and I've only shifted a handful of times since then. That was almost ten years ago."

"I see." He clenched his jaw. "And the... guy that you were with..."

It felt like a vice grip clenched around my heart. "What about him?"

"Did you tell him anything?" he asked.

"No," I snapped. "Being a werewolf had ruined so many other things in my life. I wasn't going to let it ruin things with Ted, too." I kept my eyes down as I sniffled, fighting back tears. This was dumb; he tried to kill me first. Why was I so upset over him being gone?

"I'm sorry, Lya..." he said slowly.

I took a deep breath and looked up, plastering on a smile. "I don't want to talk about him, okay?"

I was thankful our food arrived. It gave me an excuse not to talk.

OLIVER

BRINGING up her ex had clearly struck a nerve. As much as I hated the thought of that guy with her, I felt bad that I had unintentionally hurt Lya. Humans were weird. I couldn't wrap my head around how she could still be hung up on that guy.

The rest of dinner had been quiet. Every attempt I made to pull her out of the shell she had receded into failed, and she asked to go home as soon as she had finished. At this point, she was back in her room, and I was sitting in my office. I looked over at the clock. It was still early for a Friday night. Since it was only 7pm, I decided to head back out to the bar, where I was sure Kota would have migrated.

I sat in the driver's seat for a moment before starting the Land Cruiser. The smell of lilac and pine still lingered. I could get drunk off of it. Begrudgingly, I started it up, the fans of the air conditioning dispersing Lya's intoxicating scent.

Adair growled, *'Someone should be at the packhouse with her.'*

'Gregory is there,' I reminded him.

Adair accepted that, but he wasn't happy about it. I figured he'd only be happy if we had eyes on her. I pulled into a parking spot close to the bar and made my way in. I spotted Kota and claimed a chair at our usual table. He glanced up and motioned to the waitress to bring another beer over.

"What happened to the pretty little number you had with you?" he asked. The bar wasn't very full yet, so he kept his voice low.

I shrugged. "She called it an early night."

"Is there more to that story?" His eyes probed me, probably trying to read my mind.

I nodded. "Lots more."

Kota laughed. "Anything I get to know? You didn't seem like you were about to take her on a date the other night."

"Hard to go on a date with someone who doesn't realize that's what you're trying to do," I growled. Kota raised an eyebrow.

"Mate," I confirmed his unspoken question. "She resisted an Alpha command."

Kota let out a low whistle. "Well, at least you finally came around to it."

"Keep it under the radar, okay?" I asked. "She still hasn't realized it yet."

He nodded. "Guess I won't be able to encourage you to chase some tail tonight, then."

I chuckled, staring down at the beer bottle that had been dropped off for me. "It won't get you very far."

Kota leaned in and asked, "So, why do we have folks investigating hunter activity where it all originally went down?"

I stiffened. Kota was my Gamma and in charge of my warriors. In the grand scheme of things, he did need to know everything. It was wishful thinking, hoping the brief conversation of the details on Monday would placate his interest... but it still felt like a betrayal of Lya's privacy. I couldn't risk the safety of my pack, though.

"That's where she's from. Lya lost control of her wolf and killed her fiancé the night before she came here," I said quietly. "He was a Marsan. She also got attacked by a group of four hunters when she tried to make a run for it on the way out here with Trevor."

At that, he sat back and laughed. "You had to end up with the most unavailable she-wolf out there, didn't you?"

"I am well aware," I said dryly.

"But I assume this means patrols have increased?"

I nodded. "It's also probably a good time to increase training hours. War is coming, and we won't be caught with our pants down."

"It's what we always train for and hope we never need to utilize," Kota reiterated my constant mantra. "Are we worried about the rogues working with them?"

"They're always a concern," I sighed. "I'll ask Thom to keep us apprised of anything he hears."

I had worked hard to improve relations with rogues. The lands surrounding the Snow Moon territory were probably some of the safest for rogues in the entire United States, but not all of them had gotten that memo yet.

Kota ground his teeth. "Things have been quiet for too long. There haven't even been many unruly rogues recently."

"I know," I mumbled. " Have you heard about the disappearances? Sturgeon Moon even reported a dropped body. But I really don't think this family would use another wolf to get to us."

"Ya don't think?" Kota scoffed. "I wouldn't put anything past them."

"Anything is always possible," I mused. I motioned for another round from the waitress. "How are things at home?"

Kota had met his mate less than a year previously, and he rarely even mentioned her. Ellie was nearly ten years younger than him. They had met when she showed up for an initial training camp right when she turned eighteen–barely old enough to even recognize her mate. Now, she was in her first year of four of warrior training, and they frequently ran into issues related to the fact that she was barely an adult.

"I swear, she's out of control," he insisted, rolling his eyes. "I'm so excited for her to grow up."

I chuckled. "Sounds like how we were at eighteen."

Kota gave me a sideways glance. "Yeah, but we didn't have mates."

"Just because you have a mate doesn't mean your life has to completely change," I suggested, but even I knew that wasn't true.

"She doesn't even want to spend a full night yet." His tone was exasperated. "She's worried she'll lose all her independence."

"Well, will she?" I cocked an eyebrow.

"No," Kota insisted. "Although it'd be nice if she went to bed sober just like... one time."

I very nearly snorted beer out my nose. "You can't get mad at her for being exactly like you were. A match made in heaven, it sounds like."

Kota looked past me, toward the door, and smiled. I turned around to see Ellie walking toward us. The one thing this town did not have was a nightclub, so the local bar frequently became one on the weekends. Ellie was decked out in a red leather skirt, a black lace top that revealed a little too much, and black pumps. I looked over to Kota to see how he'd react to the eyes she attracted. For the time being, it seemed like he was blind to them. Ellie shot Kota a smirk, then grabbed her friends and pulled them onto the makeshift dance floor.

"This is what I deal with," he sighed, putting his head in his hands. "She dresses like that, flirts with other guys... I mean, she always comes home with me, but then she's back at her apartment by morning."

I furrowed my eyebrows. That wasn't exactly normal behavior for someone with a mate. Usually, it was hard and nearly painful to be physically too far from them. Granted, he had also confessed he wasn't happy with his mate the other night. I wondered what her wolf thought about how she acted. My mind wandered to Lya. More or less, things were like that with her, except I didn't envision her having such a wild streak. But Adair would kill anyone else who tried to make eyes at her.

I huffed. "How do you stand her not acknowledging the bond?"

"Oh, she definitely acknowledges it... on her terms." Kota laughed dryly. "She has no interest in having a mate so soon." His eyes followed his mate across the dance floor as she found her way into the arms of someone who certainly didn't know she had a mate.

"Why don't you go public with it?" I asked.

"She'd reject me."

Kota growled as my eyes roamed over Ellie. She had no mark. The sad expression I cast his way was all the conversation we needed to have.

"Don't feel bad for me, man," Kota said as he sat back with his hands up. "You're the one whose mate doesn't even realize she's yours. At least I know mine is just a tease."

My retort was cut off by a chair scraping across the floor and another person joining us.

"Word on the street is that we have a Luna," a loud voice boomed. I glanced up at the owner of the voice, surprised to see Brandon, the Gamma of mine who headed up the small town of Norridge. He was an absolute pain in the ass, but a good warrior, and, most importantly, a good friend.

"Manners maketh a man." Kota laughed. "If you didn't hear it from him, you didn't hear it at all. Who told you, anyway?"

Brandon scoffed. "Trevor, obviously. He is my cousin, don't forget. Ollie, you may be Alpha now, but don't forget your roots. I remember your first crush, first hookup, first love—"

"And how each and every one of those crashed and burned," Kota chimed in.

"Yeah, well, at the rate this is going, this relationship will, too. Keep the Woodford ready," I huffed.

Brandon cocked an eyebrow. I caught Kota out of the corner of my eye shaking his head. The simple translation was that he'd fill the newcomer in later. That was good because I had absolutely no desire to reiterate the saga again.

"Well then, I guess it's now on me to find a mate to have a normal relationship with," Brandon sighed dramatically.

"You? The normal one?" Kota chuckled. "My, how times have changed."

Brandon clapped his hands together. "Who do you think it'll be? Blondie over there? Personally, I'd like to settle down with a brunette, but whatever the fates have in store..."

"And I will take that as my cue to leave." I finished off my beer and stood up.

"Aww, but the party's just getting started," Brandon huffed. "I need my best wingmen to help me find my mate!"

I laughed. "You're on your own for this one, buddy."

I turned, heading out the door, and back to the packhouse. Back to my Luna.

THIRTEEN

Lya

OLIVER DIDN'T COMPLAIN about calling it an early night. He had offered to show me around, but I needed to be by myself. If I didn't know any better, I would think Oliver was trying to surprise me with a date, but I was certain it had to be a tactic to get answers out of me. Rose had come by shortly after I got back from dinner with Oliver and offered to hang out with me, but she was understanding when I told her I needed some time alone. I wasn't exactly upset everyone was asking nosey questions–I knew that would happen at some point–but I needed time to think and process. The past few days had been such a whirlwind; I hadn't even had time to do that.

I wondered if this was how they handled all surprise pack visitors. It didn't seem at all like the most secure setup. This pack would be very easy to infiltrate if someone harbored any amount of ill will toward them. It couldn't have happened before, though; otherwise, I probably would have been in a cell rather than the packhouse. Maybe that reputation of Oliver's really did precede him.

Curled up on the loveseat in my room with a book cracked open on my lap, I stared at the pages but hadn't read a word. It was hard to get my brain to even put thoughts together.

I didn't know what to think of anything. Maybe that's why I couldn't think. I had more questions than I could wrap my head around. The only thing I had been able to accomplish was categorizing my questions.

First, there were questions about the now. Would I actually be allowed to leave if I tried? Was I really here because of being a naive wolf, or was it because Trevor's plan got too real for him? What was Trevor's plan supposed to accomplish, and what had happened before that was threatening to happen again?

Then, of course, reading that werewolf book had created more questions rather than answering any. I didn't understand pack dynamics, or rogues, or hunters. And what was it Oliver meant when he alluded to Ted being a hunter?

Last were maybe the most important things to know. Who was I? Was it really my dad who passed the wolf thing onto me? Why didn't he tell me? And where did he go?

To be honest, I felt like a shell of myself here. I was a fish out of water and had no idea how in the world I would acclimate. I didn't even feel like I was acting like myself, but at the same time, was that the real me or a pretense of me that I had created out of self-defense? I was scared shitless about what life here would be like, but there was also a small bit of morbid curiosity. I wouldn't call it excitement yet.

I glanced over at the clock. Only 8:30. That seemed late enough for bed. I curled up in the middle of the giant bed, staring out the window, watching the moonlight dance across the part of the river I could see from my bedroom. Sleep wasn't going to come easily tonight, no matter how exhausted I was.

Tala rustled around. She had been silent since we got back from dinner, which I had been thankful for. I wasn't sure I was up for bickering with her. Now, though, that seemed like the only option.

'What do you want?' I demanded.

'I just want to run,' the wolf whined.

That confused me. 'What?'

'You know, go outside, shift, and run through the woods.' She sounded so morose, she almost had me convinced. 'Like we used to.'

'No.'

'I could make us,' she reminded me.

'Can we please wait to debate doing stuff like that tomorrow?' I asked. 'I'm exhausted and want to sleep. I don't want to deal with other people.'

'You wouldn't have to deal with them if I was in charge. I would.'

'I don't trust what you do when you're in charge. Last time, you killed someone.'

The silence in my head was strained. *'Fair point,'* Tala finally admitted. She slipped to the back of my mind, apparently admitting defeat.

I tossed and turned for what felt like hours. I desperately wanted to sneak away and soak up the near-full moonlight, but I was too nervous to start exploring the area, especially at night. Maybe something to do tomorrow, though. I settled for slipping out the French doors to the patio and curling up on one of the chairs. I couldn't remember being this cautious since I first left home at eighteen.

Home. That was a strange notion. I couldn't remember the last place that felt like home. I wondered if I would ever find a place to feel like home again.

I couldn't get a read on this place. Everything was so different from what I was used to, but of course, it would be, right? It was a town full of freaking werewolves. I wished I had other places to compare it to. Maybe I'd feel less insane if I did. Maybe I had finally had a psychotic break and this was all some crazy delusion I'd snap out of soon. I'd probably be in a mental hospital when I woke up. How would I explain the wolfy tendencies? Or was that part of the delusion, too?

Everyone I had met here was so kind and welcoming. It was unnerving, almost. It'd be easier to think this place was real if I ran into someone who acted a little more... normal.

But, all things considered, I didn't think I could leave here even if I tried, and not from being held hostage. No, it was like I was drawn to this place. It was almost magnetic. Maybe this could become my home.

If I had any hope of ever enjoying it here, my guard had to come down. Even if I had to pretend to be the old me until it felt comfortable and real. I had no idea if that tactic was going to work, but it was at least worth a try.

OLIVER

THE NIGHT DRAGGED ON. I had buried myself in work as soon as I got back from town, trying to keep myself busy. I was behind, anyway, so it was a good use of time. Patrols needed to be increased due to the imposing threat, the full moon was around the corner, and I needed to debrief all the extended leadership of the pack... The list went on and on. I didn't really trust anyone else to help Lya acclimate, and I could only go so long being stretched this thin, so it was time to delegate–not something I was good at.

'One of the Luna's unspoken duties must be to make sure you don't try and do everything yourself,' Adair mused.

I chuckled at his hypothesis, but he must have been right. Lya had only been here a few days, and already, she unknowingly had me wrapped so tightly around her little finger. I was willing to actually relinquish my hold on some of the pack management. If my dad was still around, he would have laughed.

It really wasn't fair that most transitions of power were due to the death of the previous Alpha. Not a day went by that I didn't wish for my father's guidance. Never before had I needed him around for this sort of advice, though. For some reason, needing to talk to him for a personal matter stung a little more than not having him around to help with pack matters. The Alpha gig was not all it was cracked up to be, and I could never figure out why it was so desirable to everyone. A million times over, I would give anything to be a nobody in the pack. And now, I was hoping with all my being the person who meant the most to me would stand beside me in this god-awful role. I wouldn't blame her if she was smart enough to reject me because of it. Maybe Thom had it right and the best way to have a happy, peaceful life was to completely remove yourself from a pack.

'Maybe there was no more happiness left for him here,' Adair mused. *'But we can still find it.'*

I knew what he meant. Our kind were supposed to be part of a pack, and the idea of leaving made me physically ill. I couldn't shake the feeling that being the leader of the pack wasn't what was meant for me.

'It isn't meant for you. It is meant for us. We must have a Luna. An Alpha is nothing without his Luna.'

'You speak as if you have done this before,' I griped.

'Because we have,' Adair confirmed. *'I may be the first wolf you remember, but you are not my first human. You have much to learn, young grasshopper.'*

I stood and made my way over to the couch on the other side of my office, where I plopped down and poured myself a glass of bourbon. I swirled the glass around and closed my eyes. Adair's words shook me. If what he said was true, and this wasn't his first go-round, his constant voice of reason made sense. But wouldn't it be a well-known fact if our wolves predated us?

I tried to let my mind explore the idea, but it wandered back to Lya instead. Even from here, if I thought hard enough, I could smell lilac and pine. It reminded me of the trip out to the coast of Maine a couple years before my parents passed. They were visiting an allied pack, and I had to beg to go along. Fitting, Lya was also from Maine. I wondered if Lya's parentage had ties to that pack. I glanced over to the book my grandmother had given me. I hadn't had much time to look at it yet, but I doubted any answers were there.

Adair was restless, too. For someone who had done this before, I would think he would have more composure.

'*We should go to her,*' he insisted.

'*No,*' I argued. '*We can manage.*'

'*She can't.*'

I sighed as I sipped the bourbon. Maybe my wolf really was pulling my leg and he had just as much experience as me.

'*It isn't your first time, either. You aren't in touch with your past selves the way wolves are.*'

I furrowed my brows. I couldn't say I was impressed with the conversation my wolf and I were having.

'*Stop whining,*' Adair snapped. '*You're not the concern right now.*'

'*Well then, what is the concern?*' I asked.

Adair growled and paced around, refusing to settle. I sat back and sipped more of my drink. It was becoming more and more difficult to keep Adair from pushing through and taking over. This battle of wills was not one I was familiar with; usually, we were very much on the same page.

I wasn't sure what was louder, the ear-piercing wail, or Adair's howl of despair. Before I could even think, I was on my feet and headed in the direction of the commotion—out toward the patio. I seethed at the thought of patrol letting a rogue get this far into territory without alerting me, but Adair didn't have the usual fire that lit up our bones at the possibility of a threat.

Gregory met me in the hall. "Who was that?"

"I don't know," I said curtly, quickening my pace toward the patio door. We burst through, looking left and right to find whoever screamed. There was another scream to the right, down the side of the patio that was against the Alpha wing. I rushed toward it, preparing to shift. Gregory was close behind. He almost ran into me as I screeched to a halt in front of a couple of chairs. Lya was curled up, asleep, and looked as if she was hyperventilating.

Gregory cast me a wary look, cocking an eyebrow.

"Go," I snapped. "And call off Kota."

Knowing Gregory, the first thing he would have done was alert our head of security to a threat at the packhouse.

He simply nodded as he turned to walk back inside. "Shout if you need anything."

Cautiously, I knelt down beside her. I knew what her wolf could do when she felt threatened, and I really didn't want to wake the beast right this moment... Although sometimes Tala seemed to be the more reasonable of the two.

"Hey," I said softly, trying not to startle her. I reached out to touch her when I got no reaction.

Touching Lya felt like I was catching fire. Sparks danced along my fingers. I wondered if she felt those sparks and what she thought they were. I ran my hand up her bare arm and cupped her face. "Lya," I said a little louder.

Lya's frantic breathing calmed, jaw unclenched, and body relaxed, but she still didn't wake up. I sighed. The night was cold, so I couldn't leave her out here, especially if she was going to scream bloody murder all night. I slipped my arms around her and picked her up, carrying her back to her room. I tensed as she cuddled into my chest, but Adair purred.

I set Lya down on her bed but couldn't stand as she had her hands clenched in my shirt. I uncurled her fingers and looked down at her, brushing a strand of hair out of her face.

'Let's stay here for a while,' Adair encouraged.

'No.'

Don't get me wrong, every single primal part of me wanted to wrap my arms around Lya and hold her close to me all night. But the rational, moral side reminded me that, even though mates were destined, crossing any line she had, especially before she had even recognized the bond, would ruin any hope of a future we had. Lya didn't know we were mates. She would lead every step of this, and she had not invited me to bed.

But still, every time I tried to shift or move away from the side of her bed, she clenched my shirt in her hands again or grabbed at my arm. She was asleep. Her reactions were probably caused by the faint bits of the mate bond she could pick up on craving her other half—only accessible when all her conscious walls were down.

Finally, painstakingly, I tore myself away and dragged myself back to my office. Unsurprisingly, Kota was waiting for me. He was lounged back in one of the leather chairs and swirling the tumbler.

"How's your mate?" he drawled. His southern accent always came out when he drank.

I scowled, turning to refill my own glass. "I'm sure you've been filled in on what the potential security threat really was."

"And who the knight in shining armor was," Kota added. A smirk played across his face. My grimace, however, did not change. "What? Some of us would be more than happy to fill those shoes."

I softened at his confession. While Kota didn't say as much, I knew it was in reference to the unspoken rejection he constantly received from his own mate.

I sighed. "That girl doesn't need a knight in shining armor; she just needs a sword."

"Right," he nodded, "until she has night terrors so bad it wakes the entire pack up."

Kota and I were friends. He initially came here for the warrior training the pack provided but stayed for the sense of community my father had created. He joined the pack shortly after I took over, so after my father's time, but his legacy lived on long enough to attract a few that only made this pack stronger. We had worked hand in hand to develop my father's warrior training further, as well as expand the scope of security to include more scouting and a Cyber department in the burgeoning age of technology. Kota's original pack was small, and he told most he had transferred here to find his mate, but the real reason had everything to do with who he wished his mate had been.

"I think I might reject Ellie," he blurted. There was apprehension in his tone, but certainty in his eyes.

I stared down at my glass, not knowing what to say. The mate bond was a well-known part of who we were as werewolves, but recently, there had been a growing number of the population who rejected the idea, preferring to find their partner the more human way. This very rarely worked, however, and led to problems for all parties involved. There was a significant link between rejection and the weakening of a wolf, too.

I took a sip of the scotch, trying to buy time before responding. "Have you talked to her about it?"

Kota scoffed. "About what? Her actions have made it plenty obvious."

"Have you asked her why she's stringing you along?" I clarified. "It's been a year. I would imagine, if she didn't want a mate, she would have formally rejected you by now."

Kota snorted. Before he could interject with a defense, I continued. "This pack risks a lot if you weaken or lose your wolf. I need to be prepared."

Kota sat back and sighed. "You have a point. But I'm tired of limbo."

"You and me both," I scoffed, finishing off the scotch.

Kota laughed. "Welcome to the club. Meetings are at 11 on Friday nights. We have t-shirts."

Just as I was reaching for the bottle to refill my glass, the same blood-curdling scream that initially pulled me from my office echoed down the halls of the packhouse.

"I hope she gets over that soon," Kota said as he stood up, "or you're in for some long nights."

I shot him a glare as I made my way out of the office. Soon enough, I was in front of Lya's door.

'*I told you we should have stayed,*' Adair grumbled.

'*Not now.*'

I took a deep breath and walked through the door. Lya was curled up as small as she could get, shaking and sobbing. I crouched down next to her and brushed a strand of her deep auburn hair out of her face. Sparks jolted through my fingers, making tearing them away almost painful.

"Lya," I whispered. She shuddered and let out another whimper. I shook her shoulder and called her name again, this time a little louder.

This girl was a remarkably hard sleeper, and it didn't exactly seem like sleep was treating her well.

'*We stay now,*' Adair growled.

Before I could even fight it, I felt my bones starting to crack and rearrange, and Adair seized every bit of control.

Adair wasn't like this. We shared power, neither one of us having the final say. If it wasn't an agreement, it was a discussion until it was.

'*We can't do this,*' I grumbled.

'You *can't do this because* your *mate would lose it,*' Adair said. '*But* my *mate is Tala, and Tala wants* me, *so you go away and* I *will protect our mate.*'

'*She's not in danger, though,*' I pointed out, trying to urge Adair to let Lya be.

'*Not all threats attack physically.*'

With that, I could tell the conversation was over. Adair hopped up on the bed and rested his head on Lya's side. If I knew my wolf, that's where he would stay until he decided whatever was tormenting her had passed.

Fourteen

Lya

I woke up to the sound of gentle snoring. I tried to sit up, but a weight was pinning my arm down. Fuzzy tingles ran up my arm, almost like the weight was causing it to fall asleep. I looked around, trying to figure out what the hell was going on. My eyes fell on a giant black dog sprawled out on the bed with his head on my arm.

What the hell?

I shifted around, wiggling my arm free, while keeping my eyes glued to the dog. How did it get in here? I hadn't seen one roaming around the pack-house in the days previously, and I certainly didn't remember letting one in. Granted, I also didn't remember relocating from the patio back to bed.

'Hate to break it to ya, hun, but that's not a dog.' Tala's snarky tone was about the last thing I wanted to wake up to.

I looked a little closer. I gasped in horror as I realized I had been curled up next to a wolf. Given that we were in a werewolf pack, I could only assume where there was a wolf, there was a human counterpart that went with it. I tried to fly off the bed to get out of the room, but Tala wouldn't let me budge.

'Chill. He is friend, not foe.'

'*Tala!*' I shrieked. '*Some guy is currently in our room! This is not okay! Anything could have happened!*'

'*But it didn't.*' Her cavalier attitude was possibly more disconcerting than finding the intruder in my bed.

'*This can't be happening. This can't happen again. We could have been kidnapped or raped or killed.*'

Tala scoffed. '*With your night terrors last night and how impossible you were to wake up, if any of that was going to happen, it would have already been done.*'

I eyed the big, black wolf warily. If this was the sort of thing that was acceptable, maybe I was back to coming up with a plan to run, especially if this was Tala's attitude toward such a disgusting breach of privacy.

'*I kinda like the guardian wolf,*' Tala mused. '*Good luck leaving without me.*'

I groaned, realizing for possibly the millionth time in my life how little control I had over anything with a wolf counterpart like Tala. As much as I pretended, I always knew she was stronger. I had no power, no say.

The wolf shifted, blinking its eyes. His warm, dark chocolate eyes settled on me, and it felt like they were boring straight into my soul. He furrowed his head under my hand, and a small smile flitted across my face as I tangled my fingers in his fur.

My hand slipped away, and the wolf sat up. He pressed the top of his head against my neck, hopped over me and off the bed, and nosed the sliding door to the patio open. When he stopped and looked back at me, I realized the deep brown eyes were familiar and comforting.

And with that, off he ran.

"That was weird," I mumbled to myself.

I dug some clothes out of my backpack, realizing I'd need to do laundry today. And probably get some more clothes if Tala was so adamant we weren't leaving. I'd already torn through almost half of what little I had brought.

I made my way toward the kitchen, in search of some coffee. The pack-house seemed quiet, but it was only a little past eight. Everyone must have already left for the day. Granted, I didn't know what a normal amount of activity was around here.

A woman in her late thirties or early forties bustled into the kitchen. When she saw me, she smiled brightly

"Ah, Luna!" she said, coming over and offering a hug. "It's so nice to meet you! Gregory mentioned you were here, but you've been making yourself scarce."

"Lya, actually," I mumbled, returning the hug halfheartedly. I was admittedly not a touchy-feely person, but too much of a people pleaser to leave her hanging.

She stiffened, eyes wide, then giggled. "Oh, of course, pregnancy brain. I got the first letter of your name right, though."

She turned to the counter and pulled out a K-cup. "There's normal coffee in the pot, by the way. Not this decaf garbage."

"Thanks." I smiled. "Uh... what's your name?"

"Oh, I'm sorry! I'm Allyssa, the Beta's wife. Hungry? If I'm going to eat for two, I might as well cook for three." She whipped around to give me a hard stare. "Do not tell *anyone* I am pregnant, by the way. Only you and Ollie know."

I cocked an eyebrow and chuckled. "I don't have anyone to tell, anyway."

"Oh, that will change soon enough. It's a community here. You'll make friends quickly." Allyssa pulled out a bowl and started cracking eggs in it. "So, how have you been enjoying Snow Moon?"

"Oh my God." I leaned my elbows on the counter and put my head in my hands. "It's weird... so weird."

Allyssa looked up at me with sad eyes. "I can't even begin to understand the adjustment. Just know it's in your DNA. It will get easier with time."

I looked at her quizzically, curious how much she knew. She saw my expression and laughed.

"Come on now, it's not every day the Alpha goes across the state to pick up a girl, live next to her hospital bed, then move her into the packhouse. I had to do a little bit of homework." She smirked. "You know, I think our Alpha likes you."

"He doesn't even know me," I argued, but the blush burned my cheeks.

"You'd be surprised how quickly werewolves can get a read on people." She passed me a plate with an omelet and came around to sit next to me on the breakfast bar. "I got impatient, so there's only cheese in it. I'll actually cook a good meal when I'm not hungry."

Allyssa took a bite, made a face, and quickly took my plate away. "Oh my Goddess, don't eat that!"

"Wh-uh..."

"Allyssa, I'm sure it's fine," I heard a voice over my shoulder say. I whipped around to see Oliver striding into the kitchen. He took the plate from her and took a bite of the omelet. "See? Perfectly edible. Pregnancy is playing tricks on you."

She grabbed the plate back and dumped it in the trash. "Well, I am not going to be the one responsible for poisoning our lovely guest, so we aren't eating that. And you should go make sure you didn't ingest enough to kill you."

"I'll be fine," Oliver laughed. He looked over at me, the ghost of a smile still on his face. "Lya, how did you sleep?"

I furrowed my eyebrows. "Uh... well, actually."

Oliver smiled fully, his deep brown eyes looking at me warmly. I squinted. I knew those eyes.

"Well," Allyssa clapped her hands together, breaking the strained silence, "I need food, and I don't trust myself to make it, so I'm going out. Lya, I cheated you out of breakfast, so you come with me. You..." She looked over to Oliver and shooed him away. "Go work or something."

"As you wish," he said, smiling still. Oliver's chocolate eyes found their way back to me. "Come see me when you get back. There's someone I'd like you to meet."

I nodded, breaking eye contact quickly. His hand brushed across my arm as he left the kitchen.

Allyssa grabbed her purse and motioned for me to follow. "Breakfast is on me. Come along!"

I followed her out to her car and climbed into the passenger seat of her 4Runner.

"You know, I was really hoping to get rid of this tank with almost two kids out of the house," she sighed, "but I suppose it'll be another few years. I don't particularly like driving a boat."

"A mom that doesn't like a mom-mobile?" I laughed.

Allyssa rolled her eyes. "Gregory said he'd get me a Ferrari when all the kids are grown and we don't need the space. Guess that'll be a while longer yet."

"If you don't mind me asking, how old *are* you?" I asked shyly. "Isn't your oldest daughter twenty-two?"

Allyssa gave me a sidelong glance. "Yeah, she is. She should be home in a couple weeks."

"And you're pregnant again?" I blurted. I covered my mouth, horrified at the slip of my tongue. "I'm so sorry, that was so rude!"

Allyssa waved off my comment. "No worries. I still haven't decided if I'm exactly looking forward to starting the whole baby thing over again. I'm really only forty. Greg and I got pregnant shortly after we met when I was eighteen." My eyeballs just about bugged out of my head, but she only shrugged. "It's not terribly uncommon in our society to get pregnant almost as soon as you meet your mate. Getting pregnant at forty, however, is."

"Mate?" I had heard people around here refer to their partners as their mates a few times now, but it still confused me. Maybe it was local vernacular.

"Ah." She nodded. "I forgot, you're new to the whole werewolf thing. Every werewolf has a destined soulmate, and when you meet them, it truly is love at first sight."

I scrunched up my nose. That sounded absolutely disgusting. Fate had already cursed me with life as a werewolf, and now it was going to take away my power to choose who I was with.

"What if you don't want a mate?" I asked.

"Then you reject them," she said somberly. "The mate bond dies, and you are free to choose whomever you'd rather be with. Although I've heard from people who have rejected their mates, the attraction and love do not compare, and it usually causes the relationship with the chosen mate to fail."

I thought back to my own parents, and my supposition that my father was actually a werewolf. "Are mates always other werewolves?"

Allyssa nodded as she pulled into the parking lot of a cafe and put her land-boat in park. "When the Moon Goddess creates each werewolf, she actually creates two. One soul is split in half and scattered across time and space. In my personal opinion, it was her secret trick to help keep all of us across the globe connected and create alliances."

"Does Oliver have a mate?" I covered my mouth again, not sure where the words came from, and to prevent putting my foot in my mouth anymore.

Allyssa looked over and smirked. "I can tell you the girl who owns this place desperately wants to be his mate."

The comment elicited a growl from Tala, and I desperately hoped I didn't show any of my wolf's emotions.

"But Lucy also makes amazing pancakes, so we will forgive her for today," Allyssa insisted.

The bell above the door tinkled as we walked in. The cafe was cute and quaint, as if the owner had watched a few too many Hallmark movies. The exact sort of small town charm you'd expect. The woman at the counter looked up and smiled.

"Beta Allyssa, how are you? How is Ollie?"

I took it this was Lucy.

"Alpha Oliver," Allyssa clarified, "is enjoying taking some personal time since we have the lovely Lya visiting us at the packhouse." She put her arm around me and smiled warmly, but the smile didn't reach her eyes. "The usual for me, by the way."

"Uh," I glanced up at the menu. "Could I get a soy mocha? And I heard the pancakes were good."

Lucy shot me a glare, punching my order into the register. I reached into my pocket to dig out some cash, but Allyssa slapped my hand away, giving Lucy her card.

"I ruined breakfast, so this is on me," she stated, leaving no room for negotiation. I simply nodded and grabbed the number Lucy pushed toward us without a word.

"Do she and Oliver have history or something?" I asked as we sat down.

Allyssa snorted. "Absolutely not. He's no saint, but he doesn't mess with members of his pack. Humans, or ones who have lost their mates from other packs."

I nodded. "I guess it would cause drama if he started sleeping around his own territory."

"Exactly. By the way, I heard you didn't bring much with you. Need to stop at a couple stores after breakfast?"

"Yes, please," I said emphatically.

"Good. I'm about to grow out of mine, and shopping alone is no fun."

OLIVER

ADAIR PERKED up at the sound of people coming into the packhouse. I had buried myself in work that was forgotten upon Lya's arrival at the pack. Less than a week, and I could already tell Adair was right and the pack would be best off if I started delegating sooner rather than later.

A knock came at the door, but I knew who it was before it even opened.

"You wanted to see me?" Lya asked, poking her head in.

I smiled. "Yeah. Feel up for a walk?"

"Sure, but isn't there someone you wanted me to see?"

"Yep," I confirmed. "It's a bit of a walk to her place."

I stood and walked around the desk, leading the way out of the pack-house. Lya followed in silence. Luckily, Adair and I had agreed that, if he insisted on sleeping in her room, we'd avoid shifting around her so she didn't figure out who it was, which meant I didn't have to argue with him about what form we took walking to my grandmother's house. I stuffed my hands in my pockets to keep myself from reaching out to touch her, settling for walking a little too close and blaming it on how narrow the footpath was.

"You're short," I finally commented, breaking the silence.

Lya shot me a glare. "Thanks, Captain Obvious. You're tall."

I chuckled. "Can't say I've ever been described as tall before."

"What are you? Six foot? That's a foot taller, making you tall, at least in comparison," she quipped.

"Five-ten, but close."

Lya rolled her eyes. "Two inches. Big deal. Still tall."

"Do you have a Napoleon complex or something?" I looked down at her in time to see her cheeks flush.

"No," Lya insisted. "Tall is inconvenient." I cocked an eyebrow. "Have you ever tried holding hands with someone significantly taller than you?"

"Yeah... when I was a kid," I said.

Lya nodded. "Exactly."

"So you don't like tall people because they are difficult to hold hands with?" I teased.

"There are other annoying factors," she grumbled.

"Care to elaborate?"

Lya's blush deepened. "I, uh... Never mind. Doesn't matter."

"Well," I reached an arm out and draped it over her shoulders, "I think short people make very good armrests."

Lya glared up at me through her eyelashes and ducked out from under my arm. "Where are we going?"

"To see one of the pack Elders. Figured I'd make a formal introduction."

Lya breathed in sharply. "Do we have to?"

"No," I said, "but she'd probably be a good source of information for you. Besides, I haven't seen her in a few days, so you're my excuse."

"You can't just make a social call?" she quipped.

"I could, but she won't ask me difficult questions if you come along," I mused.

Lya scoffed. "Shouldn't an Alpha be going to Elders for help in finding the answers to difficult questions?"

"Grandmothers ask much more difficult questions than plain old Elders, and their answers tend to include entirely too much logic." I looked down at her to try and gauge her reaction, but she kept her face stoic. All she did was nod.

Sooner than I would have liked, we stood outside of my grandmother's cottage. I looked down at Lya again, quickly discovering she was a master at hiding her emotions. I placed my hand on her back to guide her up to the door and knocked. Hardly realizing it, I kept my hand on her back, absently rubbing small circles.

My grandmother took her time getting to the door, but when it opened, she was smiling brightly. "Ollie! Two visits in a week? To what do I owe the pleasure?"

"Based on the smell of cookies, you knew we were coming." I chuckled, reaching out to give her a hug.

"And Lya." She reached her arms out to Lya. "This is a much better way to meet, don't you think?"

Lya's smile was small and awkward, but she agreed. "Marjorie, correct?"

"Yes, but you two come in now. The cookies are fresh." She ushered us inside and motioned for us to sit around the table. She bustled around the kitchen, bringing back a tray with tea and cookies.

"So, Lya, how have you been enjoying pack life?" she asked.

Lya reached for a teacup and sipped it before answering. "It's been an adjustment."

"But?"

"Everyone has been really nice and welcoming for the most part." She tapped her fingernail against the cup and bit her lip.

My grandmother reached over and clasped her hand. "You walk a unique path, dear. But keep walking forward; don't double back on it. Let things be different now."

Lya simply kept her eyes on her tea. It would appear she could be chatty, but she didn't like to talk. Not about things that mattered. I had to wonder what secrets she kept.

I cleared my throat. "Grandma, will you be at the full moon on Monday?"

She sighed. "It is an eclipse this month, too, isn't it?"

I nodded. "No pack run."

"Well, my creaky old bones couldn't do a pack run anyway," she said.

"What's happening on Monday?" Lya asked.

"Oh, every full moon, the pack gathers. The Alpha couple hosts dinner, and we usually have a pack run afterward. We've been doing it since my late husband and I were leading the pack," my grandmother explained. "But this month, there's an eclipse, so to honor our ancestors who were governed more closely by the moon, we do not shift."

Lya nodded, breathing a sigh of relief. I could only imagine she was relieved about not being obligated to shift and run with a bunch of other wolves.

My grandmother studied Lya. "You and your wolf haven't figured out how to get along yet, have you?"

I shot her a glare, but she ignored me. She never skirted around the topic at hand.

"It's a little better," Lya sighed. "But I imagine it's the sort of thing that just takes time."

"Make sure you spend some time with her–just her. And remember, whatever you feel about her, she feels about you. Now, Ollie," she turned to face me, "don't forget to get this girl out and about to actually experience the pack."

"I'm doing my best, Grandma," I laughed. "Allyssa took her out for breakfast today."

"Your father selected a very good Beta couple, mostly because Allyssa is such a lovely pack ambassador," she chuckled. "Now, you two head on. I'm sure you both have busy days."

Grandma shooed us out just as quickly as she rushed us in. Visits with her were usually short, ending as soon as she had said the important things.

"I see what you mean about grandmotherly advice," Lya said as soon as we were out of earshot of the cottage. "How does she know exactly what you don't want to talk about, but need to discuss?"

I shook my head. "I've stopped asking that question. I just listen to whatever she feels needs to be said."

Lya sighed, and we continued on in silence.

"So, how are you doing, really?" I hoped this question wasn't becoming redundant.

Lya stopped and looked up at me. If I looked closely, her amber eyes seemed glassy. "Honestly?"

"Honestly," I confirmed.

"I really don't know other than it's a lot and it's weird." She looked down at the ground. "One minute, I'm starting to get comfortable and think life here wouldn't be so bad, and then, I find out my best friend was plotting my murder. Then I start to relax again for some dumb reason and things get overwhelming again. I haven't even had time to stop and think about what even landed me here in the first place, and I know when I start unpacking that shit, it's going to be a whole fiasco all over again."

I reached out and pulled Lya close, locking my arms around her. She sucked in a breath and stiffened, but slowly relaxed into me. Her arms snaked out around me, and she took a few deep breaths. I grazed my lips across her hair before letting her go.

"Thanks," Lya mumbled. She kept her eyes on the ground, but the salty tang of tears pierced the air.

FIFTEEN

Lya

FOR BEING ALONE most of the day, it passed quickly. So much interaction had been jam-packed into the morning, and I was thankful for the break. I buried myself in more werewolf books, which only made it more difficult to pretend this disaster that was my life wasn't happening.

I had to wonder if the books in my room had been carefully selected. All of them pertained to werewolf history—their evolution, notable battles, and remarkable people. It frustrated me that everything seemed to make entirely too much sense. Maybe Allyssa had a point when she said it was in my DNA. Maybe the adjustment wouldn't be as rough.

Additionally, this was the most open communication with my wolf had been in years, and all desires to drive her away were quickly vanishing. The ways I had kept her out made me feel sick, and it was a relief to not feel like I had to go to that extreme anymore.

A knock at the door startled me from my book. I glanced up at the clock on the wall, seeing it was only 7:30, but it would appear I had missed lunch.

I shuffled my way over to the door and opened it, not surprised at all to find Oliver leaning casually against the doorframe.

"Hi." My voice came out a whisper. I was slowly coming to terms with the butterflies this guy gave me, and it was not fair.

I didn't deserve to have someone to make me feel like that.

"I'm ordering take-out," Oliver said, keeping his eyes on his phone. "Whatcha want?"

"Oh, uh, no, it's fine. I can figure something out for myself," I stuttered.

He glanced up at me and showed me his phone. "These places are open. What do you want?"

I shook my head. "Really, I don't mind. I can cook my own dinner."

Oliver cocked an eyebrow. "I have on good authority that I should not let you do that. So, unless you have any input, I'm ordering burritos."

I rolled my eyes. "I am not that bad of a cook. Whatever Trevor said should be ignored."

"Uh-huh," he nodded. "Burritos should be here in about half an hour."

Oliver turned and headed down the hallway toward the main area of the packhouse while I stood in the doorway watching him. I was about to close the door and return to my book when he looked back at me. "You coming?"

I sighed and walked out of the room, following him into the kitchen. I propped myself up on a barstool while he went to the fridge.

"Do you like Moscato?" Oliver asked, pulling out a bottle.

I nodded. "It's my favorite."

"I imagine Allyssa got this before she found out she was pregnant, so we should probably get rid of it for her."

I giggled and accepted the glass. "You don't seem like the wine-drinking type."

"I'm not," he agreed. "But it's Saturday, it's been a long week, and this is the only alcohol in the house."

I furrowed my eyebrows and put my glass down. "You really don't have to babysit me because I'm the new kid. I'm a big girl. I can take care of myself."

Oliver laughed, the sound music to my ears. "And give up my excuse to eat meals on time and actually take a break from all the stuff I have to do? No, thank you."

I afforded him a small smile and went back to sipping my wine.

Oliver continued watching me for a while. It was impossible to read his expression, but the silence grew thicker and thicker by the second.

"Twenty questions?" he finally asked.

"Twenty questions?" I giggled nervously. "Are we in middle school?"

He shrugged. "It's a nice icebreaker."

I shifted in my seat. "No wolf questions."

"Fair," he agreed with a nod. "What did you do for work?"

"Vet tech."

"Vet tech, huh? Do you have any pets?"

I shook my head. "I move around too much. It wouldn't be very fair to them."

"Okay, good, because I don't know what Trevor would do driving back with a cat or something." He thought for a moment. "How many places have you lived?"

I scrunched up my eyebrows and started counting on my fingers. "Maine, North Carolina, Virginia, South Carolina, Colorado, different area of Maine, Vermont, and then South Dakota."

Oliver let out a low whistle. "You on the run or something?" I nodded. "From what?"

"Me. But no wolf questions," I reminded him.

Oliver gave me a sad smile and nodded. "Your turn then. Twenty questions is supposed to be back and forth, not an interrogation."

I looked at Oliver for a minute, trying to decide how difficult I wanted my questions to be, and whether or not I was going to follow my own stipulation of no wolf questions. I wondered what no one bothered to ask him.

"You said you weren't the one who was supposed to be Alpha," I said slowly, "so what would you be doing now if things went to plan?"

Oliver cocked his head and looked at me. "No one has ever asked me that before." Bingo. Mission successful. "I was going to go out and find my mate, then join her pack. I wanted to see the world. Like you've gotten to, it seems."

"Seeing the world isn't all it's cracked up to be," I mumbled. "Why did you want to leave so badly?"

"It wasn't that I wanted to leave. I didn't want to live life as 'the Alpha's son' or 'the Alpha's younger brother.' I wanted breathing room and some time to live my life."

"And you haven't gotten that yet by the sound of it." Oliver shook his head. "Are you happy?"

I decided I would never get tired of Oliver's smile. He had a smile for everything, and his eyes always conveyed every ounce of emotion he felt. This smile felt like it was all mine.

"I am now." Oliver reached out and brushed my arm. It was almost as if his touch was electric, sending shivers across my skin. I didn't miss the glint in his eye when he noticed. I bit my lip and looked down at my wine glass. The way this guy made me feel wasn't fair. He brought a new breed of butterflies flitting through my stomach, turning my usual sarcastic, snarky persona into one of a shy, blubbery schoolgirl. "Next question, Lya?"

"The particular books in the room I'm staying in, were they put there

124

intentionally?" I demanded, forcing the words out quickly to avoid stuttering.

"Oh, very intentionally," Oliver laughed, "by my brother. That was his room growing up. He is quite the historian. You'll like him."

"Is he coming by soon?"

Oliver turned and grabbed the bottle, topping off our glasses. "Doubt it. He hasn't been back in eight years, and he's having a kid soon."

"I haven't seen my sister in almost seven years now," I said quietly.

This piqued Oliver's interest. "You have a sister? Did she ever shift?"

"No... It's only me that's the freak."

"You're not a freak." Oliver's eyes were hard and seemed darker. "If you're a freak, then what does that make me?"

"Well, I'd say it takes one to know one," I chided.

Talking with Oliver was too easy. I never really acknowledged how stressful it was to hide so much. Here, everything was already out in the open. My secret wasn't just known; it was accepted.

It was celebrated.

And right then, I knew. Sitting in the kitchen, downing a bottle of wine, having the most normal conversation with a guy who knew all my deepest darkest secrets and thought nothing of them, I would never be able to leave.

And I didn't want to.

OLIVER

HALF A BOTTLE of wine and a couple burritos later, I was starting to see Tala peeking out through Lya's eyes. The difference in your own eyes versus your wolf's was never that dramatic. Everything about your wolf reflected in you—their coat color matched your natural hair color, and eyes stayed the same except for a slight change in the shape of the pupils. As someone who had been raised in a werewolf community, spotting the presence of someone's wolf had become second nature. For Lya, I wasn't sure she couldn't see the difference.

I hadn't heard from Adair, probably distracted by attempting to get in touch with Tala. They weren't pack or marked, though, so his attempts would be futile. They already had some kind of link, but it was more like emotions being thrust upon him and an ability to feel her presence.

The more I tried to think of it from a human perspective, the more I could see how the whole mate thing would seem absolutely bizarre to Lya. For one, it was a connection amongst all four of us, never mind the whole destined other half gifted by the Moon Goddess. As much as Adair disagreed, insisting Tala would help bring her around, I knew Lya and her wolf needed to be in sync with each other before we dropped that bombshell. Ideally, she'd figure it out before I had to.

I held up the bottle of wine and cocked an eyebrow. Lya nodded and held her glass out.

"Allyssa is a woman after my own heart if she springs for the big bottles." She laughed. "My turn again?"

I nodded. By this point, we had far surpassed twenty questions, but I wasn't about to point that out. We still had another half a bottle to go.

Lya chewed on her lip, any trace of the lighthearted smile leaving her face. "What exactly was it Trevor was trying to do?"

I sighed. Logic urged me not to divulge too much pack information yet, but emotion won out. "That's a very long story."

"I don't want to hate him," Lya confessed.

I looked up at the clock. Gavin and George would be home from training soon, and they certainly didn't need to hear this. Not yet. I dumped the rest of my wine into her glass, grabbed the bottle, and stood up.

"C'mon," I said and turned to my office. Once there, I went for the scotch.

"So, it's that kind of story..." Her voice trailed off.

"And not the pack's shining moment," I confirmed. I went over to my desk and started searching for a particular file.

"Twelve years ago, a family of hunters decided they needed to take out our pack," I started. "Any idea what a hunter is?"

"I've seen *Supernatural*. I can connect the dots," she huffed.

I nodded. "Well, my father did a lot to foster positive relationships with rogues in the area, and they play a big role in pack security. Namely, covering our tracks and relaying information they gather from other rogues. One heard a rumor about this particular family of hunters and got the information back to us. They were definitely coming. There was no way to stop them, so we did what we could and tried to fool them into thinking our pack was somewhere else. Best bets were college towns because there are usually enough werewolves around to make it seem like that could be a pack, albeit a small one. Definitely not big enough population numbers to mimic the largest werewolf pack in North America, but we had reason to believe they didn't know how big our pack was."

"This is the biggest pack?" Lya choked out, looking surprised.

I smirked. "Yes, ma'am. Run by yours truly. But that's a story for another time." I dreaded when that story came up. "My father was still Alpha then, and he thought the best way to utilize the rogue wolves was to not tell them they were being used as bait. Thom and I were vehemently against the plan. Our parents kept insisting none of them would ever find out because we'd intercept the hunters before they could actually lay a hand on a rogue. But that would only work if everything went perfectly to plan, and that never happens in war. So, the Betas–Trevor's parents—went out to organize our warriors, and my parents stayed home until the last moment to make sure Thom and I didn't sound any sort of alarm within the rogue community."

I downed my scotch and refilled it before continuing, refusing to look Lya in the eye. "The hunters got there before my parents and the rest of their reinforcements could. We took out all the hunters, but at the cost of several rogues and a few of our warriors, including Trevor's parents. But the key hunters of this particular family weren't there, so I think they knew it was a ruse.

"Trevor left the pack when he turned twenty, six years after this battle. He kept hopping around for a while before he settled back down in that same college town. That's where he met you. He always claimed he was out looking for his mate, but that was bullshit because he's known who his mate was since the second she turned eighteen. I gave him the benefit of the doubt. He and his mate have been arch-enemies since they were kids, so maybe he was looking for someone to be a chosen mate. But then I found out where he was, and he went dark. From there, it was easy to figure out he'd left the pack for revenge. If he hadn't decided to bring you back here, I was about ready to send people out to bring him back. He didn't hide his scheme very well, and he was pretty dumb to think what didn't work the first time would work the second. He must have made better headway than we thought, though, because one did show up."

I shoved the file over to Lya and watched as her eyes widened reading her dead fiancé's family name. She looked up at me in shock.

"We owe you quite the debt for taking out a key player." A bit of pride bubbled up in me.

Lya's eyes glossed over with tears. "He was always going to kill me, wasn't he?"

"Eventually, probably," I mused. "I think they were going to try and utilize you to take us down from the inside, first."

"I loved him..."

I couldn't do anything to stop the growl that rumbled in my chest. "Can you actually love someone you have to hide who you are from?"

Lya looked away as a tear slipped down her cheek. I winced, knowing that statement must have hurt. I took a step toward her, but she pressed herself deeper into the couch. I settled for sitting on the other side of it; it seemed to be as close as I could get.

"And Trevor..." Lya shuddered. "He was never my friend, was he?"

"No," I said adamantly. "He is your friend. Don't forget he's the one who got you out when he saw you needed help."

"How did he know about me?"

I scrubbed my hand across my face. "Suppressing your wolf for so long has made you lose most of your wolf smell, so I don't think he even knew for certain you were a shifter for a while. But when you came into his brewery with a hunter, he started keeping an eye on you."

"Ted didn't move there until we got engaged last month," she said quietly. "Do you think he knew about me all along?"

"Absolutely," I said solemnly.

We sat in silence for a few painfully long moments. I would have given anything to know what was going through her mind.

"Lya," I said quietly. "You're safe here."

"No, we aren't," she insisted, eyes still glued on the Marsan name. "Not if Ted's plan was for me to lead them to you all along."

Maybe, somewhere deep down, this girl was Luna material. Maybe I had misread her, and my misgivings had been unfounded. I'd need to apologize for that someday.

"So, what are you going to do about it?"

Sixteen

Lya

I wasn't the least bit surprised when I woke up the next morning to a big black wolf on my bed again. He was sprawled out and snoring like the day before, and Tala was practically purring in my head.

'Do you have a thing for Mr. Stalker Wolf or something?' I demanded.

'If you only knew...' she hummed.

I shimmied my way out from under the wolf and found clothes. Then, out I went to find coffee.

The conversation from last night kept running through my mind. In fact, it had kept me up for hours last night. His last question, *"So, what are you going to do about it?"* plagued me.

I needed to run.

But how could I go about that in such a way that it drew the hunters away from this place? I could only imagine Ted's father would be solely focused on hunting me down. They were so close, after all, and if Ted knew what I was, I was certain his father did, too. The people here were innocent and had shown me nothing but kindness. They did not deserve to be caught up in the mess I'd created.

It seemed, even when everything had changed, it all found a way to stay the same.

Even worse, after not even a week in this pack–only a portion of which I'd been conscious for—I was coming to the conclusion that I liked Oliver. I wasn't his mate, but that didn't mean I didn't have feelings for him, and the people I had feelings for were not safe. The best thing I could do for him was ensure all of my problems were as far away from him as possible. I couldn't be his partner, but I could still keep him safe. Maybe my slowly blossoming feelings for Oliver that would never be reciprocated, coupled with what I knew I would have to do, was my penance for already killing someone I loved.

'*You can't take on an entire army of hunters by yourself,*' Tala scoffed. '*Besides, they didn't follow us all the way here. They still don't know exactly where you are.*'

'*There were some waiting for us in Chamberlain,*' I pointed out.

'*What's the plan then, huh?*' she demanded. '*How the hell is a little girl who doesn't even have control of her wolf and has no idea how hunters operate and think going to do a damn thing?*'

The wolf had a point.

'*Checkmate. We stay.*'

'*Just for now,*' I reluctantly agreed.

'*That will be an argument for another day.*'

I had settled out on the patio with my coffee to watch the river when I heard the door open.

"Hi!" Rose chirped as she waltzed out with her own mug. "Hope you don't mind, I grabbed some, too."

"Oh! Hey," I said, turning my attention to her.

"I wish my apartment had a view like this," she sighed, taking a sip from her own mug.

"Just trying to enjoy it while I can," I mumbled. "I imagine now that I'm all healed up, I'll need to move out soon."

Rose laughed. "Doubt it. Besides, this place is rent-free. You got a job?"

"Uh... you guys have a vet clinic?"

"Nah, only the hospital."

I shuddered. Working on humans was a totally different ballgame than working with animals. One I was completely uninterested in.

"After coffee, let's head over to the training grounds. We can work on some stuff," Rose suggested.

"I thought I wasn't supposed to train?" I asked.

She shook her head. "There's other stuff besides combat we can work on."

I furrowed my eyebrows, already dreading whatever it was that she had up her sleeve.

"But coffee first." Rose settled back in her chair and looked over at me. "So, what's your biggest question about pack life so far?"

"Oh my God, is everything a suitable answer?" I groaned.

Rose threw her head back and laughed. "Fair enough, but really." She paused to wipe a tear out of her eye. "There's gotta be something."

I sighed and thought. "Okay, I've got one." She motioned for me to go on. "The whole mate thing... does it weird you out?"

Rose scrunched up her nose. "We are a society of people who shift into wild animals, and that's your question?"

"I mean... how do I ask that question to a person who has a mate, or whose main goal in life was to leave the pack to find his mate?" I asked.

"Well, how do you know I don't have a mate?" Rose chided, wiggling her eyebrows.

I rolled my eyes. "Because you're talking to the pack's lost girl on a Sunday morning."

"Ah, fine. I guess that's fair," she admitted. "It's not really weird to me. I don't know if I feel that way because that's how I was raised, though."

"You mean you don't care about falling in love and all that stuff? You just want to find your assigned life partner?" I questioned.

"Oh, it's not that easy," she quickly corrected. "At least, I don't think so... I don't know, I don't have a mate yet."

"Do you want a mate?" I prodded.

"Oh, yes," she sighed. "Do you not?"

She had such a dreamy expression at the thought of having a mate. For me, if anything, it made me feel guilty. Some poor sap was going to be stuck with me for eternity. Let's be honest, my opinion of it was shifting. The concept in itself was quite nice. A person who was destined to be perfect for me and me for them, because we were quite literally a part of each other. But didn't so many things sound nice on paper, but work out horribly in practice?

And maybe it added to the justification that I was indeed crazy. The whole mate thing was the hardest for me to wrap my head around.

Oh no, I could shift into a wild animal, but give me a person that was meant to make me whole? Nope. That was the part that put me over the edge.

"How do you even know if someone is your mate?" I asked.

Rose leaned in like she was about to tell me a secret and raised her eyebrows. "Sparks!"

I stared blankly at her. "That's... it? Some static electricity?"

Rose laughed. "Supposedly, they smell really nice, too. And your wolf will tell you. You'll know soon enough. Now come on!"

She reached out and grabbed my hand, dragging me back through the packhouse. I blindly followed, letting her enthusiasm infect me, too.

"Hi, Alpha!" she called as we passed him in the kitchen.

I turned, flashing a smile over my shoulder. "Bye, Oliver!"

"What the hell," I heard him mumble as the door slammed behind us.

My head was on swivel as we made our way from the packhouse to the training grounds. I could only hope that I would someday be able to find my way around this pack. So far, I was lucky I could find my way from my bedroom to the kitchen, and I think that was only because I followed the smell of coffee. Luckily, someone in the pack seemed to have invested heavily in signage. There were fairly regular signs with arrows pointing in the directions of what must have been prominent locations in the territory. More than once, I saw signs pointing off into the woods with no road or path to follow.

"Alright, here we are," Rose announced as she pulled into a parking space in front of the training grounds. "Welcome to the Snow Moon Pack training grounds."

"Huh..." I didn't really know what I expected werewolf training grounds to look like, but a surprisingly mundane complex surrounding a large field was decidedly not it.

Rose looked over, taking in my expression, and laughed. "What? We didn't get to be the largest pack in North America by having shit security."

"How big is this pack, anyway?" I asked.

"About five thousand by now, I think." My eyes very nearly bugged out of my head. "We were about thirty-five hundred strong when Oliver took over as Alpha because his dad had absorbed another pack, and people kinda... don't leave. We've got more coming in than leaving."

"He took over another pack?" I squeaked. I couldn't see Oliver as being the sort that would go to war over something like territory.

Rose scrunched her nose. "Not like that. They came to us and asked to create an alliance, but they didn't have an Alpha, so we took them in."

Rose went on to explain more about how the pack functioned. I had heard some while in the hospital, but definitely not the whole story. There were four total towns within the Snow Moon Pack–the one we were in now, one about twenty minutes north, one an hour or so south, and the one over in Wyoming that used to be the Lake Solitude Pack. With the exception of the town closest, each had a smaller, satellite training complex. This one was still considered the home base and was where all the primary training took place.

Oliver's father had opened the training academy for other packs to utilize as a way to promote alliances, and Oliver had developed a fairly seamless plan for keeping the entire pack trained to fight once he took over. It truly did operate very similarly to my basic understanding of a National Guard. Once a pack member turned eighteen or an adult joined, they were required to report to "headquarters" for a six-week boot camp of sorts. After that, they returned to their own towns and had mandatory training for a few hours each week at their home training grounds.

"Now," Rose said, pointing to herself, "I am a career warrior, so I'm here all day, every day. The Academy only runs September through May and is a four-year program. Over the summers, pack members come in for their annual two-week tune-ups."

I nodded in understanding. "So, was it 'bring the new kid to work' day then?"

She rolled her eyes. "No, silly. Other than patrols, we have Sundays off. We're here to get you started!"

I stopped in my tracks and looked at her. *"What?"*

Rose tensed. "Yeah, I, um... I thought maybe you'd like a friendly face around to start working on shifting."

"Oh." I looked away. The idea of shifting into my wolf made my stomach turn. Ever since the night my mom found out, I had only ever shifted when I lost control. Sure, the ability had saved my life a couple times now, but I never really saw it as the sort of thing you did just because. Only out of necessity.

"Lya," Rose said quietly. "Bad things happen if you shut out your wolf too much. It's important you develop a seamless relationship with her, and that means being comfortable in your second skin."

I sighed and nodded, slowly becoming more and more resigned to the fate I had no choice but to accept.

OLIVER

I HAD BEEN TRYING to take Sundays off for years now. I enforced a day off for my warriors, so I should try to enforce a day off for myself, right? It had been eight years, and the closest I had gotten was a half day here and there. I could safely say the werewolf immune system and my natural instinct to pour every waking hour into the pack were the only reasons I hadn't worked myself to death.

Lya had been a breath of fresh air. My desperate attempts to carve out time to spend with her had made it abundantly clear that, although I thought I'd been delegating plenty, I was, in fact, not delegating near enough. My well-oiled machine was quickly rusting.

For that reason, I was thankful she was out of the packhouse and with Rose for the day. It provided for no distractions and no excuses to leave all the work I had to catch up on. That, and Kota sat across from me to aid in keeping me on task.

Kota let out a huff, sitting back in the chair. "I know she's your mate and all, but she's really created a lot more work for us. War is a lot of work."

"I think she actually provided us a head start," I murmured.

"Well, wars that we don't know are coming require less planning," he said.

I looked up at Kota and cocked an eyebrow. "Those are wars we lose."

Kota rolled his eyes and leaned back over the paperwork. Patrols were being increased, scouts were being sent further out, and the possibility of increasing required training for pack members looked like it was on the horizon. All of these moves would raise questions within the pack, and I really didn't want rumors to start or for word to get out about what was going on. Not yet.

"We need more information," I grumbled. "We need to attack first this time instead of waiting for them to make a move."

Kota sighed and looked up at me. "There is a person we could ask and potentially get some intel."

I clenched my jaw. The idea of drawing Lya into this didn't sit well with me at all. "She didn't even know they were hunters."

"No," he mused, "but she probably knows where their home base is, and friends her ex was close with. That'd give Cyber and scouts something to run with."

"Are they still considered your ex if they're dead?" I chuckled.

Kota laughed. "I think the murder part constitutes a break-up, personally."

I walked over to one of the bookshelves surrounding my office. Hunters had been the one topic it had been glaringly difficult to find information on. For the most part, we only had the names of key organizations and tactics they used. They were incredibly skillful at running under the radar. Hell, Trevor didn't even realize a Marsan had been under his nose for weeks.

"We really shouldn't interrogate Lya about any of this until she's pack,"

Kota said, keeping his eyes trained on the documents of training schedules on the desk. "We need to know exactly where her allegiances lie."

I shot him a dirty look. Adair growled at the accusation. My mate wouldn't be a traitor. Not intentionally, at least.

Kota held up his hands in defense. "I'm not saying she's playing for the other guys, man. She knows literally nothing, and that's dangerous. If we're being frank, she probably doesn't even realize what information she has that could be useful and needs to be shared."

I sighed and backed down. Unfortunately, he did have a point.

"So, anyway, what if we upped recruiting tactics? Try to get more career warriors in," Kota suggested. "The towns are growing, which means we need to increase the number of folks available for patrols. Artificially inflate the numbers... maybe a part-time option."

I nodded slowly. "That could work."

"I mean, you've said it yourself; you like to keep the towns small so they don't draw suspicion. With the way you're growing the pack, we need to look at developing another town. We could use that as a perfectly fine excuse," he added.

"We don't know how much time we have. I don't want to take on a project like that right now," I pointed out. I looked over at the clock, seeing it was only mid-afternoon. Time was dragging at an almost painfully slow rate. It felt like everything I'd gotten done only led to more and more things to do. I sighed. "I'll check in with Gregory on how committed he is to completely retiring. Maybe he'd be interested in being a Gamma once he steps down as Beta."

"It'll be good to have Trevor back." Kota stood and made his way toward the door. "I can't focus anymore. Sundays are for day drinking."

I smiled and followed him out. Some things never got old.

Kota beelined for the fridge, but my eyes quickly found Lya sitting out on the patio. I grabbed an extra can for her as we made our way out.

I tapped Lya on the shoulder and handed it to her.

"It's one of Trevor's sours. It'll be good," I assured her as she eyed it warily.

"Thanks," she said with a quick smile.

I flopped down and threw my arm behind her. Adair purred when she made no effort to scootch further down the couch. "Where's Rose off to?"

"Her brother apparently neglected to do a pretty big project due tomorrow, so she's helping him," she giggled.

"Is it cool if Ellie comes over?" Kota piped up, staring down at his phone.

"Sure. Brandon will be over soon," I said. "But tell someone to pick up more beer."

"Duly noted," he confirmed.

Lya shifted uncomfortably and bit her lip. "Do they know about... me?"

"Brandon is a Gamma up north, so he does," I explained. "But Ellie doesn't."

"Who's Ellie?"

"Ellie is my mate who doesn't like me," Kota spat.

Lya frowned. "Why do you want her to come over if she doesn't like you?"

I chuckled. The girl had a point. Especially given the conversation I had with Kota recently, I was as curious as Lya.

He sighed and took a long swig of his beer. "Because it'd be nice if she liked me."

Kota filled her in on the story so far, leaving out his thoughts of potentially rejecting her. I studied her, trying to gauge her reaction, but she kept her face stoic. I had hoped I'd see something, to get an idea of how the prospect of mates even made her feel, but Lya remained a remarkably closed book. A trait of a Luna, if I was being honest.

The conversation devolved into mindless banter as we waited for Brandon and Ellie to show up. It was nice to see Lya getting along so seamlessly with other higher-ups in the pack. It'd be necessary once she was Luna.

Brandon was the first to show up, lugging a case of beer. "I will say, thanks to you two, I was forced to sleep with another girl who was not my mate."

I rolled my eyes. "Yes, I am sure that was such a struggle for you."

"The horror!" he cried. "I truly hoped that a lay like her would be the one."

"Anyway," I dragged out, shooting Brandon a glare. "Lya, this is Brandon. Feel free to shut down any and all advances he tries to make."

Brandon's hand flew to his chest. He drawled, "Why, Alpha, I would never."

A scoff came from the doorway. "Brandon avoiding anything with a pulse? We must not be talking about the same guy."

I looked up and saw Ellie striding across the patio, seating herself on Kota's lap. She brought a palpable tension with her. Less than a minute with her, and I was already regretting telling Kota he could invite her.

"Who are you?" she demanded, glaring at Lya.

I had never liked Ellie. She acted before she thought, and it was out of character for her to be any semblance of nice. Truthfully, she was only a mediocre warrior, at best. Even then, with only one year out of four of training under her belt, she still acted like she was the Goddess's gift to the pack. My standards for warriors surpassed what they were able to do on the field, which resulted in her never getting selected for anything off of the territory. Her piss-poor attitude, especially to other women, would jeopardize her position as a warrior, except for the fact that she was Kota's mate. I had truly hoped the mate bond would help her back off her desperate need to fluff her ego at every corner, but so far, there'd been no such luck. I suppose she had until her full-time warrior training was completed to shape up, but if it didn't, I would have absolutely no qualms about refusing to let her pass.

"I'm Lya," she said coyly, offering Ellie a warm smile. "You must be Ellie. Kota was just telling me about you. You're a warrior, right?"

"Yes," Ellie replied smugly. "What's it to you?"

"Oh, you know," Lya shrugged, "I was hoping I could get some training in while I'm here, and it'd be nice to know a few other friendly faces around the training grounds once I'm cleared to train."

"Only pack members train," she sneered. "But if you want, I can show you a thing or two."

Ellie stood up, walking off the patio. "Let's go, then."

Lya looked down at her sundress. "I really don't think I'm dressed for it today. Rain check?"

Ellie crossed her arms, staring her down. "Fights seldom wait for appropriate attire. Let's go."

I gritted my teeth as Lya stood and walked over to her. Ellie fought dirty, and Lya wasn't trained. I stole a glance over at Kota, who sat rigid in his chair with eyes wide.

Ellie didn't even wait until Lya was facing her, but Lya quickly caught her wrist before it could make contact.

"I never agreed," Lya pointed out. "I just came over here." Ellie growled as Lya twisted her arm ever so slightly. "I'll continue if you answer a question for me real quick."

"What?" Ellie spat, trying to wiggle her arm free.

Lya's smile was kind, not the cold glare you'd expect of someone about to fight. Her tone was one of genuine curiosity. "Well, you walk into the pack-house like you own the place, but I've been here for a week and no one has even mentioned you until today. You talk and act like you're a seasoned warrior, even though I've been told you're about to complete your first year of training. And then you treat me like a threat when I have absolutely nothing you could possibly want. I would think the mate of a Gamma would handle themselves with more poise. So, tell me... exactly who do you think you are?"

Ellie's growl was more audible this time, and she flung her other arm with so much of her weight behind it that she lost her footing. Lya didn't let go of her wrist, causing Ellie's arm to twist behind her. The impromptu sparring match made me nervous, but I still had to hide my proud smile.

"Ah, a bitch. Gotcha."

'So... bets?' Brandon's voice drifted through the mind-link to Kota and me. *'Because I am putting hard money on Luna.'*

'I haven't met this Lya, actually,' I mumbled. It was like a flip had been switched. Aside from the occasional sass, Lya had presented herself as a bundle of nerves. But I had only known her for a week. I didn't know the girl very well at all. Maybe this was the Lya hiding under that hard exterior she had?

'Ellie hasn't been any good recently,' Kota offered. *'If the Luna has anything to back up her talk, she will be fine.'*

Lya was cool and calculated but lacked the organization and flow of a trained fighter. Still, she had thrown Ellie off enough that she easily maintained the upper hand. Potential and ability were clearly there, and I had no doubt she could hold her own against a much, much more skilled fighter than Ellie. Not that I wanted her to.

Lya offered a final jab of her knee to Ellie's stomach, sending Ellie to the ground. Lya crouched down beside her and whispered something none of us could hear. Given the expression on Ellie's face, it was clearly an insult. She stood up, offering Ellie her hand. "Now, back to Sunday day drinking?"

Ellie glared before struggling up by herself, bumping against Lya's shoulder as she pushed past. She stomped through the patio and back to the packhouse, stopping to glare back at Kota from the doorway.

"Are you coming?" she demanded.

Kota waved his hand, making no move to get up. "I'll stay. See ya around."

Ellie huffed and walked off. No one said anything until we heard the front door slam.

"So, Lya," Kota began, breaking the silence. "I wasn't aware you'd had training."

Lya smiled brightly. "Oh, I haven't. Just cousins."

SEVENTEEN

Lya

LAST NIGHT, the big black wolf barked at my door to be let in. I sighed when I saw him, telling him I had always wanted a dog, but it seemed like this was the closest I was going to get so he could stay. This morning, he had woken me up with a cold nose to the cheek before nosing open the sliding door to the patio and scampering out.

Tala was still riding on the high of besting a pack warrior yesterday, even though I kept trying to remind her she was a pack warrior *in training*.

Oliver had made sure to tell me he didn't want me sparring with anyone again. I was barely healed, most fighters here were actually good, blah blah blah. But she was a bitch. And I would never apologize for taking the opportunity to put a bitch in her place. I had done it before, and I would do it again.

I couldn't explain what snapped inside me yesterday. I think it was more that Tala couldn't stand the way Ellie spoke and acted, but I was still fairly certain I hadn't done anything to deserve the attitude. Last I checked, my existence wasn't a crime in this pack. That being said, it was almost a relief to run into someone who wasn't warm and welcoming. It made the place seem more real.

The packhouse was empty when I made my way out of my room, so I retrieved the book I was reading and found my way to the patio to read while drinking way more coffee than I needed. I was exceptionally good at getting lost in books, especially when trying to avoid thinking about something. I had two topics to avoid thinking of today: one being the failed attempts at shifting yesterday, and the other being the full moon party thing tonight.

Working with Rose yesterday didn't go well, to say the least. She wanted me to work on shifting at will, and that happened a grand total of zero times. She had been so upbeat and insisted it would be easy, going so far as to say it was even natural.

Rose had shifted first, explaining the process. "Envision your wolf, think about what it's like to be in your wolf form, then relax." She had shifted back to her human form, sans clothes, and exclaimed, "Your turn now! Give it a go!"

So I did. I closed my eyes, thought of the auburn fur, and tried to remember what it was like to feel the wind rustling through it. Digging paws into dirt, the intensity of sights, smells, and sounds.

'*Nope,*' Tala scoffed.

I furrowed my brows, and Rose encouraged me to try again.

'*Not happening.*'

I huffed in frustration.

"It takes a few tries," Rose insisted. "It'll happen, don't worry. Make sure you really relax and call on your wolf to come forward.

I sighed but did as I was told.

'*Please, Tala, can you please just do the wolf thing so we can shift?*' I begged.

'*Not gonna do it.*'

Tala didn't even humor me with a response after multiple failed attempts. We gave up after the sixth try. Rose tried to be encouraging, but she seemed worried, too.

"Don't stress it too much," Rose lied. "Just maybe try and focus on getting on better terms with your wolf so she wants to work with you. Remember, the wolf and human counterparts are two individuals that share a body and mind. We have to get along. If we don't get along, bad stuff really can happen."

And for that reason, I was immensely grateful there would be no shifting at the thing tonight. I wouldn't have to show off that I had absolutely no control over my wolf and could only shift when she deemed it appropriate. I didn't really know what was going to happen, other than a bunch of pack members were going to get together to celebrate the full moon. Who knew what those celebrations included, though. Maybe there would be a virgin sacrifice or something.

I heard the patio door slide open and felt the cushion dip beside me. I looked up to see Oliver sitting a little too close for comfort, bringing an onslaught of butterflies. I looked down at my book, pretending to keep reading, but really trying to hide my blush.

I needed to get control of this infatuation. He had a mate out there, and it wasn't me. It was probably better I didn't waste any time pining after other werewolves.

Was it any use pining for anyone? If I'd end up with a mate someday, even if I didn't want one, was there even a point?

I would admit, the one aspect of having a mate that was reassuring was not having to hide the wolfy thing. Maybe it'd help Tala and me figure things out if we found someone who appreciated and loved both of us the way I've always dreamed of.

"Are you going to read the day away?" Oliver asked, peeking over my shoulder at the pages.

I smirked. "I've done it before, and I'll do it again."

Oliver reached out and tucked a strand of hair that had fallen in my face behind my ear.

"Well, I regret to inform you today is not that day," he murmured. "Barbeque starts in a few minutes."

I looked up to the sky, surprised to see the sun already descending. Had I really been reading for most of the day already?

Oliver stood, reaching a hand out for me. I took it and let him lead me through the packhouse.

"Do I need to change or anything?" I asked, realizing this could be a more formal event than I was dressed for.

He looked down at my navy blue sundress covered in sunflowers and smiled. "You look beautiful."

I dropped his hand and tried to create some distance as we walked through the doors on the other side of the packhouse to a large group of people. I felt like getting caught holding hands with the Alpha would raise questions I personally didn't feel like answering.

"So, what's the whole deal tonight?" I asked, scanning the crowd for a familiar face.

"Nothing big," he assured me. I cocked an eyebrow. This certainly looked big. There were a lot of people. "The pack members all get together, have dinner, and then usually go on a pack run. Full moons are when the Moon

Goddess is closest to us, so we take the opportunity to thank her for what she has gifted us with and pay homage to our ancestors whose wolves were dictated by the cycles of the moon. It isn't required to come by any means, but as the Alpha, it also allows me to see pack members and make announcements if need be."

"Why no run tonight?" Not that it bothered me.

"Total lunar eclipse on a full moon," Oliver said. "Back when werewolves could only shift under moonlight, they wouldn't be able to shift during total lunar eclipses. They don't line up on a full moon often. This is only my third one since taking over as Alpha."

"What's it like? What do I do?" I was still waiting for the weird stuff.

Oliver looked a little confused. "You, uh… eat food… drink a beer if you want. There's cornhole set up. Have you been to a barbeque before?"

"So, no weird ritual stuff?" I confirmed.

"What? No!" Oliver laughed. "We're werewolves, not a cult."

"Some would argue that a pack of werewolves is, in fact, a cult," I chided.

Oliver slung his arm over my shoulders. "Oh, Lya. So much to learn."

Making our way through the crowd to grab a beer proved more difficult than at any other barbeque I'd been to. Oliver was stopped and pulled into a sidebar every couple strides. I suppose I could have navigated through on my own, but Oliver's arm had migrated down to my waist, pinning me to his side. I didn't really have it in me to fight it.

A hand wrapped around my wrist and pulled me away from Oliver. Tala whined in complaint, trying to stay by Oliver's side. I looked up and locked eyes with Rose.

"Let's create some distance before people start talking," she whispered in my ear. I looked back over my shoulder at Oliver. He was staring after us but made no move to follow. "If you're going to be walking around arm in arm with the Alpha, people are going to talk. I, for one, have no problem with that. I actually think you and Oliver would be really cute, but I don't think you want to be the center of attention yet, am I right?"

I nodded and followed after her, already missing the warmth and reassurance of Oliver's arm around me. Getting to the beer was much quicker this way, and lord knew I'd need a lot of it if I was going to make it through the night.

I wasn't his mate, and I owed it to whoever was to keep my hands off of him.

Oliver

Rose had mind-linked me before pulling Lya away. We had only been there for ten minutes, and she was already hearing whispers. I silently thanked Rose for being so observant and for her quick thinking. She was a tracker and a scout, though. That's what I paid her for.

I'd give anything to keep Lya tucked into my side, showing her off, and introducing the pack to their Luna. My mate. The one I had been waiting ten years for. The woman I had given up hope would show up. But I wasn't about to ruin any hope I had of Lya sticking around by throwing her in the deep end. She had been alarmingly receptive to my advances, and I was going to do my best not to blow it now.

Adair grumbled in complaint when Lya left us, but we were never too far. We could feel it all. She was tense and nervous in a crowd of so many people she didn't know. We heard every time someone called her Luna and she corrected them to Lya. It made me wonder how quickly ten minutes of selfishly keeping my arm around her would ruin the guise I was trying to maintain for her. I wondered how long we'd have to maintain the front that she was nothing other than a house guest, visiting the pack. I wondered how obvious it was to the rest of the pack that their Alpha had found his Luna.

I got a few questions, but several knowing looks. No one would dare question me and invade my privacy. When I wanted the pack to know, I would tell them. It didn't change the fact that I'd be checking in with a few people to see what was going around the rumor mill in the next few days.

I was deep in conversation with the principal of the pack school when Adair let out a deep rumbling growl I had only heard on a couple of occasions. One that signified a threat, an attack. I whipped my head around only to see Lya being chatted up by one of the unmated members of the pack.

Seth. I knew him. He was, of all people, my ex-girlfriend's older brother. Seth was tall and lanky with unkempt hair the same brown as his sister's. I remembered Sophie constantly complaining about the color of her hair, how it was so mousy, as she called it. He was an absolute genius of a software developer and headed up Cyber. As much of an asset as he was to our pack, I wanted to kill him right this instant.

"So, how does this pack stack up to the one you're from?" he asked her. Lya took a step back as he drifted toward her.

"Much more organized," she said, turning to head toward the coolers. Seth followed.

Before I could even stop myself, I was headed toward her. A hand on my shoulder stopped me, though, and Brandon's voice in my head gave me pause.

'I got this, Ollie. Go back to pretending,' he said, stepping past me. When he got to her, he threw his arm over Lya's shoulders and grabbed the can she had retrieved out of her hand.

"Thank you, dear." He chuckled, steering her away from Seth. I still wasn't happy with the interaction, but it was better than someone trying to make a legitimate advance.

Lya shot a look over her shoulder, making eye contact with me. *Thank you,* she mouthed with a smile. I responded with a wink and turned back to the pack principal who had, thankfully, been so deep into his rant about how unruly middle schoolers could be, he didn't even notice my distraction.

No run tonight meant things died down much earlier than usual. With so few people around, it was easy to find Lya sitting by herself by the firepit that had been lit as soon as the sun went down.

"How was your first full moon at Snow Moon Pack?" I asked, sitting down beside her.

Lya glanced over at me before looking back up to the sky. "I can see why you love the people here. I don't know why anyone would want to leave."

I smiled down at her. If this girl never figured out I was her mate, I'd tell her she was my chosen mate. Anything to keep her with me forever. "So, did you find something to thank the Moon Goddess for?"

"Yeah," she said quietly, looking down at the blades of grass she was uprooting. "It's really nice to not have to hide here. Everyone knows, and everyone accepts it."

"You should never have had to hide. We'll figure out why you were ever in that situation," I promised her.

Lya leaned her head against my shoulder and whispered, "I wouldn't be here if I hadn't."

"There certainly is no coincidence in the cards the Goddess deals us." I stood, pulling Lya along with me. "What do you say we take this party elsewhere?"

"Your place or mine?" she giggled.

I kept Lya's hand firmly in mine as I led her back to the packhouse. By this time, the only people still around were so drunk, they probably wouldn't even notice the Alpha bringing a girl home.

And if they did? Let them talk. She was my mate.

"Twenty questions?" I asked, stopping at the fridge to retrieve the rest of the bottle of wine from the other night.

"You go first," Lya said as she grabbed the bottle from me, taking a swig.

"What'd you think of Seth? I saw him talking to you."

Lya shrugged and passed me the bottle. "Not my type. Why wasn't Snow Moon's most desirable bachelor trying to find someone to take home?"

"I had my eye on someone." I smirked. "What does Tala think of me?"

She didn't answer immediately. "She thinks you're pretty okay. So, who's the big black wolf that's been in my bed the past few mornings?"

She knew. I knew she'd figure it out sooner rather than later. Maybe she'd figure out the other secrets I'd been keeping soon, too.

I leaned over, placing a hand on either side of her, pinning her against the counter. "The only one who can keep you from having night terrors so bad you wake the entire territory up," I murmured in her ear. I leaned back before asking my next question, wanting to see her reaction as I threw caution to the wind. "What would you do if I kissed you right now?"

We'll blame my overstep on the alcohol.

Lya tilted her chin up toward me. "Why don't you find out?"

Fire erupted across my lips as they met hers. My brain stopped, or it went into overdrive. I would never be able to kiss anyone else ever again. I'd be chasing this feeling for the rest of my life, whether she was on the other side of the bed or across the globe. With one kiss, I had lost all control, and I'd give her the world. This naive little she-wolf owned me.

And I didn't mind.

Lya's fingers weaved through my hair, pressing her body into mine. The way she molded to me felt like it was meant to be. Before I knew it, I had an arm around her waist, hoisting her up onto the counter, and Lya hooked a leg around my hip. I played with the hem of her dress that was riding up her thigh, seeking out the sensational little sparks dancing along her skin. Sundresses were my new favorite thing.

Lya put a hand on my chest and pulled back. "Wh-what happened to not messing with people who might have mates?"

"I'm not a patient man," I growled before my lips crashed down on hers again.

I should have stopped. Just lucky enough to get a kiss from my mate and I could die a happy man, but the way Lya's fingers tangled in my hair and her legs wrapped around my waist begged me to continue. Her gentle sigh against my lips had my tongue darting out to tangle with hers and my hand traveling up her leg. My lips left hers, tracing her jaw and traveling down her neck, quickly finding where my mark would someday go. She let out a moan as my teeth grazed the skin above her collarbone, careful to not puncture it.

A gentleman would take things slow, but that's never what I said I was. If there's one thing I'd learned, it's that no amount of time was ever guaranteed. Right now, at this moment, I had my world in my hands, and I would do anything to keep her there. So, I did what any sensible man would do. My hands slid under her perfectly shaped thighs, lifting her off the counter, and marched straight down the hall to her room.

The door was barely closed before Lya was tugging at my shirt. Setting her on the bed, our bodies only separated long enough for me to pull it off. My mouth and hands went right back to exploring every inch of her skin.

I don't know who was responsible, but her dress and bra joined my shirt on the floor. I sat back for a second, taking her all in. Her soft freckled skin begged to be touched. I reached out and ran my hands across her stomach, feeling the outline of each rib, all the way to cupping her breasts, rolling and pinching her pink nipples in my fingers. I leaned forward, taking one in my mouth, as my other hand explored the rest of her body. My fingers met with lace. Of course, she would wear lace.

"May I?" I murmured against her skin. I fully expected her to say no. This was probably the definition of zero to sixty. Normal for mates.

"Please, Oliver," she gasped as her hips ground into me.

I pushed the fabric aside, running a finger along her before finding her swollen clit. My fingers slowly circled around her throbbing nub before dipping inside. Lya threw her head back and moaned, arching her back as I pumped my finger in and out. I trailed light kisses down her neck, her body falling in rhythm with my hand. She whined as I pulled my hand away.

"Don't worry, I'm not done." I chuckled in her ear, nipping at the lobe.

I hooked my thumb in the band of her panties, dragging them slowly down her legs. I crouched down, quietly growling as I took in the view of her glistening folds. My hand slipped under her and kneaded her ass as I nipped and sucked my way up her thigh. I stopped before my mouth found its destination and looked up. Lya's amber eyes burned with a fiery passion.

Lya breathed heavily, hitching her leg over my shoulder and guiding me closer.

My eyes didn't leave hers as I leaned forward and ran my tongue over her. If I thought she smelled nice, she tasted better. She let out a shriek when I latched onto her clit, her legs clamping down around me.

I smiled against her. I'd never get over the sounds this girl made. I sucked and lapped up every bit I could. Her breathy moans were damn near sending me over the edge, and if her body writhing at my touch was any indication, Lya was close to that same edge, too.

I reached up, bracing a hand against her abs, holding her to the bed. With the other, I pressed two fingers inside of her. Lya's fingers knotted in my hair, pulling me closer to her. I slowly dragged my fingers out before pushing them back in.

"Oliver..." she choked out.

"Yes, Lya?" I breathed.

"Don't stop."

I chuckled, sucking and nipping harder and my fingers picking up the pace. Her walls tightened around me, but I didn't relent. Lya jerked against me, her pussy clamping down. I sat back, continuing to finger fuck her, and watched as her eyes rolled back, hips bucking against my hand, her orgasm washing over her. Listening to her moan my name over and over, I vowed to make her do that as often as I could.

Only when she began to relax did I remove my hand. I stared down at her as she fought to catch her breath. I had never felt proud of making a girl come before now.

I slipped into bed beside her and pulled her against me. Lya sighed, lacing her fingers in mine. By the time I kissed her temple, I think she was already asleep.

I prayed to whoever was listening that she'd keep me forever.

EIGHTEEN

Lya

I WOKE up in a tangle of sheets with a heavy weight across my side. I glanced around, expecting to see the big black wolf, but my eyes fell on Oliver instead.

'Same difference,' Tala mused. *'I like the wolf, though.'*

The night before came crashing back, causing me to freeze.

I stared down at Oliver, trying to decide if last night had been a mistake. Don't get me wrong, I enjoyed every minute of it. In fact, Oliver had probably ruined the possibility of me enjoying being with anyone else, and we had only gotten to third base. And it wasn't like I had coerced him into anything. I'd go so far as to say he started it. It was not my responsibility to bear the guilt of him going against his supposed rule of not messing with people who had mates. We were both consenting adults, for goodness sake. I, for one, had had my fair share of one-night stands. Letting my guard down and rolling with instinct would help me find my place here, right?

And yet, regret still formed a knot deep in my stomach.

But even still, I couldn't help myself from reaching out and touching him.

So I did. My fingers traced the contours of his face. I sighed, relishing in the fresh smell of ozone that wafted off of him, perfectly matching the light-

148

ning-like sparks that erupted wherever my skin met his. The sensation of a summer rainstorm was intoxicating.

Sparks.

I couldn't pull my hand away. As if it had a mind of its own, it trailed down his jaw, along his neck, leaving a trail of fireworks behind.

Sparks.

Oliver's eyes fluttered open and his hand caught mine, interlacing our fingers. I tried my best not to get lost in his sleepy eyes, the same warm chocolate I was growing accustomed to waking up to, and sultry smile, but I failed miserably. He had my hand pinned to the mattress and was rolled over on top of me before I could think.

"Good morning," he murmured. Oliver's voice was husky with sleep and music to my ears. His lips caught mine, but I fought it. Fighting the sparks, fighting his overwhelming scent, fighting the draw to meld our bodies into one, I wiggled out from under him. The room was too small. I needed space to breathe.

I stared at Oliver, wide-eyed in some combination of shock and awe.

"I, um, I have to go," I blurted.

I stumbled toward the patio door, yanked it open, and begged everything in my body to shift as I leaped off the porch. It had been almost a decade since I had longed to be in this form, but right now, I craved it.

Four paws hit the dirt, and I was pounding my way through the woods. The further I got, the stronger the draw to turn around and go back to the packhouse. Like a rubber band being stretched to its limits.

'Are you fucking insane?' I demanded of Tala. *'You could have told me or something!'* This wolf was going to be the death of me.

'Jeez, I live in your head, and even I didn't realize you're such a dumb fuck you can't figure out the obvious,' she remarked. *'Besides, you have quite the propensity for coming to your own conclusions. I didn't think you needed my help.'*

'This changes everything!' I shrieked.

'Does it, though?'

The terror of everything was compounding, hitting hard. Nine days ago, I killed my fiancé. This wasn't what I wanted, not yet, and far from what I deserved. I had barely gotten to the point of accepting life as a werewolf and part of a pack. But maybe I was wrong. I'd been wrong before.

I had no idea where Tala was leading me, but I soon found myself sitting on my haunches outside of Marjorie's little cottage. She was an Elder, so maybe she'd have some answers. But I also didn't have clothes. So, I sat and waited. Maybe I could glean some of that grandmotherly wisdom through osmosis.

She must have seen me, though, because the door swung open, and she placed a pile of clothes on her porch railing.

"Come on in once you're decent," she called. "I'll get tea started."

I let out a wolfy chuckle as I padded up to the porch. Old ladies and tea.

Tala gave no complaint about releasing her control. I slipped into the clothes on the porch and let myself into the cottage. There was already a cup of tea on the table, and Marjorie was bustling around the kitchen, pulling ingredients onto the counter.

"You have to stay longer if I'm baking something for you, so we'll be having scones today," the woman said with her back still to me.

I didn't know where to start, or even if I wanted to talk about what I thought was going on.

"You weren't at the full moon thing last night," I mumbled instead.

Marjorie chuckled. "No, I wasn't. There were greater things at play. Now, why don't you say what you're actually thinking."

I sighed. "Why is fate such a fickle bitch?"

"Language, dear," she reprimanded, shooting me a look. "But I do agree. Do you know much about Thom?"

Oliver's older brother wasn't exactly the guy on my mind right now. I shrugged. "Oliver's older brother who was supposed to be Alpha."

Marjorie clicked her tongue. "I suppose that is what he thinks of the situation. He hasn't yet realized Thom could never have been Alpha. You see, he has no Alpha blood. It was always going to be Ollie, one way or another."

The wheels attempted to turn in my head, but the gears weren't syncing up. "But they're brothers..."

"Half-brothers," Marjorie corrected. "The previous Luna was already pregnant with Thom when she found her fated mate. They mated with each other so quickly, though, I don't think she even realized Thom wasn't her mate's child."

"But you knew."

"Immediately, yes," she confirmed. "Alpha traits are always dominant, and he looked nothing like Oliver's father."

"Is that why he left?" I asked.

"Partly, yes. He met his mate right before going to battle, but he didn't have the opportunity to mate and mark her before she died. In a few measly hours, he lost both the man who had raised him and his mate. He came to me asking what to do, and he took my advice." She turned, sliding the baking sheet of scones into the oven. I waited for her to continue. "He knew he wasn't the rightful Alpha, and he feared disgracing the Luna while she slowly died of a broken heart, so he left instead, only disgracing himself. When your priority is to serve a pack, little things like disgrace don't matter."

"Luna." I rolled the word around on my tongue. I had read it several times in a variety of books by this point. Several people had called me Luna, and I thought they had gotten my name wrong. "That's a title, isn't it?"

Marjorie nodded. "The female mate of the Alpha."

"You were a Luna as well once, then?" I studied her features—oh-so-familiar chocolate brown eyes, a few remaining streaks of vivid black running through her silver hair, and defined cheekbones.

"Oh, no, my dear. I was Alpha," she smirked.

"Is that why nothing happened to you when your mate passed?"

"No," she mused. "He was a chosen mate. I rejected my fated mate and chose another instead. He, like the previous Luna, died of heartbreak when Ollie's father, our son, passed."

"Why didn't the same thing happen to you?" I cringed when I noticed how nosy that question was.

She didn't say anything. Maybe she didn't have the answer.

We sat in silence for a few minutes. I had no idea why she was revealing so much, but I was certain I'd figure it out, whether she told me or I connected the dots further down the line. I tapped my fingernail against the teacup, an old nervous habit.

"Rose will be wrapping up running patrol along the cottage in a few minutes, and I'm sure you have things to discuss with your friend," Marjorie said, finally breaking the silence. She turned, her eyes boring into me. "Remember, Lya. Fate deals the most difficult hands to those who can do the most with them. It is still your choice of when and how you play your cards, but the cards won't change. Hold them close to your heart and use them all."

I shifted uncomfortably, my eyes scanning the tree line out the window, looking for... I don't know. Rose's wolf was a pale cream, and I assumed patrols were done as wolves.

"Go on," she encouraged. "I need to stop by and see my dear old Ollie, so I'll bring the scones to the house."

I nodded, jumping up and making my way toward the door.

"Oh, and Lya?" I stopped in my tracks, keeping my eyes on the door. "Treat my grandson well. He's given up so much and waited a long time."

I turned back and looked at her, really noticing the similarities between her and Oliver. "Thank you, Marjorie."

I dashed out the door and very nearly ran into Rose.

"Hi!" Rose chirped. "I was told you'd be here. Wanna grab coffee?"

I nodded. I didn't trust myself to speak right now, especially so close to Oliver's grandmother. I followed Rose back to the training grounds and over to her car, wracking my brain to come up with a way to tell her about last night. I had never had girlfriends; hell, I barely had friends, but right now, I understood why people leaned so heavily on them and gossiped with them so much.

Once safely tucked into the confines of her vehicle and out of the parking lot, I buried my head in my hands and shrieked. Just shrieked, no words. It was the only thing I could come up with to convey how I felt.

The car slowed, pulling over to a stop on the side of the road. "So, maybe there's something that needs to be said before we get coffee. Am I right?"

I didn't, couldn't, look up at her. "I fooled around with Oliver last night, and-and I think... and... oh my god," I garbled into my hands.

"So, what's the problem?" Rose asked. "I mean, you could cut the sexual tension with a knife whenever you two are in the same room. Was it assault?"

I looked up into her icy blues, utter shock written all over my face. "No! God no! He was so... he asked. And I was all for it. I don't even know why things went from zero to sixty so fast. Every little bit of logic just flew out of my head, and I know I shouldn't have messed with the Alpha, but it was so... good." The words flew out of my mouth at probably the fastest rate I had ever spoken.

"So, what's the problem?" she repeated.

"Rose, I think he's my mate." There it was, out in the open. The big 'M' word I had been refusing to even think.

'Bingo! Knew you could do it, kid.'

'Not helping, Tala,' I gritted through my mental teeth at her.

Rose's eyes bugged wide and a smile played on her lips. "Oh."

"Yeah."

"That's good news, though!" Rose nodded encouragingly.

"For who?" I practically cried. "I don't want a mate yet!"

Rose cocked an eyebrow. "But you *do* want a mate, right?"

I had no idea what this girl was getting at. "Maybe. Yes. I don't know! I can't even shift yet! I hadn't thought of any of the other werewolf stuff! I guess I kind of figured, when I found the one, we'd fall in love instead of being assigned." I looked down at my hands. I could feel the tears pricking at my eyes, but I did my best to ignore them.

Did I want a mate? Equal parts yes and no. I understood and agreed with the arguments of both sides. Did I want Oliver to be my mate? I didn't even know him, really. Thus far, my feelings had been somewhere between a crush and wanting to jump his bones at any chance. But it also kind of sounded like there wasn't really time to get to know your mate before finding out; it was love at first sight. Maybe that was why I was so okay with things going too far last night. And maybe I was confused and it was something other than the mate bond I felt. I mean, he gave no indication that the sparky feelings were reciprocated.

Rose let out a deep breath and chewed on her lower lip. "You'll want to check with someone whose mated, but I don't think that's how the mate bond works. It really just makes it so you two want close proximity and want to protect each other, and, uh... procreation. You still get to fall in love."

Rose pulled the car back onto the road. "But for real now, I just got off of overnight patrols. Coffee."

There was another burning question that I was too scared to ask. Did Oliver feel it, too?

OLIVER

SHE RAN.

And to be honest, I didn't know why.

My name on Lya's lips echoed through my head all the way to the training grounds. I let Adair take over for the run there. I needed the release. I wracked my head to figure out where I went wrong. Was she not as into it as I thought? Did I push too far? Why couldn't I kiss her and then wish her goodnight?

Adair offered no words of support or encouragement in regard to Lya. He was smug and so certain he had Tala on his side that he could hardly be bothered with the human half of our mate.

We crashed into the field of the training grounds, interrupting the first-year recruits' morning session. I shifted quickly, grabbed a pair of shorts from the stash of spare clothes kept at the complex, and marched over to the head of the field. Kota was in a nonverbal pissing or eye-fucking contest with Ellie–I couldn't tell which–and didn't even bother looking my way until I cleared my throat.

"Yes, Alpha?" he grumbled when he finally turned toward me.

"How are the recruits?" I snapped, cocking an eyebrow at Ellie. She quickly turned and sauntered off, back to the warm-ups the rest of them were doing.

"Combative." He shot a glare over his shoulder at his mate. He stepped closer and lowered his voice. "What's going on?"

"I want to see how sparring is coming along," I bluffed. I needed something to keep my mind off of Lya's departure this morning. "I'm concerned that someone who has nearly completed their first year could be so easily beaten by someone with no formal training."

"Yes, Alpha." Kota flagged down the full-timers who were on the field and paired them off with the recruits to spar, then followed me over to the sidelines to watch. "You look like shit. Get much sleep?"

"No."

"Things with your mate keep you up?" he prodded.

"Yes," I huffed, scrubbing a hand down my face. If only he knew.

Kota crossed his arms and rocked back on his heels. "Well, I'm not the one to talk to about mate advice."

He was right. My circle was small, just him, Trevor, and Brandon. Even though only one of us didn't have a mate, the rest of us were all effectively single but spoken for. I gritted my teeth, cursing the Goddess for not allowing me to have one thing that went simply and easily.

But Lya was not a thing.

I turned my attention back to the recruits, taking some time to actually study their performance. One of the first things I did once taking over as Alpha was expand the school more or less for training. There were three components: warriors, scouts, and Cyber. Each program took four years, like college, and we even had contracts with other packs to allow their pack security to train with us. Since its development, the recruits we picked up were getting better and better. It truly was considered an honor to make it into one of the programs, let alone graduate.

"So, Ellie," I started, watching her flounder and take blow after blow.

"She's not good enough," he confirmed.

"I can see that."

Kota sighed. "I think it's because we butt heads so much in training."

"Don't make excuses for her," I told him. "I don't care what goes on off the field, but here, you are Gamma, and she can't refuse to listen to you."

I made my way over to her. I don't know if I was looking for a fight today, but this was sure to result in one. I nodded to Jace, signaling for him to return to whatever he was doing, and took his place.

"Alpha," she huffed, already breathing hard.

"Ellie." I didn't waste time on greetings, instead taking up a defensive stance.

I quickly saw where she struggled. She wasted so much energy, moved around too much, too slowly, and made no attempts to cover her weak side. If we actually put her in a field, it would be her blood on my hands. Most of my recruits, by the end of their first year, rivaled other packs' seasoned warriors, but not her. I genuinely thought I could put one of the pre-recruit high schoolers against her and consider it a fair fight.

I dropped my arms and straightened. "What's going on, Ellie? You were top of the class when your year started."

"Well, maybe if you didn't have some jackass in charge–"

I put up my hand, cutting off her reply. "I'll remind you once, you are speaking to your Alpha, not your mate's friend. Your Gamma is in charge of training, not your mate. He's put out too many quality fighters for me to listen to one complaint. It's a trainee problem."

Ellie crossed her arms and looked down. "It's really hard to get training like this from my mate," she mumbled to the ground.

I cocked an eyebrow at her. "If you want to be here, that shouldn't be a problem. Figure out your priorities–your ego or your pack. Your first year wrapped a couple weeks ago, and this supplemental training was required for a reason. If you haven't shaped up by the end of the summer, the decision will be made for you."

"Yes, Alpha," she agreed quietly.

I turned away from her, heading toward the building that held Kota's office. He was quick to fall in stride with me, shoving a cup of coffee in my hand once we got there.

"Thanks," I grumbled, collapsing in one of the chairs and slumping my shoulders.

Kota sat down, propped his feet up on his desk, and looked at me quizzically. "Did you talk to Lessa yesterday?"

"Yep," I said, popping the 'p.' "She and Ric will join the pack at least temporarily while this whole ordeal is seen through. Then they'll decide where to settle."

He nodded slowly. "And did you find out anything else from Lya yet?"

I sipped my coffee, delaying the answer. I'd found out plenty, but not regarding what he was asking about.

"I saw you guys in the packhouse last night. Most mates fuck as soon as they meet, so stop stressing about that."

My eyes snapped up to him. "You saw that?" I demanded.

Kota didn't look up at me. "Came by to ask if you'd seen who Ellie left with. Saw myself out pretty quick. Might be enough to get the ball rolling for you two, though."

I went back to glaring down at my coffee, still kicking myself for losing the tight hold on my control last night. I truly hoped he had a point and she had run for a reason other than regret.

Nineteen

Lya

It was Thursday, which meant I had successfully avoided Oliver for nearly three whole days. I had woken up to evidence of a black wolf in my bed each night–black wolf hair is glaringly apparent against white sheets—but he was always gone by the time I woke up. At this point, I was almost certain it was Oliver's wolf, Adair.

My attempts to avoid Oliver had resulted in spending a lot of time outside of the packhouse, meaning I was able to get more familiar with the town. Rose had shown me around a few other shops after coffee on Tuesday. She continued to try and help me tap into my ability to shift, but every time failed. I didn't tell her I had shifted to run to Marjorie's cottage. I had no idea how I had called on that, and I didn't want to give her false hope that shifting at will was a skill I possessed. Allyssa had once again made breakfast, this time successfully, on Wednesday, then dragged me along to the school to assist with substituting for some teachers while they went to the training grounds to get some of their mandatory training in. I heard rumors that the typical requirements had been increased, but no one could justify why. Some outlandish stories were surfacing, and with how little I knew, I couldn't tell how credible a two-headed rogue or a vampire able to walk in daylight were. No one had given me instructions yet to start training, but I still hadn't been cleared to train yet. It'd be another week or so before that.

Tala and I had resorted to the battle of wills I was so familiar with. She wanted nothing more than to track Oliver down and glom onto his side like an extra appendage, but I knew better. Whenever the smell of a fresh rainstorm invaded my senses, I ran the other way.

It wasn't that I didn't want to be around Oliver. Oh, no, it was damn near painful to maintain so much distance. I hadn't realized how much I looked forward to seeing him each day I was here prior to our escapades. But now? I was inclined to side with Tala on this one and give in. Which made me even more certain that what I felt, those sparks, were the mate bond talking. I was such a pro at resisting my emotions, but this time, it was proving to be too much of a challenge.

Which made the entire thing hurt even more because he didn't feel it as well. He was the one familiar with mate bonds. He would have said something. Right?

And that's exactly why, in the very late hours of Thursday night, I was still up long after I had turned the lights out and tried to go to sleep. My usual tactic of pretending to be asleep in an attempt to fool my own brain was not working, but I still tried. I was turned away from the door, squeezing my eyes shut so none of the moonlight from outside or lights from the hallway seeping under the door could interrupt my sleep masquerade when the door creaked open, bringing in the smell of a summer rainstorm. I stayed still and quiet, excited to catch my nightly intruder in the act.

I heard the telltale sounds of someone shifting, bones cracking followed by fur rustling, and the mattress dipped under the additional weight of a wolf. I sat up quickly and glared directly into his rich chocolate eyes.

'Hey, Lya,' the most annoying voice cut in. 'Mate.' I rolled my eyes.

"I am going to turn around, you are going to shift, get clothes on, and explain yourself," I said coldly.

The wolf bowed his head and whimpered. I simply crossed my arms, turned my back, and waited. Only when I heard someone clearing their throat did I get off the bed to face him. I met Oliver's gaze, maintaining my glare, but he looked guilty.

'Lya, Lya, Lya, mate, mate, mate'. I continued to ignore the wolf.

"Why have you been in my room every night?" I demanded.

Oliver dropped his eyes and shuffled his feet.

"Well?"

"You have nightmares," he mumbled, keeping his eyes on the floor.

"So?"

Oliver glanced up. "You scream... a lot. You stop screaming if I'm around."

"Why *you*?" I sneered. "Couldn't I just go have girls' nights with Rose?"

He shook his head, a small smile playing on his lips as he took a step closer. "That wouldn't work."

"Why not?"

'Because MATE!' Tala was shouting now.

Oliver closed the space between us, reaching out to cup my cheek. A small sigh escaped my lips as I leaned into his hand. I cursed myself for my stupid overactive crush. He chuckled, dropping his hand to walk past me and prop himself on the bed. "Twenty questions?"

I looked at him suspiciously all the while trying not to enjoy the sight of him leaning back against the headboard of my bed. If only it was under different circumstances. Twenty questions had gotten us into trouble last time, and we were already in a bedroom.

"You first," I said cautiously.

Oliver's smile turned smug. "What do you have nightmares about?"

It was my turn to look away, not wanting to admit it.

"The past," I said. "Why are you so concerned about my sleep?"

His eyes flitted across my face like he was trying to commit every detail to memory. "You're special, Lya. I'd think you'd realize that by now. Now, what about your past?"

I sighed. He just wasn't going to let this topic go.

"Ted," I finally admitted. "Why do you care?"

"Maybe I'm curious to see how I stack up," he drawled. "So? Do I get to hear a story?"

I cocked an eyebrow. This was, to date, the weirdest flirtationship I had been in. "You haven't tried to kill me yet, so you're doing well. Would you mind cutting the crap and just asking me what you really want?"

Oliver leaned forward, his eyes sparking with interest. "That's a loaded question." His voice was deep and husky, and the silence that followed was strained.

I turned away from him and walked out the door. I wasn't getting out of this, and maybe some information I had would be useful, although I doubted it. Oliver hadn't moved when I came back in the room, holding the decanter from his office and a couple glasses.

"That kind of story?" Oliver asked.

"Most attempted murders are," I said, pouring a glass and sitting down on the couch, facing away from him. "It's a long one, so get settled."

I heard movement behind me, and soon enough, Oliver was sitting on the other side of the couch with his own tumbler.

"Ted and I met two years ago at a hotel bar outside of Fort Wayne, Indiana, when I was driving out to South Dakota from Vermont. He said he was on a hunting trip."

Oliver nodded slowly. "There's a pack a little ways outside of Fort Wayne. They had a controlled encounter with hunters a couple years ago."

"I guess he probably wasn't lying, at least," I scoffed. "Anyway, you know the whole drill with a one-night stand. He gave me his number in the morning, and I kept it for whatever reason."

I paused, taking a minute to enjoy the flash of jealousy Oliver let slip for half a second. I couldn't help the smirk when I noticed. So, Mountain Man Alpha wasn't impressed with Ted this early on in the story. "I left Vermont because I started to get too close to people, and I really didn't want to do that here. So, when I got lonely, I'd give Ted a call. I figured it couldn't be too bad. He was so far away and seemed harmless. Just a guy who likes destination hunting trips, right?"

"Clever enough to never lie, but never tell the truth," Oliver mused.

"We both were." I swirled the scotch around in the glass. I had never liked scotch–I was more of a cheap wine or expensive beer kinda girl–but I needed the liquid fortitude. "When the brewery *finally* opened after almost a whole year of saying they'd be opening the next month, I started going almost every day. The beer was good, and Trevor was always nice. He kind of felt like the big brother I'd never had. He was my best friend because I had never really gotten close to anyone ever, even though I wasn't his. I was happy with it, but it made Ted really upset because I was calling him less. I wasn't expecting it at all when he showed up in South Dakota and proposed. I didn't know how to say no, so I said yes. He said he was only supposed to stay for a week, and I figured I'd come up with a way to break it off once he was gone. But then his entire family showed up at the end of the week for an engagement party, and he said he was staying permanently."

Oliver's eyes darkened and he furrowed his brows. "His entire family? Would you be able to recognize them?"

"Yes," I said confidently, easily picturing each face in my mind. "Ted's dad made a big show of giving him a dagger with a silver blade 'just in case I got out of hand.' He was sarcastic about it, but that's when I knew he knew. They all knew." I finished off the scotch and refilled the glass, hoping the alcohol could burn away the memory of his expression when he presented Ted with the heirloom gift. "I was so scared by it. I started a fight with Ted and spent the night at Trevor's place."

"You stayed at Trevor's?" Oliver nearly shouted. He jumped to his feet and started pacing, his anger palpable.

I slunk back into the couch, not expecting this reaction.

"We didn't do anything," I mumbled.

Oliver stopped and looked at me. "They know where he lives." He dug inside his pants pocket and pulled out his phone.

My eyes grew wide at the realization, and a small piece of my heart shattered. I hadn't found it in myself to forgive Trevor yet, but he was still the closest friend I had ever had, and I didn't want him caught up in the trouble I'd caused. I bit my lower lip, trying to keep a sob from slipping out.

Before I knew it, Oliver was pulling me to him. He ran a hand up and down my arm, leaving a trail of fireworks behind. I dug my face into the crook of his neck and breathed deep, letting the refreshing smell of a rainstorm soothe me.

OLIVER

IT WAS 7 A.M., and my office was filled with my Beta, two Gammas, *and* Luna. She didn't know, but I didn't care. Her presence alone created a completion to the leadership I had never known we needed. This pack needed her as much as I did, and although I wanted to fiercely protect her from the darker sides of this world, the Moon Goddess had carefully selected her to help lead us through it for a reason.

Adair and I were painfully aware of how carefully Lya had been avoiding us since waking up in her bed after the night of the full moon. But, oddly enough, Adair was not concerned, so I followed his lead. I knew Adair and Tala had forged ahead on some level of the mate bond, waiting for their human counterparts to catch up, and I couldn't help but feel as if he was withholding information.

Keeping Lya tightly tucked under my arm, however, was proving to be a distraction, especially when the minute traces of the bond were still so new. Fingers snapping in my face pulled my mind back to the room and the task at hand.

"If you are going to pull me out of bed at this ungodly hour with this little sleep, you are going to pay attention," Lya snapped at me.

I glanced around sheepishly, catching both Kota and Brandon chuckling. Gregory, however, maintained his stony expression.

"Sorry," I mumbled.

"As I was saying, Lu-*Lya*," Kota repeated, "if we can hack into the security footage surrounding places Trevor frequents, we can identify whether or not they are actually keeping tabs on him. It's a worthwhile assumption that they did actually follow you to his apartment, and the disappearance of their son caused enough stir for them to come back here, but we don't even know who to look out for."

Lya looked puzzled by this request. "Don't you have access to facial recognition software for things like that? More than one person has commented on how techy this pack is."

Kota nodded in confirmation. "We need to know who we're identifying, so we have to get into their footage and pull the faces first."

"But I have them all on social media, and their profile pictures have their faces. Why go through who knows how many hours of footage to maybe identify someone?"

I brushed a strand of hair behind her ear. "We werewolves don't really do the social media thing."

Lya sighed absently. "Well, maybe we should save some time and take advantage of the fact that I did."

"We can get you set up with the Cyber guy later today to get as many faces as possible," Kota suggested. "Trevor, has anything related popped up there?"

Trevor had been looped into this meeting via video conference. On his side of the state, he chewed on his thumbnail–a habit he'd had since he was a kid. "Nothing remarkable. Her boss asked about her when he stopped by for a beer, but that was it."

Lya's head snapped up, glaring into the screen. "He?"

"Yeah, the vet you worked for," he confirmed.

"The vet I worked for was a woman."

I let out a harsh breath I hadn't realized I was holding. "So, we have at least one probable suspect with boots on the ground."

"Maybe they'll think Ted and I just went on vacation and leave," Lya suggested quietly.

Kota rolled his eyes. "Lya, I think this is a good indication you need to start training."

"No," I said through gritted teeth. "Absolutely not. The doctor said two weeks, and it's barely been one."

Kota gave me a hard stare but elected against pressing the issue. For that, I was thankful. I was keeping Lya as far away from this mess as I could, which left no reason for her to go against doctor's orders and potentially injure herself by starting training early. It was for more reasons than just her recovery. She needed as much time as possible to get acquainted with her wolf and tap into Tala's abilities.

Aside from pleasantries at the beginning of the meeting, Gregory had remained silent, which was par for the course. It wasn't rare for him to sit through entire meetings without saying a word. For a long time, when he was newly appointed as my father's Beta, I believed it was because he wasn't committed enough to the protection of the pack, but the more my father involved me, the easier it was for me to notice that his gears were turning while he was listening, only speaking if his input was really necessary. So, when he lifted his head and looked up from his hands, all eyes were on him as we waited for the Beta to speak.

"You all were either not old enough to truly understand, or not a part of this pack yet," he said, voice low, "but the girl's ability to accidentally accomplish what our previous Alpha and Beta worked and planned so hard for would make them proud." My eyes snapped up to Gregory, lips pursed in a hard line. "Alpha, I know how opposed you were then, and how opposed you are now, but don't look a gift horse in the mouth, kids."

With that, Gregory stood and walked out of the office, closing the door quietly behind him. All our eyes remained locked on the closed door. The sentiment was clear. A large group of hunters, one which werewolves across the continent had been vying to take down for decades, was now gathered in a place where we could strike. Even if we weren't happy with the timing or the location, we needed to seize the opportunity to bring the fight to them before they brought it to us. It was, unfortunately, the exact thing Trevor had set out to recreate, and I had so adamantly insisted we change course. We would be fools to let them slip through our fingers now.

Trevor was the first to break the harsh silence with a wry laugh.

"I gotta get that guy to teach me how to make an exit before he steps down."

TWENTY

Lya

As it turned out, war strategy meetings weren't that bad. The remainder of it had been filled covering damage control. Trevor couldn't come back to the pack yet in fear of leading them right to us, and a group of warriors was being sent out to join the scouts. It went without saying that Oliver was furious. I personally felt like part of the reason Trevor was not allowed back at the pack yet was to keep Oliver from killing him for his award-winning *Hunters vs Werewolves: Battle of Brookings* reenactment.

I didn't expect to be in meetings by any means, but it was kind of cool and validating to be listened to and have my thoughts respected when I was the new kid on the block. Kota stuck to his word, and I was currently sitting in the Cyber Unit at the training complex with the head of the department, Kota, and Rose. After identifying the people whom I knew for certain were connected to Ted in some sort of hunter capacity on my social media friends lists, we went down the rabbit hole of cyberstalking to see if we could add more people to that list, as well as consistently adding "maybes" to the facial recognition database.

"I guess the clock is running out," I mused, trying to break the monotony of staring at a computer screen in silence.

"Yep," Kota confirmed, popping the 'p.'

I sighed. "There's gotta be a way to buy some time."

"If you come up with something, I'll be all ears," Kota growled, his hard glare falling on me. I couldn't decide if he would actually be willing to listen to ideas from someone with no battle experience. He hadn't been warm and bubbly in the few previous encounters I'd had with him, but he seemed more crotchety than usual.

I studied Kota for a minute before sharing a knowing look with Rose. And people said girls were the moody ones.

"I mean, it can't be any harder than leading a guy on," I said, deciding to ignore Kota's bad mood for now.

He scoffed. "Starting a war is a lot different than starting a relationship."

"Is it, though?" Rose piped up. "I mean, you're still trying to get the opponent's attention, but for different reasons."

"You know better than that, Rose," he snapped. "I trained you myself."

"Yes, yes," she agreed. "You taught us that it's better to be on the offensive so we are calling the shots, and we only go to battle for causes worth dying over. Personally, I like knowing exactly what's going on in a relationship, and I only waste time with the ones worth dying for."

"Ooh, okay, so what if we, like, stood them up?" I suggested. "We know they're there to figure out what happened to Ted, so what if we threw them some sort of bone? Just like you'd do if you're trying to get someone to stick around but don't want to commit yet?"

Kota grunted but gave no further input.

Rose looked lost in thought. "If we can confirm there are hunters in the area, maybe you could call Trevor or something while they're in the brewery, Lya?"

"Absolutely," I agreed. "I bet they'd love to get their hands on me after Ted's disappearance. Of course, they'd hang around and wait for me to show back up. Or the warriors there could go on a run in wolf form or something, give them the idea there is a pack presence. I bet they wouldn't make a move yet, but they might call in back-up."

"That's foolish and dumb." Kota's curt reply cut off our scheming.

"It isn't," CyberSleuth Seth, as I had named him, piped up. He turned the computer monitor toward us, and sure enough, two faces on the "for sure" list and one on the "maybe" list—Ted's younger brother, one of his two sisters, and his uncle—had popped up hanging around the brewery and Trevor's apartment.

Things seemed to snap into perspective, and I realized that this was all really happening. Up until now, none of these threats had been tangible enough, just a faint possibility, but there was no denying it now. I had a horrible feeling I would never be safe until these people were taken off the map. I wondered if, at this point, I was their main target, or if the pack was. Would they leave the pack alone if they got me?

I had gotten these people into this mess, and now I felt responsible for getting them out.

I bit my bottom lip hard, causing it to bleed. "Is it too late to pull everyone out and just pretend they're not there? They still don't know where the pack is, do they?"

"What happened to your battle strategy session?" Kota scoffed. "Too real now?"

"A little, yeah," I mumbled. "Has anyone checked the security cameras at my house?"

"You have security cameras?" Seth asked.

"Yeah." I paused. "Ted hid them pretty well and hadn't realized I found the login information for them."

Seth pushed the computer over to me. I quickly found the website and logged in, shoving the laptop back in his direction. There were four security cameras hidden around the property, giving us a view of the front, back, and sides of the house. Luckily, he had never put any inside the house. At least, none that I knew of.

"Oh, this is good," Seth cheered, smiling broadly. "I'll go over the footage and see if there's been any activity around the house over the past week."

He turned his attention back to the computer and put his headphones on. We took that as our cue to go.

Just outside the door, Kota grabbed my arm. Rose stopped and turned to us, but I waved her on, telling her I'd catch up with her at the car. I was relieved when she listened. Kota had a one-track mind, so I had to think if he was asking for my attention, it was important. And private.

"You need to start training," Kota said, very matter of fact.

I looked up at him. Given his expression, I could tell there was absolutely no room for negotiation. "I know."

"The Alpha won't let you."

I smirked. I was quickly catching on to Oliver's inner circle's use of his title when they were unhappy with his decisions. It was mostly only used when Oliver pulled rank and made a decision someone else was unhappy with. "What he doesn't know won't hurt him."

Kota nodded once and handed me a piece of paper. "Be at the training grounds at these times. Do not tell *anyone* or my head is on the line."

I rushed off to the parking lot, making sure to fold the paper up and stuff it in my pocket before I caught up with Rose.

"What was that about?" she asked when I met her at her car.

"Oh, nothing," I said, waving away her comment.

Rose nodded slowly, giving me a quizzical look. Who was I kidding? This girl was a scout. She could see through a lie. That didn't mean I wasn't going to give it my best shot.

"What do you think was up with him today?" I continued, trying to change the topic.

Rose shrugged. "I dunno. He's always kind of callus, but today he was straight-up moody."

I rolled my eyes. "I bet it's mate problems. Ellie is a bitch."

Rose whirled around to look at me.

"Ellie is his *mate*?" she shrieked. "I knew they had some weird fuck buddies thing going on, but she's his *mate*?"

I looked around, checking to make sure no one was listening. "You didn't know?"

"No! No one does, apparently!"

The whole Kota and Ellie thing confused me. Hell, I had known my maybe-mate for almost two weeks at this point, and even if the possible mate bond hadn't kicked in, I wasn't sure how long I'd be able to resist him. More power to Ellie for that talent.

"Speaking of mates," Rose began with a smirk. "What's it like being mated to the Alpha?"

I shrugged. "Don't know. I don't think I'm his mate."

"Uhm... what?"

"I mean, I know he's my mate, but I don't think I'm his," I sighed. To be honest, as fun as that night was, I was beginning to regret getting physical with Oliver. It was like whatever snapped into place had made it physically painful to be away from him, and whenever I was around him, the desire to touch him was disgusting. The last time I felt even remotely close to this way was when I lost my virginity to a guy who ghosted me the very next day. In short, this unrequited mate deal was making me feel pretty gross.

Rose blinked a few times, then burst out laughing.

"That's not how it works, Lya!" she choked out. "Your mate, it's your soulmate! Two halves of one whole, who the Moon Goddess carefully selects."

"Well, she must have gotten it wrong this time," I grumbled. "She must have mixed some up."

Rose shook her head, still laughing. "Nope, that'd be like taking the pieces out of one puzzle and putting them in another. It wouldn't work!"

I glared at her, trying to convey how unenthusiastic I was about continuing this conversation. "She clearly messes up sometimes. I mean, look at Kota and Ellie."

She shook her head. "Just talk to him. Promise me, you'll talk to him."

"You know something I don't know?"

Rose winked and gave me a sly smile. "Come on, let's go work on tapping into your wolf."

Oliver

After the meeting, I let Adair take over. We needed to run and blow off some steam. I told one of the warriors on patrol to take a couple hours off and filled in for him.

Meetings like that never brought good news. The previous night when I mind-linked Kota, he made sure to remind me that he'd told me so regarding the information Lya had shared. We all knew she knew something, even if she didn't realize she did. It was my idiotic mindset that my mate would never do me wrong that blinded me from pursuing that information.

Adair growled, *'It wasn't intentional.'*

I knew he was right about that. Since Tala had been more present with Lya, Adair had been able to maintain more of a connection with her. That gave us the privilege of at least getting an idea of her intentions. Adair would be able to pick up on it if they were dark and sinister. Right now, he only saw innocence and misunderstanding.

Something in my mind flickered and Adair perked up. He started to head away from our patrol location, but I pulled him back.

'We're on duty,' I reminded him.

By the time the warrior returned to resume his spot, whatever had piqued Adair's interest was long gone. So, I trudged over to my grandmother's cottage, shifted, found some of the clothes I left stashed over here, and let myself in. Dr. Whitledge, my grandmother, and I had a meeting arranged for this afternoon, and I was desperately hoping it would go better than this morning's.

"Ollie, how are you?" My grandmother greeted me with a warm smile.

I took a muffin from the plate she offered. "Just hoping you guys have good news. I'm a little tapped out on bad today."

"Your lucky day, then," she said, patting my cheek.

Dr. Whitledge cleared his throat, drawing my attention to where he sat at the table with my grandmother's book in front of him. "I believe I was able to identify enough markers to confirm that your mate is from this pack, but not her exact parentage, I'm afraid."

"Well, that's a start," I said, encouraged by a step in the right direction. Admittedly, this particular side venture did not matter too much right now; it could be figured out later. But I'd take any good news at this point.

"A start, yes," Dr. Whitledge agreed, "so I am returning your book to allow you and your mate to do some further research on her supposed lineage. I am still not certain, as I did not have much to go off of, but I believe it is probable. Is there any way we could get a sample and some history from her parents?"

I shook my head. "Lya's mother is a human and knew nothing of were-wolves. She thinks her father is a wolf, but she hasn't seen him since she was fourteen or fifteen. No way to contact him now."

"We need to try to dig something up," Dr. Whitledge insisted, cutting me off. "The last known traces of this bloodline died out nearly a century ago."

"What pack are we even talking about?" I demanded. "And how the hell is she from that pack if they are gone?"

"Come now, Oliver. I know Thom was the historian, but you have read your books," my grandmother sighed. "Lya is of the Wulver Pack."

I racked my brain for any information I could remember of them, but not much was known. They were one of the original packs, but they were eradicated early on, which caused an extreme loss of knowledge. Any survivors of the Wulver Pack were more of a rumor than anything. They didn't exactly have territory, but they stayed connected after their dispersal. Supposedly, they had blended quite well into human society. Especially in the region their territory used to be, they were widely accepted due to their standing with the local population.

"The pack I mentioned to you before giving you that book. It's the Wulver Pack," my grandmother clarified. "It is believed that before the entire pack could be destroyed, the remaining members escaped and found solace living amongst humans."

"Oh." That did strike a chord. I looked down at my untouched muffin. I didn't know if this information even mattered much at the moment, or if it was worth spending time on it given the other matters at hand. I tucked this information away for a rainy day. Something to deal with after the hunters were off the radar.

"You need to talk to Lya, Oliver," my grandmother said. "They were initially discovered because they were the protectors, the peacekeepers, and they still are, even from the shadows. Hunters originally came into existence to take down their pack, and the members mutated to resist their tactics. Then, they went against their natural ways of living to camouflage themselves from them. The Wulver Pack may no longer have a territory they call their own, but they are the strongest among us. The reason there has been peace for so long? It's because the remnants of the Wulvers are behind the scenes, keeping any threats at bay."

"Why would people form a coalition to destroy a group of us that were deemed protectors and peacekeepers?" I asked my grandmother in confusion. "And how do you know so much about this pack if everyone else seems to think they were successfully eradicated?"

She gave me a wan smile. "Not everyone understood that something most considered to be a monster could be good. Only the evil our kind have done gets recorded for humans to know, never the good. You know this."

I left my grandmother's cottage with the book securely wrapped in its cloth and tucked under my arm. I promised her that I'd bring Lya by soon. It was easy to see that Lya trusted my grandmother, but I wasn't so certain she trusted me. We needed to talk to her wolf and get answers from Tala, which would hopefully provide confirmation that Lya was actually from the Wulver pack. Truth be told, I hoped she wasn't. It would put a target on her head.

I wasn't quite certain how all this new information fit into the whole equation of what was going on, but given what my grandmother said, it had to.

In the time I had been Alpha, my pack had not seen much turmoil. Some disagreements with other packs, aggressive rogues, and random hunters here and there had been the extent of any upheaval. It wasn't a surprise to me that something finally came knocking on our door, but I still had absolutely no desire to put my pack through the risks of war. If they were still unaware of the location of the pack, it would be easy enough to remain hidden and wait them out. And yet, amidst it all, Gregory was right. We would be remiss if we did not do something about them now, even if lying low was the easier, and safer, option.

I didn't even realize how long I had been walking when I ended up back at the packhouse. I made my way in and knocked on Lya's door. When there was no answer, I ducked inside and placed the book on her bed. She had been reading a lot, and I hoped this one would grab her attention.

Adair perked up again once back in the kitchen, and I glanced around, trying to find what caught his attention. I spotted two wolves outside, dashing toward the packhouse. I recognized one as Rose's light blonde wolf. The deep red one wasn't as familiar, but Adair recognized his mate immediately. I strolled out the patio doors as they emerged from the tree line fully dressed.

"So, how'd you do it?" I asked, slinging my arm over Lya's shoulder. She looked down and blushed, keeping her arms crossed.

"I had to get her angry," Rose giggled. "The whole relax and release thing doesn't seem to work."

I cocked an eyebrow. I wasn't surprised; it took a long time to learn to shift without an overpowering emotion alongside it. Most forgot about that part of the learning curve. "What got you so angry it was worth shifting?"

"Nothing," Lya grumbled, keeping her eyes on the ground.

"Well, it can't be nothing if even Tala got mad about it," I chided.

Lya–or Tala, maybe–let out a low growl, encouraging me to drop it. Clearly, whatever it was, she was still quite upset. I shot a look over to Rose, but she shook her head once. Apparently, I wouldn't be getting answers from her, either.

I steered Lya inside, Rose closely following. I glanced over at the clock on the microwave to confirm I had enough time to chat before my next meeting. I wanted to hear all about how Lya finally tapped into shifting, but she was quick to head off to her room, avoiding all my attempts to start a conversation.

"What's up with her now?" I asked Rose, trying to keep the exasperation out of my voice.

Rose looked a little guilty. "I don't think Tala is upset, but Lya might still be angry with you. I am sorry, Alpha."

She put her head down and was out the door before I could ask another question. I looked over in the direction Lya went, but another glance at the clock reminded me I had only a few minutes before I needed to be at the school. With a heavy sigh, I headed out of the packhouse instead.

Twenty-One

Lya

THE NOTE KOTA had passed to me outlined times I needed to be at the training grounds, which also happened to be times he knew Oliver had prior obligations that would keep him out of the packhouse and away from the grounds. Today, he was supposed to be at the school, overseeing how the high school students were doing with their own training. It seemed like this pack revolved around being prepared, which didn't quite make sense seeing as so many people bragged about how there had been primarily peace for so long.

I trudged over to the training grounds, taking as much time as I could spare. Rose had made sure to apologize before she riled Tala and me up so we could shift, but her words still bothered me. Maybe she was right. Maybe he hadn't mentioned me being his mate because he didn't want me. Maybe he'd prefer someone who'd had a good relationship with their wolf for their whole life. Maybe I wasn't good enough for him and he was going to reject me.

And that made me feel very used. He had been in my bed every night for the past week, even if it was in wolf form. He had touched me and I had allowed it. I had never been one to get hung up on a guy. Hell, I probably used them as often as they used me, but what was the harm in having a little fun? This time, though, the thought of rejection made me want to throw up.

Tala's anger wasn't at her mate. It was at Rose for disrespecting her. Tala knew she was Luna, even if it hadn't been recognized yet, and she would defend her title and demand respect. Tala did her best to assure me that what Rose said wasn't the case at all, but I wasn't so sure.

I made my way into Kota's office, following the instructions the note indicated. He wasn't there, though, so I sat down across from his desk. I tried to throw my whole mind into the prospect of training, anything to get it off of my boy problems.

I had waited so long, I was debating leaving. I stood, and just as I was about to open the door, it flung open, bashing me in the face.

"Sorry," Kota grumbled, striding over to his desk and sitting down.

I swiped away the bit of blood trickling from my nose and walked back to the chair I had previously been in, waiting for him to say something. Kota was one of the few people I had interacted with here, but I didn't know him very well yet. I had no idea what to expect of the temper he seemed to have today. As we sat and stared at each other for a few moments, the room grew more and more tense.

"You're his mate and you know it," he finally said.

The statement caught me off guard. It wasn't that obvious, was it? "Uh... yes."

"You haven't said anything about it yet."

This was beginning to feel more like an interrogation than a conversation. Or training, for that matter.

"No," I confirmed, "but neither has he."

Kota blew out a breath. "He won't. But you are communicating more with your wolf and shifting. With you two on the same page now, she told you."

I looked at him quizzically, waiting for him to continue. "Our wolves have an inherent desire to protect us, so she wouldn't have told you until you two were a cohesive unit and she felt like the information wouldn't blow your brain."

Were Tala and I a cohesive unit? Did she actually do stuff to protect me? Personally, I felt like both those questions had the same answer: no. It felt like all we did was work against each other, and she had gotten me into a lot of trouble in the past. I mean, the other day, she wouldn't even let me shift.

That's because you didn't actually want to,' Tala chimed in. I huffed, annoyed that she was right.

"We don't always get along with our wolves," Kota continued. "But we need to always be looking out for the best interests of each other."

That part I had actually consciously been trying to improve on. This werewolf thing wasn't going away, so it was best if I accepted it and figured out how to live happily with my fate.

"What does any of this have to do with training?" I asked.

Kota smirked at my confusion. "You know you'll be Luna here shortly. You'll have as much say and authority as that Alpha of ours. We know having you training right now goes against his wishes, but if you say you want to train and learn how to fight, I have an obligation to follow my leader's demands."

Things began to click in my head. I guess I hadn't put much thought into the possibility of being a leader of this pack. I wasn't even sure I wanted to do that. Hell, I was still mostly convinced Oliver was going to reject me. But, at this moment, I could use the potential role to my advantage.

"I suppose the Luna is expected to be a skilled fighter," I mused, "to protect her pack, of course."

Kota nodded, encouraging me to continue.

I mentally thumbed through everything I remembered from the books I had been reading. "And with the threat of hunters and planning to go to war with them upon us, I should be capable of doing something, whether it's fighting in the battle or protecting and leading the members who remain at home."

He motioned for me to continue. I imagined he was getting frustrated with how long-winded I was making this, but I was having fun.

"And It's reasonable to assume the Alpha's desire to keep me from training is not in the best interest of the pack, so I do think I need to start training now."

"Is that an order, Luna?" Kota asked darkly.

I smiled broadly at his use of my maybe someday title. "Yes, Gamma, that is an order."

He nodded in confirmation, gesturing for me to follow him out of his office. "The people at the training grounds have no idea who you are, so I am not worried about them telling anyone. But we should still keep it a secret until Oliver gives his blessing."

And with that, I followed Kota out for my first session of actual training.

OLIVER

I GLANCED down at my watch, grimacing. I had another half-hour of dealing with the high school kids, and to be honest, I wasn't completely certain why I was here. The kids were developing well, and I was pleased with how they maintained themselves in their sparring. Usually, Gregory oversaw them, checking in once or twice a week, and left the majority of their training up to warriors. But I felt making an occasional appearance motivated them.

I walked around the room, occasionally making comments to critique and correct form or technique. Overall, I felt there were better uses of my time. I made my way over to Colin to let him know I'd be ducking out early.

"Alpha." He nodded as I approached.

"Will you be here next Thursday?" I asked, getting right to the point.

Colin shook his head. "No, Ellie and I alternate. This week, I have Tuesday and Thursday, next week, I'll have Monday, Wednesday, and Friday."

I furrowed my brow. To my knowledge, I hadn't signed off on warriors in training leading the kids. I wasn't exactly enthused with Ellie doing any training with this group, especially after seeing her recent performances. "Since when is she involved at the school?"

"I asked her to," Colin said sheepishly. "I thought it'd be good if there was a female leader as well, and she was the only one I could get to say yes."

"You should have come to me. I could have assigned someone," I told him. Off the top of my head, I could think of several more qualified women to help out here. On top of that, I had a hard time believing many people would turn down spending their time helping our next generation.

"She only started leading it by herself this past week, Alpha," he quickly added. "I used to also be here with her."

"Well, I'll leave you for the rest of today. I'm headed over to the training grounds. I need to check in over there, too," I said. I also planned on talking with Kota, as this change had probably been approved by him, and I wasn't thrilled about it.

"Yes, Alpha," he called as I headed toward the exit.

Once in the Land Cruiser, it wasn't too long of a drive to the training grounds. I saw Kota's car wasn't in the parking lot. His apartment in the warrior housing wasn't far away, and sometimes he walked in for the day instead of driving. I decided to check the field first, but no such luck. I caught the attention of someone and asked if they had seen him around.

"He was here working with a new person, but I think he headed to his office," the warrior said.

"A new person?" I asked, hoping for clarification.

"Yeah," he confirmed. "Some girl. I hadn't seen her before, but I haven't been out of this town much."

I thanked him for the information and headed in the direction of Kota's office, hoping to catch him before he headed out for the day. His office door was cracked, and I could hear the rustling of papers as I approached.

"Hey, man," I said, walking to one of the chairs. Kota glanced up but didn't give much more in the way of a greeting. "Heard you're working with a new person. How's that going?"

Kota shrugged. "Just someone who wants to join the ranks. Shows potential."

I nodded, curious as to who it was. "Is she interested in enrolling in the program?"

"Might be a back-up plan," he grunted.

I ran through who I knew in the pack but couldn't think of anyone who might be interested in making a career change into the warrior ranks. But I wasn't as familiar with the people from different towns. New recruits usually started applying this time of year, though, so it wasn't unusual for people to come and train for a little bit to get a taste of it. Almost like humans touring college campuses.

"Why didn't you tell me Ellie was helping Colin train the high schoolers?" I asked, changing the subject to why I was really here.

Kota looked up from his paperwork, anger flashing across his face. "What?"

"I was over at the high school, and Colin said Ellie has taken over half of the training. Why didn't you tell me?"

He clenched his jaw. "I wouldn't have approved that. She's only a first year, and she's not that good."

I nodded slowly. "I figured you might have made an exception because she's your mate."

"She's not my mate," he said through clenched teeth.

I lifted an eyebrow but decided to ignore the comment for now. He'd go into detail when he felt like it. "Well, Colin said—"

"Fuck Colin and whatever he said." Kota stood and started pacing the room. "No requests for an additional trainer at the school ever came across my desk."

"Ellie's leading training—"

"Fuck her!" he roared. "She's a shit warrior who can't follow directions and has no business training them!"

I stood up, commanding his attention. "Colin suggested a female assisting with training would do the kids good. I don't disagree, but I do need you to find someone more suitable for it."

Kota sat back down behind his desk, defeated, and grumbled out, "I'll find someone else."

I sat back down and watched as he stared blankly at the papers in front of him. I trusted that Kota hadn't actually approved Ellie to lead training of the kids; he wasn't a liar. But he had been in a remarkable mood the past few days, and outbursts were not his style. I was also not one to pry and knew he would come forward with whatever information he was withholding when he felt ready to. If it had something to do with the safety of the pack, he would have told me by now.

"I don't think we should send more people East River," Kota said, breaking the silence. "At least, not for now."

"Oh? Want to expound on that?" It was an idea that had been playing around in my mind, but if I wasn't the only one thinking about it, maybe the thought held some merit.

Kota picked up a pen and twirled it between his fingers. "Your mate had a good idea to buy us some time. It's reasonable to assume their primary motive is getting their hands on her, and they will probably hang around until she makes an appearance."

"Lya isn't going back there," I insisted. That was non-negotiable. There was no way I'd put her in harm's way.

Kota held up his hand to stop my train of thought. "I'm not saying she actually shows up there. But maybe we could do something to convince them she'd be back there at a particular time."

I nodded slowly. "That might draw even more hunters in for back-up, too."

"Possibly," Kota muttered. "Depends how many they would think it'd take to collect her. But the more wolves there, the less likely they'll hang around."

"So, how do we guarantee the most hunters get drawn in as possible?" I asked. If we were going to set up to take out as many hunters as possible, we needed to make sure they'd be there. This whole endeavor wasn't worth just a couple.

Kota gave me a sly grin. "Lya and I came up with some ideas."

I cocked an eyebrow. "Should I be worried about you spending time with my mate without me around?"

"You better get used to it," he chuckled. "She will be Luna, you know. That's going to require a lot of communication with male pack members."

I grimaced, annoyed that he was right.

"How do you deal with it?" I asked. "I mean, Ellie is a warrior, and a solid seventy percent of the warriors are men. And she's a flirt."

"I don't, not anymore," Kota huffed, reaching for the bottle of Woodford he kept stashed in his desk drawer. "She cheated on me. I'm going to reject her."

My eyes grew wide, stunned that a fated mate would do something like that. It wasn't unheard of with chosen mates, but fated mates were a different ballgame. His foul mood made sense now.

"I'm surprised it took this long for her to do something like that, to be honest," he admitted, taking a swig directly from the bottle. "Betcha it was that guy who decided to let her train the high schoolers."

"How do you know?" I asked, hoping he was mistaken and Ellie's behavior had simply gotten out of hand.

"You can feel it, man," Kota scoffed. "It's like someone's got a vice grip around your heart and is slowly squeezing harder and harder."

I sighed, scrubbing my hand across my face. "I don't know what to say." I grabbed the offered bottle from him and took a drink.

"I was dumb for not realizing it was coming," he said with a shrug. "No mate for me, I guess."

I stood and made my way to the door. "Just let me know when you need some time. I've heard rejecting hurts."

"Can't hurt any more than feeling her fuck another guy," he jeered, taking another pull of whiskey. "And we don't have time for me to take a break. I've got enough to distract me for now."

I made sure to close the door behind me. In light of Kota's experiences with his mate, it seemed as if I needed to have a conversation with my own.

TWENTY-TWO

Lya

THE BOOK I had found on my bed was interesting, to say the least. It had been wrapped in an old cloth, and the warmth under my skin when I skimmed my hand over the cover confirmed it was embossed with silver. Given it seemed to be a book about werewolves, and we had a sensitivity to silver, that was a peculiar choice. I wondered if it was filled with information they didn't want just anyone reading.

I hadn't gotten much into the book—having barely read the introduction of the Wulver Pack, its location, and when it came into existence—when there was a knock on the door. I went over to open it, not at all surprised to find Oliver was on the other side.

'*Lya, mate!*' Tala piped up. I rolled my eyes at her. Ever since I had chastised her for not telling me Oliver was our mate, she had made a point of announcing it every time we saw him. It was getting annoying.

'*I get it, now leave me alone,*' I growled, frustrated by her nagging.

'*But mate! Mate is right there!*'

"Hi," Oliver said with a lopsided boyish grin. "Am I interrupting something?"

"Depends on who you ask," I huffed. I couldn't help it, my eyes raked over him. His blue t-shirt struggled to contain his muscles, and it was drool-worthy. "Do you need something?"

Oliver shrugged. "It's getting late. I figured it was time for bed."

I raised my eyebrows. Sure, he'd spent every night here recently, but was that really necessary? "Don't you have your own room?"

"I mean, I'll be back in here when your night terrors start up, but if you'd prefer..." He turned to leave, making it a few feet down the hall.

Some sort of sound caught in my throat, causing him to turn back and look questioningly at me. I opened the door a little wider, relishing in his smile as he walked back toward me. He caught my hand in his, dragging me over to the bed with him.

I couldn't stand this. Why did he have the power to turn me into putty in his hands?

'*Well, mate. Duh,*' Tala piped up. I didn't humor her with a response, focusing on the static electricity on steroids zapping between us.

I perched on the edge of the bed, not quite willing to get too close. "Are my night terrors really that bad still?"

"It's normal, Lya," Oliver insisted, sprawling out on his side of the bed–when did we develop designated sides of the bed?–and lacing his fingers behind his head. "It's your brain's defense mechanism. We have professionals at the hospital you could talk to at any time if you so choose."

I scrunched up my nose but decided to return to the book I was trying to read.

Oliver sat up, scooting over to where I was, which had been as far away from him as I could get. "Are you liking the book?"

"I don't know, I haven't really had the chance to read much," I said point-edly. I closed the book, taking a moment to look at the intricacies of the cover. Oliver held his hand out for it, but as soon as it hit his skin, he hissed, drop-ping it quickly.

"Careful! It's old!" I reached for his hand, examining the welts that quickly developed where his skin came in contact with the silver emboss-ment. "Will my sensitivity to silver get worse the more in touch with my wolf I get?"

Oliver kept his eyes closely on me as I reached down to retrieve the book from the floor. He flinched when I picked it up, but all I felt was a warm sensation.

"No, I don't think so," he said quietly. "Does that silver seriously not bother you at all?"

I shrugged. "It feels a little warm. I imagine if I left my hand on it for a while it would get itchy or zingy, kind of like when I'd wear the silver bracelet or earrings for long periods of time."

"Interesting," Oliver said slowly, like he was trying to taste every letter of the word. "I wonder how you would react to wolfsbane. Let me know if that comes up in the book."

"Why would it be in the book?" I asked. "It's just about some pack over in Scotland. Although, it's the region of Scotland my dad's side of the family is from, which is kind of cool. How did you know that?"

A small smile flitted across Oliver's lips. "We're trying to get some more information on that pack, trying to connect some dots. Speaking of, my grandmother wants to talk to you more about that."

I furrowed my eyebrows. "What's so important about this pack, though? Aren't there a bunch of packs around?"

"Usually, it wouldn't matter, but this is one we don't know much about yet. You're what we'd call a rogue, by the way, given that you aren't in a pack. Until you join mine, anyway," he said with a smirk.

"What makes you so certain I'll join your pack?" I chided, even though I knew I would. The possessive look was adorable on him, so I continued. "Maybe I like this whole rogue thing. No responsibility, no one to tell me what to do."

"Trust me." Oliver reached out, snaking his arm around my waist. He pushed me down onto the bed, caging me in with his arms as he moved to hover over me. "If I have it my way, you will."

His lips crashed down on mine, greedy and demanding. I turned away, giggling, and rolled out from under him. "Oh, no, Mr. Alpha, I'm not about to give up all this independence I so recently discovered. I'm a lone wolf until I decide otherwise."

I picked the book up and moved to rest against the headboard. I felt the bed move but refused to take my eyes off the pages. Oliver's arm came around me, pulling me against him, and he placed featherlight kisses along my neck.

"What do I have to do to convince you?" His voice was dark and husky and hard to resist.

"I-I'll think about it," I stuttered.

Oliver settled in with his chin resting on my shoulder, reading over me. Occasionally, he'd ask me to wait to turn a page, and I could tell he read faster than me when his lips found their way to my skin, which only made me read slower.

I could get used to this.

Tala purred in contentment, but the way she was flitting around, I could tell she was trying to reach out to Adair. I wondered how it worked for our wolves. Did they have their own way of communicating, or did they rely on their human counterparts to pass on messages, like a game of telephone? None of the books I had found talked much about mates, so I didn't know a lot about them other than what Rose, Allyssa, and Marjorie had told me.

"Is what Kota and Ellie are like normal for mates?" I found myself asking after a good half-hour of very distracted reading.

"No," Oliver said quickly. "I have honestly never even heard of mates being like that. Gregory and Allyssa are normal."

I thought of them dancing in the kitchen a couple mornings ago while their kids ate breakfast before school. Every time I saw the two of them together, they seemed so happily in love, even twenty something years and three and a half kids later. Gregory was so reverent of Allyssa, and Allyssa clearly cherished him. The thought of that being my future with a mate filled me with warmth, and made the idea seem less scary than it had been.

"What's wrong with Kota and Ellie, then?" I continued, still not able to get a hold on my brain's programming to latch onto the bad.

Oliver leaned back to lie down, pulling me with him. "I don't know. But he told me today he's planning on rejecting her."

"That would explain his mood," I mused. "Did your grandmother reject her mate for a reason like that?"

"What?" he snapped. "My grandmother would not have rejected her mate."

"Y-you didn't know?" I sat up and looked at him. The look on his face made me feel guilty for divulging some dark family secret. "Ollie, I'm sorry, I didn't mean—"

Oliver reached up and pulled me back down to him. He kissed me again, but this time it was slow, with a passion that simmered just beneath the surface.

"I don't let many people call me Ollie," he murmured, placing another kiss on the corner of my mouth. "But to answer your question, my grandmother can be a very scary woman. If she rejected her mate, it wouldn't have been because he acted like Ellie. I don't think anyone would have dared to treat her like that."

I snuggled down into the pillow, keeping my eyes on Oliver. Tala let out a contented hum, and for once, I had to agree with her. The quiet and peace of this moment was something I wanted to hold on to forever.

For a brief moment, I wondered if I would have changed the way I approached the whole wolf thing if I had known this was what life could have been like. But I had other people to hold responsible for not having access to this. I was pretty certain my own father was a werewolf, for crying out loud. I had talked to him a couple times after he saw me shift. He could have made sure I knew, but he made no attempts to fill me in.

And then, the nagging acceptance of fate crept in. How in the world would I have ever ended up here if things had been managed correctly?

OLIVER

AS LYA SLEPT SOUNDLY, I reached to brush a strand of hair away from her face. I was about to drift off myself when my phone vibrated against the nightstand, jolting me from my thoughts. I reached over and grabbed it before the sound could wake her. I groaned, noticing it was an incoming call, and not one I felt like I could refuse. I got up from the bed, quietly making my way out of her room.

"Hey, man," I greeted, keeping my voice low and closing the door as quietly as possible. Lya wasn't historically a light sleeper, but I tiptoed to my office anyway. "Make it quick."

"Am I interrupting something?" My brother chuckled.

"No, Lya has night terrors."

Thom cleared his throat. "Right. Mate bonds are the cure for all maladies."

I could hear the sorrow in his voice. I knew he was happy with his life now, but I imagined the pain of losing your fated never quite went away.

"Trevor called. Heard things aren't shaping up too well."

"On which front?" I scoffed.

"Fair point."

I scrubbed my hand over my face, trying to focus. "It sounds like it's going to be exactly like twelve years ago, and with how connected Trevor is to that, I am fucking furious with him for getting us into this mess."

"I don't think you can blame him for this, actually," Thom said slowly. "I don't think they want anything to do with the pack, just your girl. Trevor was in the wrong place at the wrong time."

"What makes you think that?" I snapped. Trevor was the one who set out to replay this whole game of cat and mouse with the hunters, and I wanted, needed, to place blame on someone.

"Think about it, Ollie," he chided. "We are naturally drawn to our mates, however far they are. It makes sense that she'd be migrating in a direction closer to you, and that guy followed her here."

I sat back against the overstuffed chair, pondering his comment. It made sense, and deep down, I already knew that. It hurt that my mate would be the subject of a hunt across the country.

"Why her, though? There are tons of other wolves out there for them to choose from."

Thom barked out a dry laugh. "The Wulver clan is small. They are hard to come by, and they are very, very good at not being found. That meeting in Maine ten years ago, Ollie. It was about her. Packs caught wind of how her dad was hiding her, and they wanted to step in. Just as the pack in Maine was about to make a move, her father did what Wulvers do best and disappeared with her. To be honest, I'm surprised it took hunters this long to find her."

"Wait, you knew the Wulver pack was still around?" I asked, puzzled that he had that information and I didn't.

Thom grunted in confirmation. "This is a conversation for another time. I'll be back in a couple days. Make sure my room is ready for me, will ya?"

Thom ended the call, leaving me to sit alone in my dark office, lost in thought. And like it was yesterday, I was back on that stormy, pebbly beach on the midcoast of Maine. It wasn't a trip I had been invited on, but I insisted on going. I was newly eighteen and took every opportunity to get out of the pack in hopes of finding my mate. I had this gut feeling she'd be there.

The agreement was that I could tag along, but I wasn't allowed in any of the meetings. Those were exclusively for the Alphas and Lunas. As my older brother was the Alpha-to-be of the Snow Moon Pack, he was allowed to join. But me? I may have been of Alpha blood, but due to birth order, I was a nobody. That was exactly how, on an overcast late May morning, I found myself sitting on a stoney beach behind a restaurant that was technically still closed for the off season, throwing rocks into the Atlantic Ocean, while the rest of my family sat inside discussing an issue I wasn't privy to.

I looked down the beach and spotted a figure walking toward me. The grayness of the day made her long, auburn hair stand out, the wind causing it to swirl around her in an almost mystical way. I didn't think she'd noticed my presence as she made her way closer to me. The girl seemed lost in thought, smiling to herself and humming a tune I didn't recognize.

Another gust of wind from behind the girl pushed the heady scent of the nearby lilac bushes pine forest toward me, along with the unmistakable scent of wolf. As she got closer, it was clear she carried the overwhelming smell with her. I wondered if maybe she had recently gone for a run in the woods, and the smell clung to her. I wondered if someone had devised how to turn that smell into a perfume or a candle, and where I could buy it. It caused Adair to stir, insistent on us getting closer.

She very nearly tripped over the driftwood log I sat on, only noticing me when she looked up, shocked out of whatever thoughts were consuming her. I stood to help her up, but she rebalanced quickly. She looked up at me, bright amber eyes exuding her innocence. She was young, and I wanted to wrap her up and protect her from all the dangers of our world. My wolf preened under her gaze, and I could tell he was reaching out trying to sense hers.

"Hi!" the girl chirped. "I'm sorry, I didn't see you."

I smiled down at her, catching myself trying to make constellations out of the freckles smattered across her face. She was a child, and as such, too good for this dark world.

"There's a better view over there," she said, motioning further down the beach. "You can walk with me, if you'd like."

I nodded, stuffing my hands in my pockets as I followed her. She was too young; I wouldn't dare reach out to feel the sparks I knew would be there. Adair didn't push, which made me think maybe my assessment was wrong. But her scent, the overwhelming desire to stay by her side, this need to keep her safe—it had to be. She was a child, and maybe Adair recognized that. No mate bond could surface for years yet.

"Are you part of the Strawberry Moon Pack?" I stumbled over my feet as much as I stumbled over my words. I couldn't take my eyes off of her, even if hers remained locked on the ocean before us.

"What?" She giggled. "I mean, the strawberry moon isn't until June, and my birthday is in June. How did you know?"

I shook my head, brushing off the question I had asked. Clearly, she wasn't a member of the local pack. Maybe her parents hadn't familiarized her with the packs in this area yet. Strawberry Moon was the only one, but it was prominent across the nation. The secluded location and unique landscape made it a place our kind flocked to.

"Rogue, then?" She didn't smell like a rogue.

She furrowed her eyebrows. The frown lines didn't suit her angelic face. "My mom always says I should do better at following rules, I guess."

I sat down on the outcropping of rocks she had led us to, careful to keep some distance.

"This is my favorite place," she sighed. "I'm moving this weekend, though."

"Oh?" My heart panged at the thought of not knowing where she would be. "Where to?"

She shrugged her shoulders. "Some place down south. Dad said it wasn't working out around here, and he got a job somewhere else."

We sat in silence for a while, staring out at the ocean. With the way she looked at it, I prayed she would be able to see it wherever she ended up. I had so many questions, and no idea what to ask at the same time.

"How old are you?" I finally settled on. It seemed better than asking how long I had to wait to find her again.

"Fourteen," she announced. "My birthday is in a month, though. I've heard a big change is supposed to happen when I turn fifteen."

If innocence and slyness could team together, that was the look she shot at me. I chuckled, certain her wolf had told her that was when she would first shift.

Three years and one month. In three years and one month, I would track her down. Adair rumbled in approval, and that was all the confirmation I needed that my suspicions were correct, even if he had stayed mostly silent.

She stood, turning back down the beach, without so much as a goodbye.

"Hey, wait!" I called after her. "What's your name?"

The girl turned, flashing me a devious smile. "I'm Lya. I'll see you some-day, Oliver."

"Lya," I repeated, committing the name to memory as I watched her walk away.

Three years and one month later, I was still in the throes of mourning my parents' deaths a year prior, tangled up in the sheets with a she-wolf who had lost her mate in the same battle I lost my father. I felt it; I felt her wolf reach out, searching for her mate. I felt the pang of betrayal as her wolf pulled away, refusing to let her human feel that pain. Adair had done his best to shield the memory of her from me, but the infiltrating presence brought it all back. My eyes snapped open, pulling away from the woman, as I let Adair try and follow that link, trying to grasp for a name long since forgotten in the corners of my mind. But she was gone.

The door pushed open, the dim light of the hallway leaking into the room and pulling me from my memories.

"Ollie?" a familiar voice croaked.

"Lya," I breathed, striding over to her. I reached out, pulling my mate to me, and crushed my lips down on hers.

Twenty-Three

Lya

I BLINKED MY EYES OPEN, praying to whatever was out there that it was morning. Sleep hadn't come easily, and I hoped with everything in me that it'd be late enough to start the day, but only moonlight seeped in from the windows. I reached across the bed for the familiar warmth I had relied on whenever I woke up the past few nights, but nothing was there. I sat up, looking around. It slowly hit me that I was alone. While I wished for that when I was awake, it was something I dreaded overnight.

I understood exactly why. He was my mate, whether I wanted him or not, and a part of me would always need him. But I did want him. I wanted all of him. Even if I didn't want to admit it to anyone yet.

I stumbled out of bed, following the smell of an incoming rainstorm down the hall.

I opened the door, breathing in as his scent wafted toward me.

"Ollie?" I asked hesitantly, hoping he wouldn't turn me away for intruding.

"Lya." He said my name as a reverent whisper. He was on his feet and in front of me in an instant, wrapping me in his arms. His lips pressed against mine, expressing a hunger I had refused to admit to myself.

I moaned against his lips as he backed me up to the wall next to the door.

187

He took advantage, his tongue slipping between my lips and tangling with my own. I reached up and fisted my fingers in his hair, arching my chest into him, pushing myself as close to him as I could get.

"Don't leave me again," he murmured against my lips as his hands traced lower down my hips, hoisting me up to pin me against the wall.

I wrapped my legs around his waist, holding him to me. I smiled against his lips but refused to make a promise I couldn't keep. For now, though, I was here. I was all here.

His teeth grazed against my neck, making me shiver. "Wrap up."

I locked my arms around his neck as he secured his hands at the back of my thighs. He kicked the door open further, making his way back down the hall with me hanging off of him by his mouth. The next thing I knew, I was being pressed against a soft mattress and his hands were slipping up under the oversized shirt I had worn to bed. I was fairly certain the shirt was his; it was one I had found on my floor one morning, and stashed away because it smelled like him.

Hands slipped down, trailing closer and closer to the apex of my thighs. I moaned his name as his lips left mine, exploring the skin along my neck and collarbone. I struggled with the shirt that clung to him, wanting it off. We separated long enough for him to tear it off, allowing my hands to freely roam his chest. He growled, tugging me into a sitting position to peel my, or his, shirt off of me.

His hands returned to my skin, pushing me back down onto the bed, leaving an absolutely addicting sense of fireworks in their wake. His mouth wrapped around my breast, taking a nipple in his teeth. I hitched a leg around him, grinding my hips into his. I could feel his length pulsing against me, confirming I wasn't the only one desperate for this.

A thumb hooked in the band of my underwear. He lifted up off of me, looking me in the eye, hands frozen.

"Tell me," he breathed. "Tell me what you want."

"I want you, Oliver," I whined. And I truly meant that. I wanted him. Not just physically, not just in this moment. I wanted my mate.

He smirked down at me, and my underwear was shredded. He pulled away, tearing away his own pants, but he was quick to press back down into me. His shaft pressed against my wet folds, giving away how much I wanted him. For a second, I was mortified at the fact that absolutely no pregaming was necessary when he had his hands on me. His tip pressing against my entrance quickly eradicated that thought. He stayed still, breathing against the crook of my neck. The sensation sent shivers throughout my body, awakening a whole new feeling. I mewled, grinding against him.

"You're mine," he growled, lips crashing down on mine once more as he plunged into me.

And I agreed.

His hips rocked back and forth, and my body quickly found a rhythm with his. With each thrust, I felt the tension in my core growing more taut. I wasn't new to this. It wasn't like I had sat around waiting for my 'one and only' to come along. But this was the first time I had felt like my wolf was present with me. And maybe that's why, the closer I got to orgasm, the more evident the new feeling became. He pulled out, nearly to the tip, and as he thrust back in, I felt myself toppling closer to the edge.

I tried not to think about the fact that my gums were tingling more and more with each thrust. He already had me crumbling to pieces quicker than I ever had before; I didn't need him giving my orgasms even more tantalizing sensations, even if I was fairly certain I'd never climax with anyone else ever again.

"Mine," he rumbled again.

"Oliver," I gasped, breath hitching in my throat. Canines punctured through my gums. My eyes rolled back, and I curled around him, my entire body shaking. My teeth sank down, puncturing the skin right where his neck met his shoulder, crushing through tissue and muscle, and try as I might, I couldn't pull back.

As I pulled my teeth out, a surge of energy that put the tingles, sparks, and fireworks to shame rushed through me. Something in my mind opened up, like a door to a part of my brain I didn't know existed had been unlocked. A rush of emotions that mimicked my own, but were not mine, flooded me. I gasped, collapsing back on the bed.

The rumbling in Oliver's chest grew to a roar as he found his release too, collapsing on top of me. Our breathing was heavy. I was recovering from the best orgasm of my life, fated to never climax again. I could only hope he felt somewhere close to the same.

Oliver leaned his head down, forehead pressed against mine, panting heavily. "You-you marked me."

"I... what?" I sat up, confused by what he said. "What did I do?"

I could feel the smile as he pressed his lips to mine. "You gave me a mate mark."

My hands shook, worried that I had done something wrong. I reached up and stroked the impression of my wolf's teeth that was somehow already healing. "I'm sorry."

"That's not something you need to apologize for." Oliver chuckled, placing a kiss in the same place on me. He rolled over beside me and pulled me to his chest. "I hope you let me mark you someday."

I nodded against him. I wasn't completely certain what I had done, nor the significance of it. It hadn't even felt like it was something I had done. It was more like Tala took over and just... bit him. Why would she bite him? I thought she adored him?

There was a contented purr resounding in my head. It wasn't Tala, and it most definitely wasn't me. I was plenty happy, but I didn't purr. That was an animal thing. I looked up at Oliver a little shocked. "Do I hear Adair?"

Oliver nodded slowly. "You should be able to feel how I feel, too."

He smiled down at my expression, probably understanding my worry that he could feel how I felt, too. "Don't worry, I haven't marked you. I don't have the same privileges... yet."

I nodded, contemplating that idea. Maybe marking him wasn't a great thing like he seemed to think it was. It didn't seem reversible. What if something happened, and we ended up not being compatible? Would I be stuck feeling his emotions forever?

But, at the same time, he was mine, and that was all I wanted.

"We can talk about it more tomorrow," Oliver insisted. "For now, sleep."

I took his advice, wanting to turn my brain off at this point and focus on the incomparable bliss I'd experienced.

OLIVER

LYA MARKED ME.

I didn't think she realized what she had done, but I was ecstatic. You could only mark your fated mate, which meant that at least some part of her knew I was made for her. I would deal with the repercussions of that tomorrow. For now, I got to hold her.

I knew without a shadow of a doubt, there was absolutely no going back now. If she decided to leave, I would die a lonely man, unable to find someone to fill the void created by her loss. But now that she had marked me, leaving would be nearly impossible for her.

As much as I was proud to bear her mark, if I had known that might have happened, I wouldn't have let her. She deserved that option. If she decided she didn't want this, want us, I'd do everything in my power to fix it for her, even if it killed me.

Mate bonds sucked.

Morning came too soon, the buzzing of an alarm startling me out of sleep I hadn't realized I had fallen into. Lya's back was pressed against my chest, and I had an arm draped over her waist. I looked around, realizing I had taken us to my room instead of hers. Given Thom would be returning, I wondered if, maybe, she'd decide to stay in here with me instead of relocating to another room. Realistically, I could easily put Thom in a different room, but I was going to try my luck at getting her in my—our—bed, in our room.

I detangled myself from Lya and the sheets, leaving her to sleep while I went off to make coffee. I leaned against the counter, waiting for it to brew, and waved absently at Anna as she walked through the kitchen. I quickly did a double take when I realized who I saw.

Anna scrunched her nose at me. "You should really wear a shirt. If I can't walk around topless, neither should you."

"You're back! What brought you home early?" I asked.

Anna shrugged, walking over and snagging the pot of coffee to fill her own mug. "Dad called and said to get back sooner than later."

She turned and squinted her eyes at me. Specifically, at my mark. "Is that..."

I nodded, unable to keep the smile from my face. "You'll like her. Lya will make an amazing Luna."

Anna sighed. "I had really hoped to have met my mate by now."

I chuckled, reaching past her to grab two mugs of coffee. I dropped a peck on her forehead before making my way out of the kitchen. "You'd be surprised by the curveballs the Goddess throws. Trevor might be back this weekend, by the way."

"Great," she spat sarcastically, adding an eye roll for extra emphasis.

Lya was sitting up, wearing my shirt from the night before. She reached out for a mug, sighing with her first sip. I settled back in bed beside her, doing my best to memorize the details of her face. I smiled softly when she looked up at me.

"Do you want to go for a run today?" I asked tentatively.

Lya furrowed her eyebrows. "In wolf form?"

"Yes, spending more time in wolf form is important." And it would give our wolves a chance to formally meet. "I have a meeting in a few minutes, but after that?"

She nodded slowly, nibbling on her lower lip. I leaned over, kissing the corner of her mouth delicately, then headed off to get a shower.

Lya was gone by the time I came out of the bathroom. I carefully chose a shirt that would hide my mark for the day, not wanting to show it off until she understood what it was. Kota and Gregory were already waiting in my office, Trevor on the monitor.

"No Luna today?" Trevor asked with a sly grin.

I shook my head. "Can we loop Thom in on this call?"

Kota gave me a puzzled look but walked over to the computer and sent the meeting information to him. A couple minutes later, he joined as well.

"Thom, could you share your justification as to why you think this hunter situation has nothing to do with the pack and everything to do with Lya?" I asked, forgoing a greeting.

"Well, hello to you, too, brother," he joked. "But yes. Ten years ago, our parents included me in a meeting with several other Alphas and Lunas. This would have been shortly after Gregory took over as Beta, before you came to the pack, Kota. And Trevor, obviously, you were still a kid. This meeting was regarding a half-blood wolf pup who was intentionally being raised as if werewolves were not a thing."

Kota sat up a little straighter. "And you think that pup was Lya," he clarified. "What would make you think that?"

"I can confirm they were discussing Lya," I said darkly.

"And what makes you so sure?" Kota challenged.

"Because I saw her there."

"Wait," Trevor said slowly. "Was this when you came back from Maine freaking out that you thought you met your mate and she was some fourteen year old kid?"

I nodded slowly. Trevor and Kota were the only people I had told about her, absolutely positive I must have been wrong. I had tried desperately to put the memory out of my head, convinced that I couldn't feel any semblance of a mate bond for a child. Even if, at that time, it was the need to protect her.

Trevor shrugged his shoulders. "I knew I was right. Lya would have just gotten her wolf, still lived in Maine."

Thom cleared his throat, wordlessly asking for everyone's attention so he could continue. "The pup in discussion was such a high priority concern that required Alphas and Lunas from across the country to meet at her closest known location because she's a Wulver, and the Wulver Pack has historically provided too much assistance that all concerns need to be handled carefully.

We don't exactly want to piss them off, especially when they have never asked for anything in return."

"And we have confirmed that Lya is from the Wulver Pack, as well," I added.

Kota and Trevor looked at me in confusion while Gregory sat in the background with a knowing smile.

"But the Wulver Pack is dead," Trevor stated.

"No," Gregory said slowly. "They are not. The Wulver Pack is interesting because they have no territory and live as nomads, usually amidst humans, ever since they fled from their territory in Scotland so long ago. While we may also hold them responsible for the development of hunters because they lived so seamlessly among the local towns once upon a time, they are the pack most widely revered for clinging to a werewolf's purpose on this earth. They protected locals from both supernatural and natural threats, taught hunting skills, and were looked to as healers."

"Yes, we have all heard the legends," Trevor huffed. "But then hunters decided to band together, take them out, and they were killed off."

"Oh, no," Gregory said. "The Goddess gifted them with the ability to evolve quickly because of their work to uphold goodness and protect this earth's inhabitants. They are resistant to most things that would harm a werewolf, most famously silver. I had my suspicions when you told me Lya had been shot with silver bullets, and she made such a quick recovery."

"So, then, why didn't they integrate into another pack when they fled?" Trevor asked. "Wouldn't that have been safest?"

"For them, yes, but the Wulvers were not going to turn their backs on their morals and let the blessing of the Goddess go to waste. They dispersed, and they can now be found, if you look carefully, all over the globe, taking out hunters, keeping vampires in check, removing serial killers from the populace, and hunting for areas going through famine. Much more, too." Having said his peace, Gregory sat back, giving us a moment to digest the information. I had heard bits and pieces before, but having it all laid out linearly helped it make more sense. They were, after all, only a legend.

Trevor shifted around, looking as if he was trying to find the words to phrase his question. "So, then, why not go to the Wulver Pack Alpha and bring up the concern that someone was breaking werewolf law with how they were raising a pup?"

Thom shook his head. "That wasn't an option because the child was the daughter of their Alpha."

Kota visibly stiffened, grinding his teeth.

"And that's not to say Lya is of Alpha blood," Gregory jumped in. "The Wulver Pack chooses their Alpha. It is not inherited."

"Exactly," Thom agreed. "The meeting was to try and figure out how to reach out to the rest of the Wulver Pack so we could convince them to name a new Alpha. That way, we could simply go to the new Alpha and hedge our complaint, instead of doing something like kidnap and properly integrate her, which would also break werewolf law. But then they disappeared."

I sat back, debating whether or not nine in the morning was too early for scotch.

"And why is this the first I am hearing of this pack being real?" I demanded. "Especially given how much mercenary work our pack does."

"To be fair, most everyone was in the same boat until that pack in Maine called the meeting," Thom said with a shrug.

"I assume, in order for them to remain as successful as they are, they must remain in the shadows," Kota grumbled.

I whirled around, looking at Gregory. "How do you know so much about them, then?"

Gregory gave a sly smile but made no effort to explain himself.

Trevor cleared his throat, pulling my attention away from the daggers I shot toward Gregory. "So, we have enough background to assume they are only after Lya, and given the circumstances that she and Ted came to be together, they intentionally sought her out. But why her?"

The question ping-ponged around my brain, only settling on worst-case scenarios.

"Regardless of the why, I believe this changes our approach to the whole situation," I said slowly. "Trevor, take your time getting back here, and make sure you aren't followed. The handful of scouts we have over there now should stay to keep us apprised of the situation. Warriors should be pulled out over the next couple of weeks."

Kota nodded in agreement. "We make no moves on the hunters until we have a better plan."

"I think we need to find more folks from her pack."

Twenty-Four

Lya

I DRAGGED myself out of the training ground. Three more hours of grueling work for the second day in a row had been tough. Yeah, I was pretty athletic, but this was a whole different ball game than kickboxing a couple times a week.

"You're better than I thought," Kota said with a pat on the back. "Whatever your cousins taught you was pretty good."

I smiled sheepishly. "I haven't seen them in a few years at this point. Maybe if I ever see them again, I can kick their asses instead of them pulverizing me."

He cocked an eyebrow at me. "Whose side of your family were they on?"

"My dad's," I answered, a little confused by the question. "They made sure to stay in touch even after he hightailed it."

Kota nodded slowly but made no attempts to cue me in on his thoughts. "Tomorrow, wolf form."

I looked up at him a little shocked. "I-I'm not sure how reliably I can shift."

He shrugged. "Gotta figure it out sometime, kid." He turned, walking back toward the training grounds. I ever so slowly started the long walk back toward the packhouse.

A little red Corolla pulled up next to me, rolling down the window. "Need a ride?" Rose laughed with a sly grin.

I pulled open the door and flopped down in the passenger seat with a groan. I had been starting to look forward to a run with Oliver, but at this point, I was absolutely dreading it. I was absolutely beat, figuratively and literally.

"Are you feeling okay?" Rose gave me a concerned look. "Do you need to go get checked out? You could still be healing."

"No!" I quickly snapped, cutting her off.

"Then what's going on? You were exhausted when we worked on shifting, too."

I glanced over at her. "Can you keep a secret?"

Rose chewed on her lip. "Oliver isn't usually one to give commands like that, so probably."

I rolled my eyes. I had read about the Alpha command. It seemed like a thing that could easily be abused. "As Luna, can I ask that you keep this secret?"

Rose's eyes lit up. "I like the way you think!"

I wasn't sure how well this tactic would hold up. From what I'd read, I wouldn't get the power to command until I was officially Luna, so I hoped Oliver was a good enough guy to not pull out a dick move like using the Alpha command on his own pack members.

"I started training with Kota yesterday," I said hesitantly. "We figured with whatever is coming, I need to be as prepared as possible."

Rose lifted her eyebrows. "Behind Oliver's back?" I nodded in confirmation. "You guys are going to get in a lot of trouble when he finds out."

"It's only another few days he needs to not find out," I sighed. "I think we can keep it under wraps for five more days."

Rose pulled up to the packhouse. "Your secret is safe with me, but I am warning you to be careful."

"I'll do my best," I agreed, getting out of the car.

I trudged up the steps to the packhouse, Rose close behind, desperate to find food. I must have not been paying much attention, because as I was pulling the door open, I ran into someone. I looked up, a little shocked, ready to apologize. I knew I was new here, and I was a far cry from knowing everyone, but I recognized everyone who seemed to frequent the packhouse. This person was decidedly not a packhouse regular.

"Hi!" the girl said excitedly. "You must be Lya! Do you want to join us for lunch?"

I looked at her quizzically. She was quite a bit taller than me, but that wasn't hard. She was the spitting image of Allyssa, with the same dark brunette hair and hazel green eyes.

"Are you Anna?" I asked cautiously.

The girl smiled broadly. "I got back last night. My dad told me we had a visitor at the house. This is so exciting! What pack are you from?"

My head reeled at the bombardment of questions. This girl was way too perky and cheerful. I didn't know how long I could stand it. "I, uh, I actually didn't grow up in a pack."

Anna hooked her arm through mine and dragged me back down the porch steps. "Well, it's good you came for a visit. I'm so happy Ollie finally found his mate! You know, I used to dream about being his mate. I can guarantee I'm not the only girl in this pack who cried on their eighteenth birthday when we figured out we weren't his."

"I was going to meet Oliver for a run," I told her, trying to pull away.

"He's in a meeting with the Gamma from Wyoming. It hasn't been going great, so I'm sure he won't mind if I steal you for a little while," she enthused.

I nodded and allowed myself to be pulled toward her car. I didn't say much during the car ride, letting her and Rose catch up. It would seem they were old friends. We pulled into a parking spot in front of Lucy's and made our way inside.

Rose leaned in toward us, keeping her voice low and nodding her head toward Lucy behind the counter. "Do we want to go somewhere else?"

"Nonsense!" Anna insisted. "They're marked! Lucy's shit out of luck, and I have missed the food here."

Rose looked at me, eyes wide. "You two marked each other? That's so great!"

I shook my head slowly. To be honest, I was planning on having a panic attack about this with Rose around to talk me down, but I didn't know this Anna character. I didn't want to divulge my secrets to her.

Rose furrowed her brows, studying me for a moment. "Then how does he have a mark and you don't?"

"I didn't really realize I did it until after," I grumbled.

Anna's lighthearted giggle tinkled across the restaurant. "Heat of the moment, right? I wonder how he was able to hold it together and not mark you."

I tried not to let it show how much her offhand comment bothered me. But it added credence to my thought that maybe he didn't care about me. I mean, wouldn't I have a mark if he did? I did my best to shove the thought from my head, participating in the lunch conversation as much as I could. Luckily, the conversation quickly drifted away from whatever it was that Oliver and I were or were not.

Lucy stopped by the table a couple times to check on how we were doing, something she notably didn't do with other tables, and asked Anna pointed questions about how "Ollie" was doing, causing Tala and me to bristle. The two were quick to deflect her comments, assuring her that "Alpha Oliver" would not be free that night, and no, he was not starting to look for a chosen mate.

I was all too ready to leave when Anna and Rose finally decided they had finished their lunch. They were old friends, and I felt like a third wheel. I gladly took the back seat and tried to fade into the background on the drive back to the packhouse. I quickly scrambled out of the car, dismissing myself for a nap, and left the girls to continue doing whatever lifelong girlfriends did. Given my hour or so of experience, I realized it wasn't intriguing enough to supersede my introverted ways.

I flopped down face-first on my bed, feeling more exhausted now than right after training with Kota. Groups of friends were not a thing I was vastly familiar with. In my previous life, sure, there were people I'd grab a drink with every once in a while, but we were never close. Getting close to me had been dangerous. It was going to take a while to get used to the fact that was not the case anymore.

I was drifting off to sleep when the door creaked open. I smiled into the pillow as his familiar scent wafted around me like a warm hug. I laughed to myself at the thought of a rainstorm being akin to a warm hug, but to me, it was. The bed dipped under his weight, and I felt an arm around my waist pulling me against his hard chest.

"I heard you got to meet Anna today," Oliver said, his breath tickling the nape of my neck.

I nodded, still trying to pull myself out of my brush with sleep.

His chuckle rumbled against my back. "I am sorry. You don't strike me as the sort that handles constant sunshine and daisies very well. But Trevor should be back soon, and they'll be distracted enough by each other."

And in that moment, it struck me how little I knew about Oliver. How little he had told me, anyway. Sure, I'd heard some stories here and there, but he hadn't told me any of the important, monumental tidbits. Part of me wondered how much those really mattered in learning who someone was. Maybe the little things, how they were day to day, what they decided was worth remembering and repeating, were more important.

All I really knew was somehow, in the past couple of weeks, this guy had seen all sides of me. He held me while I cried, broke down my walls and made me laugh, gave me a home and community and friends, and convinced me I was worthy of feeling things I had previously always thought I didn't deserve. He made me happy, and I did a piss poor job of showing him that.

But I trusted him with my life.

And I loved him.

Even if he didn't love me.

"Hey, Oliver," I whispered, my voice hazy with sleep.

"Yes, love?"

I tried not to let the term of endearment distract me. That's all it was, right? Just a term of endearment, not a confession.

"What was it like growing up here?"

OLIVER

LYA'S QUESTION shocked me a little. I didn't expect it to be so innocent. I was prepared and willing to divulge all my deepest, darkest secrets to her, and she just wanted to hear about my childhood. The conversations twenty questions had started usually had an agenda, anyway.

"That's a difficult question to answer," I admitted. "I don't really have anything to compare it to."

"Tell me a story then," she sighed sleepily. "A happy memory."

I stayed quiet, my mind going blank. Twenty-eight years of memories went out the window when put on the spot.

Lya opened her eyes, looking up at me through thick lashes. "You and Trevor have always been friends, right?"

I brushed the hair out of her face, tucking it behind her ear. "He grew up in the packhouse, like me. He used to live in the Beta wing, but after his parents died, he needed to move over to the Alpha wing as my parents essentially adopted him and the new Beta family was moving in. They needed all four rooms, too."

I paused, thinking back. Running around this place without a care in the world felt like a different lifetime. The memories didn't even feel like they were mine anymore, things had changed so much. "He refused to give up his old room, which was supposed to be Anna's new room. Eventually, Anna just started sleeping in there with him."

Lya giggled at that. "He's such a player. I'd think he wouldn't mind a pretty girl crashing with him."

"He still had some self-respect when he was fourteen," I told her with a chuckle. "Besides, Anna was only ten then."

"I forget he was that young when they died."

"He was pretty dark and twisty for a while," I confirmed. "But really, I think having Anna around to constantly haze him helped distract him for a long time."

I told Lya stories about the antics Trevor and Anna used to pull to drive each other, and everyone else living in the house, up a wall until she drifted off to sleep. I slipped off the bed, certain after a taste of Anna at her finest, her nap was well-deserved. Lya cuddled deeper into the sea of pillows, latching onto the one I had been laying on. I smiled to myself and slipped out the door. I was fairly convinced she would be around forever. We would have time for a run another time.

I was not surprised to find someone in my office, waiting to speak with me. I was, however, surprised that the person was Rose. I looked at her questioningly as I made my way behind my desk.

"Alpha," Rose said with a nod.

"Rose."

She sat quietly for a moment, keeping her eyes trained on her hands. "Alpha, I need to know what side I'm supposed to be on."

"Side?" I asked. "I wasn't aware there were supposed to be sides."

Rose tapped her foot impatiently. "Am I first and foremost Lya's friend, or do I need to report matters back to you?"

"Oh." I sat back, pondering the question. The last thing I wanted to do was betray Lya's trust, but I also wanted to know all the details she didn't share with me. It had already been proven that she had valuable information she didn't realize was important. "In your professional opinion, does it jeopardize the safety of the pack?"

"Safety? No," Rose considered. "But I know this pack will fare better with a Luna, and what I know could expedite the process."

"But that would be cheating, wouldn't it?" I said with a sad smile. "Rose, I appreciate the offer, but I believe, on this matter in particular, you need to remain Lya's friend first. Only come to me if it is a safety concern."

"A safety concern for the pack."

"Yes," I confirmed. "Is there anything you need to share, Rose?"

Rose stood. "No, I don't think so. Thank you for your time, Alpha."

The conversation didn't sit right with me, but I could worry about benign secrets that would eventually find their way into the open another time. There was a tickling in the back of my mind that maybe it deserved more thought, but I couldn't dwell on it now.

The Wulver Pack name stood out to me, and I needed to figure out why. They were a fable amongst pups, serving as an example as to what the Moon Goddess created us werewolves for, so of course I remembered hearing about them all through childhood and during history lessons in school. But I couldn't shake the feeling that, at some point in years previous, the name had found its way across my desk. I found it odd. Granted, if they were as integral in present-day werewolf society as Gregory and Thom led us all to believe earlier today, I felt like I should probably know more about them. And now that my mate seemed to be entangled with them, it was even more imperative, especially considering that was probably the aspect about her the hunters were most interested in.

I turned to the filing cabinet filled with records of pack members that had transferred into this pack, having no better idea of where to start. The Wulver Pack was actually a pack, so it was possible someone from them had transferred in. The other options I had were to search through my father's old emails and contact the other Alphas at that meeting in Maine, but I felt like those routes wouldn't bring up any new information.

Staring at that filing cabinet was daunting. This pack had over doubled in size since I had assumed my position, and it would take months to go through each and every file. I was kicking myself for not accepting the Cyber Unit's offer to digitize records. I let out an exasperated sigh and decided to track down people to do this for me. The Beta's children would want a summer job. Figuring out more about the Wulver Pack would, after all, not change the situation my mate was in. She would still have hunters after her, and I would still have a duty to protect her. All on top of running a huge pack that spanned multiple states.

A better use of my time would be determining if the town up in Wyoming actually had a violent rogue problem like the Gamma there claimed. Rumor had it he was executing peaceful rogues in cold blood. So, tearing my mind from my mate, I made my way over to the training grounds. Kota and I needed to determine which scouts to send out that way.

TWENTY-FIVE

Lya

TIME at the pack passed in such an odd way. Things that would seem so small to others, like a spur-of-the-moment lunch date with a stranger, were a huge deal, while monumental things came across as expected and ordinary. Maybe it was how my brain processed things, not how pack life was different.

Oliver and I didn't get our run in the day before yesterday, and for that, I felt bad. Instead, we went over to his grandmother's cottage so she could talk to my wolf. It was so interesting, willingly letting Tala come forward and take control while I sat back and watched from the sidelines. All she wanted to know was how exactly silver affected Tala. Tala's answer surprised me, too. Basically, it seemed like the silver just suppressed her presence, making my more human traits come forward—my scent, my senses, all the way down to silver coming across as an allergic reaction. It was more humanesque. It hurt her significantly, but it didn't shut her out like I thought for so long. She was the one who had made the choice to sit quietly in the background, not healing me at appropriate speeds, keeping things like having a mate a secret. She always had the power to come forward, as made evident by her killing my fiancé, but very rarely chose to. Her logic was, if I didn't want her around, she could appease me and not be around... because she also didn't want to be around me if I was going to hurt her.

Yesterday, fear was the modus operandi to get me to shift while training in wolf form. I tried to shift on command, I really did. But I ended up standing on the field butt-naked for ages. The only thing that worked was Kota charging at me as his wolf when my back was turned.

After training, Kota had been extremely curious about my past, specifically my family on my dad's side. The ones who had taught me how to fight. He wanted answers, and so did I. He made several good arguments, too.

"You're telling me you are almost certain your dad is a werewolf," he said, looking for clarification. I nodded in confirmation. "And you saw your family on his side regularly, even after your dad left you guys?" Another nod. "So, that means your cousins are almost definitely also werewolves, which would explain why you fight like a trained wolf."

I just shrugged. To be honest, the thought that they might share the same genetic anomaly my dad and I had never crossed my mind.

"I think my mom sent me to them for the summers so she wouldn't have to deal with me," I told him sadly. "She was scared of me, don't forget."

"With good reason," he scoffed. "I wouldn't want to meet you in a dark alley, wolf or not."

I rolled my eyes. "Sure."

"Really," he insisted. "Do they know you're a wolf? Your cousins are good. I want to know what pack they're from."

"I never told them. But how would I know about their pack?" I laughed. "I didn't even know the pack my dad was in until Oliver planted a book in my room and Marjorie started asking too specific questions."

Kota narrowed his eyes at me. The look was one that was full of suspicion, not curiosity. "You know what pack you're from?"

I shifted uncomfortably. "It was pretty easy to connect the dots."

"So, you know." It wasn't a question, so I didn't bother to answer. He turned, leaving me standing by myself in the middle of the training field. I quickly gathered the rest of my clothes and rushed back to the packhouse.

And like yesterday morning, getting out from under Anna's thumb and away from the packhouse so I could make it to the training grounds in time was a feat that should count for training in and of itself. The more I got to know Anna, the less she intimidated me... but she still exhausted me. She was big energy, all the time.

"What do you and Mr. Alpha have planned for today, huh?" she insisted. "He's got me reading through and scanning a bunch of files of people who have joined the pack. I bet you have more fun plans."

I smiled and continued sipping my coffee.

"And when are you officially joining the pack, anyway?" she demanded.

That question caught me a little off guard. It had kind of been the elephant in the room for a few days now. I was not at all opposed to it, but at the same time, I didn't want to give up that last bit of independence I had. But if Oliver and I were going to work out, I was going to end up as this pack's Luna, and I'd have to be a member of the pack for that. I couldn't lead a pack I wasn't a member of.

I wondered how that all fit into the Wulver Pack equation. According to the book, wolves didn't lose their Wulver Pack status, even if they joined others.

I rushed into Kota's office a couple minutes late. He glared at me over his cup of coffee and motioned to the chair across from his desk.

"Sit," he growled.

I sat down cautiously, not particularly interested in getting reamed for trying to stay under the radar. I had a good excuse for being late. Anna had a big mouth, and if I had told her I had to leave because I needed to sneak off to training, that would have undoubtedly gotten back to Oliver. I knew for a fact he would be less than thrilled if he found out his Gamma and his mate were going behind his back to train.

Kota snapped me out of my internal panic. "I don't care what little secrets you and your mate keep from each other. That doesn't concern me. But this pack and the safety of both of you is my first—my only—priority. You don't keep secrets from me."

"Wh-what?" I stuttered.

"You know you're a part of the Wulver Pack, which means your family is, too."

"I don't see how any of that makes a difference," I said slowly, noting that I had never told him that was the pack I was fairly certain I was a part of.

"It makes a hell of a lot of difference," he scoffed. "The Wulver Pack are the best fighters out there, and a few summers training with them goes a long way. I'm putting you up against one of our trained fighters today."

"What?" I choked out. "They'll kill me!"

Sure, I could hold my own, but I wasn't *that* good.

"No, they won't," Kota assured me. "I need a proper baseline for where you're at. And handing Ellie's ass to her certainly doesn't tell me much."

Part of me thought about whipping out the 'hey, I'm Luna' line, but I also knew Kota was smart enough to know when to let me play that card versus remind me of my lack of place. So, not really having any other options, I begrudgingly followed him out to the back corner of the field. Even though

Kota insisted no one would recognize me, we had still made sure to keep our distance and train as far away as possible from the rest of the warriors. If anyone asked, I was interested in potentially joining the ranks. He skillfully left out which exact rank that was.

Kota coached me through a brief warm-up before waving over a hulky guy who I'm sure ate half-pints like me for breakfast. I craned my head up to look at him and gulped in fear. I was certain he had ditched his shirt because his flexing muscles had torn it.

I suddenly regretted agreeing with Kota to start training. This was it. This was how it ended. I had wolfed out and taken out a hunter that had nearly two years of preparation and planning to kill me, but this beast was going to snap me like a twig and he probably wouldn't even notice. I glanced around, trying to find the cameras. Was *Punk'D* back on air?

I didn't miss his visual assessment of me, his sullen gray eyes taking in his next victim. He had to be thinking this was a joke as much as I was. I tried to offer a smile but failed miserably. How exactly was Kota going to get a baseline from this? A flatline, maybe, but then he'd have to deal with Oliver.

He pushed the deep brown hair off of his face and offered me a nod before taking up a defensive stance. I shot Kota one last glance, hoping he'd call it and say he was joking, before following suit.

Fear—legitimate fear—twisted into knots in my stomach. Give me a normal-sized human, and I'd probably willingly give it a go. This person, though, I was convinced was a descendant of mythical giants.

He made the first move. I was not about to initiate a fight with this guy. I was happily surprised with how slow he seemed to be, easily dodging his advances. I had to figure out how in the world I was going to land any sort of blow.

Opportunity struck when he threw all his weight at me, and I ducked around him, grabbing his arm and pulling it with me. I moved with him as he stumbled to the ground. With an arm pinned behind his back and a knee at his neck, I was able to land a couple of blows, even though I was certain he hardly felt them.

A prickling sensation alerted me that we were being watched. Not surprising; I was sure everyone was morbidly curious how long I'd last. I was glad I hadn't taken any bets because I had already made it longer than I thought.

The feeling of being watched shifted from prickles to feeling more like stabs. I spared Kota a glance, hoping for some reassurance, but he was focused on something past us. I didn't risk hazarding a glance over my shoulder to see what had his attention. I had this guy pinned. He used my distraction against me, though, and we were back to circling, ducking, diving, striking.

I didn't need to look around; I could feel we were attracting more and more eyes. It didn't matter who. Smallest versus largest was probably a pretty silly fight to watch, but at least we were putting on a show.

I shouldn't have been so surprised when a familiar voice boomed over the field. The voice was angry, and it was easy to be more scared of it than the man in front of me.

"What in the ever-loving hell is going on?"

OLIVER

TREVOR AND THOM would be getting to the pack today. I was on a call with them, orchestrating exactly how they'd get here. They were under instructions to take the most convoluted path possible, which required extra time. Trevor was driving south before making his way back our direction, and Thom had taken a plane to Wyoming and then rented a car the day before. It was probably an extraneous measure, but I wasn't willing to risk the pack's safety.

A sudden stroke of fear racked my bones. I gulped it down, unfamiliar with a relatively standard thing rattling me so much. Adair stirred, growling in defense.

'*What has you so bothered?*' I asked.

Another shudder of nerves ran down my spine. There was an overarching, gut-wrenching, loathing of what was going on, but fear at this one particular instance? That was far stretched.

'*That's not ours,*' he insisted.

I frowned, trying to place where the feeling could possibly be coming from. Instinctively, my hand went to the mark I had kept carefully covered. I pushed the feeling down, deciding to head over to the training grounds. Clearly, I had some pent-up emotions to deal with, and for as long as I had known, training was the best way to deal with that.

Running there provided a good warmup, but driving was faster. I elected for faster today. My time would be limited with my brother and friend getting into town.

Lya's scent was so ingrained in me. No number of showers or clean changes of clothes could erase it from my mind. Even walking out onto the field, it was easy to confuse the faint scent of incoming summer for her unmistakable lilac and pine.

I whipped my head around, convinced the smell was actually her. I caught sight of Kota watching over Jeremy sparring with an incredibly small girl. Must have been a new recruit. I chuckled to myself. It seemed incredibly unfair, but it was the typical rite of passage. He was big and lumbering and slow, but his size alone could strike fear into the hearts of anyone. If a new or potential recruit would stand up to a fight with him, even if they knew they would lose, they at the very least had what it took to be worth our effort to train up. I stood for a moment, impressed by how the tiny little spitfire held her own. A small, morbid part of me was excited to see how she progressed up the ranks.

I hoped my own little spitfire would face a fight like that when she inevitably started training. But she wasn't training right now for a reason, and if I had it my way, I'd push that off for as long as I could.

Kota glanced across the field, eyes locking with mine. A look of dread overcame his expression.

Wait a minute.

Lilac and pine.

My spitfire.

A gentle gust of wind pushed her scent in my direction, forcing it into my lungs, and for hopefully the only time in my life, it was the absolute last thing I wanted to smell. It was all the confirmation I needed.

I seethed. Adair raged. She had no business being here. I had specifically said she wasn't to train yet. Lya went behind my back, and my Gamma broke my orders. This was not acceptable.

I stormed across the pitch, fists clenched. Claws broke through and pierced the palms of my hands. This was a fierce brand of rage I was not completely familiar with, and it all stemmed from keeping Jeremy's filthy paws as far from my mate as possible.

The voice that came out of my mouth was not my own. Adair was possibly more furious than I was but for a very different reason.

"What in the ever-loving hell is going on?"

Lya's eyes snapped up to me, her expression mimicking Kota's.

I marched up to Kota, grabbing the front of his shirt. "What the fuck is wrong with you? I told you! I told you she wasn't to train!"

"Alpha, I—"

"She just got out of the hospital and barely has a wolf!" Spittle flew. I was on the verge of shifting.

"Alpha, she—"

"Oliver, for fuck's sake, I can make my own choices!" Her sharp voice rang over the both of us, bringing all eyes to her.

I spun around, pulling her to me, trying to convince myself she hadn't gotten hurt. "Not in my pack, you don't."

Lya pushed away from me. "Last I checked, I actually do."

She turned, rushing off the field toward the tree line. She jumped over a log, a lithe auburn wolf landing in her place. I stared after her, and a small part of me wondered if maybe I had overstepped.

I had overstepped before, though, and it had always been for good reason. Keeping Lya safe was a very good reason.

Adair's anger dwindled away quickly. All it took was Lya pointing out her rightful place of power, whether she realized it or not. I knew him. He was never angry that she was sparring. Truthfully, he was anxious to see how it played out. He was angry the Gamma we had hand-selected had gone against our wishes.

I desperately wanted to chase after Lya and give Adair a chance to actually meet Tala in the flesh, but Lya's anger was directed toward me, and I had already learned she wanted to stay away from whomever she was angry at. Instead, I whirled around to face Kota. "Office. Now."

I stomped my way toward his office, wanting to get this conversation over with as soon as possible. I took the chair behind his desk—I was in charge, not him—and glared over at him.

"Why?" I demanded.

Kota gave me a sly look. There was little to no remorse for what he had done, which infuriated me. "Her request to train superseded your wishes to keep her grounded."

"She barely has a wolf, and without full access to her wolf, she can't heal as quickly," I reminded him. "The physical combat that comes with training is actively putting your Luna at risk."

Kota cocked an eyebrow at me. "The girl converses with her wolf regularly, shifts daily, and accepted life as a werewolf a while ago. What makes you think she 'barely has a wolf'?"

"Because if she was actually fully reintegrated with her wolf, she would have noticed I was her mate," I scoffed.

"And what makes you so certain she hasn't?"

Blood pulsed in my ears. Kota's accusation that she would keep something like that a secret infuriated me. I wanted to put him in his place, but it was Adair who reminded me part of the reason we chose him as Gamma was because he was willing to go toe to toe with me.

"Don't assume you don't need to clean up your own house when you and your mate are keeping secrets from each other," Kota growled at me.

Again, it was Adair who kept me from lunging across the desk. Adair reminded me of the truths behind his words. I slumped in defeat, unwilling to be the Alpha who took anger out on his own pack.

"You talk as if you're harboring secrets," I said dully.

Kota held his hands up in innocence. "You two need to clear the air before it drives a wedge between you two. The whole pack will start to feel it soon."

I shrugged, knowing exactly what he was talking about. "Her pack might be a useless piece to the puzzle. Finding out her identity was kept from her might do more harm than good."

"She already knows, Oliver. The future Luna is many things, but dumb is not one of them. And it is important. It is in her DNA to do the utmost. You never actually leave the Wulver Pack, even if you join another. She needs to know her responsibilities to her pack," Kota insisted. "You can't keep her a secret, especially if you make her Luna. The rest of us will come looking for her sooner or later. Do you want to have that conversation on your own terms or when strangers—her family—are vying for her to come back?"

I looked up at him quizzically. "The rest of us?"

"I wondered if you didn't know when I transferred into the pack." Kota chuckled. "Marjorie knows, and Greg and Thom caught it. Figured they'd fill you in."

I motioned for him to continue

"Just like Lya, I am destined to be the silent protector residing in the shadows. The guardian of peace and the unsung bringer of hope. The gladiator of goodwill." A smile flitted across his face, the first one I'd seen in nearly a week. "Secrets aren't very fun, are they?"

Twenty-Six

Lya

I STOOD naked in the hallway of the Alpha wing. My room was completely empty of all my things. My clothes had been moved out, all my toiletries had been removed from the bathroom, and the book on the Wulver Pack was gone.

'*Well, that didn't take very long,*' I grumbled to Tala. '*I didn't realize we had pissed him off that bad.*'

She giggled but provided me no guidance on where to maybe go.

I heard the door to the packhouse open, so instead of being caught with my pants down—or off, for that matter—I slipped back into what was apparently my old room. As much as I didn't want him to see me completely naked at the moment, I really hoped it was Oliver so he could tell me where my clothes were.

The door to my room creaked open. I shrieked when I realized it was decidedly not Oliver. This guy bore almost no resemblance to him, either.

"Well, this is quite the greeting, but I'm married," the guy said nonchalantly. He had a pleasant lilt to his voice that at least made me feel like he wasn't mad.

"I, um, I... Where's my stuff?" I blurted.

The guy chuckled. "The only thing I can tell you is you're standing in my room."

My eyes grew wide and my jaw dropped. Oliver had mentioned I'd been using his brother's room. "You're Thom."

"The one and only," he confirmed. He set his bag down and rifled through it, finally pulling out a shirt he handed to me. "I take it you're Lya?"

I nodded, still uneasy. I was slowly growing accustomed to nudity not being a huge deal here, but it was still unsettling that the guy who had seen me on full display was the brother of the person I was fucking.

Thom ushered me back out the door and down the hall, stopping outside the room Oliver and I had ended up in the other night. "If I know my brother, your stuff will be in his room."

I sighed in annoyance before pushing my way through. Just like he said, my stuff was all neatly laid out on the bed. I assessed how little I had left from my recent shopping spree. At the rate I was tearing out of my clothes, I'd have to buy more soon. Thank goodness cheap, fast fashion was the rage for werewolves; it made replacing everything easier. I quickly changed before heading back to knock on Thom's door and return the shirt.

"Thanks," I mumbled as he took the shirt from me. "Sorry."

"Not a problem," he assured me. "But let's not tell Ollie about this encounter. I haven't seen him in a few years, and I don't feel like fighting with him."

I nodded and rushed off, making my way outside with *A History* clutched to my chest. I found the path that led down to Marjorie's, but I followed the stream along a barely visible fork I'd instead of going to her cottage. I wandered along slowly, enjoying the tranquility. The tree line broke, and I walked out into a sea of bluebells, going right up to the edge of the water. I smiled to myself. This place was perfect. This could be my new place.

I found a rock and sat down, dangling my feet in the water. It was still chilly from snowmelt, and it would probably never get comfortably warm. But I could handle frostbitten toes in exchange for some peace.

Hours passed by blissfully. The sun was beginning to set when I reached the final page. I laughed to myself. It was a little cheesy, but it was a creed. A promise. And one I figured I was intended to uphold.

The Wulver is destined to be the silent protector residing in the shadows. The guardian of peace and the unsung bringer of hope. The gladiator of goodwill.

And then it ended.

I'd need a whole other book to answer all the questions this one created.

The book had only gone over the origins and works of the pack, how they were responsible for the rise of hunters, and then chronicled the exodus of the Wulver Pack from their territory to living among humans, hidden in plain sight. Were they still a pack? Where were they now? Were they upholding their promise? How much guilt did they carry? Was I expected to fill a role with them? How did I go about doing that?

Kota had alluded to it, but no one had told me for sure. It was painfully obvious this pack was where I was from, and I could tell Tala was proud of us and who we were. She was puffing her coat and preparing for whatever battle called on us.

I resented my dad a lot for the way he left my family. But maybe there was a bigger reason for him leaving. I didn't even have his number anymore. Equal parts starting my new life and closing his access to me. Right now, he was the only connection I had to what I was supposed to be, and I needed some guidance.

I took as much time as I could to get back to the packhouse. I really wasn't prepared to deal with the wrath of Oliver. I wasn't sure why I was so certain there would be wrath. Oliver had had plenty of opportunities to show me a side of him that included fury, but I had never seen it. Maybe he wouldn't be angry, just disappointed. But disappointment was worse.

Light poured out of the giant windows of the packhouse. Gathered around the kitchen island were: the person who tried to use me as bait, the person who had just seen me naked, and the person who was my mate and was potentially furious with me. They were laughing, smiling, and seemed so genuine and happy. They were a family.

I smiled to myself and snuck through the patio entrance to Oliver's room. I didn't exactly feel like crashing the three musketeers' reunion. Oliver had mentioned Thom would be here for a few days, so I was sure there would be other opportunities to make a better impression.

I'd take the excuse to not face Oliver yet. I knew I had made him mad, and I was not sorry in the least. Even if he wasn't going to tear into me, that conversation would be a long one. Sure, Trevor was also there, but knowing all sides of the story, it was really hard to be angry at him. Especially when I would have done the same. From the sound of it, it didn't seem like it was his doing that landed hunters on my trail, anyway.

Someone slipped into the room. I ignored it, knowing exactly who it was. Ever since I marked him, whatever that entailed, his presence and proximity had become even more overwhelming. I thought it was bad before, but now I felt like the little red string binding us had shortened, the tension of distance becoming a physical, painful feeling, only much more dramatic than before. It would take some time to get used to that part.

I was putting clothes away in an empty drawer I had found when his arm slipped around my waist, pulling me into his chest.

"You didn't really think you could sneak in without me noticing, did you?" Oliver murmured against my ear.

"One could always hope," I said, spinning around to face him. His grip didn't loosen, keeping us much too close, but I didn't have it in me to pull away. "Why'd you move me to your room?"

Lips fluttered against my cheek. I tried my best not to sigh and sink into his touch, but I was failing. "What's the point of putting you in a spare room if I'll still track you down every night?"

I offered no response. He wasn't wrong. The night terrors hadn't reared their ugly head recently, but there was no denying I slept much more soundly with him by my side, and who was to say where the line between fitful sleep and night terrors was.

Oliver leaned down and kissed me, and I quite happily let go of the little bit of self-control I barely maintained. This was not how I envisioned the conversation going, but I wasn't about to complain. Maybe we could skip the fighting part.

Oliver pulled away abruptly. "Thom is making dinner. Come on."

OLIVER

FOR THIS ONE NIGHT, I had agreed to cut Trevor a break. I had pulled some strings and gotten Rose to agree to get Anna out of the house by whatever means necessary. Rose had tried to get Lya in on the deal for a night out, but I wasn't about to let her out of my sight, especially off of pack territory when we knew there were people after her. It didn't exactly sit well with me to encourage my mate's best friend and the Beta's daughter off territory as is, but Trevor refused to set foot on our land until she was gone. I couldn't keep them separated forever, but I could allow him one night.

Trevor's head popped up when we walked into the kitchen, eyes locked on my mate. "Do you still hate me?"

I didn't miss Lya's pained expression. Her anger at him had been justified, and if she could overlook it, she was a better person than me. The only thing that had kept Trevor in my good graces was a lifetime of friendship, and he came clean.

"No," she said quietly. "Just don't do anything like that again."

"I'll have an entire pack after me if I do." He set a beer in front of Lya. "Peace offering?"

Lya smiled up at him before glancing around the room. I breathed a sigh of relief. It'd be difficult to have a Beta the Luna disapproved of.

Her eyes fell on Thom, color rising to her cheeks. He shot her a wink, and if he hadn't already told me the pretenses of their initial run-in, I would have been jealous that he could bring color to her cheeks with only a look.

"Nice to see you with clothes on, Lya," he greeted with a chuckle.

She glanced down at her beer. "It would've been nice if someone had told me my room had been moved," she grumbled. "What are you doing here, anyway? Don't you have a wife that's about to have your kid?"

Thom's laughter roared through the kitchen. "I like you. You know, you're the first person who has asked about Maggie since I got here. But she'll get here in a couple days. With the possibility of it being a werewolf pup, we want to make sure we're at a hospital that can handle it if something goes wrong."

"Oh, so nothing to do with wanting to see your brother?" I asked with mock-hurt.

Thom glanced up at me. "No, but the excuse to make sure you're treating your kidnapping victim well did cross my mind."

"She's not being held here against her will," I snarked back, my arm instinctually wrapping around her.

Thom cocked an eyebrow at me. "Is that so?"

He placed plates in front of us, and I reveled in how naturally and easily the banter continued over dinner. The feeling of being surrounded by family for the first time in a long time was comforting and soothed the pang of loneliness I was so familiar with. Losing my mom and dad had gotten easier to deal with, but I never missed them any less. My brother disappearing immediately after made it all the more difficult to deal with, and even my best friend hadn't stuck around, finding an excuse to leave for longer and longer stretches.

I owed Lya for more than being my other half. When she was brought to the pack, she unknowingly dragged my family back with her.

Trevor quickly ushered us out of the kitchen as soon as dinner was over, worried Anna would show up at any moment. He led us to the farthest point from the entrance to the house where Anna would have absolutely no reason to go—the den in the Alpha's wing.

"Can you seriously not cope with seeing her?" Lya sighed. "I mean, I can deal with you, and you very nearly had me killed."

"It's not that simple, Lya," he said tersely.

I rolled my eyes. "It's extremely simple. Trevor doesn't want Anna to find out that they are mates."

Hurt flashed across Trevor's face, but I didn't care so much anymore. "Trevor has been a very good liar for the past four years, and he doesn't want to actually own up to it yet."

"Oh, like you're one to talk," Trevor snapped at me, sending a very pointed look Lya's way.

I glanced over at Thom, but he didn't look the least bit surprised. I would not have been shocked if he was in on the whole ordeal. Lya, however, seemed very confused.

"Trevor left six years ago," I said, filling her in. "He told everyone it was to find his mate, which was believable. He used to come back regularly. Then at Anna's eighteenth birthday four years ago, he was here for ten minutes, then left. He's only come back once in the past four years. I believed him for a while, that he wanted to find his mate, but after he accepted the Beta position, said he wanted to start a life with Anna, and then backed out, I started connecting the dots. He wanted revenge for the death of his parents. If he actually found his mate, he wouldn't have an excuse to leave and do that. It took me a long time to figure out why he would agree to come back, then not."

Trevor looked down at his beer. "It wasn't a good plan, but at least it was a plan."

"A good plan would have been being up front with your Alpha," I shot back.

"Well, Alpha, I'm going to bed. You have fun with your own secrets."

We all watched as he stormed out of the room. I expected Lya to ask for clarification, but she kept quiet. It surprised me when she got up to follow him, but she was ever the Luna already.

"You know, if you're going to be angry at him, you also need to be angry at me," Thom said. "I'm the one who told him if he was going to pursue the hunters behind your back, he needed to stay away from the pack, make sure none of it got back home. Her blood would be on his hands if any harm came to his mate."

I looked over at him, but he didn't make eye contact. "He almost brought harm to my mate."

"But he didn't," he pointed out. "And would you really be this angry with him if it was just some random rogue she-wolf caught in the crossfire?"

That comment gave me pause. A good Alpha would have been angry either way, but I truly didn't know if I would have been. I had to wonder if Lya ever would have stumbled into my life if it weren't for Trevor.

"Besides," Thom added, "I was keeping an eye on him. He never actually did anything to attract any hunters. He only turned that town into a hub for rogues. It would've taken a few more years or so for it to even show up on the hunters' radar."

"Then why are there hunters sniffing around that town now?" I asked.

Thom shook his head. "You have your mate to thank for that. They have been tracking the lost Wulver for years now."

The confirmation of what we had been thinking felt like a punch to the stomach. Lya wasn't safe, and I had to wonder if she ever would be. I'd have to start thinking about how much danger I brought to the pack by harboring her sooner rather than later.

"You know, the entire pack likes her," Thom continued, as if he had read my thoughts. We hadn't been able to mind-link in a long time, but we were still brothers. "They'll help protect their Luna."

"And who have you been talking to? I thought you had severed ties with the pack."

"The pack, yes," he agreed. "But not my friends. Everyone's hoping your public appearance with her at the last full moon means she's your mate. They think she's brave for jumping into training without even understanding what she's training to do. And you haven't exactly done a good job of hiding your mark."

"I don't want to mark her until she actually knows what it means," I confessed.

Thom chuckled. "I figured. You two weren't all over each other the way mated couples are."

He stood up, heading for the door. "I really can't believe you guys. I'd give anything to have my mate."

I sat in the den, alone with my thoughts. Thom had always had a way of presenting uncomfortable truths, and right now, I resented him for it. He was always right, too. He really should have been Alpha. Not me.

TWENTY-SEVEN

Lya

TREVOR AND THOM were my new shadows. Oliver had given in, accepting that I overruled him, and was letting me continue to train. He knew me well; even without his blessing, I would have continued. The stipulation he thought I wasn't aware of was Trevor or Thom would tag along to make sure I was never actually at risk. Both were coming with me today under the pretense of wanting to catch up with Kota. I knew Trevor wanted to avoid Anna as much as humanly possible, and Thom... I wasn't exactly sure what Thom's excuse was. Maybe he did just want to see Kota.

Training today had been tough. That's not to say it had been easy before, but I was pushed further past the limits of my previous sessions. Kota said it was because I was clearly a better fighter than he had initially thought. After running over some new maneuvers, he left me with the other warriors to work on them, telling us to find him after we were done. I had desperately hoped a couple times that maybe Trevor or Thom would jump in and say something was too rough, but they never did. Kicks and punches were being landed on me at a much higher rate than I was delivering them, and absolutely no mercy was being shown for the future Luna. Granted, I had to wonder if I'd get any useful training at all if the people I sparred with knew I was the future Luna. If I actually wanted to get good at fighting, it was probably best this way.

"What happened to you two last night?" Thom asked as we headed toward Kota's office.

I shrugged. "Nothing. We sat out on the patio for a couple hours."

Trevor still hadn't talked to me since dinner last night. I had tried to get him to after he unceremoniously left, but he kept quiet. It would all come clean eventually. He wasn't much for the silent treatment, though, so it had to be a big deal.

I wasn't surprised to find Kota sitting behind his desk, glaring cooly at the door as we entered. It was the way I always found him. A few people had mentioned he had been exceptionally moody and angsty recently, but I didn't really know him well enough to make that call.

Kota stood, shutting and locking the door behind us. "This conversation does not leave this room, under any circumstances."

He sat back behind his desk, pulling out tumblers and a bottle. He must have forgotten I was small, and half-human. The pour he handed me was much more than three fingers.

"Well, good to see you too, Kota." Thom chuckled, taking a seat across from his desk.

"Isn't it a little early for drinking?" I asked hesitantly, not exactly wanting to poke the bear, but also worried about what sort of topic would warrant drinking at three in the afternoon.

"No. Now sit." He shoved the drink across the desk, and I did as instructed. I glanced at Thom and Trevor on either side of me while taking a sip. I really wanted water, but anything to relieve my parched throat after training. The whiskey burned on the way down, but I wasn't about to piss him off by refuting his offer. He seemed to be in an exceptionally bad mood today.

The strained silence only lessened when Kota finally spoke up. "Lya knows she's Luna, and she knows she's from the Wulver Pack. She isn't telling Oliver she knows these things, and I have no clue why, but I also don't care."

"Is this secret meeting only about our dysfunctional Alpha couple?" Trevor asked.

"No," he said, turning to his computer and pulling up a screen, "but we can use their dysfunction to our advantage."

Kota turned the screen toward us. Each quarter showed the feed from one of the security cameras around my house. Three of them showed a quiet, abandoned house. In the last one, however, was the camera that would have shown if there was regular surveillance of the house along the street. All that could be seen was a note in front of the camera.

Time to come out and play.

The silence was deafening as we took in the ominous request. My mind raced with everything this could entail. One thing was for certain, though; there was absolutely no avoiding the problem. Not anymore.

"So, what's the plan?" Trevor finally asked.

"That's why we're here," Kota said, "to come up with a plan without Oliver sitting in the corner having a conniption that his little mate is in danger. Whatever we come up with that will actually work, Lya, you will be in danger."

Thom shook his head. "I can't sit by and be a part of coming up with a hit or miss scheme. We have to keep Lya as far from this as possible. If something happens to her, we'll lose Ollie, too."

Kota's eyes never left mine. "She's a Wulver. She is going to do what's best for the greater good, with or without our help. Best to be in on it so she has more protection."

I narrowed my eyes at him. I mean, he was right. I wasn't going to let anyone else get hurt when it could potentially just be me at risk, but I wanted to hear his justification. "What makes you think that?"

"Because I'm a Wulver, too." His expression glowed with pride. "I know the way you think because it's the way all of us think. It's the same line of thinking that had you constantly ostracizing yourself. So, best we all come up with a plan that includes that rather than you coming up with your own."

I blinked but kept my initial thoughts to myself, deciding it was better if I tracked him down some other time to ask questions.

Thom seemed to recover the quickest. "First, we need to figure out how much time we have. As much time as possible to get her fighting up to snuff."

Kota nodded in agreement. "And then, the strategy we'll pitch to the Alpha to cover our tracks."

"I don't know if I can lie to Oliver again, especially if it risks her," Trevor said quietly. "He'd never forgive me, especially if she got hurt."

I looked over at Trevor. He was tired. The weight of what was happening, what he was convinced he had caused, was taking its toll. I felt bad for him, but I wasn't about to let others take part in a fight that was not their own.

"If this is too big for you, you need to leave now. You leave now, you won't have anything to lie to Oliver about. You stay, and I'll have to figure out how to do that command thing so you don't talk when you start feeling guilty. Either way works for me."

I could feel Thom and Kota looking at me, but I didn't take my eyes off of Trevor. I watched the internal battle play out on his face, trying to decide where his allegiances lay.

"I'd listen to your Luna if I were you, Trevor," Thom said gravely. "She scares me more than Ollie Pop does."

Trevor nodded once, indicating we could continue. "Yes, Luna."

The term knotted my stomach, emotions rolling through. It felt wrong. I felt like an imposter. It was everything I was meant to be. It was right.

"We'll meet again after training tomorrow," Kota announced. "I'll get the scouts over there to give me an idea how long we can drag this out, and all of us will have an idea by then to bring to the table. Once we have a better plan, we can move forward with what we need to tell Oliver."

Thom and Trevor stood up to leave, and I followed suit.

"Lya, a moment," Kota called. I slipped back into the room, closing the door in Trevor's face.

"This is going to be dangerous," he warned me.

"I know," I said with a nod.

"I can't guarantee you'll make it out alive."

"I know."

"You'll need to make sure we don't lose the Alpha in all this, too. I know you marked him, but you can't let him mark you and complete the bond," he stated. "If you want to back out, you need to say so now."

I didn't break eye contact, and I knew. I knew what my decision was, and I hated it. "I have spent my entire life running, Kota. Running from what I am and who I am all for the sake of protecting those I care about. I am still going to protect those people, and to do that, I cannot run just because things are a little tough. I won't let this pack suffer."

Kota gave me a small smile that was far from reaching his eyes. "Well spoken, Luna."

I turned and left, not even bothering to say goodbye. Time was becoming something we didn't have much of, and I wanted to spend the rest of the guaranteed time I did have with my mate.

OLIVER

THE ENTIRE TIME Lya was away at training, I got exactly no work done. All I did was worry about her. Dr. Whitledge had specifically said two weeks until she could train, and while those two weeks were almost over, she had already been training for nearly a week. The idea of her getting hurt, even a minor injury that was common in training, made me a ball of nerves. Adair tried to talk me down, insisting that when she officially became Luna, she would have to also be a warrior in some capacity to stand up and protect her pack, but it still didn't sit well with me.

I wanted to mark her. I wanted to feel what she felt more clearly, instead of only when it was all-consuming. This half-bond was miserable to deal with, and that was one thing Adair and I agreed on.

My office door creaked open, and I breathed a sigh of relief when I looked up to see Lya. She walked around the desk and sat down in my lap, pulling her knees up to her chest and resting her head on my shoulder. Hesitantly, I pulled her closer against me. Up until this point, Lya had not been the touchy feely type, so a small part of me worried something was wrong.

"Hi," I said, smiling into her hair. "What's this about?"

"Weird day," she breathed.

I pulled back and looked down at her, biting my tongue when I took in the already fading bruise on her cheek. I stood with her and set her on my desk.

"What's the damage today?" I asked, scanning the rest of her exposed skin.

"Most are fading already, thanks to Tala."

I placed a hand on either side of her and looked down at her. "I really don't like you training."

Lya sighed. "I know, but I do."

"Please don't get hurt," I insisted.

Lya didn't respond, instead pulling my face down to hers and kissing me.

"Are you trying to distract me?" I mumbled against her lips.

"That depends, is it working?"

Her tongue skimmed my lower lip, and I was quick to relent. I pushed her knees apart, pressing my body as close to hers as I could. My hands traveled underneath her shirt, finding the heat of another bruise on her side. "It's working very well."

I pushed Lya back down on the desk, letting my hands roam under her shirt. Part of me worried about the unlocked door to my office, but it was quickly overridden by the irresistible little spitfire sprawled out on my desk.

This was the sort of work I could easily wrap my head around.

My hands drifted down to her legging-clad legs, skimming up the inside of her thighs. I kissed down her neck, eliciting a small moan, and the sweet smell of her arousal flooded my office.

Lya reached for my shirt, but I caught her wrists and held them above her head. She was eager, and I couldn't help but tease. "No, ma'am, I think I'll take my time."

And take my time, I did. I needed a distraction from doing nothing, and I was going to drag these few moments of bliss out as long as I could. Her shirt fell to the floor, and my mouth quickly returned to exploring every inch of her shoulders, chest, and stomach. Her hands strained against my hold when I reached the waistband of her leggings.

"Do you want me to stop?" I breathed against her.

Lya lifted her hips and spread her legs wider as I stayed motionless, waiting for a response.

"Please," she begged.

"Please, what?" I asked, watching her face as I slid one hand past the waistband of her pants.

Lya continued to squirm against me. "Please don't stop."

"Don't move, then. I'm enjoying taking my time."

Lya stilled. I slowly removed my other hand from her wrists and pulled the leggings off of her, kissing and nipping at her ankles and all the way up to her thighs. Her whimpers as I got closer to her core made it clear I was going too slow for her, yet I still stopped and stood.

"Quiet," I told her. The packhouse was full, and no one else needed to overhear.

I leaned down and kissed her while one hand found her wet folds and the other unbuttoned my pants. I kept my lips on hers as one finger slowly dipped inside. Lya's legs tensed on either side of me, but I maintained the slowest pace I could.

She gasped against my lips when the head of my cock pressed against her instead of my fingers. I pushed into her slowly, kissing her harder as she mewled. Lya's back arched as I began to thrust, both of us freezing and glancing toward the door when commotion was heard outside. I clapped my hand over her mouth to keep her quiet.

"Just ignore it," I whispered. All thoughts of going slow went out the window, and I pounded into her, the sound of skin slapping and muffled cries hidden by the argument going on down the hall.

Lya reached back and clutched the edge of the desk. She gasped, arching her back, and her walls clamped down around me. A sensation in my gums urging me to mark her rattled my teeth, but I kept my jaw clamped shut, growling out as I released.

Lya stared up at me, eyes wide and chest still heaving. I marveled back at her, unwilling to move and wanting to prolong the moment.

"You okay with me training yet?" she huffed.

I smiled down at her and placed one last kiss on her jaw. "You might have to remind me sometimes."

Whoever was screaming in the hall made its way closer to the door, causing Lya to jump up and start searching for her clothes. She had barely gotten all the necessary clothing on when the door flew open, revealing an absolutely distraught Anna.

"What's that smell?" she demanded. "Where's it coming from?"

"Anna," I growled. I shot a glance over at Lya, who was trying to inconspicuously fix her hair. "You can't just barge into my office."

"Lock the door, then. What have you even been doing in here that's so secret?" Anna scoffed. She glanced over at Lya and scrunched her nose. "Your shirt's on backwards."

The color Lya's face turned put the deep red of her hair to shame. "Oh, uh, must've put it on wrong after training. I need to go shower anyway."

She stumbled out of the room, Anna hot on her heels, continuing the rant I wasn't going to listen to. I sat back down in my chair, reaching out to straighten a few things, counting down the minutes until the scent in question found me. Trevor walked over to open the window before reaching for the bottle of scotch. If the drama didn't calm down soon, I was going to have to hide my stash.

"I am not handling any paperwork that has touched that desk," he stated.

I ran my hands through my hair and glanced around, desperately trying not to make eye contact. I bit back a smile to myself when I caught sight of some lace under the desk.

"The Beta has his own office, anyway," I mumbled.

He rolled his eyes. "You say that as if this'll be reprised."

If I had it my way, it would. "Sounds like your time is almost up."

Trevor finished off his scotch in a gulp and stood. "Might wanna zip your pants before you leave. And doors do have locks, you know."

"I will make absolutely certain to walk in on you two at some point, I promise," I told him as he left, going out the window. He had to realize the fight that would ensue when Anna finally tracked him down.

TWENTY-EIGHT

Lya

ANNA TRAILED behind me all the way to my room, talking nonstop about a smell of intense spices, certain it was her mate and he was close and he had been in the packhouse recently and she had to find him. I peeled off my clothes, noting my shirt truly was on backwards, and stepped into the shower while she continued to chatter outside the door.

"I get it! I truly get it!" she insisted. "I totally understand why you can't keep your hands off of Ollie, because as soon as I find this person, I swear I am going to eat him alive. He smells so good. In fact, I have no idea how you control yourself as much as you do."

I cringed. I really thought I had been relatively successful in my restraint, keeping PDA to a minimum. It was Oliver who either wasn't trying or was having a really difficult time keeping his hands off of me.

"Do you have any guesses?" I called out over the sound of the water.

Anna was quiet for a moment, a rare occurrence. "I feel like I've smelled it before, but not this intense," she finally mused.

"So, who do you know that you haven't seen in a long time?"

"A lot of people," she laughed. "I hardly came back here when I was in college."

I stepped out of the shower, dried quickly, and threw on a sundress before

225

emerging from the bathroom. "So, of those people, who would have any business being in the packhouse?"

Anna shrugged. "I guess anyone could at this point. Who has gotten promotions in the past four years?"

I shot Anna a look over my shoulder as I made my way toward the kitchen, on the hunt for a beer. It'd be so easy to tell her exactly who she was looking for. "Pray tell, exactly how would I know that?"

"Good point."

"Why don't you maybe try checking rooms to see if there's a particular room that smells more like your mate's scent than others?" I offered, figuring I'd throw her a bone.

Anna perked up at that. "Good idea!"

And as quickly as she had glommed onto me, she was off, headed up the stairs to the guest rooms. No one had stayed up there in the past few weeks I had been here, but I wasn't about to tell her that. It would at least keep her occupied for a few minutes.

I caught sight of Allyssa out of the corner of my eye. I turned to greet her, feeling a little guilty that I was drinking a beer in front of her.

"You know who it is, don't you?" she said accusingly.

I nodded sheepishly, sending a glance in the direction of the Alpha wing. There were three males living that way, only one of which was a possibility for her. Hopefully, Allyssa got the point.

Allyssa let out an exasperated sigh. "I knew it. This house will never sleep again."

"Should we just tell her?" I asked tentatively.

"No," she said quickly. "Anna will be furious enough when she finds him."

I had heard several stories by this point about the two of them growing up. It was very easy to see that would be the case. Allyssa was probably right; there would be no sleep once Anna finally tracked Trevor down, but for which reason I couldn't decide. "How long do you think it will take?"

"Oh, not long." Allyssa's eyes looked past me, over my shoulder. I turned to follow her gaze and saw Trevor standing in between Oliver and Thom, one holding each arm.

"Go put him in his room," I suggested to Thom. "Anna's checking rooms to find one that smells like him."

"He tried climbing through the window to make a run for it," Oliver informed us, making his way into the kitchen. Allysa rolled her eyes, almost as if she expected the behavior.

"Is that normal?" I asked. The whole mate thing still confused me, and I could only imagine the way it was going for me was far from normal, meaning I had no idea what sort of show I was in for when they finally did run into each other.

"No," Oliver said, eyes searing into me. "Most mates are overjoyed to find each other, glued at the hip, and have no qualms showing the world they have found the one who belongs to them."

His words cut into me, feeling like they carried much more meaning than explaining what was going wrong between Trevor and Anna. His words were directed toward me and what was supposed to be happening with us.

But it took two, sweetheart.

If he wasn't going to talk about it, neither was I. I was the newbie here, so he could take the lead. 'Hey, Lya, love of my life, gift from the Goddess, I want to make sure you know those sparky feelings are because we were made for each other.' It wasn't that hard.

But then again, it wasn't that hard for me to say something, either.

Easier said than done.

Allyssa's glance shifted between the two of us. "I'm sure they will figure it out sooner or later. Sometimes it takes an adjustment when there's history that predates discovering your mate."

Her comment didn't sound like it was exclusive to Anna and Trevor, either. It felt like everyone knew. Our mutually unrequited mateship was quickly becoming the elephant in the room.

"I'll go track down Greg to give him a quick heads up," she decided, slinking out of the kitchen.

Oliver stalked toward me, almost predatory. "Do you ever think about what it'll be like to meet your mate?"

With each step Oliver took toward me, I took one back. In no time, I was backed up to the refrigerator with no space between us, leaving no room to breathe.

"I could ask you the same," I choked out.

"They say there are sparks." He reached a hand up, brushing his fingers along my cheek, the electricity making me jump. "And an irresistible scent that only you can smell." Oliver's nose grazed along my jaw and down my neck. "And it's nearly impossible to not mark them when close to them." Teeth—canines—grazed along where my shoulder met my neck, right where I had marked him.

Barely a prick. A canine ever so slightly broke the skin, releasing a trickle of blood to run over my collarbone. His tongue flitted out, sealing the wound. I clamped my hand down on my neck, feeling for the mark I hoped he hadn't bitten deep enough to leave.

Oliver kissed me like it could be our last, or like it was a kiss he had waited his whole life for. It said everything he hadn't put into words. Fire burned across my lips, and I couldn't live without it.

"Don't worry, I won't mark you without asking first. But I'm still going to stake my claim. Over and over again until you let me mark you."

I wanted his mark. I wanted to be only his. But I bore too much responsibility to succumb to temptation and selfish desires. I felt guilty for marking him so prematurely, especially when he was so willing to afford me a courtesy I denied him. But he wanted me as his, and that was all I needed to know.

Oliver buried his nose in my neck again, breathing deeply. "You smell like lilac and pine carried on an ocean breeze, like a beach in Maine I went to once."

My breathing hitched. If I thought hard enough, I could almost remember a perfectly overcast late spring morning, my last day in Maine, visiting my favorite place for one last time. Before my first shift. But there had been something that had caused my wolf to surge forward, coming closer to the surface than I had ever experienced before. I barely made it off the beach that day, shifting for the first time as soon as I hit the tree line. She had told me it would happen after my fifteenth birthday, but it came prematurely. It had been a long and agonizingly painful experience, overshadowing nearly everything else. He had changed since then. Lived more. But if I thought hard enough, I could remember him.

"Mate!"

OLIVER

I SMILED into Lya's neck, pretending for a moment that it was Lya who'd said my favorite four-letter word I so desperately wanted to hear tumbling from her lips. This was Anna's moment, though. One that would go correctly. She wouldn't be able to see it at first, and maybe not ever, but Trevor had kept his distance from her so he could come to her with no demons. He probably felt as if it'd be wrong to bring all the baggage he still carried from unfinished business to a mate, but Anna knew it all already. And a mate was supposed to help you heal.

"Come on," I said, taking Lya's hand. "Let's go watch."

I pulled Lya toward the Alpha's wing, in view of Trevor's doorway. Watching someone find their mate was a beautiful thing, and I wanted Lya to see.

Anna stood at the end of the hall, her back toward us, eyes on Trevor's door. She was frozen in place, and I was certain Trevor could smell her, too. Thom had probably stayed in there to make sure he didn't try and escape through a window or something again. And like it was scripted, the door swung open and Thom shoved him out. I wasn't surprised; he had already made it four years of resisting the bond.

This was different from Kota and Ellie. Trevor had resisted the bond, not rejected it. But sometimes, resistance could result in rejection. He wouldn't be able to hide from Anna that he had denied her four years, and there was no telling what her reaction would be. But then again, she was only eighteen when he discovered they were mates, still a child. Maybe it would work out for the best that he held off.

Still, I was jealous. That moment of perfect clarity, where everything that mattered snapped into place.

I leaned against the wall, pulling Lya's back to my chest. This was the first time she had seen mates meet. She seemed almost as absorbed in it as Trevor and Anna. My eyes never strayed from her, though.

Like a coordinated dance, they stepped toward each other, their wolves at the forefront. It was undeniable what was happening, four fractions of a soul becoming one.

"Let's go," I murmured into my own mate's neck. It was selfish to have her watch. I was grasping at any possible opportunity to spur her to confess what I knew she had to know by now. Lya was unmoving, though, completely engrossed in their moment. I dragged her along behind me in an effort to give them the more intimate parts of their moment in peace. She snapped to attention when they were out of sight, willingly following along behind me.

Adair and I had found her scent lingering in the clearing she had spent the previous afternoon in. It suited her perfectly, tranquil enough to quiet the over-workings of her mind. She had mentioned finding safe havens in each place she had lived before, and it was easy to see this place becoming one for her here. It felt natural to bring her to this spot, too.

Riverbanks were her thing. She sank down on a rock, dangling her feet in the stream. I wished I had thought ahead enough to grab some beers to set in the cool water.

"I feel like you don't lie to me," Lya said cautiously, eyes following the current. "You simply don't speak on things until you fully understand them."

I sat down and tugged her onto my lap. "It's hard to put into words things you can't wrap your head around."

"What's a mate bond to you?"

Lya's question stopped my mind in its tracks. I replayed it a few times, examining each syllable.

"Evolving," I finally admitted. "Everything I need and nothing I expect."

"You've met her already, then?" The hurt was palpable in Lya's voice. As if she didn't already know.

"I met her before she turned eighteen," I confessed. "It felt... different then. There was no lust yet." I didn't know the best way to navigate this conversation. All the doors were wide open for me to admit to Lya it was her, that she was my world. But I was convinced Lya would bring it up when she was ready. If she wasn't talking, there had to be a reason. "Back then, she was my motivation to make this world safe. I failed her in that, but I have to hope that what I did for her resulted in better lives for others."

"I thought you couldn't meet your mate until you were eighteen?" I quickly thought through the books Thom had in his room. None of them discussed the intricacies of mate bonds. My girl had been asking questions.

"I think the signs people expect out of a mate bond don't crop up until we're eighteen and the Moon Goddess sees us as fit to mate. I think it's a fallacy that your mate is first and foremost your romantic partner. Your mate is supposed to complete you." I, at least, was not completed by who I went to bed with every night. The person who would willingly point out when I was wrong, challenged my ego, gave me a safe space to confess my secrets and fears–that was who completed me. Of course, you'd fall in love with the person uniquely designed to provide that. "I swear, I am about to make it so schooling ends a year earlier... It's gross seeing so many kids in high school all wrapped up with their life partner because their sex drive kicks in at eighteen."

"I'd have to agree," Lya giggled. "I imagine it's a big distraction from school, too."

"Maybe it'd be better to make sure their basic education is complete before all the additional hormones of mating kick in," I added, chuckling.

Lya shrugged. "Maybe it's because I'm half-human, but I still went through puberty at a normal time."

"That's not what I'm talking about, love," I said, placing a kiss on her shoulder. "You'll start going into heat once you're marked."

"Heat?" she squeaked. "Like an animal?"

"Like a wolf, yes," I told her. My teeth grazed along the nape of her neck, sending shivers down her spine. "Would you like me to mark you so you can find out?"

Lya didn't turn to look at me as she spoke, but her body betrayed her, pressing closer into me. "I don't even know what the mark is for, anyway."

"It's to let everyone know our souls are bound," I told her. "You felt it when you marked me. You can sense my emotions easily. You could read my thoughts if you tried. I can feel yours now, if they're overwhelming enough, but it would become a two-way street." I looked down at her, trying to gauge her reaction. "When I mark you and our bond is completed, we'll be able to mind-link, even if you aren't pack yet. And once you are Luna, you'll have as much control over the pack as I do."

"I don't think I'm ready for that yet," she said quietly. I knew that would be her answer, but it was worth a try.

I quickly shifted us around so she was under me and I was between her legs, pressing my hips into hers. I fought to keep my canines from surfacing, but if I couldn't mark her permanently, I'd leave whatever marks she would allow. I nipped and sucked at the skin along her collarbone, leaving bruising marks behind as my hands pushed the hemline of her skirt upward. Sundresses were my new favorite thing.

"Everyone is still going to know you're mine."

My hands slipped under her dress, disposing of it and leaving her exposed. I inhaled sharply. If sundresses were nice, the lingerie they always hid was better.

"Oh, but where to start?" I muttered before sucking on her neck, only a little disgruntled it was a hickey instead of a mate mark.

"Oliver!" Lya giggled. "What are you doing? I don't think anyone is going to argue that I'm yours."

"Mmm." My hands had a mind of their own, running up her ribs and skimming under the fabric of her bra to undo the clasp. "They still need to see proof. But say that again?" I pinched her nipple, her resulting gasp eliciting a growl from myself.

"What? That I'm yours?"

I dragged my teeth down her collarbone and sternum, leaving red trails behind. With one hand still kneading her breast, the other tore away her underwear. "Again," I growled. I pushed a finger inside of her, rumbling in approval at how wet she was.

"I'm yours," she breathed.

I sat up, admiring my handiwork thus far while casting my clothes to the side. This girl would either be wearing turtlenecks or showing off all the ways her Alpha could mark her.

I leaned over her again, biting down on her shoulder. Another mark her sundresses couldn't hide. Before I could nestle myself back between her legs, Lya's hands were on my chest, pushing me over. I reached up, digging my fingers into her hips to pull her closer, but she resisted. With the sly glint in her eyes, I was absolutely done for.

"If I'm yours, though, what are you, Alpha?" she asked.

I grasped her hips harder, claws nearly puncturing her soft skin. I was certain Lya could see the animalistic shift in my eyes. "All yours, love."

Lya purred in approval, slowly lowering herself down onto me. I pushed my hips up to meet her, groaning at the feel of her core. "What was that, Alpha? I don't think I heard you."

"Fuck, Lya, you own me," I rumbled. I held her still and began thrusting up into her. I couldn't take her taunting because I knew she would use her body for it. Primal was what I needed.

Without warning, I pulled out of her and rearranged us so she was on her hands and knees, ass on full display. I positioned myself at her opening, teasing her with my tip. My hand smacked down on her ass, causing Lya to jump, but quickly returned to massage away the sting as I plunged into her. I found a pace that had her writhing and moaning, doing my best to commit all her sounds to memory.

She clenched down around me, and my balls tightened. Feeling her climax pushed me over the edge, releasing into her. I reached forward, fisted my hand in her hair, and pulled her up so her back was flush against my chest. I buried my nose in her neck and took in as much of her scent as I could.

"So, whose are you, love?" I murmured into her ear.

She was breathless. I could hear her heart pounding. "I'm yours."

The rumbling in my chest reverberated through us. "That's right."

Twenty-Nine

Lya

TELL a girl she's your mate without telling her she's your mate. That's what this felt like.

Oliver was my mate and I was his. Of that, I was certain. Pretty much everyone in the packhouse knew, but we still weren't fessing up. We were the epitome of dysfunction. Too much depended on me keeping Oliver at arm's length, but that was getting more and more difficult by the moment.

A whole week had passed since the secret meeting with Thom, Trevor, and Kota. We had a plan, and it was a good one. The scouts out there were confident we could put things off for another couple weeks, and we were going to fudge things as long as we could. That provided more time for training, to perfect the plan, and ideally for Thom's wife to have their baby. I had no idea how I was going to hold out for so long.

If Oliver had any suspicions, he wasn't letting on. That, or he was running me ragged to try and make it so I was too exhausted to scheme behind his back. He kept to his word; it was painfully obvious to everyone that I was spoken for. A hickey here, teeth marks there, and he never let the love bite fade where his mark would someday be. It was embarrassing. But you wouldn't hear a single complaint from me. He had given up hiding—or was showing off, I couldn't decide—his mark, too. It didn't take long for people to start talking, easily connecting the dots.

I stumbled out of the bedroom to hunt down coffee. Oliver had disappeared a few minutes earlier to prepare for a meeting with the Gammas, and he was thankfully including me. Given how large this meeting would be, it would be held in the formal dining room, which we had been using more regularly with how busy the packhouse was becoming.

At the moment, there were two functionally mated couples that were both expecting, two children, Oliver and me, and Trevor and Anna. It wasn't uncommon for Brandon to crash in one of the rooms upstairs, either. Allyssa was constantly celebrating how full of life the packhouse was, but I personally was looking forward to quieter times.

I weaved my way through the sea of people in the kitchen to get to the coffee maker, only to find it empty. My shoulders slumped as I began reaching for things to make another pot. I'd be late at this point. A hand reached out and snagged mine. The tantalizing sensation of sparks that would never get old gave away the culprit who pulled me out of the fray. Oliver placed a kiss on my forehead and shoved a large mug into my hands.

"Don't say I never did anything for you," he razzed as I reveled in the smell.

I had seen Oliver a few minutes previously, but he came bringing gifts of coffee and salvation from crowds, making him a sight for sore eyes.

"Your mark is showing," I whispered to him. Oliver caught my hand as I ran my fingers over the portion that was visible.

"Yours isn't."

"I don't have one," I replied, arching a brow. We had brushed on that conversation a few times, and it was getting more and more difficult to dodge it by the day. I wanted him to mark me, but I also had to heed Kota's advice.

"We should change that." Oliver's voice was husky and low, and I could already tell his mind was far from the meeting at hand.

I grabbed his hand and started pulling him toward the dining room, the opposite direction of our bedroom. "Come on, I don't want to be the last one there."

All four Gammas were already seated around the table. Gregory was still seeing the kids off to school, Thom was spending a couple extra minutes with his wife, and Trevor was trying to talk Anna off of her most recent cliff that would undoubtedly devolve into an argument.

Kota and one of the Gammas I had not met were caught in a glaring contest. His foul mood over the past couple weeks had not resolved, and I was now absolutely certain it was his personality. The only thing that seemed to pull him out of it was strategizing for the upcoming war. I thought he was really enjoying going behind his Alpha's back, too. If I didn't know better, I'd think he had Alpha blood. Some intrinsic drive to lead.

"What's the girl doing here?" the Gamma Kota was glaring at grumbled.

I shifted uncomfortably under his scrutiny as he gave me a once over. Oliver had warned me the Gamma from Wyoming would be the least receptive to this meeting, so I figured this was him.

"Hello, Derek." Oliver had dropped my hand before we walked in, but the comfort of his touch would have been nice right now. "Thom, Trevor, and Gregory are already apprised of the situation, so let's get started."

I sat quietly while Oliver recounted for possibly the millionth time my relationship with my wolf, how I came to be at the pack, the hunters we believed to have been trailing me for years, and my connections to the Wulver Pack. Kota filled them in on the surveillance footage, including the note that had been left. The three others had trickled in, providing an extra detail here and there.

"So, why exactly are we here?" Derek asked. "The pack has ended up with a broken Wulver, and I'm going to go out on a limb and guess it's she who marked you, so we are obligated to protect her until you decide whether or not you'll make her Luna."

Oliver's growl reverberated through the room, shaking my bones, and causing me to jump.

"I'd suggest you speak with a little more respect," Trevor rumbled. His defenses seemed to be going up, too.

"Why?" he scoffed. "Clearly, she isn't marked. That's either because she hasn't accepted him, or he doesn't think she's good enough. Why would the pack want a Luna raised like that? How would that be good for the pack? And if it's taking the Alpha so long to decide whether or not she's worth marking, she probably isn't. My vote is to let the hunters have her."

Oliver was across the table in a heartbeat, Derek pinned to the wall by his throat. Kota and Brandon were quick to follow, requiring them both to pull Oliver off. I remained where I was, studying the reactions of everyone else in the room.

"Don't forget, Gamma, you're the one who came to us for sanctuary. I can take it away as quickly as my father gave it," Oliver spat.

"Maybe you should go see my daughter and wife in the kitchen, Derek,"

Gregory said quietly. "This is a strategizing meeting, not a Luna selection approval."

"He should stay, actually," I cut in, stopping Derek in his beeline for the door. "He should stay, or he should be dismissed from his Gamma duties, I would think."

All eyes fell on me, the silence consuming the room. It must have been a nonverbal agreement I wasn't privy to, putting me in charge. "Well, Derek? Are you here to help us determine how to neutralize the most hunters possible, or scrutinize the Alpha's assessment of my suitability to sit in this room?"

"Here to help, Luna," Derek said sullenly. He returned to the table, eyes downcast.

It was easy enough for Kota to steer the plan the way we needed everyone to think it was going. There had been hunters sighted lingering around the town the entire time, meaning the wolves we already had there could easily make their presence known. There had been a lot of back and forth on whether that was the proper approach, but from what the scouts had observed, it was a move that would undoubtedly bring more hunters in. Once enough were there, the pack would strike.

They were after me, though, so the scene? Well, obviously, my friends were planning a surprise early birthday party for me, just in time for when I'd be getting back from an extended vacation. Throw in the scouts and warriors stationed over there having a pack run with a few rogues to boost numbers, and the werewolf presence would be obvious to anyone who knew what they were looking for.

I had very little faith they would fall for it, but it was the best idea we had. Almost exactly like the battle plan from twelve years prior.

Derek had stayed silent for the rest of the meeting and was the first to leave, the Gamma from down south quickly following. It didn't take long until only Oliver, Kota, Brandon, Trevor, and I remained. The four of them were old friends. Brandon was a year younger than his cousin Trevor, and Kota had joined the group when he came to the pack to take advantage of the training program ten years ago. They meant the world to each other, and I knew for a fact Oliver wouldn't have survived the last eight years without them. I wondered how torn their group would be after all was said and done.

"I want Derek monitored," Oliver grumbled. "He's causing too many problems."

"What's his deal, anyway?" I asked, curiosity getting the better of me.

Oliver let out a sigh, scrubbing his hand across his face. "How much have you been told about the rogue who killed my father?"

"Not much," I said, shaking my head. It seemed like a rather taboo subject around here. His parents were rarely talked about at all, let alone the intricacies of why they were no longer with us. "Just that there was a battle."

He nodded slowly, taking a sip of his coffee before starting in.

"Ten or so years ago, a rogue came on the radar, targeting and attacking smaller packs. Recent information has come to light that his wolf side took him over, probably because he tried to shut the wolf out completely." Oliver didn't look at me, but I could feel the turmoil wreaking havoc in him. I gulped, understanding dawning on me why it was so imperative to him I integrated with my wolf. "One of the packs he attacked was a smaller pack in Wyoming, killing the Alpha and Beta. The Alpha had no heir, and Derek was only an adopted son of the Beta. He had no hope of taking over the pack with no Alpha blood, so he came to us, asking for protection. Dad welcomed them with open arms, instating him as a Gamma to oversee the town, and tried to let them keep their individuality. Once, uh... Once Dad died, Derek got fussy about the transition of power."

"He didn't get fussy," Kota scoffed. "He tried to challenge you. I told you then, and I'm telling you now, your idea to keep him close to keep an eye on him was faulty."

"Yeah, probably," Oliver huffed. "I should have at least moved which town he was based in. But anyway, now there are a lot of mixed messages coming out of that town. Derek is saying they are inundated with violent rogues, but scouts are reporting he's killing first, asking questions later."

"I thought this pack tried to maintain good relations with rogues?" That had been something everyone talked about, a fact that set this pack and its allies apart. Rogues were not considered guilty until proven innocent.

"We are," he confirmed, "but the pack they were before was not. And I wouldn't be surprised if the events that caused the demise of his pack solidified his views."

I nodded, understanding. I really did. And it made Derek's feelings toward me even more reasonable. Hearing your entire ideology had flipflopped was something that took time to process. The more pressure, the harder it was to accept. I knew that better than anyone.

I felt like I had come a long way with only being part of a pack for less than a month, but I struggled plenty with trying to change my mindset. Right now, what got me through was focusing wholeheartedly on keeping my problems away from this pack.

OLIVER

As soon as it was out in the open that Lya was training, she threw herself into it wholeheartedly. The meeting with the Gammas had not helped the matter. It seemed her suitability being questioned only fueled her commitment. Kota had integrated her in with the second year recruits putting in extra time over the summer, and she was holding her own easily. Rising to the top, actually. I still didn't like the fact that she was training, and I'd somehow received a ban from the Luna herself not to set foot on the training grounds while she was there. She was making quite a name for herself already, but only snippets of her performance were being passed on to me.

With her spending all day training, I saw her less and less. I tried to convince her it was a matter that could be dealt with once the impending battle was over. Or maybe she could join the first years when a new group started in August. Every suggestion was shot down.

Kota wasn't helping, either. She had gotten her claws and command into him before I could, so he was obligated to follow her word over mine. Realistically, I didn't think hers was a proper command, but Adair wouldn't allow me to muster a single word to override her.

I had to get used to spending days without her, anyway. This was what life would be like when everything calmed down. It'd be easier once my mark was on her neck, though.

"I don't see why you can't march over there and see what's going on for yourself," Brandon quipped. He, along with the other Gammas from out of town, had stuck around to brush up on training under Kota's direction in preparation for next week. With Kota and Thom preoccupied with training my mate, and Trevor wrapped up with his own, Brandon was the only one of my circle typically around.

I shot Brandon a glare. "I can't."

"Aw, c'mon," he teased. "She'll be upset for a while, but she'll get over it."

"No, Brandon, I really can't," I huffed. "She figured out a command."

Brandon's lighthearted expression quickly fell away to reveal confusion. "But she can't do that yet. She isn't even pack yet, right?"

"Her dad is an Alpha," I reminded him.

Brandon shook his head. "Kota insisted that isn't how the Wulver Pack works. She shouldn't be able to do that."

"Well, maybe it's because she's my fated mate, not chosen." I sat back with a huff, trying to get control of my frustration.

RUN.

"And Derek doubted the Moon Goddess's command," he chuckled. "Maybe you need to quit with those temporary marks. Just get it over with and mark her."

I stood up and made my way over to the decanter sitting by the couch. That thing had been utilized much too frequently recently. "I'll get to it."

"Have you two still not talked to each other about that yet?" he asked. "Dude, you were sunshine and daisies after you found her. Now, you're starting to get dark and broody again. Just man up, will ya?"

I slung the liquor back, draining my glass before speaking. "I have hunters threatening my pack and my mate. I'll deal with it after that threat is resolved. Besides, I can't have her going into heat now."

"Fair point." Brandon retrieved a glass for himself and settled in on the couch. "You're getting mean again. You two could, at the very least, have a conversation and get on the same page."

"Easier said than done."

Brandon seemed to have the easiest time of my friends determining when he was talking to his friend versus his Alpha. He always knew when to back down, whereas Trevor and Kota would continue to push. It surprised me when he continued to talk on this particular subject.

"The longer you wait, the more time you're losing with her," he pointed out.

I turned away, not willing to admit he was right. "I can't do this right now. I have a war to plan."

"I don't even get why you're stressing so much. If everything goes well, you'll be back in time for dinner that night. Pop out there, off a handful of hunters, then get back home to mark your mate."

"You don't know that," I snapped. Every fiber of my being anticipated things going wildly awry.

"Fine, fine," he huffed, standing up. "Mates change people, man. And I'm beginning to think it isn't always for the better."

The words cut, but he was right. Lya and I deserved an award for how well we ignored the elephant in the room. She seemed to be coming out on top, too. None of it seemed to be bothering her at all. Maybe because she had already marked me. Maybe she still couldn't feel the mate bond yet. My hand went up to the mark on my neck. Her wolf knew, at least.

The door clicked closed behind Brandon, leaving me alone with my thoughts. Even my wolf wasn't around to talk to, not that he would provide words of encouragement. He would have agreed with Brandon. Hell, I agreed with Brandon.

239

Silence was my enemy, providing too much time to think. Without the interruption of my wolf, my mind drifted to problems. I had been lucky these past eight years; in all my time running the pack, problems were small. The largest issues we ever dealt with were problems other packs roped us into. Those, I had the option to pull out if it put my pack in too much danger. Now, though? Retreat was not an option.

To retreat would be to turn my back on my mate. With all I had already lost, she was the one thing I would not let slip through my fingers.

I looked up to the clock, desperately hoping enough time had passed. Seeing it was 5 pm, I breathed out a sigh. Lya should be wrapped up with training, meaning she was all mine for the rest of the night. I beelined for the door, not even giving my desk covered in paperwork a second glance.

"What do you want?" I huffed, catching sight of Kota making his way down the hall.

"Time's up, Alpha."

My shoulders slumped. He didn't need to clarify anything. Eight days had already passed since our first strategy meeting. "Two weeks was wishful thinking, wasn't it?"

Kota clapped me on the shoulder, offering a somber smile. "We gotta roll out the day after tomorrow. The number of hunters that have shown up, it'll be conspicuous if we don't make a move soon. They'll know it's a set-up."

"We were supposed to have more time."

I didn't feel like an Alpha right now. I felt pathetic and weak, begging to have back the very thing I hadn't been utilizing. In the grand scheme of things, hunters didn't scare us. Just a couple here and there were the sort of things we classified as controlled encounters, barely worth reporting. A large group of them together at once? We truly didn't know what to expect. The Marsans weren't your typical hunter, either. We didn't even have a semblance of an idea how far their connections stretched. We could end up blindsided.

If Thom and Kota were right, they weren't after the pack. They wanted the lost Wulver. If even one of them got through and they were able to track us back, that put her at too much risk. I didn't think my mind would be completely on the battlefield if she stayed at the pack, either. I had thirty-six hours. Maybe that would be enough time to convince her to let me mark her. I'd be more at peace if I could keep tabs on her wellbeing.

I caught sight of my little spitfire, engrossed in conversation with Rose and Trevor. Her smile had become more commonplace recently, shining through more and more with each crack to her walls.

Amber eyes fell on me, a mischievous glint calling back the wolf I had been searching for all day. She turned her back to her friends, stepping toward the tree line. She afforded me one last taunting glance over her shoulder before shifting quickly and dashing off.

I stood frozen in place, hypnotized by the sea of red fur. But Adair quickly surged forward, my large black wolf closing the space between him and his mate.

THIRTY

Lya

WE VIGILANTES HAD MET ALMOST DAILY the past two weeks, refining and perfecting the plan. Oliver had nearly found us out, but it was not a wolf my anger and fear brought forward. A roll of power surged through me, similar to the one that hit when I marked him, and filled my words.

"Just stay away from the training grounds while I am here, Oliver," I demanded. "You can't act on every worry, and you know I am safe here."

Hurt flashed across Oliver's face and consumed my thoughts, but I did my best to push it aside. I'd be hurting him a lot more soon enough. But right now, this was for the best.

When I got home that afternoon, we didn't talk about it. Thom mentioned I shouldn't be able to muster a command yet, especially one an Alpha had to obey, but I didn't quite care why or how. It provided the means to an end. Oliver had been getting closer and closer to finding out what was going on right under his nose, and we couldn't let that happen.

I had been at the pack for over a month now, and it was safe to say I was quite easily finding my place here. I owed them a debt for the new lease on life they gave me, and I would repay them, no matter the cost.

Maybe I hadn't changed as much as I thought.

Kota had been doing his best to answer any and all questions I had about the Wulver Pack we were a part of. Unfortunately, the Alpha, my father, had vanished several years ago, leaving them to find their own direction. The pack had not felt his passing, but no one could find him. The only way to replace an Alpha was in the event of their death, leaving the position open for someone else to assume, or by challenge, where the winner took control. You couldn't exactly challenge someone you couldn't find, though. Kota had tried to press me for any sort of information that might lead to my dad's whereabouts, but I had not laid eyes on him since that night when I was fifteen. Aside from a few phone calls over the years, I hadn't even spoken to him. The last time he called had been a couple phone number changes ago, too.

Thom had some affiliations with the Wulvers, too, thanks to Kota. He may have left Snow Moon, but he was nowhere near ready to abandon all of werewolf kind. He wasn't considering joining them, but was always willing to assist when asked. Kota said that made him an honorary Wulver, at least.

They would never tell Oliver, or any other pack for that matter, but the reason our particular area had known peace for so long was because of their unknown frontline of three - Kota, Thom, and Gregory. Even Trevor had helped them out during his hiatus from pack life.

Gregory was the one who actually made the most sense to me. Quiet and unassuming, passionate about protection and preparation, he carried the Beta role because of a duty to protect and serve. If it weren't for his mate, he wouldn't have ever joined a pack. Kota said he was apprised of the plan we had, but not to expect his input unless he saw a legitimate flaw.

This was the first time Gregory had appeared for one of our secret meetings, and his presence made me nervous. We had planned so carefully up until now, and I wasn't prepared for everything to come tumbling down.

Trevor, Thom, Gregory, and I sat quietly in Kota's office, waiting for him to get back from his meeting with the scouts. I glanced around nervously, thankful when Gregory cleared his throat to speak.

"Thom," he began, "how is Maggie doing?"

Thom glanced up, smiling at the mention of his wife. "Very ready to be done with pregnancy. I'd put money on her going into labor while you guys are gone."

Oliver had quickly agreed to Thom staying behind to oversee the pack for the day or two he, the old and new Betas, and Gammas would be out East River. Someone needed to be around in case things went south, and Thom knew how to lead. Derek would stay behind also, but Oliver wasn't about to put him in charge. That, and Thom needed to be close to Maggie if the pup came. Everyone was worried about her, too, with her being human and all. It wouldn't be fair to put him in the line of fire.

"The first pup is always the most stressful," Gregory offered. "You two will do fine."

Kota barged into the room, interrupting whatever it was Thom had for a response.

"I don't think we can wait any longer," he said quickly, demanding everyone's attention. "There are eight confirmed hunters milling around, and I'm sure there are others we don't know about."

"Can you remind me why we are doing it this way?" Trevor asked, pinching the bridge of his nose. "I really don't understand why we can't take the eight or more that are there out and call it a day."

"Because we can end this for good now if we play our cards right," Kota reminded him. "Hunters will always come back into play, but removing a dozen or so of them isn't going to hurt their ranks enough. We need to maximize the impact, and we need to know their plans. If they've been tracking her but not striking for years, there's got to be a reason, and we have to know. It's not only our Luna and pack we are trying to protect."

Gregory turned to me. We had hardly spoken, even though I had been in the packhouse for so long. He was quite happy to keep his distance, only offering pleasantries on occasion. At first, I thought he didn't like me, but I quickly learned that's just who he was. It was always the silent ones you needed to look out for, right? I was one of the silent ones. Before, at least. He slid a carefully wrapped package across the desk, a somber look on his face.

I gulped down the nausea the contents of that package brought up. "Is this really the best way?" I asked feebly.

"It's the only way," Gregory said sadly. "You'll need to start tonight."

I snatched it up, stuffing it in my backpack quickly. I stood, leaving the office. I wasn't sure if the meeting was finished, but I was done.

I had expected arguments from Tala about this, but she seemed as resigned to the necessity of it as I was. It would be her that was impacted the most, her that would shield me from feeling any of it. Comparatively, my part was easy.

Oh, how times had changed.

'I'm so sorry,' I whispered to her.

'You don't want to do it this time,' she said quietly.

Tala and I were still figuring out how to forge a new path ahead. It was difficult trying to figure out how to happily share my brain, but we seemed to be getting closer every day. Shifting regularly, along with our proximity to our mate, helped. It was beginning to feel more natural. I resented what I'd have to put her through.

'We will be okay,' she assured me. If only I could believe it.

Rose caught up to me as I was leaving the training grounds, falling in step beside me. It was rare I didn't enjoy her company, but now was one of those times.

"Guess what!?" she shrieked

I glanced up at her, trying not to let my inner turmoil show. No response was apparently invitation enough to continue.

"I got an assignment!" Joy bubbled over on Rose's face, making it hard not to smile with her. "I mean, I'm kind of upset that I didn't get selected to go out to your old place and help over there, but I am going to work!"

"I wouldn't be too upset about sitting that one out if I were you," I said slowly. Hell, I would sit it out if I could have it my way.

"This will be a longer assignment, anyway," Rose explained. "I'm keeping tabs on that Wyoming Gamma! Do you think he's really as bad as Oliver thinks he is?"

"Yeah," I snorted. "He's a prick at the very least. He was all for just handing me over to the hunters."

Rose looked over at me, wide-eyed. "No! He said that?"

"Right to Oliver's face," I confirmed. A small part of me warmed, remembering how Oliver jumped to my defense. "That's why he's not being included on the East River assignment. Oliver doesn't think he can trust him. But you knew that already if you'll be trailing him."

"I never thought this pack had issues like that," she mused. "I guess they don't really let pack members in on the leadership drama, though."

"I guess not." Come to think of it, even the East River assignment was being kept relatively quiet. Oliver hadn't done anything to publicly alert the pack to the threat. Of course, everyone knew there was something big going on because the warriors were apprised of it and mandatory training had increased. It was big enough to call on some of the non-warriors to take over patrols and such while everyone would be gone. But overall, the extremity of the situation had been kept quiet.

Granted, if we had covered our tracks well enough, Oliver shouldn't think it was a big deal, either. They were projecting three or four wolves to each hunter present, meaning, aside from us rebels, everyone should be under the impression that it wouldn't be a hassle to go in, neutralize the threat, and leave. It actually seemed like a lot of manpower to me. I mean, Trevor and Rose didn't seem to have any problem with the four hunters in Chamberlain.

At some point, Trevor had joined us in our walk back to the packhouse. I glanced over at him, offering a small smile. I knew this weighed on him heavily, and the guilt of lying to his best friend was eating him alive. At least he had a new mate to keep him distracted.

We came to a stop in front of the Lincoln Log mansion. Kota had made it here before us, and it looked like he was breaking the news to Oliver that the timeline had been moved up.

I could feel Oliver's eyes on me, but I tried to ignore them—just for a moment.

"Mind stashing this?" I asked Trevor, passing my backpack over to him. "I want to go on a run one last time."

He took the backpack gingerly. I wondered if he could feel its contents through the fabric. I really hoped I'd be able to find that backpack again. I knew he wasn't completely on board with the plan; he'd already thrown a fit about it.

I finally caved, locking eyes with my mate. A smile crept over my face, pulling at the corners of my mouth, and I felt Tala push forward.

OLIVER

ONE OF MY favorite parts of the past couple weeks had been runs with Tala. Lya's shifts were getting easier, and Tala lived for the chase. Tala was quite the small wolf, but she was exceptionally agile. She could stay remarkably quiet, too, which surprised me given how little experience she had in wolf form. And she was fast.

Adair assured me this was due to her lineage. Wulvers, rumored to be genetically produced protectors and defenders, would of course have more natural inclinations to the traits warriors trained so hard to learn. Maybe she'd become a tracker or scout once she progressed through training.

So much about Lya was defined by something she had no clue about. All we had was one book that didn't even provide much information, and one person who provided equally little knowledge.

I wondered about the girl Trevor told me about before she came to the pack, because I certainly didn't know her. I had heard about a lost little girl who acted akin to a feral cat someone got too close to, but the woman I knew was headstrong, feisty, and set out to get exactly what she wanted, and she was rarely selfish with her wants. All she needed to unlock that door was the permission to do so. It'd be easy to try and take credit for the growth she had experienced here, but all I had done was try to put some of her insecurities to sleep. She was the one who set out to fix herself.

The girl didn't need a knight in shining armor; she just needed a sword. And from what I could see, she had found her Excalibur.

Adair came screeching to a halt in Lya's favorite clearing, nose in the air, trying to catch Tala's scent. The little red wolf had given us the slip. Again. Some Alpha we were.

The snap of a twig had us whirling around, lunging for our mate. Let's be honest, the chase was fun, but catching the prize was the best part.

Tala didn't back down, instead lunging forward to meet us head-on. The wolves grappled for a bit, but Adair eventually pinned Tala. He licked her muzzle and nibbled at her neck until a giggling Lya lay underneath him. I quickly shifted as well, rolling to the side and pulling Lya with me.

I lost track of how long we lay there in comfortable silence. Slowly but surely, though, the crushing weight of anxiety crept back into my chest. The feeling had been omnipresent the past week, and I hated it more and more by the day. It wasn't a feeling I was used to, and I desperately hoped it would disappear when I got back from East River.

That isn't ours,' Adair's voice rumbled in the back of my head.

'What?'

'It isn't your fear,' he clarified. *'It is mate's.'*

I breathed a small sigh of relief, thankful to know I hadn't just gone soft. I looked down, trying to get a good view of my weakness.

"Are you worried about the hunters?" I asked her, brushing a lock of hair out of her face. Lya nodded but didn't say a word. "You don't need to," I tried to reassure her. "We're leaving the day after tomorrow, and we should be back just the day after that. You'll be here and safe, and we'll be back before you know it."

"We'll see," she said quietly.

"Really," I insisted, tipping her head up to look at me. "There's no reason why this should take long or even be that dangerous. It's just a handful of hunters, and we are more than prepared for them." Lya's eyes darted around, but she refused to look at me. "You'll be able to feel if something goes wrong, too, you know."

Her brows furrowed. "What?"

I chuckled and brought her hand up to my mark, letting her feel the energy surge between us. "You marked me. We are connected, remember?"

She smiled, but it didn't quite reach her eyes. "Everything will be fine, Lya. I promise."

Lya breathed out a sigh and looked up at me. Her eyes told me Tala was just as present as she was. "Let's just not talk, please?"

A new emotion laced with the fear in my chest. It was one I was all too familiar with.

Sorrow.

Fear and heartbreak. It was a lethal combination.

When Lya kissed me, it wasn't filled with the hot and fiery passion I had come to anticipate and look forward to with her. It was low and smoldering and communicated everything she couldn't find the words to say. Her lips moved slowly, and her skin felt like fire against me.

I rolled over, supporting my weight on my elbows so I hovered over Lya. Looking down, I studied her expression carefully.

My gums tingled. It was a sensation I was growing all too used to. Every moment with her made it harder and harder to maintain my self-control. Marking was an intimate thing, almost always taking place during mating, but the need to do so surfaced when the connection was closest.

The mate bond didn't lie.

My soul was bound to this woman, and the way she needed me most was as her protector. In all reality, it had surprised me when the sexual desire for this little spitfire crept up on me. I wasn't about to regret a single part of our bond, though.

Your mate was always who you needed.

One soul, divided amongst two humans and two wolves, with the red string of fate pulling them together, just waiting for paths to converge. Of course, the bond would supersede the need to mate and produce offspring, but it made sense that the closeness, the intimacy of knowing thoughts, the willingness to lay down your life for them would also cause the burgeoning of love.

The mate bond, I was discovering, was not love. But it was designed to foster love. The existence of our race depended on it in more ways than one. We were a dying breed, and we mated for life. Each of us needed a sworn protector, a confidant, our own personal judge and jury. Of course, we had to be cut from the same cloth. She was mine and I was hers.

Skin on skin, hearts beating in time, electricity zapping through the air so palpable I was certain an onlooker would feel it, too.

I felt my canines elongating. I couldn't even find the words to condense all of what I felt and thought, but the look in her eyes told me she knew.

Lya gave me a small nod and rolled her head to the side, exposing the delicately freckled skin on her neck where my mark would go. Will go.

The reality of what I was about to do consumed me, making me tremble. It was Adair who pushed forward, bringing my mouth to her neck and sinking teeth into flesh.

Nothing would have prepared me for the freight train that hit. It was all-consuming, flooding my mind with swirling emotions and need. Lya etched herself upon my soul, claimed permanently as mine. There was no going back, and I didn't want to.

My canines retracted, and I pulled away from her, anxious to see her reaction. I reached out, trying to search her mind for the reason behind her approval that now was the right time but was met by a wall, blocking off all answers.

She reached up and cupped my face, running her thumb along my cheekbone.

"You just have to trust me, alright?" she whispered.

I only nodded once. She wouldn't have to ask me twice.

THIRTY-ONE

Lya

SUCH LOVELY LITTLE four-letter words that could change your life.

Love.

Hate.

Wolf.

Mate.

Bond.

Lies.

I looked up at Oliver, trying desperately to shove away the desire to tell him everything. Let him know what was coming. But if I told him, everything up until this point would have been for naught. He would never let me risk it all like that.

"You just stay safe, okay?" I begged. "This pack needs you. You need to come back."

"Nothing could keep me away," he insisted, the corner of his mouth quirking up in a half-smile. "I have too much waiting for me back home."

He would certainly have plenty waiting for him here, that was for sure. I was absolutely certain he would not be impressed with what was left.

He brushed his lips against mine one last time, a soft kiss that left me wanting more. "I love you, Lya."

I stared up at him, a culmination of emotions I couldn't quite put my finger on flowing through me.

Love. That's what it was.

It was a foreign feeling. I didn't think I had ever been loved before. Not truly, anyway, and not in years. I had certainly never loved anyone.

Oliver shot me a wink before getting into his FJ60. "I'll see you soon, love. I'll be back in time for the full moon run tomorrow night if everything goes well."

All I could offer was a smile and a small wave. *Please, just trust me,* I begged, hoping he could feel that notion through the little fragments of the bond I could still feel.

I turned away, unwilling to watch him leave. He was so hopeful. If only he knew.

I was about to ruin everything.

My hand went to my mark. I had been careful to keep it covered the past day, but I was constantly painfully aware of its presence. Every time I was on Oliver's mind, it seemed to emit the sparks mate bonds were known for. Right now, it was practically burning.

I adjusted my shirt to make sure it was covered and found my way over to Thom. We had about an hour until shit really got started.

"You ready?" I asked.

"As ready as I'll ever be," he huffed. "I just wish you weren't my brother's mate. He doesn't deserve what we're going to put him through."

I looked out at the caravan of vehicles headed off pack lands. "If suffering for one means safety for all, it's the best choice."

Thom shook his head. "If something happens to you, this pack is in trouble. Suffering for an Alpha is suffering for an entire pack. Don't forget this is the largest pack in the country."

"Well, it's too late to come up with a different plan," I argued.

"I don't think there could even be another plan."

He was right. We had explored every option. At the end of the day, this was the best we had.

We turned and headed back into the packhouse. The wheels were officially in motion, and there was no turning back.

The hour passed way too slowly. I had agreed to this, but that didn't change the sense of dread coming over me now that it was happening. Any notions I had of being the one to save the day were quickly vanishing, replaced by the reminder of my own mortality. On top of the sense of impending doom, the further Oliver got from the pack, the more I felt the strain of a rubber band being stretched to its limits. Damn mate bond.

I glanced up at the clock, begging time to pass more quickly. If anything, watching the second hand just slowed it down. I trudged over to the parcel Gregory had given me and pulled out the box inside. Glaring down at the teabag, I brought it with me to the kitchen and made one last cup of tea, my throat itching as I gulped it down.

I breathed out a sigh when Thom finally knocked on the door. I gave a quick glance around the room. There was nothing I needed to take. I grabbed Oliver's sweatshirt, intending to keep as much of him with me as I could, and headed out the door, following behind Thom in silence.

Neither of us spoke for the first hour of the drive. I felt like I had forgotten how to talk. All I could do was focus on the mixtape crackling through the stereo.

"I see the bad moon a-risin'."

"So." My voice cracked, almost as if it was radio static. "You can't mind-link anymore, right?"

Thom shot a glance in my direction. "No. Why?"

"I see trouble on the way."

"Just wondering," I shrugged. "Not even Maggie? Isn't she your mate?"

"Chosen mate," he corrected. "Chosen mates don't get fated mate privileges. You can't even mark a chosen mate."

"I see earthquakes and lightnin'."

I nodded slowly, not really concerned about the particulars of their mateship. "And with South Dakota's reception, you really can't call anyone, either."

The car slowed, coming to a stop on the shoulder. "What are you getting at, Lya?" Thom demanded, turning to glare at me.

"I see bad times today."

I refused to look at him, but I could feel his eyes searing holes in me. All I did was pull down the collar of my shirt, so my mark was on full display.

"Oh, fuck."

"Don't go around tonight
Well, it's bound to take your life
There's a bad moon on the rise."

I nodded in agreement, although feeling guilty that, for just a split second, I regretted letting him mark me. It was selfish of me.

"When?"

"Day before yesterday," I gulped. "It would have been too late to change the plan. When everyone gets back, you have to tell them. You have to make sure everything goes perfectly. If I don't get out, we lose Ollie, too."

I finally looked up at Thom. The look on his face made it seem like he was reliving the loss of his own mate, and already mourning the very probable loss his brother was destined to experience. I was surprised when he pulled back onto the road, still heading east.

The stakes had just gotten higher, putting a lot more of the onus on the small group running the show back home. I chuckled, trying to figure out if I feared more for them as they fended off an overprotective Alpha with a lost mate, or for the hunters we were trying to eradicate.

We didn't talk again, the music on the radio dancing along with the tension. I would have taken this drive continuing on forever over what waited for us at the end, though.

I knew how to run. It was my greatest gift. I could run from what I loved, what I lost, what I hated, what I needed. I could run from anything.

But I couldn't run from this.

The car stopped, but I refused to move. Something about out of the frying pan and into the fire.

"Don't forget, Lya, he has to see you. He has to know you've been captured." I nodded. If I spoke, my voice would crack and I would cry. "Avoid everything that would bring the presence of your wolf forward. You can't smell like a wolf. You haven't spoken to your wolf or mind-linked or shifted since you started drinking the silver tea, right?" I shook my head, still scared to talk. "Good. Don't take off the silver jewelry if at all possible. They have got to think you're human, Lya, until we give you the go ahead."

"I know," I squeaked.

I didn't say goodbye. Just slipped out the door, closed it quietly behind me, and started the trek to my old house.

I tried to look oblivious to what was going on around me, but I could still smell the wolves nearby, occasionally seeing their eyes glinting in the near full moon light. Kota had been careful to select the ones for this mission, ensuring none of them would be able to recognize me. And if Kota and Trevor were doing their job correctly, Oliver wouldn't get here until it was too late. There was no one to jump out and stop what was about to happen. Brandon was the only outlier, but I was certain Gregory had a good handle on him.

I strolled down the block, looking for anyone I could possibly recognize. Anyone human, that is. I stopped in my tracks, heart skipping a beat when I caught a face from my past out of the corner of my eye, standing just across the street from my old house.

Ted.

No, not Ted. Will, Ted's younger brother.

"Will!" I called, trying to put on as happy a front as possible. "What are you doing here? Is Ted with you?"

Will looked up and started walking toward me, closing the distance quickly.

"Hi, Lya." His voice held none of the jovial, upbeat tones I was used to. "Why haven't you been answering any calls?"

"Oh, you know," I shrugged, "Ted told me he needed some space. I decided maybe that'd be good for me, too. I've just kind of tried to unplug completely. It's been really nice, actually."

Easy enough lie. Unplugging was what all the cool kids were doing these days.

"Ted hasn't answered any calls, either," Will pointed out. "We haven't heard from him in weeks."

"Oh." I blanched, furrowing my eyebrows. "I figured he'd go straight back home."

I started glancing around. If Kota's predictions had been correct, the hunters would be close, probably just out of sight.

"Do you think maybe you'd want to go grab a drink with me, have a chat, see if we can figure out where he might be off to?" Will asked.

I swallowed hard. This seemed like it was all going just a little too easily. Everyone was confident they'd want me alive. Me going willingly would be their preferred way of kidnapping. I caught headlights in my peripheral vision, and I was certain the car they belonged to was Oliver's Land Cruiser.

"Uh, yeah," I agreed. I shot another glance over to the car, hoping it really was Oliver. I looked back at Will. His smile was cold and menacing. "Yeah, that'd be fine."

"Good. Because you weren't going to get much of a choice."

I whipped my head around, back to Oliver. Fingers crossed he'd remember when I asked him to just trust me.

He was out of the car, running toward me before I could even blink.

"Lya, run!" Oliver shouted.

And for the first time in my life, running was the last thing on my mind.

A large black wolf was the last thing I saw.

OLIVER

I HADN'T STUCK AROUND LONG ENOUGH for the clean-up. Hell, I probably shouldn't have stuck around at all. There weren't as many hunters there as I'd hoped; they could have spared me so I could have followed my mate. Anger had consumed me, though. That kid's arms around her with a silver knife to her neck, taking what was mine, made him an impossible target without risking her life.

I damn near tore the door of the packhouse off its hinges.

"Thomas!" I shouted. I needed answers.

Padded feet came rushing down the hall. Decidedly not Thom.

"You're back!" Anna cried. "It's 5 in the morning. What are you doing back so soon? Is Trevor here, too? Is he okay?"

"Shut *up*, Anna! Where the fuck is my brother?" I demanded.

She took a step back, a look of shock crossing her face. "I-I'm sorry, Alpha. He's probably still sleeping."

I stormed down the hall, not sparing her a second glance. Just as I lifted my fist to start banging, the door swung open. Thom looked like he hadn't slept at all, eyes haggard and hair sticking up in all directions, as if he'd been running his fingers through it all night. He took a cautious step into the hall, quietly closing the door behind him.

Before he could say a word, I had my hands around his throat and pinned him to the wall. "How the fuck did Lya end up at the battle, Thom?"

Thom held his hands up in surrender and choked out, "I'll talk when the others get here."

I tightened my hands. "What the fuck do they have to do with it? She snuck out from under your nose! If you had been keeping an eye on her, she wouldn't have gotten out there! They took her, Thom! She's gone!"

Hands grabbed at my arms, pulling me back.

"Let go of him, Ollie," a voice I knew but couldn't be bothered to recognize said.

"Oliver," Gregory called. My head snapped around; hearing my name instead of my title out of him was just barely enough to get my attention. "Office, now."

I turned and walked toward my office. I felt like a zombie. The string connecting Lya and me felt stretched to its breaking point, wrapped so tightly around my heart it was suffocating. I sat down at my desk, head in my hands.

This couldn't be happening. Someone put an overfull glass of scotch in front of me. I couldn't even be bothered to give it a second glance.

I sat still, trying to drown out everything around me. People slowly filtered in, but I couldn't think clearly enough to distinguish who they were. I couldn't tell if it had been hours or milliseconds, but I still didn't have answers.

"Someone needs to start talking." I hardly recognized my own voice.

Gregory stood, walked over to the decanter, and poured himself a glass. I hardly ever saw him drink. Come to think of it, the last time was at my father's funeral. "Oliver, can you tell me why exactly you chose the people in this room to stand by you as you lead this pack?"

I looked up, eyes unable to focus. "I don't understand the question."

"Why are we all here, Oliver?" Gregory asked. "Do we boost your ego? Is it just to agree with you and tell you your choices are correct? Or do we serve a more important purpose?"

I furrowed my eyebrows, taking a second to think. "No one would be able to lead a pack alone, especially a pack this size."

"Good, you got that answer correct." Gregory chuckled. "Now, you need to shut up and sit quietly while the circle you selected explains what is going on and why you were not involved in it."

I looked around the room, but no one seemed the least bit excited to begin explaining. I cleared my throat. "The Marsan family and their connections make up the largest hunter contingent in North America. We have over one hundred members cataloged, but it's likely their numbers are much higher. We took out seven tonight, keeping only one survivor." I shot everyone another glance before continuing. "We know they've been searching for the lost Wulver girl for years, but we do not know why. In a twisted turn of events, that girl is also mated to the Alpha of the largest pack on the continent. If they discovered she was mated to that Alpha, they would surely be after that pack as well. Do I have the story right so far?"

Soft laughter started in the back of the room. I looked up to see Trevor's face contorting as it progressed to manic guffaws.

"Oh, and you thought my first plan was bad," he hooted. "You are going to murder us all when you find out what's going on."

Kota reached over, smacking the back of his skull. "No, he won't. We're the ones who got her into this mess, and without us, he can't get her out."

Kota got up and started pacing. "Look, Lya is a plant. We've got people following her, figuring out where the hell these guys even hole up to hide from us. She shut out her wolf so they shouldn't be able to realize she's anything but human. When we have enough information figured out and have picked off enough of the hunters to make it an easier job, we'll go in and get her. For right now, we need you to get on the phone and start calling in every favor you have."

I looked at him, absolutely dumbfounded. "And you actually think that is going to work?"

"No fucking clue." He laughed coldly. "But she's a Wulver. Just like me, just like Gregory, and just like your brother. If we didn't facilitate the plan, she would've gone and done it herself. At least, this way, we know she has a minimum of two packs backing her up."

I grabbed the glass of scotch and took a long swallow. "When this is over, I'm killing all of you."

"No, you won't. The hunters came into existence to destroy the Wulvers. Now, the Wulvers are rising to destroy the hunters. We have come full circle, and our leader is our MIA Alpha's daughter," Kota detailed.

Gregory's glass clinked down on the table. "I am not scared of you, Ollie boy, but I am scared of that girl's father when he finds out we did not uphold his very last request of us to keep his daughter away from our kind."

"What are you even talking about?" I asked, looking at Gregory. "Who even are you? How are you and Kota in this pack if you're also in the Wulver Pack?"

"The pack isn't technically a pack since they don't have an Alpha blood-line," I heard. It was Thom cutting in this time, helping bring me up to speed. "No one really knows why they can still maintain a pack link, but because they don't have a true Alpha line tying them together, they can join other packs."

"There's a Wulver in almost every pack," Kota agreed. "We are small in numbers, but we have our hands in everything, directing everything where it needs to go."

I sat back in my chair and took a deep breath. "I never had any control here, did I?"

"No, you've always had all the control, called all the shots," Gregory said. "We don't get involved in pack matters unless it's breaching werewolf law."

"And it's just you four in on it?" I asked.

"And the rest of the Wulvers," Kota said, "and a few rogues like Thom we've picked up along the way."

I finished off my scotch, staring blankly at the glass for a moment. None of it felt real. I just wanted to wake up from this horrible dream.

"This is too much," I mumbled. "I just want my mate back."

"We'll get her back, Ollie," Trevor promised.

Glass shattered against the wall, sending shards cascading through the room. I looked down at my hand, not even realizing that was where it had originated from.

"I marked her!" I roared. "I can't even feel the bond anymore!"

Kota quickly strode over to me, tearing the collar of my shirt down to reveal my mark. The thought to fight him off was somewhere in Neverland. This wasn't a good position for an Alpha to be in.

"She's still alive," he offered, relief evident in his voice. "She's fine for now."

"You won't feel it, anyway," Gregory said nonchalantly. "She's been drinking silver-laced tea for two days now."

"Why would you have her doing that?" I spat at my Beta.

"Because of the way silver works for a Wulver," he explained. "We are resistant to silver, but not immune. Her wolf will recede to avoid it, taking the scent, the ability to mind-link, even the mate bond with it. The wolf is still there, watching and waiting in case it needs to come forward. It isn't going to hurt her."

I rolled my eyes. "Yeah, the same way silver didn't hurt her before. You've seen all her scars!"

"None were permanent, and all healed. Any human would have bled out or overdosed from her past wounds, but her wolf didn't let her," he pointed out. "Oliver, she chose this. All of this was her plan."

I looked around the room, trying to find someone to stand by me. But I was a lone wolf here.

Something inside of me knew this was going to happen. Once I knew where she came from, it had seemed inevitable that she would take matters into her own hands. She knew me well enough to know I would have never let her do that, too. I had a sudden realization that learning about the Wulver Pack and my mate's origin story should have been a priority.

Some Alpha I was.

I slumped back down in my chair, squeezing my eyes shut, hoping that when I opened them it would be Lya in front of me instead of a room full of betrayal.

"Does she even realize we are fated mates?" I asked quietly. I bore her mark, but maybe she truly didn't realize what her wolf staking her claim meant.

"She's known for a month now," Trevor mumbled. His voice was dull and lifeless, exactly how I felt. "She was pretty hurt that you never said anything about it."

The weight of that truth hit me like a ton of bricks. Maybe if I had been up front with her, none of this would be happening.

"Wait," Kota cut into my train of thought. "You're both marked, but neither of you have accepted the bond?"

I kept my eyes down but shook my head.

"Oh, thank the Goddess," he breathed out. "Even if we don't get her out alive, we won't lose you, too."

"Oh, no, we will still lose him," my brother murmured. "He'll still physically be here, but Alpha Oliver will be gone."

THIRTY-TWO

Lya

MY HEAD WAS POUNDING. I tried to lift my hands to my head to hold it together, but my hands were bound tightly behind me. I shifted around, trying to loosen them, but whoever tied them was really good at knots. I settled for pressing my head against a cooler part of the leather.

I had to catch myself before reaching out to Tala to make sure she was okay.

I hadn't gotten brave enough to open my eyes yet, but I wanted an idea of just how far we were from the pack. The idea of sunlight made me cringe, so I just listened. It was hard to hear past the pounding in my head, but I still tried. Luckily, the silver tea didn't affect my senses too much.

The road rumbled like it needed to be redone. I didn't hear any cars around, so it must have just been us on the road, and judging by the fact that I could only smell one other scent, it was just me and Will in the car. I wondered if anyone other than us made it out alive. Given how angry Oliver was when he saw me, I doubted it.

I smiled to myself. At least one thing had gone right so far.

I took a deep breath. Time to open my eyes. I could do it.

This was going to make my head hurt worse, I knew it. I only cracked them open at first, bracing myself for the inevitable searing pain.

What I really wasn't prepared for, however, was the darkness that engulfed me. I could make out a glow from the stereo, but that was it. Was it still night?

I sat up a little, trying to get a better visual of my surroundings. It didn't help much, seeing as we were apparently still driving across the barren wastelands of the Midwest. Every once in a while, I could make out the outline of a tree. Definitely still the Midwest, but headed westward, which meant we couldn't have been driving for long. Had it really happened only hours ago?

"Ah, you're awake," Will said. "We should be coming up on a town here shortly. We can stop and grab some food."

I needed water, and being able to move around would be nice. I had been rather rudely crammed in the back seat of his car, and I was starting to get sore.

"Where are we?" I croaked.

"Almost to Kennebec."

Kennebec. Headed back to where I'd just come from. Why exactly did I leave? I could have just met them on the road. But they couldn't know that.

"Lya, I think we need to talk." Of all Ted's family, Will was probably the one I got along with the best. Maybe that's why he was the one collecting me. "You wanna tell me what's happened to my brother?"

"I-I don't know," I stuttered. "Is this why you kidnapped me? You know, we could have just talked."

"Oh, no," he chuckled. "You know something. And life is going to be pretty hard for you until you talk. How is it connected to all the werewolves roaming around your place?"

"What?" I sputtered while sitting up a little straighter, trying to get comfortable. This was going to be a very, very long drive. "What do you mean, werewolves?"

Will glanced back in the rearview mirror, making eye contact with me. I tore my eyes away, looking toward the lights of the upcoming town. "Don't play dumb. I know you know what I'm talking about."

I tried to force out a laugh. "I know you're crazy. You have to let me go!"

"Do you hear voices, Lya?" he asked. "Specifically, just one voice."

I shook my head frantically. "If I did, I'd be talking to a therapist about it, not you!"

"Oh, yeah, I guess so. Unless shifting into a wild animal accompanied that voice." He shot a pointed look in my direction that sent a shudder up my spine. He pulled the car into the parking lot of the local dive in Kennebec, putting it in park before turning to me. "Now, we're going to go in there, grab a drink with some friends of mine, and if you play nice, we can make life real easy for you. Ya hear?"

When I nodded, he got out of the car, coming around to where I was to pull me out. He kept one hand firmly on my upper arm, guiding me through the parking lot. I glanced around, trying to keep my head as still as possible.

There was a couple laughing and chatting across the parking lot, and a few guys were gathered around some larger than necessary trucks smoking, but other than that, the place was pretty dead. My eyes bounced between the people around, waiting for a sign.

Everyone here must be in on what was going on. Why else would they just ignore a girl with her hands tied up being dragged around?

I caught the eye of one of the guys with the 'making up for something' trucks. He gave me a curt nod and tapped his foot twice. Such a small thing, but I let out a huge sigh of relief because of it. I was being tracked. The pack would know where I was soon enough.

I wondered if this guy was a Wulver or Snow Moon. With the proximity to the pack, I assumed Snow Moon. There were a few solid possibilities of where they would take me, giving us a good idea of where people needed to be to drop off and pick up tracking, but I had hard money on Bakersfield, California. That's where Ted and his family were from, so it'd make sense for their headquarters to be located there. Or maybe they'd want to take me somewhere more out of the way?

"Keep walking," Will growled in my ear, shoving me through the door of the bar.

Given no other choice, I stumbled in. I could feel all eyes on me, yet no one got up to help. I was certainly, utterly fucked. I looked up at the bartender with pleading eyes, but all she did was point to a more secluded back room. I walked as slowly as Will would allow, trying to drag this out as long as I could.

I was shoved down into a chair. I kept my head down, not willing to see who surrounded me. Who was deciding my fate.

"Lya, dear, I haven't seen you in a long time. How are you?"

I cringed at the voice. I could never forget that voice. It grated against my skin, making my hackles bristle. "Hello, Mr. Marsan."

"Oh, please, call me Alexander." His voice was sickly sweet, and it made me want to vomit. "Will, untie your sister-in-law. That's really no way to treat family, is it?"

As soon as my hands were free, I stretched my shoulders and rubbed my wrists. From what I could tell, no silver laced the ropes they were using. A glass of water was placed in front of me, but I refused to touch it. I had a sneaking suspicion there would be more than just water in it. I hazarded a glance up at my almost father-in-law, but his expression revealed nothing. He was a good actor.

"So, Lya, could you tell me what you've been up to since you and my oldest got engaged?" he asked. "I was really thinking I would have heard more from you two."

I just shrugged my shoulders. "I think Ted got cold feet. He said he needed some time and left. I took a pretty long vacation to do some soul searching after that."

Alex hmphed. "I would really think that's the sort of thing my son would have told me. Do you have any idea where he took off to?"

"No." I shook my head. "I just figured he'd come back when he was ready. Maybe he went on a hunting trip?"

He nodded slowly, a pensive look on his face. "And did you discover anything while you were off soul searching?"

I smiled, affording myself just a moment to think of my summer so far. "Just that I didn't know myself as well as I thought. Kind of an *Eat, Pray, Love* adventure."

Alex leaned in to me, his expression turning icy. I allowed myself to slink back to the scared little girl I used to be, ready to run at any given moment. I had to keep up pretenses.

"Here's the thing, dear," he cooed. "I haven't heard from my son in six weeks. He vanished right when you did. We come out to ask questions, and your area is swarmed with werewolves. I know you're hiding something, and I will find out what it is. I'll give you one chance to come clean, and I promise I won't be angry. We could even work together here. But you have to tell me what happened for that arrangement to work. You finally snap, lose control of your wolf, and kill my kid? Get claimed by your mate and he had it out for my son? I know what you are, Lya, and I will not stand for the abominations of your kind. So, what do you say?"

My mind raced. There was a truth to his words that was tempting to pursue. We needed to know exactly what he was planning, and this would be the best way. The trackers still had eyes on me, so they'd still be able to find me.

I looked up at Alexander, eyes wide. "Werewolves aren't real, Mr. Marsan."

OLIVER

EVERYONE WAS SO certain they would lose me in one way or another if we didn't get Lya back in one piece, but I felt like I was already gone. The way she had locked away her wolf, I could hardly feel the mate bond anymore, and it scared me that I might not be the first to know if something did happen to her.

I hadn't moved in hours. I stayed sitting in my office chair, staring at the wall. Someone had cleaned up the broken glass, and Kota stopped in regularly to give updates.

My own pack members were tracking her for a while. I wanted to rip each person who had aided and abetted in this scheme limb for limb. But I wouldn't get her back if I did that.

I understood the reasoning. I understood why it had to be Lya. But nothing would make me agree with jeopardizing my mate.

There was strength in numbers. Our pack had stayed safe and not experienced any issues, but hunters were ramping up. Over the past three years, five packs had been decimated by them. Sure, you could chalk it up to those packs being quite small, necessitating higher levels of integration with human communities, but the fact of the matter was they were striking more often and harder. It would only be a matter of time before they set their sights on bigger game. We were at the very top of the food chain, but that made us all the more responsible to look out for the ones further down.

But it was my mate on the line. And I could do nothing to protect her. She was already in the fire.

I heard the door open, but I didn't even look over, making no effort to discern who entered. Delicate footsteps tapped along the floor, and a hand reached out, taking the now empty decanter from my grip.

"What do you want?" I growled at the presence.

"I want you to listen." The response was stern and familiar. I glanced up, a little surprised to see my grandmother. "Oliver, your time as Alpha has been painfully simple, and now? Now, you need to step up and actually show your pack that you are worth your salt and worth the dedication and commitment they show to you."

I let out a huff. "My pack has betrayed me, Grandma."

The Elder sat down in a chair and began playing with the ring she wore on a chain around her neck. The one her first mate, her fated mate, gifted her. "Our family line is very new to the Alpha position of this pack."

"I know, I've read the history books," I mumbled. "You transitioned from Luna to Alpha when your mate was challenged and lost the pack."

"Yes, but do you know what the history books and pack records leave out?" she asked. I just shook my head. "They don't tell you who challenged the Alpha, or why. I made sure those details were left out."

I watched as the ring glinted in the pale light of morning. "Those are important details, Grandma."

"I wouldn't dishonor my fated mate by letting the world know I betrayed him."

I furrowed my brows. "You challenged your own mate?"

"Well, of course," my grandmother said. "You see, he started making choices that affected the entire pack based around the comfort of me, not what was actually best. I ignored it for a little while, but then he elected to ignore a rogue threat to a pack south of us. The rogues had been kidnapping Lunas, and he didn't want me to be targeted by getting involved."

"Is that not reasonable?" I muttered. "As an Alpha, you need to look out for your own."

"I agree, but as an Alpha, who is your own?" She spoke as if she was lecturing a child, and at this moment, I felt like one. Just a lost puppy, really. "The entire pack. All of werewolf kind. That is your own. Rogues destroyed a large portion of that pack, and when I found out, I was disgusted. Our pack has always been exceptionally large and strong. We could have easily jumped in to stop them and save many, many lives. Instead, my mate just increased our own border security."

I barked out a dark laugh. "Where were the Wulvers then?"

She shook her head. "You misunderstand their purpose if you think they are the ones exclusively responsible for solving and preventing problems. They seem to have the gift of knowing when something needs to play out instead of being covered up. When something is not their responsibility."

I stood up, walking over to the bookcase filled with pack records. I needed to reread about this transition. "So, what did you do?"

"Well, I went to the Wulvers. I presented the issue, declared our Alpha was blinded and no longer fit to lead a pack." She paused for a moment, voice caught in her throat. "They told me I clearly knew the solution, so I needed to fix it."

"I'm guessing that's when you rejected him as your mate and challenged him."

"Yes," my grandmother confirmed. "I was really hoping I would die in that fight, but he couldn't even defend his leadership of the pack if it meant hurting me. He just conceded and left. I took the pack south of us in, claimed them as our own, and began remedying our relationships with rogues. My pillar as Alpha was that all of werewolf kind is our own. The same as I taught your father, and thought I taught you."

I pulled the record off the shelf, aimlessly flipping through pages. She was right. No reference to the wolf that challenged her first mate was there.

"Does Lya know this story?" Lya had spent quite a bit of time with my grandmother, and I wouldn't be surprised if she knew more about this woman than me.

"No," she said. "She knows the mate I had my child with was a chosen mate, and that I rejected my fated mate. Lya is strong, Oliver. If you don't turn yourself around, I will encourage her to do the same as I did. A person who can manage a feat like this? Well, that is an individual fit to be an Alpha."

I looked up at her, pain written all over my face. I couldn't even claim she didn't know the pain I was going through, because she probably understood it better than me. "She is protecting the pack and all of our kind in a way I wish I could personally do myself."

"But you can't," she reminded me. "It's incredibly easy to demonize the ones who step up when you are unable to. Just remember your pack and your mate did not go behind your back to spite you. They did it to make sure the good of all was upheld first and foremost, even when it would be too difficult of a decision for you."

"I would have backed the plan if it was anyone else," I insisted.

My grandmother stood and walked over to me, giving my hand a supportive squeeze. "The Goddess knew what she was doing when she selected the lost Wulver for you. All you can do is trust not only your mate, but the ones you have hand-picked to surround you and your decisions."

I gave her a quick nod. Tears pricked my eyes, and I knew if I spoke, the floodgates would open. She left me standing in my office, alone with my thoughts. I wished I could just turn my brain off for a moment, something not even the alcohol had been able to accomplish.

I sat back in my chair and closed my eyes, willing myself to go back in time. Maybe when I opened them, it would be two weeks ago and Lya would be perched on the arm of the couch, reading pack records again.

"What in the world are you still doing in here?" I had asked. "Weren't you girls going out for lunch?"

"Hiding from Anna," she confessed with a giggle. "She's really angry at Trevor."

"Rightfully so." I nodded, walking over to her and pulling her to her feet. "Stick around for lunch with me?"

Lya laced her fingers with mine and pulled me out of the office. "Much preferable."

"What do you think of the whole Anna and Trevor thing?" I asked her, studying her face for a reaction. Her expressions typically said more than her words.

Lya bit her lip, focused on perusing the refrigerator. Her brow creased, and I quickly noticed she wasn't really seeing what was in front of her. The girl got lost in her own thoughts so easily. "I understand why he hid everything from her, but she needs to forgive him. Anger won't turn back time and change the past."

I reached past her and pulled out some leftovers, stashing them in the picnic basket she had grabbed. "I understand why Anna is so upset. Four years is a long time they could have been happy together."

"Yeah, I guess," Lya mused. "But what's arguing about it going to fix now? Her point has been made."

"It sounds like we are talking about a lot more than just Trevor and Anna."

"Maybe," Lya said with a shrug of her shoulders. "The same logic can be applied to most anything. I dunno, I just get wanting to keep the people you love at arm's length so they don't get wrapped up in your messes."

She looked up at me with such sincerity in her eyes that I just couldn't argue. In that moment, I understood every time she ran, every secret she kept, and the intensity of everything she deemed worth words.

I leaned down and kissed her, taking my time to memorize the outline of her lips.

"You're a better person than most, Lya," I murmured when we finally separated. "Most wouldn't be able to look past something like that."

"It's just the same courtesy I hope others give me," she whispered.

I slipped my arm around her waist, pulling her toward the patio doors. "C'mon, let's go find a place for an Anna-free picnic."

Lya looked up at me, one of the corners of her mouth curving upwards. Her amber eyes were soft and warm, and I was certain they could see right into my soul. Her soft, absentminded smiles were a thing I would never forget.

Thirty-Three

Lya

THE FIRST DAY HERE, I was left mostly alone. I had an open invitation. If I ever wanted out of the cell block, all I had to do was come clean about my transgressions. I hadn't spoken a word since the late dinner with Alexander Marsan, though.

Aside from myself and a guard, the cell block was empty. I had kept insisting I was human, and tried to poking fun at the guard who had to watch over an imprisoned little girl, but he was stone-faced and never gave in to conversation. I didn't even have Tala to talk to, and I'd just started to really enjoy her presence. The past month and a half at the pack had changed me, and I felt it was for the better. I could comfortably be myself, make friends, and have relationships that didn't require hiding a huge portion of who I was. The downside was I missed those things even more now.

It took about two days for me to come to terms with the fact that I was getting lonely. Lonely was a feeling I was quite familiar with, but resenting it was a new development. I guess sometimes you really did have to lose everything to appreciate it.

Don't get me wrong, I knew this would be a difficult venture, but I hadn't really thought of how it would impact me personally. My thoughts had been consumed by how it would hurt Oliver. Alone with my thoughts for twenty-four hours a day, the only thing I had to do was admit to myself everything I had been avoiding thinking.

That's how I'd always been, though. Thinking of others but forgetting myself. Maybe I was a Luna.

My heart hurt, thinking of Oliver and how this must be eating him alive. At least I had the advantage of knowing he was physically safe. For now, at least. I couldn't imagine what it was like to know your mate was risking themselves, and I hoped I would never have to. Every single moment, I felt probing at the edge of my mind, begging me to let him in. But I couldn't. I wasn't about to give him a little bit of hope when nobody knew how this would really end. It was cruel, but it was my last act of kindness.

Day three started with interrogations. It started simple, just asking a question, and if I gave an answer I got food. It didn't matter if the answer was what they felt was right or wrong. It only took two missed meals to catch on to that drift.

And yesterday? Yesterday, I cried. I hadn't cried yet, and it was probably well overdue. It was cathartic and horrible. The guard stayed motionless, not reacting at all. I hadn't met many people who could maintain a stoney appearance when someone was ugly crying in front of them, but the ones I had, I was fairly certain were sociopaths.

But today was the fifth day. I sat quietly in the far corner, waiting patiently for whatever their question would be today. 'Are you a wolf?' again? No. Not quite a lie. 'What does silver do to you?' maybe? Nothing. That was true. 'What happened to Ted Marsan?' was also on the table, and I didn't know what happened... to his corpse. Everything had been too ambiguous thus far.

Today, though, was different. The person who usually came with breakfast was running late. Not that it was really something for concern; I was certain maintaining my meal schedule was very low on their priority list, but the reason for their tardiness was. Nearly an hour after I usually got fed, someone came storming in, dragging a person that reeked of wolf behind them.

I studied the newest prisoner carefully. This girl was practically a child still. She couldn't have been any older than eighteen, and that made my heart sink. She was just so young to experience a life changing ordeal. I tried to look past that, though, because Kota had promised me I would have someone on the inside looking out for me. I had specifically asked not to know who it was so I could keep my guard up more easily, but that only made me question the loyalty of every single person I encountered, a false sense of hope rising up with each new face. This girl couldn't be my insider.

She was a rogue, though. Rogues always had a very particular smell. The smell had been explained to me as the smell of the death of a bond. Old, decaying, rotting. Whether it was the bond and link to a pack, your mate, or even your own humanity. The smell of death followed you, alerting everyone that you had lost something.

When I asked why Thom didn't smell like a rogue, Kota's quick answer was because he never truly severed ties completely with either of the packs he was affiliated with. When I asked why I never smelled like a rogue, Kota thought it was because I was a Wulver through and through. Personally, I thought it was because I had never actually been in a pack, and a link that had never existed couldn't die. Sure, by blood I was supposed to be a Wulver, but I had never joined them. The Wulvers were a pack based solely on honor, not right. The Wulver Pack chose you.

When the poor kid got dumped in the cell across from me, I got a chance to study her face. She was beaten up and bloody. I was a little disgusted that they hadn't even done something for her broken face before casting her away, but at least werewolf healing should take care of it. I slid over to the cell door and leaned against it, trying to get as close to the girl as possible.

"Hey," I whispered. Whispering was probably unnecessary, but feeling secretive wasn't so bad. The girl looked up at me but didn't respond.

"Hey," I said again. "My name is Lya."

"How are you touching that?" Her voice quivered, motioning toward the cell door.

I glanced down at it, realizing that it did, in fact, smell of silver.

"Oh, uh..." I thought fast. This kid was like me, but the ones who were inevitably listening didn't know that. "Is it supposed to have a chemical on it or something? It just seems like a normal steel door."

"It's silver!" she insisted. "How is it not burning your skin off?"

"Huh..." I mumbled. "I guess I never really had a silver allergy or anything."

"Are you not a werewolf?" she asked, confusion etched across her face. "Why would they have a human locked up in here?"

"No, not a werewolf." I tried to laugh. I was still insisting they weren't real. "I truly couldn't tell you why I'm here, either."

That part wasn't a lie, at least. I really didn't know what they wanted with me so badly. It would have been so easy for them to just kill me, and I was still a little shocked they hadn't yet. That's one of the things we were gambling on.

This couldn't be my person on the inside to report back to the pack, could it? I had long ago learned to never judge a book by its cover, but it wasn't her ability to do the job I was questioning. This was really, truly, genuinely a child, and if Kota had elected a child to be my link to the outside world while in here, I would never forgive him. That, and she was clearly a rogue. She wouldn't be able to mind-link with a pack to provide them updates.

"So, what are you doing here?" I asked.

The girl shrugged. "Got caught hunting for food."

I looked at her quizzically. "Were you eating humans or something?"

"No," she hissed, recoiling. "I was just at the national forest, and they found me."

A fire burned in my gut. I could understand hunters patrolling for werewolves that posed a danger to society, but to take one that was peacefully minding its own business, trying to find its next meal? That wasn't acceptable.

"My name's Danica, by the way," she whispered.

"Hi, Danica," I said with a smile. "Where is this prison located exactly?"

Danica looked up to the frosted glass window, not that she would be able to see anything out of it. "We can't be too far outside of Cheyenne. It wasn't that long of a drive from where they got me."

I nodded slowly, turning away from Danica so she couldn't see the look of disappointment on my face. Cheyenne, Wyoming, was not one of the places Kota had targeted as a potential place they would take me. I truly hoped this didn't alter the plan too much. I had been in here only five days, and I didn't know how much longer I could take. But, Cheyenne wasn't one of our targeted locations. It would take at least a few extra days to move people here.

I took a deep breath, reminding myself that somehow, some way, things would work out for the best. Even if they weren't the version of the best that I would have chosen.

Oliver

"You gotta stop pacing, man," Trevor grouched. "Your stress is stressing me out."

"Yeah, well, I might just snap if I don't do something," I quipped. "If you haven't noticed, Lya isn't back yet, and my sister-in-law has been in labor too long."

"We know where Lya is, and we have someone keeping an eye on her. As for Maggie, human labors generally take longer than wolf labors," Trevor sighed. "If you need to get out some pent-up rage, go train or something. Stop wearing a hole in the hospital floor."

I turned on my heel without saying a word and stalked out of the hospital. I had been doing my best to heed my grandmother's advice, but I was still out for blood. Knowing Lya's location was the only good news I had gotten in the past five days, but Kota and Gregory insisted on stalling until making the next move.

The main goal here was to decimate as much of the Marsan contingency as possible. Pulling her out too soon would only make them angry and put a target on our heads. The person we had on the inside feeding us information wasn't getting much, though. He had joined their ranks only a couple weeks ago, and had been kept widely out of the loop. He had, however, been able to share a few locations we could send teams out to, which we corroborated with the social media and cyber stalking Lya had suggested. Most seemed to be flocking to the new location outside of Cheyenne, which confirmed our suspicion that their reasoning for needing Lya had something to do with using her to infiltrate packs from the inside.

I had to hand it to my girl. She had devised a good plan.

The training grounds were looking sparse. Our ranks were not small— about a thousand of our pack members were part of the security contingent —but those were dispersed throughout four towns. Right now, we had a group of scouts out around Lya's location, and had sent some teams to the locations we had a lead on, too, leaving few at our home base.

I marched across the pitch, not offering greetings to any of the folks there, and straight into Kota's office. He had been steering clear of me unless he brought an update, which was a good move on his part, but I was quickly losing hold on my restraint.

"Let's go," I snapped, gesturing for Kota to leave his office.

He glanced up at me. "What?"

"Let's go," I repeated. "Training field, now."

The second my feet hit the grass, I whirled around and landed a punch to his jaw. I didn't relent, landing blows wherever I could. Kota, for the most part, remained on the defensive, only blocking and trying not to lose ground. I could tell a crowd was forming, but I didn't change my tune. Kota had blood streaming from his nose, and my knuckles had broken open. I wasn't holding back.

Finally, he shifted his stance.

This was the fight I needed.

I wasn't really thinking about the fight. I just wanted to pulverize him, not kill him. I wasn't the Alpha getting in some training; I was a heartbroken man begging for physical pain to manifest how my heart felt. That's probably how he got the upper hand, pinning me to the ground. I stared up at him, my resolve crumbling. Lya was my weakness. I understood why some Alphas refused to accept their fated mates.

Kota stood, offering me a hand to pull me off the ground. "Let's go grab a beer."

I laid there for a moment, just looking up at him. The tension in the air was still thick.

"Yeah," I finally agreed, letting him pull me up and walking with him to his truck.

The drive was silent. I hadn't had much to say to him, for fear of losing my cool, but this couldn't go on forever.

We trudged in, taking up our normal table, both ignoring the looks people tried to hide. The Alpha and Gamma, walking in for a beer while all bruised and bloody. Of course, everyone would be nervous.

"How's Maggie?" Kota asked once we had drinks in front of us.

"Still in labor," I told him. "It's been rough."

Kota's face twisted. Part-bred births were hard for humans. With how long it had been going on, everyone was worried.

"So, can ya give me an update?" I asked, needing something to calm my mind.

Kota took a swig and started in. "Teams got sent out yesterday to check out the other locations we were told they have. If there are few enough around, they'll neutralize 'em. Scouts up in Cheyenne have reported more hunters coming in by the day, as well as them taking some rogue hostages, which supports the idea that they probably wanted to get their hands on Lya to put on their own sting operations within packs."

I sat back and nodded. "How long do you think until we can move forward realistically?"

"Realistically?" Kota paused. "We know there are about a hundred to one-fifty in their little hunter club."

"We took out seven the other night," I reminded him.

"Yeah," he agreed, "and another five in Kennebec. I wanna see these next few ambushes go well, and we need to get someone to interrogate out of it."

I nodded slowly. "So, right now, we sit and wait."

"Unless you feel like heading up the team I'm sending out tomorrow," he suggested.

"No," I snapped. "I'm staying so I can leave for Cheyenne the second it's time."

"Ollie!" a shrill voice called behind me.

I put my head in my hands. "Oh, Goddess," I muttered. "Yes, Lucy?"

Lucy sauntered up, taking up one of the spare seats at our table. "I heard about your break up, and I just wanted to say I'm so sorry."

Her voice dripped with insincerity, and I had to stop myself from clenching my fists. "There was no break up."

"Oh!" She flashed her sickly sweet smile I had done a good job of avoiding for the past year or so. "Well then, no judgment if you were just having some fun with that Lya girl."

I turned to her, narrowing my eyes. "What are you talking about?"

"That girl that you had living at the packhouse," Lucy clarified. "Rumor has it she just ghosted you."

I glared at her, gritting my teeth. I couldn't lose it on a pack member, no matter how much they made my skin crawl.

"Fuck off, Lucy," Kota grunted.

The bartender appeared at our table with another round for me and Kota. Spotting Lucy, he asked, "Can I get you something, too?"

"Yeah, I—"

"She's not joining us," I quickly cut in. "Lucy was just on her way."

Lucy's eyes flashed back to me, a small amount of hurt visible, but I didn't care. She slunk away, and I breathed a sigh of relief.

"Lucy still up your ass?" Brandon asked, slipping into the spot she had previously occupied.

"Apparently," I huffed.

"You could always just show off the mark," he joked. "Where is my dear cousin, by the way?"

I flagged the bartender down, getting a beer for Brandon as well. "At the hospital still. I got kicked out."

Brandon took a second to assess the damage between Kota and I, but must have decided not to press the topic further. "Have things calmed down between Trevor and Anna yet?"

I shrugged. "Lya disappearing was a little sobering for both of them, I guess."

Smiling to myself, I thought of when Lya gave Anna a piece of her mind regarding the disconnect between them. I hadn't pegged Lya as one to defend the mate bond, especially when she seemed so opposed to it at first, but she respected it at the very least.

I had walked out onto the patio in search of Lya. It was over a week or so after Anna had discovered she and Trevor were mates, so I was certain they had worked through their disagreements about how Trevor handled it. But, in true Anna fashion, she wouldn't let it go when she felt she was right.

I quickly determined it wasn't the sort of conversation I wanted to intrude on. Hell, some of Anna's anger was directed at me for not forcing Trevor to come clean. I stayed at the door, though, wanting to hear what Lya's input would be.

"Look, Anna, you're one of my closest friends here, but if you don't move on from this, I am going to stop talking to you," she snapped.

The look on Anna's face was priceless. I truly don't think anyone had ever pointed out to her how annoying her constant ranting could be. Being the Beta's daughter had gotten her some protections from that.

Rose shifted uncomfortably in her seat. Rose and Anna had been friends since they were young, and it warmed my heart how they both took Lya under their wing. "She's right, Anna... It's getting redundant."

Lya swirled the ice cubes around in her spiked lemonade. "Constantly dwelling on the past is only going to impact your future. So, either reject him and move on, or accept him and move on."

"Sorry," Anna mumbled.

That had been the last anyone heard of the disagreements between the two, but it was obvious they were still arguing behind closed doors. But then Lya ran off with the hunters. My personal opinion was that it made it apparent to Anna just how quickly the good things could be taken away, causing her to really think about whether her anger was worth it.

Trevor pulling out a chair and joining us pulled me from my memories and back to the present.

"Baby yet?" I asked.

Trevor shook his head. "They were about to start a c-section. Thom asked everyone but Marjorie to leave."

"It's a good thing they came to the pack hospital," I mumbled.

Thirty-Four

Lya

IF MY COUNTING WAS CORRECT, today was the summer solstice. My birthday.

Interrogations were well underway.

I wanted to go home.

I understood what the shackles on the walls were for. It was so I couldn't try to get away or fight back when they tried beating answers out of me.

Lying was getting harder.

Tala continued to play her part, obediently staying locked away and not healing anything, but I could tell she was struggling.

The silver earrings, necklace, and bracelet set I had on had been torn away. I knew what they wanted; they wanted me to shift, admit I was a werewolf, and then ideally comply with their demands when they threatened to kill me. But we had suspected that when we came up with this plan, and I would let myself be killed before I gave up my pack.

The longer I was here, though, the more I wondered why we didn't go with Trevor's suggestion—lead them to the pack, and then destroy them on our own turf. At the time, I had adamantly refused that notion. I wasn't about to agree to putting the entire pack at risk. I still stood by that, but man would this be easier if we had planned for that.

I hadn't seen outside, so I didn't know the exact topography we were dealing with, but I knew this area was just prairie land. That would make blowing this popsicle stand all the harder.

It was impossible to get an idea of how many hunters were here, too. The only people I really saw were Alexander Marsan and the silent guard who seemed to be around twenty-four-seven. It seemed there must be a handful of other hunters here, though, because a menagerie of different people brought food.

The last time I saw Alexander, he brought a silver knife with him. I recognized it. It was only a few weeks ago I was staring it down from my bed, begging and pleading with a deranged fiancé. He cut deep into my skin. I screamed because getting fileted hurts, but he insisted it was the silver bothering me.

"Can't you see she's human?" Danica shrieked. "Stop with the torture and just let her go!"

I felt bad. Her defense of me resulted in her getting thrown against a wall and nearly knocked out. At least her wolf was fully present to patch her up.

I cringed as the door to our cell block opened, stuffing myself deeper into the corner farthest from the door. I was still bruised and bloody from the previous day's interrogation, and I was not ready for more. What was the likelihood I could ask for a shower and some stitches for my birthday? I hid my face in the oversized sweatshirt I refused to take off. Oliver's scent had long worn off, but I could still pretend it smelled like him.

"Lya," Alexander sneered, looking down on me through the bars. "You know, maybe I was a little unfair to you. I should have told you from the get-go that we know you're lying, and how we know you're lying."

I tensed. The pack. They couldn't have actually gotten their hands on anyone from the pack, could they? My mind immediately went to Oliver. In all his rage, did he end up getting captured? I bit down on my lower lip, scared to hear what exactly they had over my head.

"That right there, that reaction is all we needed." He chuckled, crouching to get on eye level with me. "But why lie, my dear? We've told you how much more comfortable life here will be if you just work with us."

I lifted my lip and growled at him. "What you want me to do is genocide, and I will not be a part of that."

"Genocide, you say?" He paused, looking as if he was actually contemplating what I said. "I would actually argue we are doing the human race a favor, removing their only predator."

I scoffed. Werewolves, a predator? All we did was look out for our own.

The only humans that ever got killed in that endeavor were the ones hunting us. We didn't start the war, but we were more than willing to end it.

"Is that why you hunters decided they needed to destroy a pack that was keeping the local communities alive?" I spat. I stood up. At that moment, I was willing to go toe to toe with him. "What was it that caused a group of humans to torture and destroy an entire pack of do-gooders? You know, those people they helped fell into famine and entire towns fell to rot after that. Was it jealousy? If the history books got it right, you went after the pups and the sick first. Even then, they didn't seek retribution. They just tried to escape, giving you hunters space. What's your reasoning now? Are you just scared? Worried some werewolf will come knocking on your door to collect on their debts?"

"Ah, the Wulvers," he said with a smile. "So, you know. Well, Lya, we do have a birthday present for you. He should be by soon. I look forward to our next chat."

Alexander turned and left the cell block, leaving just us two prisoners and our guard. I scanned my eyes over the room, looking for a reaction. The usually statue-like guard leaned back against the wall, offering me one curt nod. I kept my eyes on him for a moment longer. Two foot taps. I let out a sigh of relief.

But Danica was wide-eyed and confused.

"Y-you're a werewolf," she stuttered.

I just shrugged my shoulders, neither confirming nor denying.

"How do you hide your wolf? You just smell human."

I offered the kid a half-smile. "Maybe I'm just an ally, then. You don't have to be a werewolf to think kidnapping and killing innocents is wrong, no matter the species."

Danica sat back against the wall, clearly lost in thought. Carefully, I started poking around the walls built up closing off Tala, making sure there were no cracks or holes she could slip through.

That had been close.

It was one thing for them to know I was a werewolf. It was another thing for me to wolf out and make them think I was an unstable werewolf. Tala was on my side here, though, and I truly believed she would do her best to maintain control. Unfortunately, we both had the disadvantage of the same things pissing us off.

I leaned against the bars of the cell, trying to get a closer look at Danica. Her eyes grew hard, though.

"I don't believe you're a werewolf if you can touch silver like that," she stated.

I let out a long sigh. This kid was definitely not my insider. "Danica, did you grow up in a pack?"

"Yeah, I did," she muttered, eyes glazing over. "It was a really nice pack, too."

This piqued my curiosity. Since living at Snow Moon, the reasons people left pack life interested me. "What happened?"

"Rogue attack. About nine years ago now."

I wanted to press for details, but I felt like they wouldn't come, so I let it be. So, my birthday slipped away slowly. I bit back a flash of resentment that raged through me. Why did it have to be me here?

Life at the pack was supposed to be when I changed my life for myself. No more moping and hiding. Start putting myself first sometimes. Make real friends. For the most part, I had made pretty good headway on fixing myself, yet here I was, taking one for the team I'd only figured out I was on less than two months ago.

Thoughts of Oliver swarmed my mind. We were going to take a mini vacation up to Norridge for my birthday. Maybe he went without me. I wondered if he would move on now that I was out of the picture.

Jealousy reared its ugly head, curling its claws around my chest. How long would it take for him to kiss someone else? Would he take them to our spot along the river? Flames roared across my body, but not the kind Oliver's touch would ignite. These were a raging inferno, threatening to burn me alive.

I could feel Tala pacing, begging to be let out. Her anxiety creeped in and mingled with my own. I fell to my knees, fighting the urge to shift and hunt down whatever was causing this insufferable pain. As the clawing in my chest dug in and the burning across my body took over, I felt canines descending and claws breaking skin.

It was so all-consuming that I didn't even notice someone entering my cell. All I could think about was the fur sprouting along my arms. The feeling of freedom, and I craved it.

My head hitting the wall and hands around my throat, cutting off my oxygen, pulled me out of the oblivion just enough for me to get a handle on my wolf. My tongue and throat burned as something metallic was stuffed in my mouth.

"Control yourself, Luna," the person ground out through his teeth. "You know he wouldn't betray his fated."

And just like that, I was free from his grip. I crumpled up on the floor and watched as the guard turned and exited the cell, returning to his position, again unmoving.

One curt nod and two foot taps.

I'd get out of here.

And then I would kill her.

"L-Luna?" Danica stuttered. "How did you get here?"

I shot a glare over at her. "It's a long story.

"What pack?" she asked. "Why didn't you smell like a wolf?"

I let out a sigh. "That's for me to know. Please just trust me."

I was asking a whole lot of people to trust me recently, and to be honest, I was starting to wonder if I was worth trusting. It sure seemed like this mess had become a lot more difficult than we signed up for.

Danica glanced over to the guard. "Is he part of your pack, too?"

I bit my lip, thinking over this response. Our mole was a Wulver, I knew that. I was definitely linked to the Wulver Pack, but was I actually in the pack?

"Yes," I said slowly. "Kind of."

Danica looked frantic. "Really, Lya, I have to know. What pack? They'll come for you, and I don't know if I'll be safe here when they do."

I let out a short laugh. "You seriously think you're safer with hunters than with a werewolf pack?"

"I'm a rogue, Lya!" she hissed.

"Oh." I bit my lip. "You'll be just fine with my pack, I can promise you that."

Danica scoffed, turning away from me. "Not likely. I can think of exactly one pack that doesn't have it out for rogues, and that's the pack that took mine over when my dad died."

I studied the girl carefully, dots starting to connect. I let it be, though. I didn't exactly want to talk, either. I just curled up in the corner of the cell, nursing my wounds.

OLIVER

LYA TEETERED ON a moss covered rock, out in the middle of the river running behind the packhouse. I watched, mesmerized as she giggled at fireflies blinking around her. I couldn't tell if the heady scent of lilac was her or the bushes around us, now in full bloom.

This wasn't the same girl who had initially arrived at the packhouse, nervous and scared of everything. I still hadn't figured out why, but after only a few weeks of being here, it was like a switch had been flipped and a beautiful, loving personality emerged. It wasn't even a subtle evolution.

"When's your birthday again?" I asked.

She looked over at me, her eyes nearly glowing as the last remnants of the sunset reflected against them. "June twenty-first. I'll be twenty-five."

She was a solstice baby; of course she'd be special. Born with the light within and prosperity at her fingertips.

Lya made her way back to the riverbank, snagging her can of beer from the water's edge. "Are you making plans for it or something?"

"Maybe I am," I teased. I reached out for her, but she took a step back.

My eyes stayed transfixed as Lya reached for the hem of her sundress, pulling it over her head to reveal every inch of fair, sun-kissed skin. She smiled coyly at me before dashing off further downstream to a swimming hole Rose and Anna had shown her a while back. I didn't think twice, quickly trailing after her and shedding clothes as I went. I dove in, snatching her by the waist and pulling her to me. She planted her lips on mine, and I couldn't help but let my hands wander.

We floated along for a while. Lya watched the moon replace the sun as I watched her. I'd have given anything for the moment to never end. I was running into more and more moments I wanted to last forever with this girl, and I hoped that would never change.

Lya finally broke the comfortable silence. "Hey, Oliver?"

"Yes, love?" I murmured.

"I love it here."

I couldn't help but smile. "Let me know what you think of the place once you've been here for a few years."

Lya bit down on her lip, the dark clouds returning to her eyes, threatening to rain on her joy. I knew something had been weighing on her, but I also knew if I pushed, she'd be less likely to tell me what it was. "I will, I promise."

We planned a trip up to Norridge for her birthday. There was a waterfall with a swimming hole she would love up there, and it'd be easy to convince her friends to tag along. The sun came too soon, alerting us to the fact that we had fallen asleep in a tangled mess of flesh and sweat on the riverbank.

I had started counting down the days to when I could whisk her away and pretend responsibility didn't exist for just a little bit, and here we were. June twenty-first. Lya's birthday.

Instead of sitting by a waterfall with homebrew, I was back at that same riverbank with a bottle of Woodford I had every intention of finishing off before the night ended. Silence cast a thick, suffocating blanket over me but did nothing to drown out the echoes of her tinkling laughter in my mind.

I didn't even pay any heed to the person who came and sat beside me. So many people tried to ensure I always had someone around, but I really just wanted to be alone with my best memories.

"I'd really like to be alone," I huffed before taking another pull from the bottle. It was only halfway empty, but the night was still young.

A hand caressed my arm. If it weren't for the lack of sparks, I could almost imagine it was her.

"Really?" a voice I didn't want to hear cooed. "You don't want something to take your mind off of it?"

I gritted my teeth but refused to move. I didn't trust myself, especially when I could already feel claws surfacing and gripping into the dirt. I hadn't shifted since the night Lya was taken, and I couldn't let my first shift in over a week be out of anger. "You aren't who I want touching me."

The hand traveled further up, running along my neck. A sick feeling twisted in my gut when it grazed over my mate's mark. This was decidedly not my mate.

"You would really rather string along that rogue?"

A growl slipped between my lips, but that apparently wasn't enough warning to keep the intruder from turning my head and plastering their lips on mine.

That was when I lost it.

Before I could even think to hold him back, Adair was on top of Lucy with his teeth positioned at her throat. At the very least, he had his wits about him enough to not kill her.

'Touch me again and you won't have a pack.'

Adair backed off of her slowly, watching as she sat up and rubbed her throat. She looked up with horror-stricken eyes, but I felt no shame at all.

'Go.'

Lucy didn't need any more encouragement. She was on her feet and running back to the packhouse before Adair could growl at her again.

I let out a breath, expelled the rest of Lucy's scent from my lungs, and tried to pull Adair back. But, now that he was in control, he wasn't about to let go. He leaned his head back to the solstice moon and let out a howl. One that sang the ballad of heartbreak. The pack called back, validating their Alpha's suffering.

We ran for hours. Part of me questioned why I had held off on shifting, but every time we neared the border and Adair tried to push me over, in pursuit of his mate, I was reminded. When I finally collapsed back on the riverbank, next to my bottle of liquor, I felt absolutely spent. The emotions of the past several days were overwhelming, and the way the wolf forced me to bring them to the forefront of my mind was painful. I grabbed the bottle and stumbled back to the packhouse.

Oh, how the mighty had fallen.

Some Alpha I was.

Kota and Brandon met me at the door, one grabbing each of my arms and guiding me over to the kitchen island.

"How the fuck are you going to march into battle if you're doing shit like this?" Kota grumbled.

I winced at the truth behind his words. "Sorry."

He exchanged the Woodford for a glass of water and sat down beside me. "You're lucky we have a few more days yet. The parties we sent out have been successful for the most part. Lya's idea of utilizing social media to figure out who to track made things so much easier."

"Any casualties?" I slurred.

Kota wasn't quite the animal I was; he poured himself a glass. "Just a few, but we surprised them."

"And just a few days until we head over?"

"Yep," he confirmed. "And you'll have explaining to do."

I grabbed the bottle back from him. "What?"

"You remember how I said you can feel when your mate cheats on you?" I nodded, my mind instantly going to Lucy. "Well, Lya nearly wolfed out when she felt it. It's a good thing our Jenko is her guard."

I squeezed my eyes shut and scrubbed my hand across my face. "I almost killed Lucy."

"Should've gone public with being mated," Brandon scoffed. "Might've been better for her if you did take her out. We're going to have one angry she-wolf on our hands when she gets out."

"Yeah." I chuckled, studying the condensation on the water glass intently, trying to pull myself together and maintain a straight face.

Brandon nudged me in the ribs. "You think she's going to be silent and deadly scary angry, or everyone knows Hurricane Lya is on its way angry?"

"Goddess, we have a better bet of surviving Hurricane Lya." I grinned.

We dissolved into fits of laughter, loud enough to lure Thom out of his room.

"What the hell are you guys doing?" he groaned, glancing between us. "We just got Kai to sleep."

I offered the bottle to Thom. "You look like you need a drink."

"Fatherhood will do that," he agreed. "But seriously, if you wake Maggie or Kai, I'm going to kill you. Maybe before Lya gets the chance."

"So bets," Kota said. "What version of angry Lya are we pulling out of Hunterville?"

"Well, that depends," a new voice piped up. "What happened to piss her off so bad?"

I turned to look at Trevor. "Lucy kissed me, and I did her the disservice of letting her live so Lya can have her."

Trevor let out a low whistle and snagged the Woodford from Thom. "Fires of hell froze over. We are all fucked."

"When do we go pick her up?" Thom asked. "I'll make sure our bags are packed and we're moved out."

We tried to keep our laughter quieter this time but weren't very successful.

By the end of the night—or start of the morning, rather—the bottle of Woodford was gone.

THIRTY-FIVE

Lya

IT WAS impossible to keep track of time in here, so I gave up trying. There was a window in each cell covered by frosted glass that let just enough light in to give a faint idea of the time. Overall, the days revolved around when meals were brought. Even those weren't consistent, though.

I was beginning to think my "birthday present" was just a bit of blackmail. More than likely, they didn't have anything they could hold over my head.

Paranoia had begun to sink in. Was the guard really truly working on my side, or had the hunters won him over? He was a Wulver, of course, he wouldn't betray us. Was Danica in here just to try and get information out of me? It was always possible, but her eyes screamed truth and naivety. Was Oliver moving on with someone new already? He wouldn't. I'd know. My days were filled with constant internal debates, and nights trying to fight off memories of Oliver and the pack I had come to love. It was easier if I didn't think of the good times, but I was rarely successful.

It had come full circle. I was back to resenting the mate bond. Every once in a while, tendrils of how Oliver felt would sneak through, bringing on waves of heartbreak. The wall I had up to keep all aspects of my wolf at bay was crumbling, and it was only a matter of time before everyone here knew for sure.

I had gotten up and started pacing a while ago. I was probably driving Danica and the guard insane, but I didn't care. I didn't even look up when the door opened. More than likely, it was just food, and that person wouldn't even make eye contact with me. However, when I smelled the faint traces of wolf, it was impossible to keep my eyes on the floor.

"Dad," I gasped, eyes wide.

My father offered me a sad smile. "Hello, sweetheart."

I rushed over to the front of the cell, grasping the bars tightly in my hands. If I thought hard enough, the silver prickled my skin. "Dad, you've got to get us out of here! Please!"

He reached through the bars and cupped my cheek in his hand. "I believe you have been told the terms to get out of here, yes?"

"Yeah, but I can't do that! You wouldn't either, would you?" I looked up at him. I could feel the tears pricking my eyes. "Would you?"

"Could you unlock the cell please, son?" my dad asked softly. The guard reached over to a power box beside him and pressed a button, triggering the locking mechanism in the door to click open.

I felt numb as I followed him. My entire world seemed to be crashing down around me. My dad, the Alpha of the Wulver Pack, the sworn protector, the gladiator of goodwill, was in on this scheme with the hunters? The hunters that had kidnapped his daughter? I had so many questions, but I refused to speak. In the grand scheme of things, the answers probably didn't matter.

My dad led me through rooms and halls. I tried to keep count of the number of people we passed, but I quickly stopped caring. It seemed like a lot, though. More than we predicted. Finally, we entered a conference room of sorts. Alexander and Will were there, as well as others I hadn't seen before. I shuddered just thinking about how big this hunter operation was.

"Lya, dear," Alexander crooned. "Please, sit. I'm sure you and your father are well overdue for a chat."

I begrudgingly sat down, trying to figure out how I could get anywhere but here. Even back to the cell to be interrogated and tortured again. I looked around, trying to find an ally, but it seemed like I was on my own. So, I just directed my eyes to the table and refused to make eye contact.

"What pack have you been with, Lya?" my dad asked softly. I stayed quiet. He let out a groan. "I guess I do know you better than to think you would actually be so forthcoming."

I dragged my eyes from the table. "Why did you leave us, Dad?"

"The same reason I'm trying to include you in our endeavors now," he said with a smile. "Werewolves are a threat to humanity. You've experienced it, too. Do you remember how horrified your mother was of you? And then imagine the turmoil that would be unleashed if our kind became public knowledge. No one would be safe."

I furrowed my eyebrows. "But werewolves have lived in secret for hundreds of years. Why are they becoming such a concern now?"

"Oh, it's always been a concern, honey. The age of technology, though. That makes it a lot harder to put rumors to bed before they truly take hold." His tone was that of a teacher explaining simple truths to a child, but none of this was simple or true, and I was not a child.

"You're the Alpha of the Wulver Pack." My voice caught in my throat, causing me to stumble over my words. "Why would you join forces with hunters?"

Another sad smile, but with condescending notes. "As a Wulver, we have always protected those around us. A war has been brewing amongst the werewolf packs for years. The best way to keep humans safe is by the extinction of our kind. It's sad, but it is the reality. A sacrifice any true Wulver would be willing to make."

I shook my head, refusing to believe him. "Even in war, genocide is not the answer."

"Oh, child," my dad patronized. "You do not know enough about werewolves to make that judgment."

I gritted my teeth, refusing to humor him with a response.

"You know, I truly wished that by mating with a human, my children would not inherit the werewolf gene," he lamented.

"Why?" I scoffed. "So you could raise up little mercenaries for your hunter army?"

"Exactly." His smile became wicked. "I already had to kill your sister because she refused to join forces against you. I'd really like to not have to end my bloodline altogether, so please do us all a favor and make the right choice."

My blood ran cold. My sister. Dead. I knew I should have looked for her.

I looked up at my father, mimicking his menacing grin. The others in the room would not know what was happening, but my father would. I let the wall locking Tala away come tumbling down, the familiar scent of wolf flooding the room. My eyes flashed as Tala's, showing him the wolf was ever present.

"Oh, but Daddy, I did make the right choice."

287

"Fine," he growled, eyes hardening. "If that's your choice, I will personally guarantee you don't make it out of here alive."

I shrugged, trying not to let my fear show. "Do it now then."

I maintained my eye contact, letting the challenge take time to register. Tala was poking around, but she didn't sense another wolf in the room. "By the way, when was the last time you shifted?"

He stiffened in his chair, fists clenched. "I would not allow that beast to ruin me."

"Oh," I said, realization hitting. "You know, I read of instances where your wolf can leave you. Betrayal is the primary force, right? You don't have a wolf anymore, do you?"

My dad stood, reaching over and pulling me to my feet by Oliver's sweatshirt I had yet to take off. The sweatshirt shifted, and his eyes seared into me before landing on my neck.

"She's claimed," he growled, tossing me across the room and into the wall. I might have had inhuman strength, but strength didn't stop velocity.

A couple of the hunters who had been standing around the room picked me up, quickly shackling silver cuffs around my wrists.

"You do realize those don't do anything to me, right?" I laughed. Imprisonment was making me feel deranged. "I'm gonna make the suggestion you guys relocate your hideout. I do have the Wulver Pack on my side, and I don't think they'll be thrilled their Alpha has betrayed them!"

This was a dangerous game. I had no idea what the pack's plans for striking were, and I was not exactly confident I could get in touch with them. Who was to say how many from Snow Moon were already around the compound, or if they could even get here in time.

"Maybe we should just kill you now, then," the person on my right spat in my ear.

"No," my dad quickly interjected. "Her mate will feel the bond die. Keep her alive until her pack shows up."

I had to bite back my smile. If only they knew we had them exactly where we wanted them.

Will took me from the people stationed on either side of me and dragged me back to my cell.

"I don't think you actually understand the predicament you're in," he mused. "Who are you to threaten us when you are the one being held as a prisoner?"

"Prisoner, you think?" I bit back. "Prisoners have the right to a trial."

"You just had yours. You were deemed guilty."

I rolled my eyes, letting all the sass and spunk I had been holding back rear its ugly head. "You really think an ultimatum is a trial?"

"Good enough for me," he snarked. "We all know you killed my brother, so you're guilty of that, too."

The door to my cell clanged open, and I was shoved back inside. I waited until I heard the cell block door close before turning around.

"Now," I told the guard. "It has to be tonight."

There were two realistic options the hunters could pursue. One was to move us, and the other was to sit and wait for an ambush. If they moved us, who knew how long it would take to restructure the plan. If the plan was to wait around, they wouldn't be prepared as early as tonight.

He didn't say anything in return, just one nod and two foot taps before his eyes glazed over.

I looked over to Danica. "I'm a Wulver. That's why I can hide my wolf and silver doesn't affect me. My mate is also the Alpha of the Snow Moon Pack."

I sat down on the floor of the cell and leaned back against the wall. I closed my eyes, forcing myself to sleep. The last thing I did before drifting off was break down the boarded up mate bond, pushing every ounce of love I had down it.

OLIVER

WE HAD CELLS HERE. They were probably my least favorite place to be. But here I sat, for the third day in a row, trying to get information out of a hostage. Kota and Trevor had both offered to take over for me, but I had refused. It was my responsibility as both Alpha and Lya's mate. I'd get her safely back to this territory if it was the last thing I did. Besides, I had dropped the responsibility my Alpha title demanded too much. It was time to reclaim it.

We had never had a human in these cells before, but the warriors we'd sent to the hunters' Oklahoma outpost had brought back a hostage. The usual tactics, silver and wolfsbane, weren't working, and as I sat and stared at my bloody and bruised hands, I had to wonder if this guy even knew anything at all.

A wicked smile crossed my face as I came up with one last idea before I handed this project off to someone else.

"Let's try one more time," I decided, staring him down. His eyes were swollen nearly shut, but he still tried to maintain eye contact. "You hate were-wolves, right?"

He spat a mouthful of blood at my feet and choked out, "Scum of the earth."

"So, I imagine you'd do anything to avoid being turned?" I mused.

A look of abject horror crossed his face. "Y-you can do that?"

I cocked an eyebrow. He didn't need to know it was impossible to turn someone into a werewolf; it was all in the DNA. "How do you think we keep our numbers up so successfully, especially with the likes of you guys running around?"

"You're lying."

"Fine, then," I shrugged. "Keep withholding information and you'll find out."

For a little extra flare, I let my canines descend and slowly approached. How exactly was it that all the stories said you could be turned? I gripped his hair, exposing his neck.

"Wait!" he cried. "What do you want to know?"

"That's better," I sneered, backing away from him. "Now, how many of you are in the Marsan ranks?"

"Couple hundred," he declared proudly.

I nodded, thinking through how many we had targeted the past week. There would be no way for him to know about all our recent hits. We had timed things too well. Still, the number was higher than we wanted to deal with.

"The Cheyenne location you have," I began, choosing my words care-fully. "How many are stationed there?"

"Dunno," he answered, coughing. "We got a new recruit who was gonna be based there, and we were all supposed to report for orders." He looked up at me, blood oozing out of his cracked lips. "Can ya believe it? A wolf girl who wants to get rid of you guys."

I let out a low snarl. There was no way Lya would have betrayed us. "What makes you so sure?"

"Her daddy's been workin' with us. No way you'll beat us when we have wolves on the inside," he said triumphantly.

"Oh, don't you worry about that," I chuckled. "We have people on the inside, too."

His expression sank at the realization we were prepared. I placed a hand on either side of his face and twisted violently, snapping his neck, his down-cast expression frozen forever.

I turned and walked out of the room, not exactly wanting to take the extra time to study my handiwork. I made it only a few steps out of the building before being hit by a freight train, bringing me to my knees and leaving me gasping. I braced myself against the ground as I struggled for breath, tears pricking my eyes while trying to place what the hell this feeling was.

Lya.

The mate bond had been completely cut off for so long, and when every ounce of it returned, it was like being hit by a ton of bricks. It was damn near painful. Was this how it felt to die a slow death from a mate bond?

As the feeling of drowning subsided and the missing piece of me clicked back into place, I could finally place what was happening. She was alive. She was hurt and weak, but she was alive. I let out a strangled sob and fought back as Adair tried to take over. He wanted to run to her right this second, and as much as I wanted to endorse that, it would only risk her life if I showed up without an army.

Fear took hold. Why did she let down the wall?

I struggled to my feet, opening up the link to the pack. Adair found the words I couldn't.

'All warriors heading to Cheyenne, be ready within the hour. It's time to bring our Luna home.'

My mind was reeling faster than my legs were moving toward the pack-house. Our strategy was well rehearsed, but there were so many places things could go wrong.

I was met at the door by Gregory, guiding me into the living room and into a chair. Someone put a glass of water in my hand and encouraged me to drink.

"Man, are you okay?" Trevor asked, grasping my face and peering into my eyes. I was sure he could see my wolf and me struggling for control.

Anna shoved him aside, examining me.

"Adair, back off," she snapped. I felt him begrudgingly pull back, allowing me to focus and regain more control. "Okay, now follow my finger. The mate bond just hit you so hard you're all fucked up."

I nodded absently as I followed the instructions she gave to–what? Check for a concussion?

"Liam linked us right before she slammed you with the bond. I don't think anyone warned her what that would do," Kota supplied.

"Who's Liam?" I rasped.

"Her brother," Kota said. "Half-brother whom she's never met. He has been her guard."

I nodded again, barely processing what they'd said. I sat back, the shock now practically immobilizing me. Somehow, someway, I was going to have to find a way up off this chair and get my ass in gear. It was funny how the mate bond could be your greatest strength and ultimate weakness, all rolled into one. I scanned the room, trying to find something to ground me. I glanced to Gregory, who was studying me carefully.

"This is normal," he reassured me. "It's like eating too much after being starved."

I closed my eyes and sat back, claws digging into the arms of the chair. I fought my way down the bond, digging into Lya's mind. I refuted the flashes of what she had experienced there, seeking out her smile, her eyes, the way she set her jaw when there was no changing her mind, every piece of her I needed to bring back home intact. Anything to provide a small stepping stone back to the light.

My eyes snapped open, and Adair's voice rumbled out of me. "Patrols here confirmed?"

"You solidified them the day before yesterday," Kota said.

"Vehicles loaded?"

"You loaded them yourself four days ago," he reminded me.

"Back-up wave knows to roll out two hours after us?"

Trevor let out a harsh laugh. "You know we won't need them, but yes. You also have a third and fourth wave scheduled."

"What about a medic team?"

Brandon rolled his eyes. "Just get in the damn car, which has a restocked, expanded, and tripled first aid kit."

I stood abruptly, storming toward the door. "We'll review the strategy on the way."

"We all know the plan, and the back-up plan, and the back-up plan to the back-up plan," Trevor sighed, following me out the door.

I glanced to the back seat of the Land Cruiser, taking in the blood stains that were too set to be scrubbed out by the time I remembered the car needed to be detailed after Chamberlain. I vowed to not let another drop of Lya's blood grace this vehicle.

Kota, Brandon, and Trevor were barely in the vehicle as I pulled away from the packhouse.

"Where's Thom?" Brandon asked.

"Taking a separate car," I mumbled. "It makes more sense with him going north to meet up with the rogues."

Brandon nodded slowly. "And the pack closing in from the west is...?"

"Beaver Moon. Smaller pack that sends all their warriors to us for training." I glanced in the rearview mirror back at him. "Do you not actually know these things, or are you trying to get my mind off of something?"

Brandon scrubbed his hand across his face, avoiding eye contact. I didn't get a response, but I didn't expect one.

Thirty-Six

Lya

MY EYES nearly rolled back in my head, the sensation of Oliver's presence again all-consuming. I had missed this. I could practically hear the missing piece of me clinking back into place. A smile flitted across my face as lightning danced across my skin, embracing me like a warm hug. I could almost smell him.

'*Might as well get a chance to feel all warm and fuzzy again,*' my wolf sighed. '*It has been too long.*'

'*Never again,*' I agreed.

That familiar wolfy chuckle. I had missed even that. '*Don't make promises you can't keep.*'

I pulled my legs up to my chest and rested my head on my knees. Tala may have thought she was helping, but it really just made me sad. I missed home. I missed my mate. It was a cruel reminder that, even if everything went to plan, there was a very high likelihood I would never see him again. Part of me wanted to see if I could reach out to him, but the other part didn't want that small glimmer of hope.

My heart broke for Danica. I hadn't heard much about her life, but I was certain it had been filled with more suffering than she deserved, just like mine. At least I had gotten almost two full months of happiness before ending up here. I'd be lying if I said she would have an opportunity to find that after we got out of here. I was fairly certain we would be leaving in body bags, if at all.

No one ever really spoke about just how deafening silence could be. Sure, 'resounding silence' was a descriptor, but until you'd been truly submersed in unequivocal silence, you didn't realize just how loud and all-consuming it was.

That's what I noticed first. Everything was silent. No hum of electricity or regular beeps acknowledging the electronics keeping our cells locked shut were still working. I imagined all three of us were subconsciously holding our breath just to avoid being the first to threaten the lack of noise. I lifted my head out of my arms and slowly opened my eyes. I hadn't noticed the blackness behind my closed lids. It was so impermeable, if it weren't for the frosted glass windows letting moonlight in, I wouldn't be able to see at all. As it were, my werewolf eyesight was able to amplify the small bits of light available so I could distinguish what was going on around me, which was admittedly not much.

The silence continued for either seconds or hours, I couldn't determine which, with the three of us barely risking taking a breath. Slowly, I stood up and made my way to the cell door. I didn't expect it to budge when I pushed against it, but it swung open.

"You'd think they'd come and make sure we were still secure if we were that important to them," I mused, my voice clanging against the walls. I took a few steps out, the sense of freedom nearly crippling me.

'Can we just get the fuck out of here now?' Tala demanded.

I turned around, looking at the others. Danica shuffled to the front of her cell, standing as close to the door as she dared. I offered a small smile and pulled it open for her, keeping in mind she wasn't one of us blessed enough to be able to touch silver. The guard still stood nearly unmoving and conveniently blocking our exit.

The cracking and explosion of what sounded like fireworks at first rattled the building. My head snapped around as one of the windows blew out and a bullet went whizzing over our heads. Danica shrieked and threw herself to the ground, crawling over to where I stood facing our guard.

It had been tempting to put off training all the times Oliver begged me to, exchanging sweaty brawls on the field for days spent with him, but I was glad I hadn't. The few weeks in a cell would have definitely made me a little rusty, but I was going to pretend courage was a skill that never quite went away. Just like riding a bike. I'd sure need those skills now.

I looked up to the guard with pleading eyes. "Please tell me this is part of the plan."

'Avoid the windows,' his gruff voice echoed in my head.

"Danica can't mind-link. She's a rogue," I reminded him.

He pursed his lips and looked down at me. *'I'm only responsible for you.'*

I furrowed my eyebrows and followed the link he created, trying my best to mind-link for the very first time. *'Well, I'm going to be responsible for her, so your job will be a lot easier if you include her in this.'*

He was a man of little words. All he did was nod and turn to lead us through the door. I crept along obediently, Danica right on our heels.

"Do you know him?" Danica whispered to me.

I spared a glance back over my shoulder. "He's part of the Wulver Pack."

"Yeah, but do you know him?" she repeated. "Like, what's his name?"

I bit my lip. "Uh... no. Hey, what's your name?"

"Liam," he muttered gruffly.

I turned back to Danica. "His name's Liam."

"And you trust him?" she demanded.

"It's the only choice we have."

Liam stopped us short at a doorway and grabbed my arm, pulling me forward and leaning down to whisper in my ear. "Stay as clear of everything as you can. You don't know battle, and everyone out there is seasoned. Your one and only job right now is to stay alive. You keep yourself hidden."

"Fat chance," I scoffed. I'd go down fighting with all the other people I'd dragged into this.

I got just the hint of a smile out of Liam. "I know."

He stepped through the doorway and swiftly shifted into a large, auburn wolf, dashing off in the direction of war cries.

I beckoned Danica over to me and gave her a once over. "Do you know anything about how to fight?" She just shook her head. "And you're scared shitless?" She nodded. "So, you're planning a getaway as soon as you see an opening?"

"Please don't judge me," she whispered.

"I'm not," I assured her. "I'm scared shitless, too."

Danica's hands shook as she gripped my arm. "I-I've got things I need to do before I die."

"Then don't die," I instructed, giving her as reassuring a smile as I could muster. Maybe it was because we were imprisoned together, but I felt obligated to make sure this kid got out alive. She didn't have any dog in this fight. "You need to make sure when you run you aren't followed, though. They'll kill you if they get you alone. Strength in numbers."

I looked around the hallway, trying to find something I could use for defense.

Bingo.

May the Goddess bless whoever's brilliant idea it was to have this building up to code once upon a time. I marched over to the emergency box and drove my elbow into the glass. I pulled out the axe, the beginnings of a smirk developing with my probably horrible idea.

I wasn't sure if the look of horror on Danica's face was because of my expression, or the axe I was holding. "I don't think I like what you're thinking."

"We're closer to the hunters than the wolves, right?" I asked, glancing up at her. "We have to get through them somehow. I'm not going in defenseless, and I'm not shifting and drawing too much attention to myself."

Danica nodded in understanding. "What do I do then?"

"Skirt the perimeter. Stay as far out of the fray as possible," I told her. "When you find an opening with no one at your back, you run." I studied her for a moment. What should be such childlike innocence was marred with too much trauma. "When you're sure you aren't being followed, you go to Snow Moon Pack. Got it?"

Oh, to run. A skill I was oh so familiar with. Formerly just a lost girl who ran away from every little problem under the guise of protecting those I loved. This time around, the best way to protect them was to run into the problem head on.

My, how times had changed.

"Why don't you do the same?" Danica asked.

I flipped the axe over in my hands, studying its weight and balance. I didn't know anything about axes, but I figured if I'd be lobbing it around, I needed to get as good an idea of how it felt as possible. I stepped out of the doorway, looking out to the battle that was just beginning. The smell of blood was thick in the air, and already bodies had fallen on both sides. Battle was probably a thing I'd never have to get used to because I doubted I'd make it out of this alive.

I bit my lip. Staying alive was so important because my life was linked to Ollie's. Maybe Liam was right, and I should just stay in the safety of cover and wait for people to come find me. Or I could escape from it all with Danica.

A howl resounded from just outside the door. I smiled. It was a howl I would always recognize. Tala clawed at the edges of my mind to get out, but we had our plan.

"I can't run away anymore."

OLIVER

OVER TWO HUNDRED wolves surrounded the hunters' compound. In another four hours, there would be another three hundred and fifty more. We were overprepared, but I didn't care. Every single wolf here knew exactly why and who they were here for. Given the way her story was told, I truly hoped they would be here even if she wasn't their Alpha's mate.

I would have to make sure Lya knew that everyone knew now. She was the girl who overcame her upbringing only to put her life on the line for an entire population she barely knew. She was the girl who didn't need a knight in shining armor. She just needed a sword, and she forged her own. I never even stuttered when I declared she was my mate.

I couldn't muster the courage to try and mind-link with Lya, but Kota had filled me in on what little Liam had been able to pass on, including the fact that in some way or another, her dad was involved in this whole mess. No one was quite sure what Lya had done to set the wheels in motion, but it was chaos when we arrived. The scene before us did not support the image of the hunters we all had in our heads. We thought them to be calculated and sinister, not running around the place, screaming at each other, and fighting amongst themselves. Whatever was going on, people were in disagreement of how it should be managed.

'*What the hell did your girl do, Ollie?*' Kota whispered through the mind-link.

I smiled. '*Whatever it was, it's helping us out.*'

We steadily crept closer, slowly closing in on their compound. There was barely a sliver of a moon left, and the lights glaring from the building left plenty of shadows for us to stay hidden in. The closer we got, the more we could overhear.

"You're seriously listening to that guy?" a younger man shouted in the face of one a generation or so his senior. "He's a fucking werewolf! We can't trust a werewolf!"

"Used to be," the older hunter hissed. "He don't have a wolf now. That kid of his got herself marked, and she'll have wolves comin' after her. Easy kills."

I shot a glance at Kota. We had little information to go off of, but it was reasonable to assume they were discussing Lya's father, the missing Wulver Alpha. Kota seemed to radiate anger at what he heard about his other Alpha.

Losing your wolf was the ultimate dishonor, and certainly not something one of the Wulver Pack would suffer, I would think.

The younger one scoffed, "That's assuming she's not linked to a big pack. We could easily be outnumbered."

"A pack'd know better than to send out all their wolves jus' to pick up a girl."

Oh, if only he knew this was just a fraction of our wolves.

"She's the daughter of the Alpha of the strongest pack known to man and beast," the younger said through gritted teeth. "The only one more powerful than her mate is probably her. We don't stand a chance."

'Don't worry,' Adair growled, *'we are the beast.'*

"You gonna desert then, boy?" the older man asked. "Go on, we don't need the help of someone who can't follow orders. You young bucks ain't no better than rogues."

The younger one lunged at the man, knocking him to the ground and grappling with him. The scene caught the attention of the others in the area, the hunters who were supposed to keep an eye out for intruders like us. So, I started sifting through all the links, looking for the particular line I needed.

'Seth?' I called. *'Cut the lights.'*

'Yes, Alpha.'

Not a second later, the compound went dark. This was our party trick because we hadn't assumed there would be turmoil already. Cyber had hacked their power grid, cutting all electricity. Not only did this leave them in the dark, but Liam had tipped us off that the cells had fail-safe electromagnetic locks, so as soon as the power went out, Lya would be free. We could only assume they had generators that would kick in within a few minutes, but it would give us the upper hand to start, at least.

The plan had been reviewed ad nauseum. I didn't need to send out orders to everyone; they all knew the parts they'd play. The second the lights went out, those of us who had shifted hit the ground, staying as low as possible as we crawled on our stomachs closer to the compound. Bullets zipped over us, taking out the majority of hunters standing around the outside of the building, the sound drawing out more.

I smirked to myself. I had gotten pushback when I decided warriors needed to be able to shoot. It sure was coming in handy now.

The smell of gun smoke filled the air as the hunters drew their only form of defense. The gunfire was blinding for them at night, though, giving us the opportunity to charge forward.

I paid no regard to who was in my way. If they smelled human, they fell.

Copper and iron filled my nose as the rank smell of blood permeated the air. But it wasn't quite enough to drown out my mate's scent. Instead, it was like smelling it for the very first time.

Adair let out a howl, calling for his mate. The ones who could joined, offering a response to his song, but the battle raged on. I leapt over a body, paws skidding in the coagulated, sticky puddle salting the earth when I landed. Adair tore his way closer and closer to where she was, thankfully not losing regard for the task at hand.

Something mauled me from the side, sending me off balance and skittering through the dirt. Lya's scent nearly forgotten, I stood up and shook myself off, looking around for the culprit. I zeroed in on the big, burly man who had just tried to bodycheck a wolf. He was brave, but not smart enough. I lifted my lip and growled at him, providing him just a second too long. The gun was aimed and cocked, pointing right between my eyes.

The bullet never came, though. I crouched back on my haunches, ready to attack, but paused another second to study the frozen form. Blood bubbled up through his lips, and he teetered on his feet before falling face first. His solid form had hidden a small figure with a raving mess of unkempt red curls in an oversized sweatshirt. She brandished an axe, the pick of it stained red.

Our eyes locked. Her amber eyes looked like little balls of fire out here on the battlefield. I took a step toward her, trying to close the distance, but an injured wolf with a hunter on its trail stumbled between us. I lunged for the hunter, bone and sinew crunching under my jaw and blood leaking down my throat. The taste was repulsive, but the glory of another threat removed was sweet. I looked over to the wolf to ensure they were okay. I quickly noticed it was one of the newly graduated females. This particular battle had seen a lot of women stepping up, and I had to think they saw some inspiration in the way Lya put herself on the line for the pack. And she wasn't even a pack member yet.

I glanced around, taking a moment to assess the damage. Bodies had fallen on both sides, but significantly fewer wolves than humans. With nearly a one-to-one ratio, we had been making quick work. My pack's particular talent on the battlefield was showing.

When I looked back to my mate, she was gone.

THIRTY-SEVEN

Lya

MY MIND WAS MADE UP. I knew exactly what my role in this fight would be.

If I had learned anything about my father, it was that he was a coward. He wouldn't be out on the field participating. Maybe he was who I got my ability to run away from problems from. Even still, I was drawn outside.

The sight was horrifying, and the smell of war made me gag. Guns rang out, teeth clashed, screams and howls resounded. What my eyes honed in on, though, was none other than Will barreling into my mate. I careened toward them faster than I could think. If anyone died here, it was supposed to be me.

"NO!" I screamed, but the sound was drowned out.

Oliver waited too long, giving Will the opportunity to aim his gun. I didn't have time to shift, but I still had the axe. I flung it with every ounce of strength I had, burying the pick deep in his back. I was certain the pick of a fireman's axe wouldn't be enough to actually kill him, so I twisted it for good measure. If I was lucky, I'd maim him enough for Oliver to go in for the kill.

Will toppled over, leaving me staring at Oliver. Every bit of the mate bond I had been hiding from the past couple weeks hit me full force, nearly bringing me to my knees.

'*MATE!*' Tala screamed in my head, trying her best to drag me to him.

But this war wasn't over yet, so I did the only thing I could think of. I shoved Tala back to the farthest point of my mind I could get her and ran the other way. There had been a facility map next to the emergency box, and I tried to follow it to the best of my memory.

I waded my way through the sea of bodies, swinging my axe at whoever crossed my path. I didn't kill anyone by any means—aiming an axe accurately when you haven't even held one before is just not possible—but it still hurt like a bitch.

When I finally found the garage, it was swarming. It was more than I could handle by myself. I didn't really know how to mind-link, but I could feel the presence of wolves around me. I followed those connections.

'*We could use some folks in the garage, please,*' I stuttered.

I kept to the periphery, trying to stay out of sight as best I could until more help showed up. It didn't take long, though. The door crashed open, and wolves came barreling in. I recognized Oliver and Kota, but not the others.

The entrance of the additional wolves grabbed the hunters' attention, giving me the cover I needed. I ducked under one of their vehicles, trying to stay out of the way. I looked up at all the hoses and belts and had an idea. I reached up and started pulling and disconnecting them, letting my claws slip free to cut a few. When the coast looked clear enough, I rolled over to the next one and did the same. Presumably, the hunters in the garage were here because they wanted to get away. At least I was ruining their easiest escape plan, as well as getting closer and closer to my destination.

'*Lya, where are you?*' a voice crackled through my head. I recognized it as Kota.

'*Under an SUV,*' I said. '*Who all's here?*'

There was a pause, and I heard another body hit the floor. '*Wulvers and Oliver.*'

That made sense. I wasn't part of the Snow Moon Pack yet, so they wouldn't have been able to hear my mind-link. And Oliver and I were mated, giving him unfettered access to my head.

Things were quieting down. Of the twenty or so hunters that were in the garage, it seemed like the number of wolves that inundated them took them out pretty quickly. I rolled over to the last vehicle in the line and started pulling at hoses. I watched out of the corner of my eye as a set of shoes stomped past me. I didn't stop working, though.

But then there was a hand fisting my hair, dragging me out from under the vehicle and pulling me to my feet.

"What did you do, Lya?" my father growled. He'd be menacing, but he lacked the wolf to back him up.

I offered a sinister smirk back at him. "Cars needed a little maintenance. Remember that Chevelle you said I could keep if I got running? I didn't have a dad around to teach me how, so I don't know how well I did."

He let go of me and took a step back. "You'll regret this."

I could feel the wolves around me looking on, bristling at his threat, but not making a move. I could only imagine how angry the Wulver Pack was with him, although I wasn't sure if they were aware he no longer had a wolf.

"You will, too," I told him. "In fact, I think I speak for all your pack when I say you are not fit to be the Wulver Alpha. Daddy, I'm challenging your Alpha title."

I heard scuffling behind me, but I ignored it. My vision had honed in on my father, who had his fists clenched behind him. I let the axe fall by my side and took a step back, creating enough room.

For just a moment, I thought I saw a flash of pain cross my father's face. Good, he deserved it.

"You don't know what you're doing, child," he ground out.

"Maybe not," I conceded, "but I do know this pack deserves better than you."

And with that, I lunged, shifting in the air. My paws landed on my father's chest, pushing him to the ground. This would be a fight to the death, and to be perfectly honest, I wasn't completely certain it'd be me walking away. Kota had said he could kill a wolf with his bare hands, but could he kill his own daughter?

Who was I kidding? He had already killed my sister.

He reached up to shove me off, but I locked my jaw around his arm and shook violently. I wasn't a big wolf, though, and he pushed me over easily. I was on my back, making ribbons of his flesh until I could get my hind legs positioned well enough to shove him off.

As soon as the weight was off of me, I sprung back up on my feet. I stalked over to my father, watching as he writhed on the ground. He had nothing—no wolf, no healing, not even a weapon. I looked down, seeing the axe I had previously used. I nosed it over to him.

And just like that, the prickling sensation of another wolf entering the room crawled up my skin. One that was all too familiar, yet I had never known.

'You fight,' I insisted, all Wulvers—all of them—able to hear.

My dad glanced at the axe but shook his head. I sat back on my haunches and waited. Killing a human like this was murder, not a challenge. He laid there for a moment, gasping for breath, before finally reaching for the axe and getting to his feet. I stayed still, waiting for him to take up some sort of stance.

When he finally took up the defense, I lunged again, this time going for his throat. Before I connected, his eyes flashed to that of his long lost wolf, and he dropped the weapon, but it was too late. I pummeled into him, latching down and snapping his neck.

I don't know how long I stood over him, looking down at what I had done. I wasn't proud.

I could feel numerous sets of eyes burning holes in my back, but I still took a couple extra moments before I shifted, turning slowly to face the crowd.

I almost completely ignored the wolves surrounding me on one knee, only having eyes for Oliver. It felt like Tala and I melded into one, reaching out for him.

"Mate."

And then everything went black.

OLIVER

I SAW RED.

The first I heard from Lya in weeks, and it was a plea for help.

I followed my nose, bursting through the door blocking me from her. I couldn't see her anywhere, but I knew she was here. There were countless other wolves from her birth pack on my tail, and we immediately set to work dispatching the stragglers looking to escape us, dragging most out of cars that refused to start.

I finally spotted her, underneath one of the vehicles, disabling it. I took half a second to let out a breath of relief and smile. Smart girl.

I lost track of her again when my focus shifted to keeping others away from her. It wasn't until I had no one else in my sights and everything had fallen quiet that I heard her voice ringing through the garage, filled with confidence and conviction.

"Daddy, I'm challenging your Alpha title."

I spun around, charging for where she stood. I wasn't going to let her risk her life like this. But I was stopped by Kota and Gregory.

'She initiated the challenge,' Gregory insisted. *'There's nothing we can do.'*

I snapped at him. In that moment, I'd take out anyone who stood in my way of protecting my mate, and right now, that included those I had hand chosen to stand by me.

The wolves formed a wall, blocking me from her, forcing me to just sit by and watch. I tried to push past, attempting to take her place, but again I was stopped.

'*She isn't strong enough to challenge an Alpha!*' I pleaded with Kota and Gregory, but they offered no support. '*Let me fight for her!*'

'*It has to be a Wulver,*' Kota deadpanned.

'*Then one of you step up!*' I begged. '*You can't let her do this! She'll die!*'

Kota turned to me, his wolf's eyes boring into mine. '*You know the rules of an Alpha challenge. Besides, Wulvers trained her. She will be fine.*'

Kota was right. I knew the rules. As soon as the challenge was issued, there could be no interference. If there was, the challenged Alpha would keep their title. In a pack like the Wulvers, where there was no Alpha line and passing on the title relied on challenges, their rule that it must be a Wulver made sense.

She maneuvered around her father effectively, Kota's training proving its worth. This hadn't been part of the grand plan, though. No one had known he would be here. She had elected this on her own. If she was anyone other than my mate, I would be furious.

I couldn't peel my eyes away, needing to know the second something went wrong so I could jump in and save her. I had been here before, and I refused to watch her nearly die again. My claws dug into the ground, scraping against the cement floor as Lya was flung to the ground. Even without a wolf, her father was still strong. His own training showed.

Adair pushed me to the back of our mind, antsy as he watched. Pinned to the ground like that, her fear was gut-wrenching. Just as he was about to spring forward and pull the Wulver Alpha off of Lya, she turned the tables.

Fate had chosen this woman to stand by my side and lead a pack. Around every corner, the Luna she was meant to be took its opportunity to shine through. The fight in her opponent was gone, but even still, she held out for a fair fight, not going in for the kill until her father was on his feet.

It was curious, the way he chose to surrender. He could have easily conceded and gotten away with his life, but he held his ground until the very last moment. No, the very last millisecond. The wolf's jaws were around his throat when he dropped the weapon she had forced on him, too late for her to change her trajectory and spare his life.

Lya shifted back quickly, sparing barely a second to look at the body before her. She looked past her new pack that was on its knees with necks barred for her.

And I saw her for the first time.

Adair howled, and her scent overwhelmed me. I hadn't even realized I had shifted back to my human form. It was a feat in and of itself to stay upright, but I found myself moving through the crowd toward her.

"Mate."

Lya was breathless, but her voice was music to my ears. Mine hitched in my throat, barely able to get the word out.

I was too blind to see it, but a shot rang out. I couldn't even tell you which direction it came from. Her eyes stayed on me until she hit the ground, head clunking against the vehicle beside her, causing her amber eyes to go glassy.

By the time I got to her, I could tell she was unconscious. I paid no attention to the commotion going on around me, intent on stopping the bleeding. I was completely and utterly consumed by her, but the need to keep her alive overrode succumbing to the tendrils of the bond reinforcing their presence throughout me.

We had been here before.

Hands were pulling me to my feet, but I refused to move.

"Let's go!" someone yelled. "Brandon's got the car."

I was moving through a haze. The only thing on my mind was her blood seeping through my fingers and not having something to stop the bleeding with. Our skin-on-skin contact lit me up like a bottle rocket just like it had the first time I touched her. The scuffle behind me sounded like it had died down, so I just assumed they had found the shooter. Even if that one had gotten away, I didn't care. The Marsan legacy was no more.

I found myself struggling to my feet, holding her close and following blindly. Maybe it was just her adrenaline crashing, or maybe she was really losing that much blood, but the slowing tempo of her heartbeat was the only thing fueling me through the fog that seemed to slow time and hold me back. I had been here before, and I refused to watch her die.

At some point, Trevor fell in stride beside me. The sense of Déjà-vu hit hard. "Is now too soon to make a joke about full circle?"

I shot a glare over at him but couldn't find the words to speak.

"Well, we thought to bring the doc along with us this time, so Lessa will get her bandaged up enough to at least get back to the pack," he offered. "Besides, her wolf is on her side this time."

I nodded, hardly able to take my eyes off her to see where I was going.

When my Land Cruiser rolled up to us, it was Brandon driving this time, not Rose. Rose had begged to come, but her orders to monitor Derek superseded this, especially with how many others we had.

I slid in, still cradling Lya, and once again started layering on all the bandaging material in the SUV. Brandon pulled out of the compound, slowly making our way across the rolling hills of the prairie. If she could hold on for another twenty minutes, we would be at the base we had set up.

"We'll get her all patched up, Ollie," Brandon promised.

"Just drive," I grumbled.

This was exactly the same. I had secretly wished for a second chance to see my mate for the first time—a time when she would recognize me as her mate, I had my head out of my ass, and we got it right—but not like this. This was too familiar. I didn't want her nearly dying again. She was much stronger now, but that didn't change the fact that even wolves couldn't heal some injuries.

My heart fell as we rolled up to our base. There were too many injured wolves surrounding it. Anna was running around, helping patch up the less serious injuries and getting people out of the way, but the doctor was nowhere in sight and not responding to mind-links.

I hadn't had time to assess damages and losses yet, but the bodies being loaded into vehicles seemed to be rapidly growing. Our general rule of thumb was to bring back every wolf we lost, giving their families a chance to say goodbye. In this instance, we would also bring back the rogues who had stood with us and give them a pack burial.

I didn't risk moving Lya more than necessary, instead sending Trevor out to see if there was even a gurney to put her in.

"Alpha Oliver!" a voice called as they pulled open the door. "Over here!"

I turned, attempting to see through my foggy vision. Was this what panic did? Where was Adair to take over when I needed him?

"Bring Alpha Lya here," the person said. I couldn't focus, couldn't see who it was.

Alpha Lya. My Luna was also an Alpha. Could she even be my Luna now? Lya was an Alpha. My mate was strong enough to be Alpha. No one contested it or complained.

Hands began reaching for Lya to pull her away from me, snapping everything into focus.

"Don't touch her," I growled, pulling her back to me and exiting the vehicle. I followed along, but the person was leading me in the wrong direction. "Where are we going?"

"Wulvers brought their medics as well," he said. "I'm Liam, by the way. One of Lya's relatives."

"You were her guard," I said dumbly. "Did she not recognize you?"

Liam chuckled. "She hadn't met me before."

"She spent summers with your family, though." Lya had told me countless stories of the summers she spent with her twin cousins growing up, including how she severed ties with them all when she turned eighteen. "Why didn't you all tell her about being a werewolf?"

"She never met me. Everyone thought she was human. Her mom's human, you know." He paused for a moment, waving another person over. "Jade!"

I placed my mate gently on the table Liam had led me to, but kept a firm hold on her hand. I needed to feel the magic sparking across her skin. It was the only thing letting me know she was still alive.

The girl rushed over to us, throwing her arms around Liam. "Oh my Goddess, I'm so glad you're okay!"

He pushed her away, directing her attention to Lya. "Get our new Alpha stable to be moved to a hospital, please."

Jade looked up at me, hardly sparing Lya a glance. "You need to leave. I can't have an Alpha mate standing over me. She's with family here. We'll take care of her."

I was prepared for that, relinquishing my hold on her hand and backing away.

Liam gave me a quizzical look. "Thought there'd be an argument there."

"We've done this before," I grumbled.

Thirty-Eight

Lya

Endings were hard.

Beginnings, though? Well, beginnings were easy. They sneaked up on you, and you found yourself halfway into the storyline before you even realized the plot. Truth be told, I couldn't even tell you when this story began. Was it my first shift? The first time I slit my wrist? Maybe when I met Ted Marsan, or when I killed him. What about when I finally ended up in this pack?

I could tell you one thing, though, and that was this was the end.

Endings were hard. They always came too soon, leaving plot holes and unanswered questions in their wake. There was so much more to say, to do. My story was ending, and it felt like it had only just begun.

Fate was a fickle bitch. I was still resentful it had taken her this long to let me find my way to this pack. Six weeks just didn't seem like enough time to be happy. Oh, how I would have changed those six weeks if I had known how quickly it would all end. I had known death was a possibility when I signed up for this gig, but it hadn't seemed real until just now.

People knew what they were talking about when they kept saying this whole werewolf thing was in my DNA. It had seemed like a switch flipped shortly after ending up at Snow Moon. Acceptance was easy, and molding to this life was second nature. But the six weeks I had with the pack? It felt like the first six weeks of my life I'd actually lived. Maybe it all happened so quickly because I had never had what this pack offered.

Home.

And I'd give anything for my home, even if I didn't get to keep it when the dust finally settled.

The world was dark. I tried to move my limbs, but they felt as heavy as lead. I couldn't even open my eyes. The gentle rocking and occasional bumps made me think we were on the road. Thinking was too much energy, though, so I just settled in to focus on the warmth zinging through my hand.

I reached out cautiously, searching for that familiar presence I had missed. *'Tala?'*

'We're sedated,' she told me. *'You got us shot again.'*

'What?'

'Yeah, another bullet removal surgery incoming. But just try and listen right now. The grown-ups are talking,' she instructed.

Thinking was hard, but Tala was rarely wrong, so I did my best to listen.

"We've got another three hours until we are back at the pack, so someone better start talking," a familiar voice grumbled. I smiled to myself, but I was sure it didn't actually reach my face. Oliver.

"What do you want to know?" I heard Kota say.

His hand tightened around mine. I could tell he was about to snap at them. And I was right. "Everything. You all have kept me in the dark, and if I'm supposed to trust you Wulvers, you aren't doing a very good job of instilling it. All you have done is make me feel like I have absolutely no control over my pack this past month, and I am done with it."

Someone else cleared their throat. "We'd been devising plans to target the Marsan operation for over a year now. We needed an in, and a pack with more manpower to back us. I'll have you know, not once did anyone push this on your mate. She chose it. She understood she was the lost Wulver the hunters were actively seeking, and provided the perfect opportunity for that in."

"And, Ollie," Kota quickly added, "I don't think anyone could have changed her mind, no matter how hard they tried. She was born to be a Luna, after all. She knew the hunters would find her eventually, and she'd die to protect her pack."

It was Adair that let out the growl. "You're saying my mate is your Alpha now. I don't trust you with her."

"She challenged Dad and she won. Of course she's now Alpha," the mysterious person said. I racked my brain, trying to place the voice, but came up blank. "And to be honest, we don't really care if you trust us."

'*Focusing on the wrong thing, Lya,*' Tala cut in, interrupting my thoughts. '*You are a freaking Alpha now!*'

If I hadn't been on all the drugs, my breathing would have caught. How was I supposed to know killing my own father would land me as Alpha? If I had known that, I wouldn't have challenged him. I was just hoping to get him out of the position so someone else, someone worthy, could take over. Not me! I was not at all suitable or worthy for the job, and I didn't want it.

I tried to open my eyes, tried to sit up, even tried to mind-link so I could protest. It couldn't be me. I didn't want it. I wasn't going to do it.

My mate must have sensed my distress because his hand traveled up my arm to rub soothing circles, attempting to bring me back into my body.

"She barely wants to be a werewolf. What if she doesn't want to be Alpha?" Oliver asked.

I took offense to that. I loved being a werewolf. The Alpha thing could go, though.

Kota huffed. "You know as well as anyone, Oliver. Those who don't want it are the best ones to lead. She can give up her title about as easily as you can."

There was a pregnant silence that fell over the vehicle. "She was supposed to be my Luna."

"And she will," the nameless voice assured him. "You already have a Wulver Beta and Gamma; what's a Luna, too? Most of us have a home pack, and it's not unusual for us to find ourselves rising up the ranks."

"Who even are you?" Oliver snapped.

There was shuffling in the front seat. I imagined the person was turning to look at Oliver. "I am her older brother. Half-brother."

I didn't have a brother.

"Lya never mentioned a brother," Oliver told him for me.

He chuckled. "She never met me. Doubt she even knew I existed."

"You've called her the lost Wulver several times. How was she so lost if she was spending summers with her cousins?" he asked.

"She was never that lost," the other person, my supposed brother, offered. "We didn't know for certain she was a wolf, and we couldn't risk asking her about it in case she wasn't. When she turned eighteen, that's when she became lost."

"And no one looked for her?" Oliver demanded. Without even seeing him, I knew exactly the thunder and rage flashing across his face.

"Of course, we looked for her," my brother barked back. "I've spent the past seven fucking years of my life trying to find her. As soon as I found out he killed Lindy, I've been trying to find her!"

My heart sank. My baby sister. I had desperately hoped my father had been lying when he had said he'd killed her. I hadn't spoken to her or my mother since I moved away, and it had been in the back of my mind to track her down and see how she was doing. My poor mother. She had lost both her children now.

"Well, great job you did there," Oliver spat. "You've heard how fucked up she was when she got to me."

My brother let out a dark laugh. "I could say the same about you. An Alpha who can't even keep his mate from being kidnapped by hunters?"

I pushed hard against the darkness keeping me down. I tried to grab on to any little tether of light I could and drag myself out.

"Stop," I mumbled. The words barely passed my lips, but I hoped it was enough because I tumbled back down into the dark abyss of drugged unconsciousness.

OLIVER

Lya's own little army sat in the waiting room as she underwent surgery. Again. Everyone seemed to be glaring at someone. Liam and I continued our silent argument through looks alone. Jade and Jason, Lya's supposed cousins, were arguing about whose fault it was they hadn't realized Lya was a wolf. Thom kept his eyes locked on them as he rocked Kai, silently begging them to be quiet. Then there were Anna and Trevor, still in a staring contest about his refusal to let her start warrior training. Kota curiously enough kept shooting daggers at Jade. Marjorie was the only one sitting quietly, observing everything. Brandon waltzed back into the room, returning from his mission for "supplies."

"You all need to take a chill pill," he informed us, handing everyone a beer. "We're all on the same side here, don't forget."

I sighed and sat back, cracking my beer. "You're right."

"I mean, really, you can be as angry as you want that Lya accidentally landed herself an Alpha gig, but think of why you're angry," Brandon pointed out. "It's just because she's in the same shoes you were in eight years ago."

"Hey, Thom," I scoffed. "You sure you don't wanna be Alpha? I'll just go be the Wulver Luna."

Thom looked up, a morose expression on his face. "I can't, Ollie. I don't have Alpha blood."

"You're my brother," I reminded him. "You have just as much Alpha blood as me."

Thom shook his head. "Think about it, Ollie. I don't look like Dad at all, and Alpha genetics take over. Just look at Lya and Liam. And when he died, it was you the Alpha link went to, not me."

I glanced over to Liam, noticing for the first time that Thom was right. He had the same striking amber eyes and mess of bright auburn curls. There was no denying he and Lya were at the very least closely related.

The Alpha link, though. When Dad died, a surge of power hit me, and I had no idea what it was. I wasn't the one who had been trained to be the next Alpha. Thom was. In the moment it happened, I took over calling the shots for the pack because I was the only one with the power to do so. I always assumed it would transfer over to Thom as soon as he recovered from his injuries from that battle. It never did, but again, I thought it was just because he'd abandoned the pack.

Now that I thought of it, there was no denying it. Thom was not an Alpha by blood. It always would have been me, no matter how much I didn't want it.

"Mom's boyfriend when she met dad..." I trailed off, the dots all starting to connect.

Thom nodded. "I tracked him down when I left the pack and lived with him for a while. Beta of Mom's old pack now. Ended up being mated to her sister of all people."

I laughed at that. "Had fun causing family drama, did you?"

"Just for a little bit." Thom shrugged. "You know us wolves though, always forgiving of pasts prior to mates."

Liam looked over to the door leading down the hallway to surgical suites. "Would you mind if my mom came by to meet Lya?"

I didn't expect formalities from him. He struck me as the sort who asked forgiveness, not permission. Much like his sister. "It's your pack. I won't over-step. But I feel like she'd like to meet her."

I studied him cautiously. "Why?"

Liam took a pull from his beer before speaking. "Our father was my mother's fated mate. He rejected her very early on. She's always been curious."

"Lya's mother was not good to her once she found out she was a wolf," I said slowly. "She is not welcome if she will place any blame on Lya."

He nodded, peeling at the label of his beer. "This a pack brewery?"

"Brewed it myself," Trevor piped up, smiling proudly.

Anna reached over, thwacking him over the head. "Don't get distracted. We're still talking."

"Anna," I cut in, before Trevor could respond, "you can train to be a warrior."

Anna let out a sigh of relief. She'd wanted to train for forever. Her father had pushed her to do anything but, and with the addition of a couple words of encouragement from Trevor years ago, I had refused her application, forcing her into school. We needed another pack doctor, but if Anna was a Wulver by blood, like Lya, she needed to be a trained warrior. I wondered if Gregory had kept Anna in the dark, like Lya had been.

My mind had never wandered far from Lya, opened up on an operating table again, but I now thought of her own warrior training. By ability standards, she was wrapping up her second year, thanks to how Jade and Jason trained her. I'd need to sit the two of them down for a chat regarding her childhood, but that was a problem for another day. Similar to general education, after the second year was when specialties were determined. I had no idea which direction she would go, and I worried it would be something that would put her on the front lines. And I had to imagine, given her heritage, she would be all too willing to find her way to the front lines at every chance.

"Where's Rose?" I blurted out.

Trevor glanced up to me, pursing his lips. "I think we all forgot to tell her."

I looked over to Kota, who had yet to take his eyes off of Jade. That was another thing I was curious about. There was history there, and I was worried I knew it.

"Get someone to replace her on trailing Derek, and then get her over here," I instructed. He looked like he needed a distraction.

The room fell silent again, all of us now glaring at the door instead of each other. Brandon's theory that alcohol fixed all problems seemed to be correct, at least this time. I reached for the cooler, grabbing another one, anxious for a distraction until there was an update.

It felt like hours had passed when Dr. Whitledge finally emerged. He scanned the room, giving me a quick nod. I was on my feet, ready to burst through the doors and see my mate almost instantly. Before I could even ask what the damage was, the doctor spoke up.

"The bullet went through the right side of her chest. She lost a lot of blood, but nothing a transfusion couldn't help. By the time we got in for surgery, her wolf was clearly already working on healing her. We just helped speed things along, as well as put in a chest tube to remove some air. That was removed already, so I foresee her being able to go home tomorrow." He turned to give me a stern look. "I will not let her go home tonight. This is the fourth bullet wound injury she has incurred. I do not care that she seems to be immune to silver. She will stay here for the night."

I didn't miss the pointed look I got from Liam.

I smiled at the doctor, clapping him on the shoulder. "Then I will, too."

"I would expect nothing less, Alpha." The relief written on his face was evident. He hadn't been impressed with me when I pulled her out early last time, but in my mate's words, she wanted to blow this popsicle stand, and I'd give her anything in this world.

"If you'll follow me, Alpha."

I stopped in front of her door, feeling the familiar insecurities to actually face her once again. She was my mate; I had known that for so long. She had admitted it, too, and that made me anxious. I was thankful when Adair pushed forward, shoving me through the door and to her side.

Lya looked so fragile and delicate lying there. She had lost weight, her skin was pale, lips dry and cracked. I took her hand in mine, relishing in the sparks I thought I would never feel again. I pulled her hand up to me and kissed her palm, silently begging her to wake up.

Dr. Whitledge cleared his throat. I had forgotten he was even there. "I'll leave you be then. Someone will be by periodically to see if she's woken up." He turned to leave before throwing one last look at me. "She stays until tomorrow."

I didn't even bother with a response, so caught up in the sight before me. Nothing could ever change that she was the most beautiful thing I had ever seen. Adair purred in my head, content to finally be in her presence. He had been so absent for the past few weeks, constantly trying to seek his mate out. It was good to have him back again. It seemed we were as out of the woods as we would ever be, and with that, the weight of the past few weeks without her lifted off my shoulders, leaving a consuming tiredness in its wake.

I slipped into bed next to her, delicately running my fingers across her exposed skin, relishing in her slow, even breaths. I laid there for hours, not even taking my eyes off of her when nurses came in to check on her. They made comments about how remarkable her healing was, especially compared to last time. It took a really close relationship with both your wolf and your mate to heal this quickly. I didn't care, though. I could only think of her. I was very nearly asleep when I finally heard her voice.

"You know, I really think we need to stop meeting like this."

"Lya," I breathed through a grin, her name music on my tongue. "I believe I asked you not to try bleeding out in my car again?"

THIRTY-NINE

Lya

OLIVER'S LIPS CRUSHED MINE, awakening a hunger and need and wholeness I had tried to forget about while I was the hunters' hostage. Tears pricked my eyes, but he was quick to brush them away. He pulled back, looking down at me.

"Why are you crying?" Oliver murmured. "You're back home now."

I reached up, pulling him back down to me. "I missed you."

"Scoot over?" Oliver asked.

I made space quickly, anxious for him to be as close as possible. I quickly found myself tucked under his arm.

"Can we go home?" I asked. "Back to the packhouse?"

"Tomorrow," he promised, brushing his lips across my hair. "The doc says you're healing better with your wolf around."

"Tala only held back like that as a punishment, apparently," I said, furrowing my brows. My relationship with my wolf had grown immensely, and she had plenty of confessions for me. That was one of them.

Oliver placed his thumb on my chin, turning my face toward him so I could see his glower. "Don't ever do that again."

"I won't," I promised, burying my face in his chest and breathing deep.

Summer lightning storms were always my favorite, and now I'd never need to be disappointed I missed out on them again.

Oliver settled back into the bed, absentmindedly playing with my hair. He stared off into space, lost in thought it seemed.

"You know, we met before," he finally confessed. "Before you came to the pack."

"I know," I said quietly. "In Maine. Tala told me your name."

"I felt it that day."

"I did, too," I whispered. "I shifted for the first time."

Oliver chuckled quietly. "If you hadn't told me you were moving, I would have stayed and transferred into that pack just to be around you."

"I was never part of that pack," I mumbled.

"But your dad was. And I would have been close enough to you to maybe see you again. Keep you safe..." His voice trailed off, but I knew where that comment was headed.

I bit my lip, thinking about his words. "It's hard to keep someone safe from themselves."

"I should have stayed and followed you," Oliver insisted.

I quickly shook my head, refuting his suggestion. "You couldn't have done that. You have a pack to run here."

Oliver offered up a morose smile. I would never get tired of his smile for everything—the good, the bad, and the ugly. "It's no surprise you were destined to not just be a Luna, but an Alpha, too."

"But I don't want to be an Alpha," I argued, my voice shaking. "I just thought it would give someone else the option to step up."

Oliver rolled over onto his side, propping himself up on his elbow. "I don't know if I can trust you, Lya."

I gritted my teeth, refusing to make eye contact. "I know."

"You're my mate. You're supposed to lead beside me." His voice cracked, and he took a sharp breath in before continuing. "I need my Luna to be someone who works with me, not against me."

I swallowed hard, trying to rid the lump in my throat, but it didn't budge. "Can you trust me to make decisions for the best of the pack, even if it's not ideal for us?"

"That's all you've done, Lya," he choked out. "You were a better Alpha to a pack that isn't even yours than I was when I was so wrapped up with finally finding my mate."

I nodded, biting my lip. "Then we have something to work with. It's just us that needs fixing."

"You're the Alpha of another pack, Lya. I don't know how this is going to work, or if it's even... fixable."

I tore through my lip, tears stinging my eyes. Was this rejection? Could he even do that at this point? "C-can we table this-this discussion? Just for now? Just one night of being here with you before reality has to kick in?"

Oliver brushed away the tear making its way down my cheek. He brushed his lips against mine but didn't say anything.

Silence used to be my friend. But now, it was just an enemy.

"We are marked and mated. The Moon Goddess chose us for each other, and she chose you to be an Alpha as well. We will find a way for this to work," he promised.

We lay there in silence for a while. I at least was scared to speak, scared to even move. I had never shared my life before, and this was uncharted territory for me. Part of me was more scared than when I was imprisoned by hunters. And for all I knew, it was going to come to a screeching halt. The thing I wanted most.

"Twenty questions?" I finally squeaked out, desperate to fill the silence.

Oliver smirked at my suggestion of our 'I don't know what to say but we need to talk' game, the tension in the room dissipating. "You go first."

"When did you know I was your mate? The second time." I asked hesitantly.

"Chamberlain." Oliver was confident and resolute. "I wish... I was so stuck on this girl I couldn't quite remember, I refused to believe it."

I bit back a giggle. "Too hard to believe it was me?

He looked down at me before taking his turn. "What was it like for you when you realized?"

"Horrifying," I groaned, burying my head in his chest. "I spent days convincing myself it wasn't worth my time having a crush on you because we both had mates out there waiting for us, but then the full moon..."

"The full moon." Oliver chuckled, pulling me closer to him. "That was a good night. I'm sorry I didn't take things slower. I'd spent the week before trying not to overwhelm you, and I just... I don't know."

"Lost it?" I supplied. "Me too. Would you have ever told me, or waited for me to say something?"

"The full moon in June," he said, again quite certain in his words. "I wasn't going to let it go on any longer without telling you. I couldn't. Do you wish we'd handled it differently?"

I sat up some, rubbing my chest where the bandages were. I thought about his question, digesting it.

"I don't know," I said slowly. "Part of me wonders how important the words would have been when it was so painfully obvious. But your pack has known for a while now, haven't they?"

Oliver nodded, the hint of a smug grin flitting across his lips. "I didn't want to keep it a secret bad enough to hide it." He reached out and delicately traced the features of my face. I closed my eyes, fireworks dancing behind my lids. "Do you wish I had?"

I offered a sly smile. "No, it got me tons of privileges. But I bet everyone hated us. Like poor Rose, I imagine you told her I was your mate, and then I told her you were mine, and we both must have insisted she keep it a secret."

"Great minds think alike. But that explains why she kept asking me what side she was supposed to be on. Your question."

I bit my lip and looked up at Oliver. "The night of my birthday. What did I feel?"

Some of the residual pain must have been evident in my eyes because he turned away quickly and created a centimeter or so of space between us.

"I was at the swimming hole getting sloppy drunk, and Lucy showed up and kissed me. I almost killed her," he blurted.

I let out a deep breath and tucked myself back into his side. Tala stirred, excited for the next time we could drag Allyssa over to the cafe for pancakes. "Your question."

"Yeah. I saw the cells. They didn't look too comfortable, and you just nearly died on me again. Aren't you tired?"

"Mm. Can I ask one more question, though?" I let Oliver nod before I continued. "Can you take me home now?"

He let out an exasperated sigh and looked down at his watch. "Oh, what the hell. it's close enough to tomorrow."

I looked around, noticing I wasn't hooked up to anything this time, and slid off the bed behind Oliver. I tried to take a couple steps, but he scooped me up.

"You're still healing," he murmured against my ear.

Oliver carried me silently through the hospital, carefully peeking around each corner. I couldn't help but laugh silently when he had to duck down a hall to avoid being seen by an oncoming nurse. I clapped my hands over my mouth to keep the sound in, but the irony of the Alpha and Luna hiding from people we should have control over was not lost on me.

When we finally made it to his Land Cruiser, he double and triple-checked I was buckled before he pulled out of the parking lot. So much could happen on the half-mile drive where we never went above twenty-five miles per hour, he insisted. He also promised me he'd be hearing from Dr. Whitledge within five minutes of getting back.

He walked me up the steps, insisting that if I refused to be carried we were going to go painfully slow. I could hear the muffled voices of my friends in the kitchen, or maybe the patio if the back doors were open. I pulled away from Oliver and rushed through the house, anxious to see the faces I thought I'd never get the chance to again.

"Lya!" Anna squealed, rushing to her feet to wrap me in a hug that was maybe a little too rough, but I didn't quite care.

Trevor was close behind her, ruffling my hair. "Glad you're back, kid."

"Had to," I insisted. "Your head would be on a stick otherwise, right?"

Oliver was quick to wrap his arms around me, pulling me back to his chest. "Can we resume the welcome party tomorrow? She needs a chance to sleep and recover more."

My eyes flitted across the room. The usual suspects were of course present, minus Rose. I smiled warmly at my cousins, not at all surprised to see them here. What surprised me the most, was the guard from back at the compound. I knew he was a Wulver, but Oliver was not one to welcome just anyone into the living areas of the pack house, claiming even leaders needed some privacy. What had he done to gain entry past the communal areas?

With a small smile, I tugged Oliver over to the last available chair, curling up on his lap.

OLIVER

I IGNORED Dr. Whitledge's request to know where his patient was. He was a smart man, he could figure it out. What was the point of sitting and relaxing in a hospital bed when she could easily do the same thing at home? I had no intention of letting her out of my sight, either.

It was a noble effort, but Lya only lasted half an hour before she passed out, slumped over against my chest. The firepit was still burning, and the Woodford was still being passed around. I had watched her closely before she fell asleep. There was a dam that was going to break, and I wanted as much warning as I could get. She was handling things alarmingly well for now, too well. The only person she truly strayed away from talking to was Liam.

I had to wonder if she even realized who he was. My eyes danced back and forth between them, picking out their similarities. They had the same wild mess of red curly hair, freckles, and features, the same eyes that seemed to change colors with their moods. He was tall, though, and I imagined if he were human without all the werewolf muscle, he would be lanky.

Anna and Trevor disappeared first, making their way down the Alpha wing. Liam, Jade, and Jason were staying at the packhouse, and Brandon crashed in his perpetually prepared room for whenever he got too drunk to make the drive back to Norridge. Kota promised he could walk home, and with how he couldn't stop glaring at Jade, I figured he'd want to get out of here sooner rather than later. And Lya snuggled into bed with me again? Well, I hadn't slept that well since the first time Adair forced me to shift and we spent the night curled up with her. Adair purred all night long.

I let her sleep in and enjoyed spending my morning sitting across the bed from her with a cup of coffee, watching her sleep. I felt guilty that, as soon as she woke, she would be thrust right back into work, this time as both Luna and Alpha.

Lya groaned lightly and rolled over, slowly blinking her eyes open. Her eyes flashed over to Tala's for just a second when she saw me. She smiled brightly and reached out, but knowing her, I handed her my cup of coffee.

"Good morning, love," I smiled.

Lya breathed in deep. "Oh my Goddess, I love you."

"Are you talking to me or the coffee?" I laughed.

She sat back, taking another sip. "Haven't decided yet. I can't remember my last cup of coffee."

I wanted to kiss her, but I knew it wouldn't end there if I did.

"Well, you get ready," I told her. "Welcome to Luna life... and Alpha life, I guess."

I slipped out of the room, not quite ready to be tempted by her showering and changing. We had a track record of getting distracted. I thought about which sundress she would choose today.

Liam was perched at the island, chatting away with Allyssa when I made it to the kitchen. He was another one I couldn't get a read on. I knew he was an ally, but I couldn't put my finger on why. I still hesitated to think the Wulvers were good just for goodness' sake.

Well, some of them might be. But not all.

"You find her yet?" I asked Liam when there was a lull in the conversation.

Liam shook his head. "Haven't seen her. Still, give Lya a chance to look so she knows, too."

"Thanks for mentioning her, at least," I grumbled.

"Ollie!" Allyssa chirped, pulling my attention away from Liam. "Do we get to acknowledge that you two are mates yet?"

I couldn't hold in my smile. "You can go ahead and go hog wild with planning a Luna ceremony."

Allyssa waved her hand. "No worries, I have most ideas already together. Will Rose be back anytime soon? I'm sure Lya will want her to join for dress shopping."

"Still on the Derek detail, but Kota is working on swapping her out so she can see Lya."

Allyssa scrunched her nose. "We'll plan for a couple of weeks, then. Every single scout has been working so hard, and they need a chance to recover."

Liam looked over at me, narrowing his eyes. "Why do you have one of your top scouts following one of your Gammas?"

I studied him for a minute, not exactly certain how much I wanted to divulge. It bothered me he didn't need to ask who my people were. But it was easy to assume the only way to keep him from knowing the goings on of my pack politics was to also remove both Kota and Gregory from their positions.

"Mistreatment of rogues," I finally admitted. "I want to see if the rumors are true before taking action."

He nodded thoughtfully. "I can do it. This weekend?"

"This is a pack matter, Liam," I insisted.

"Is it, though?" he challenged. "Rogues don't belong to a pack."

I glared back at him, coming to the final conclusion that he was one to watch, Lya's brother or not.

The shuffling of feet brought all of our attention to the person walking into the kitchen, and my heart melted at the sight.

Lya offered us a tentative smile, finding a spot at the island.

"H-hi," she stuttered.

Allyssa beamed over at her, passing her an omelet. "Welcome home, Luna."

"Alpha, actually," I corrected, wrapping my arms protectively around Lya. A blush stained her cheeks and she dropped her eyes. I placed a finger under her chin, tipping her head back up. "None of that, Little Alpha."

I caught Liam studying us out of the corner of my eye. He stood, offered a nod, and made his way out of the packhouse.

"Who is that?" Lya asked, leaning back into me. "He was the guard back at the compound, but why is he here?"

"Supposedly, he is your brother," I grumbled.

Lya nodded slowly and turned to her food. She picked at it, eating slowly.

I traced the outline of my mark on her neck, enjoying the electricity that coursed from it. "Please actually eat, love. You've lost weight."

"Yeah," Lya scoffed. "One meal a day for a couple weeks will do that."

"You should have stayed at the hospital," I mumbled into her hair.

Lya shook her head, refusing my suggestion. "We have stuff to do."

"But you could take a few days..."

"No," she said adamantly. "Do you know who all died? Rogues included? There was a girl..."

"Your cellmate," I confirmed. "Liam told me. Eat, and then we can discuss it."

Lya returned to her food, finishing slowly.

The dam was getting closer to breaking.

FORTY

Lya

APPARENTLY, the pack had a morgue. I shouldn't have been surprised by this, but I was.

Also apparently, the pack had brought all the rogues' bodies back, as well as pack members. This didn't surprise me.

Oliver claimed it was because they died fighting with and for a pack, so they should be treated in death as one.

"I don't understand your mentality toward rogues," I mumbled. Danica filled me in on the way most packs treated rogues, and with what happened to Oliver's father, I was genuinely shocked he did not feel the same.

"People should be treated as individuals," he stated, offering no further clarity.

Getting to the morgue took forever because people kept stopping us to thank me, congratulate me, or praise me. And I didn't deserve any of it.

I had been the catalyst.

And now I was being rewarded for starting a war.

My eyes scanned the room, expressionless eyes staring into the abyss of nothingness that now consumed them. A lump rose in my throat, hating that so many people died. Died for me.

I knew logically that this was not about me. This was about removing the primary threat to werewolves. And from my understanding, most of the Marsan group had been eradicated. Of course, there were other, smaller contingencies that would need to be watched, and a few outstanding members that had gotten away—Alexander Marsan included —but the largest hunter organization in the United States was, more or less, no more. We knew they would rebuild, but that would take years and years.

But I had been the one at the center of it all.

Wars were not uncommon. This was just another one for the history books.

Oliver rubbed soothing circles up and down my spine and whispered, "You know this isn't your fault. This would have happened one way or another, and the outcome could have been so much worse."

I nodded, feigning understanding.

I walked down the rows of bodies. It felt like I had murdered each and every one of them. Their blood was on my hands.

I studied each face, searching for the murky brown hair and dull gray eyes. She had always looked like a stray, even in human form. And true to my bleeding heart, I had chosen to take her in, in whatever way I could, even if I had little to offer. At the time, it had been solidarity. Now, though, it could be a home in a pack.

How had two months changed my life so much?

The love of my life.

A true home.

Leadership.

And I deserved none of it.

I came to the last face, breathing out a sigh. "She's not here."

Oliver took my hand, pulling me away from the scene. I could only imagine which of my emotions he was sensing. Hell, he would probably be able to feel it all even without a mate bond.

"That's good," he attempted. "She more than likely made it out alive, then."

"Or you guys missed a body."

"Liam specifically looked for her," Oliver insisted. "He knows her scent. If she was still out there, she would have been found."

I pursed my lips, thinking of all the other possibilities. Maybe she hadn't made it quite far enough away, and the remaining hunters recaptured her. Maybe she wouldn't be able to reestablish living on her own again, but I had told her to come here. Maybe...

"Sure." I looked up at him, doing my best to mask the pain and uncertainty on my face.

Oliver put his arm around me, giving my waist a reassuring squeeze. "C'mon, love. Please, let's just have a moment to be thankful you're back."

I nodded slowly, letting him pull me toward his Land Cruiser. "You know, you really don't have to jump back into things immediately."

I looked up at him, letting the grief show through my expression. "Oliver, with some of the things I heard in there, we don't have time to sit back."

Oliver studied me for a moment before lifting me up and placing me in the passenger seat. I tried to utilize the bond to interpret what his expression meant, but it provided no answers. "Just an afternoon, please."

The drive back to the packhouse was silent, but not uncomfortably so. I barely noticed as he led me out to the patio. The July sun beat down on us, but I wasn't about to be upset about being outside, and it wasn't quite scorching enough to force me to pull myself out of Oliver's arms.

"Tell me what you're thinking," he murmured into my hair.

I shifted slowly to face him, keeping his hands in my lap. "I'm just scared, Ollie." I paused, trying to figure out how to put into words everything that scared me. "I feel like I wasted time. The time I was here before should have been utilized accepting our bond, not whatever it was we were doing. I absolutely don't want to be an Alpha. I have no idea how to be a Luna, and if I don't know how to be a Luna, how the hell will I also be an Alpha?"

Oliver smiled softly down at me, running his fingers along my mark, causing me to shudder under his touch. "Lya, it wasn't wasted time. We never said the word mate, but we both knew and we didn't fight it."

"But we could have—"

"Do you actually think anything would have been different if we had said just one measly word?" he asked me. "If anything, I think that would have just scared you off. You were here, with me, acting like my mate, *my Luna*. It was exactly perfect for us."

"But other mated couples—"

"We aren't other mated couples, Lya."

I looked down at our hands. He was right. It was no use comparing.

Oliver tipped my chin up so I looked him in the eye. "And you do know how to be a Luna. You knew the exact times to challenge me and put me in my place. You worked cohesively to plan a war. Do you remember how you put Derek in his place without lifting a finger or raising your voice? You were *made* to be my Luna, and you've already been given the perfect opportunities to show you have exactly what it takes."

He paused, probably expecting me to say something, but I had no words. "If you can be that exceptional of a Luna without any knowledge or training, I think you'll be able to figure out being an Alpha just fine."

"But there's so much I don't know," I whined.

Oliver chuckled. "Then it's a good thing you're mated to an Alpha who can show you the ropes."

He shifted, pulling my back to his chest, arms protectively wrapping around me. "Stop overthinking everything, Little Alpha."

"Is that my new nickname or something?" I giggled.

"Behind closed doors, yes," he confirmed. "We wouldn't want anyone using it as a slight on your position."

"Does it bother you that I'm a Luna and an Alpha?"

Oliver's hands stilled, tensing against my skin. I didn't have to look back at him to know his face was pinched. "I don't know how it'll work. Especially with how difficult it is for mates to be apart."

"Luckily, the Wulver Alpha is usually more of a delegate than a warrior," a voice I was learning to recognize said from behind us. I turned to see Liam leaning against the door, arms crossed. "The Wulver Alpha is the one who decides which problems we actually get involved in, devises the plans, and handles diplomacy."

"How long have you been standing there?" I asked, concerned I hadn't smelled him or noticed another presence.

Liam's eyes glinted mischievously. "Long enough, Little Alpha."

He strode over, taking a seat across from us. "Come to think of it, a Luna is a perfect fit for the Wulver Alpha."

I chewed on my lip. Part of me wanted to doubt he was actually my brother, but the way Tala warmed to his wolf immediately, and the fact that I felt like I was staring into a fucking mirror confirmed it. "Do you want to be Alpha instead? I didn't want it. I didn't realize a challenge would make me Alpha."

"Fuck no," he scoffed. "I pretended I was long enough. I'd much rather be on the field."

Worry crashed down on me. The impending doom of losing my home hit hard again. "Will I be able to stay here?"

"It would be most beneficial, actually," he confirmed. "We worked hard to build up a significant presence in the pack that most closely aligned with what Wulvers stand for."

I let out a sigh of relief, melting back into Oliver's chest. He absentmindedly caressed my shoulders, but I could tell something was bothering him.

"When did you figure out Lya was a wolf?" he blurted, pulling Liam's attention away from the river.

"Well, my baby sister seems to have inherited the family trait for keeping things, including herself, hidden." He smirked. "Thom called and told me. And when Kota and Gregory filled me in on her plan, I knew I could step down as acting Alpha, even if she hadn't challenged dear old Dad."

"Lya!"

I turned abruptly, smiling broadly at the two pairs of emerald eyes staring back. My twin cousins had been who I had missed most about my old life. I'd have to take it up with Tala later for not letting me know I didn't have to hide from them.

"That's Alpha Lya to you, Jade," I chided. She rolled her eyes at me, quickly taking up a spot next to us.

OLIVER

IN THE HOURS THAT PASSED, the entire crew had filtered onto the patio. Trevor and Brandon had ensured everyone, aside from Allyssa and Maggie, always had a beer in hand. Every one of Lya's questions got answered, and she had given up trying to pass off her newfound Alpha title. Her grand plan that someone should challenge her and she would concede before the first punch was thrown was laughed off. It was a well-known fact that Alphas who had leadership thrust upon them upheld the title the best.

Lya reached over, grabbing another beer. "So, the Beta I choose, do they have to have Wulver blood?"

"No," Kota said. "In fact, there are only a few families left with any Wulver blood at all. I don't."

"But," Gregory added, "the Alpha always somehow does. When our previous Alpha fell, it was between your father and me who would take up the gamut."

"Why didn't it go to you?" she asked.

Gregory offered a rare smile down at Allyssa, wrapping an arm around her shoulders. "I had met someone."

Allyssa reached up to him, kissing his cheek. "It'd be a fight all over again if the Little Alpha had died at the hands of her father, though."

I cringed at the term. These people used it endearingly, but I could only foresee it being used as an insult. Lya may be an Alpha now, but she was still my mate. I would defend her honor, even if she didn't need me to.

Lya glanced over to Thom. "So, I need a Beta. Preferably someone who could assist with figuring out how to be an Alpha and has experience with the inner workings of the Wulver Pack."

I followed her gaze, watching as Thom's eyes darkened. A smile flitted across my face, knowing exactly what she was getting at.

Lya glanced sympathetically to Maggie, who was rocking Kai. "And I think it would probably be best if my Beta was someone who wouldn't suffer being too far from a fated mate should they need to go somewhere."

Maggie offered Lya a warm smile. "You also never know when someone who has past hunter affiliations could come in handy."

"So, we are all agreed then," Lya said, clapping her hands against her knees. "Thom is my Beta."

"What?" he sputtered.

Maggie placed her hand on Thom's arm. "Honey, Kai has a wolf. He needs to grow up with some sort of affiliation with a pack."

"Yeah, but we were just going to move back here!" he insisted.

I let out a long sigh. "I dunno, man. The pack's getting pretty full. I don't know if I'd be able to accept another rogue. If you were already part of a pack that had been heavily involved in the direction our warrior training program has gone... I might be able to make a concession."

Thom sat back, chewing his lip.

"Fine," he finally conceded. "On the condition that I have a good fleet of Gammas under me."

Lya smiled brightly. "I think I can make that happen."

"And with that," Liam said, standing up. "I'm out."

Lya looked up at him, worry on her face. "Where are you going?"

I pulled Lya closer, tucking a strand of hair behind her ear. "He's going to take over for Rose for a while so she can come see you. You guys do have a Luna ceremony to plan."

'And you're actually okay with that?' Lya asked through our mind-link. *'I know you don't like him.'*

'My reasons for not liking him are personal, not a slight on his allegiances or abilities,' I confessed.

Over the course of the evening, I had come to terms with the fact that there needed to be a line in the sand with Liam. Liam the brother-in-law and Liam the Wulver needed to be two separate people in my mind. You never were supposed to get along with your in-laws, right?

As the sun set and conversation dwindled, people filtered out. Soon enough, it was only Lya's twin cousins that remained.

"What is your plan from here?" I asked. I had greatly enjoyed the two of them, and I could feel that Lya appreciated having some of her past with her.

Jason shrugged. "Head back to Sturgeon Moon, I guess. But Jade, she's the primary medic for the Wulvers. I don't know what she needs to do."

"Sturgeon Moon? That's the pack Kota transferred from, correct?"

"Yep!" Jade giggled. "He officially transferred here right after my eighteenth. We were so disappointed when we figured out we weren't mates..."

I didn't miss the way Jade's face fell, and I saw the way wheels started turning in Lya's head.

"Have you met your mate then, yet?" Lya asked.

Jade shook her head. "You'd think, with how I'm all over the place, I'd have run into him by now."

I picked up on what Lya was putting down, taking over for her. "You know, Lessa's talking about transferring to her mate's pack now that the hunters have been put to sleep."

"Maybe we could bring Jade on as a doctor here," Lya supplied, looking up at me. "Maybe even get Anna all trained up as a field medic while she does her warrior training."

The love and warmth that filled me was all-consuming. I only had eyes for my little mate, my Luna, my Little Alpha. "I like the way you think, love."

I leaned down and pressed my lips to hers. It was a kiss that quickly got too heated, weeks of missing my mate catching up to the both of us.

"I can't watch this," Jason huffed, standing up abruptly and slamming the door behind him.

Without taking my lips off of my mate's, I saw Jade bounce up off her seat out of the corner of my eyes. "Well, I accept! Thank you, Alpha and Luna. I look forward to joining the Snow Moon Pack."

Just like that, Lya had another piece of home with her. Jade quickly followed her twin, leaving Lya and me alone. Something I had desperately needed.

I pulled back, taking the time to look down at Lya. I studied the outline of her swollen lips and the fire in her eyes. I traced the contours of her face before tugging her into my lap.

"Whatever am I going to do with you now, Little Alpha?"

Lya giggled, leaning down for a chaste kiss. "I have a couple of suggestions."

"Is that so?" My hands crept up her thighs, finding the hem of her dress. "Have I ever told you how much I love sundresses?"

She sat back, pretending to ponder my question. "You know, I don't think you have. But maybe you could remind me?"

I stood abruptly, holding Lya over my shoulder. I kept my hand much too high on her thigh, confirming my suspicions that her affinity for lace had not changed in the weeks she had been gone. We were through the kitchen and behind our bedroom door in record time. I placed her gently on her feet and pulled my shirt off before I spoke again.

"My favorite thing about sundresses is how they look on the floor," I growled, tearing through the little number hiding her sun-kissed skin. She looked up at me, eyes wide as I stared down at her with a hunger only one thing could sate. "We have a bit of time to make up for, don't you think?"

Lya didn't say a word, instead sinking to her knees in front of me, hands fumbling with my jeans. Her eyes didn't leave mine as my pants and boxers slid to the floor, revealing that I had been half-cocked all afternoon. A primal sound rumbled out of me as she wrapped her hands around my cock. I reached out, fisting her hair to guide her closer.

"Words, my Luna," I reminded her. "You don't owe me this simply because you've been gone. I can find another sundress to put back on you."

"Just so you can rip it off again?" she asked with a sly smile before sliding her lips over my shaft. I gave her a moment, one short moment, to swirl her tongue over the tip before fisting my hand tighter in her hair and pushing myself further into her mouth. She moaned around me, the vibration eliciting a rumble of satisfaction from me.

Lya nearly gagged, encouraging me to pull back. She released my tip with a pop, and I pulled her up to her feet without a word. With each predatory step I took toward her, she took one back. When her legs bumped into the bed, I shoved.

"Oliver!" she giggled, bouncing on the mattress.

I leaned over her, pressing her further into the bed. "I love you, Luna Lya."

Lya reached up, knotting her fingers in my hair, purring in response, "I love you, Alpha Oliver."

I grasped behind her knees and pulled her legs apart, pinning her there with my hips.

"Let me show you how much," I murmured into her neck, taking in her scent.

Lya tugged on my hair, pulling my face up to hers, and kissed me deeply. I slid my tip along her slit before pushing into her and rocking. My movements were slow, drawn out, milking every ounce of passion out of each thrust.

Lya and I had fucked. We had made love, we'd had angry sex, and we'd had quickies. I'd taken her pinned to walls, in the shower, on my desk on more than one occasion, and even a time or two sprawled out on the kitchen counter. Nearly every room in the packhouse and every area of our territory had been christened. We had not wasted time, oftentimes avoiding saying a few imperative four-letter words in favor of some version of fucking. But nothing, absolutely nothing compared to worshiping my marked mate's body for the first time.

Reader, I marked her.

Again.

Acknowledgments

For a long time, *Run.* was a secret venture. Apparently, at the rehearsal dinner the night before our wedding, I got *very* drunk and proclaimed I was an author because I was publishing a book. If we're being honest, the only reason you're reading this now is because I am incredibly stubborn. There was no way in hell I was going to backtrack on that, especially when my friends started reaching out to ask how the publishing process was going.

Prior to my drunken escapades, this book was only on some internet sites where it did get awesome reviews. I still think of jestrada_17, JCBisme, and all the other readers who left all the good comments and support. CJ Primer, an author who also originated on those platforms, also left me so much feedback and encouragement. I feel really cool because I got to interact with an author who is a big shot now. There are a lot of people in real life that I owe this book to, though.

It's easy to say those who deserve my thanks know who they are, but they really don't. I'm sure some of those people don't want to, either. I mean, who wants to get a thank you card in the mail for inspiring the bad guy in a book?

I pulled so much inspiration from my own life for this book. I wrote it when I was in the midst of a messy divorce in 2020 and I wanted to be anywhere but here. At a time where I felt like I was nothing more than the villain, I needed to be a hero. So, I made Lya. I gave her the power to do something about her pain, and in turn, she taught me being the tortured victim is a choice. Maybe that's why I let myself meet an Oliver. I kid you not, about halfway through writing this piece, I met my now husband. From appearance to personality, he is Oliver. Part of me thinks I manifested him. He spent countless nights brainstorming with me, working through plot holes, and editing scenes for me. Whenever I was ready to print the manuscript out just so I could burn it (that's much more dramatic than deleting the file), he was my cheerleader. This book would not exist without him. Also, he cooks dinner every night to keep us alive, so we should all thank him for that. Where do y'all think Lya got her inability to cook?

My friends are absolutely priceless. If I needed a book suggestion to get my mind off of what was going on in Snow Moon, they had one. If I needed to rant, they were all ears. If I needed to know if a scene was so totally cringe, they were honest. I think they even pre-ordered this book even though they know full well they're getting a free, signed copy.

My poor, sweet editor, Kendra Gaither, deserves a medal. I may have gone to school for literature, but it certainly isn't what I do now. The draft of this book I sent her had the word 'just' in it 805 times. It's down to 345, and it'd be lower if she had her way.

But mostly, I need to thank my readers. From my beta readers who went gaga over it to the people I will never get the opportunity to talk to, it's you guys who appreciate my work that keep the imposter syndrome at bay. Whether you read the first couple chapters back in 2020 or are buying a copy now, if you're staying up until 3 a.m. to finish or chucking it in your DNF pile. You are taking a chance on me, and I could never thank you enough for that.

I'm headed back to Snow Moon soon. Hope to see you there.

ABOUT THE AUTHOR

Lydia Maine spent her childhood building fairy houses and arguing the existence of dragons. A few decades into that childhood, and life doesn't look much different. She writes in cursive and drives stick shift. Some days, she wears all black with purple lipstick and goes to seedy dive bars, while others she dons vibrant sundresses and dances through fields of wildflowers. Everything, to her, is an adventure, so it's no surprise she now writes about such. It's only a shame she has to add in the description of "paranormal" or "fantasy" now.

Lydia's writing is either the cause or result of her insomnia. Her books reflect traumas she has experienced and some she will never know. She draws on the mundane to further glorify the fantastical lives she would rather be living, leaving small pieces of herself in each story she tells.